PENGUIN BOOKS
Disobedient

Elizabeth Fremantle is the acclaimed author of four Tudor historical novels: *Queen's Gambit* (soon to be the feature film *Firebrand*), *Sisters of Treason*, *Watch the Lady* and *The Girl in the Glass Tower*. As E.C. Fremantle she has written two gripping historical thrillers: *The Poison Bed* and *The Honey and the Sting*. She lives in London.

For all the survivors

Disobedient

ELIZABETH FREMANTLE

PENGUIN BOOKS

PENGUIN BOOKS

UK | USA | Canada | Ireland | Australia
India | New Zealand | South Africa

Penguin Books is part of the Penguin Random House group of companies
whose addresses can be found at global.penguinrandomhouse.com.

First published by Penguin Michael Joseph 2023
Published in Penguin Books 2024

006

Copyright © Elizabeth Fremantle, 2023

The moral right of the author has been asserted

Typeset by Jouve (UK), Milton Keynes
Printed and bound in Great Britain by Clays Ltd, Elcograf S.p.A.

The authorized representative in the EEA is Penguin Random House Ireland,
Morrison Chambers, 32 Nassau Street, Dublin D02 YH68

A CIP catalogue record for this book is available from the British Library

ISBN: 978–1–405–95281–1

www.greenpenguin.co.uk

A note on the text

I have chosen to anglicize the titles of Artemisia Gentileschi's paintings and also the names of the saints, while
my characters' names are kept in Italian. With very few
exceptions the characters are inspired by historical figures
though in some cases I have changed their names for flu-
ency. Tuzia Medaglia I have called Zita and her baby Diego,
Luca. Of the Stiatessi family, Pierantonio is shortened to
Piero and Giovanni-Battista, simply Giovanni. Michelangelo
Merisi, more familiar to us as Caravaggio, I refer to as
simply Merisi. The Palazzo Conscente is a place of my
own invention.

PART I

I'll show you what a woman can do.

Artemisia Gentileschi

1. Beatrice Cenci

Rome, September 1599 . . .

The studio smells of minerals and linseed. It is silent, save for the rhythmic grinding of the pestle and mortar as an assistant mills pigments at a bench: gaudy splats of colour, glossy with oil.

Artemisia sits motionless. She is trussed up uncomfortably, like a joint of mutton, in a puce silk dress that belongs to another girl. A loose wire in her jewelled headband torments her.

She musters all her self-discipline to keep still, waiting for the moment her father turns away to discuss something with the assistant. Quick as a fly, she digs her nails into her scalp – an instant of blessed relief.

'Don't move,' he blasts. She snatches her hand back into position. It must be true, his warning that he has eyes in the back of his head. She squints at the dark hair hanging to his shoulders, wondering how those invisible eyes can see through such a mane.

She has taken the place of a child whose portrait he is finishing. Artemisia hasn't seen the girl in real life but knows she is the Pope's great-great-niece, or something like it. That is why she is wearing the elaborate, scratchy lace and jewels – so her father can add the final touches without 'further imposing on the young lady'. She is very

3

glad not to be the Pope's great-great-niece and have to wear such uncomfortable things every day.

The quiet is shattered as the door bangs open and her father's friend strides in, bellowing a greeting.

'You're early, Merisi.' She can see her father's irritation in the red flush blossoming on his cheeks. He is usually quick to temper but not with Merisi, or not to his face anyway. Behind his back he calls him 'that vile miscreant' and worse things she is not supposed to have overheard: 'The devil's taking all my commissions. Everyone calls him a genius. He's not a genius, he's a plague sore.'

'Early? On the contrary' – Merisi is wearing a grin – 'we'll miss all the fun if we don't hurry.' He steps towards Artemisia, removing his hat with a flourish and stooping into a deep bow. 'Michelangelo Merisi de Caravaggio at your service, my lady.'

'I'm not . . .' She stops, unable to remember the Pope's great-great-niece's name. 'It's me, Arte –' Realizing that Merisi is teasing, she laughs.

The angelus bells ring across the city. 'See, it's already noon.' Merisi is animated. 'Help your daughter out of that absurd dress and let's go.'

'We're not taking her with us.' Orazio hands his palette and brushes to the assistant to tidy away.

'Why ever not?'

'It's not a suitable occasion for a six-year-old.'

'You wouldn't say that if she was a boy.' Merisi winks at her, his thick-lashed eyes black and shiny. 'Let her learn what becomes of girls who disobey their fathers.'

She wonders what he means.

Merisi removes the jewelled band from her hair.

4

'Her mother would never allow it. Be careful with that. It's worth more than you earn in a year.' Her father loosens her ties and lifts the heavy dress over her head, leaving her in her shift, comfortable at last.

'I didn't know your wife was your keeper.' Merisi is standing in the doorway, tapping the jamb.

Artemisia watches her father relent with a sigh, as she climbs into her ordinary clothes.

'Where are we going, Papa?' She wonders if it will be one of the puppet shows in the Piazza del Popolo. She remembers the man puppet, big red circles painted on his cheeks, beating his puppet wife with a truncheon. Everybody thought it was funny.

'Isn't it much more exciting if it is a surprise?' says Merisi.

'No!'

He laughs at her. Not in a way that makes her feel silly, like some adults do, but more in a way that draws her in, as if he counts her as one of his friends.

'Look!' He is holding out both of his hands. His fingers are long, nails clogged with paint. One hand is fisted, the other open, a coin cupped in the palm. 'Pick one. You can keep what's in it.'

She considers for some time which hand to choose, glancing at her father for help. He merely shrugs. She has never had a coin of her own. She could buy something with it.

Her mouth waters as she thinks of the cones of sugared nuts sold in the market that her mother says are too expensive. She is on the brink of making her choice but something stops her. Perhaps there are two coins hidden in his fist. She could buy the sugared nuts *and* a bag of seed to feed the little birds, or a length of silk ribbon, or a *bombolone*. She can already taste the sweet creamy ooze of its filling. 'That one.' She points at Merisi's closed hand.

He unfurls it slowly with a low chuckle.

It is empty.

Disappointment washes away her small dreams. Another girl might cry, but not her.

'Honestly, Merisi.' Her father is frowning. 'Getting her hopes up like that. She's just a child.'

Merisi ignores her father, asking her, 'What does that teach you?' as he caches his coin.

She has to think very hard to come up with the lesson she has learned.

'Not to want more than I am offered?' she suggests quietly.

She has the feeling of being wrong but her father says, 'Good girl. That's right. The moral is that we must all learn to limit our expectations.'

'I suppose that's one way of taking it,' Merisi says. 'But it's not what I intended.'

Even though he frightens her a little, there is something about Merisi that Artemisia can't help feeling thrilled by.

'What is it that makes you want the thing you can't see?' Merisi thrusts forward his clenched hand once more.

Her mind churns for an answer. 'It might be something even more special.'

Merisi is smiling at her. 'No one can resist a mystery.' He turns to Orazio. 'Not a moral but an observation. Your daughter is uncommonly perceptive. How old did you say she was? Six? You might well have a prodigy on your hands!'

6

She isn't entirely sure what a prodigy is but from his expression it must be something good.

'I wouldn't know about that.' Orazio passes Artemisia her coat. 'One doesn't really want precocity in a daughter.'

When her father isn't looking, Merisi slips two coins into her hand, lifting his forefinger to cross his mouth. She hides the treasure in her pocket. The idea of keeping such a secret gives her a warm feeling inside.

Her father takes her elbow as they leave. His grip is tight and she has to run to keep up, weaving through the narrow streets. The crowds become dense, the atmosphere high with excitement, as they jostle forward towards the river. All Artemisia can see are backsides and shirt-tails, the hilt of a knife stuffed into a belt, a baby bundled in a woman's arms, a donkey leaving a pungent trail of dung in its wake.

They grind to a halt and people begin to shout and push. Somewhere ahead she can hear a great roar go up.

'Sounds like we've missed the wife,' Merisi says. 'I told you we'd be late.'

Artemisia, pressed too tightly between strange bodies, feels the fizz of panic. Something hot and wet slides over her hand. She recoils. It is only a dog licking the salt from her skin. She strokes its head, glad of the distraction. It pushes its cool damp nose into her palm.

The throng begins to move. She stumbles on a broken cobble, falling, grazing her palms. A boot stamps, narrowly missing her head. She struggles to get to her feet, the press of the crowd preventing it. Large hands grip beneath her arms and, before she knows it, she is catapulted up, above the crowd, and onto Merisi's shoulders.

7

Her father is grumbling. 'I told you we shouldn't have brought her.'

Artemisia looks down on the sea of heads surging forward below. Tiny beads of blood are forming on the soft cushions of flesh beneath her thumbs. She blots them on her coat.

Perched up high she can see where the street opens out into a large piazza from where the bridge spans the river. The water sparkles and writhes, boats cluster, jouncing on its surface, sails flapping like Friday washing. The Castel Sant'Angelo squats on the other side, its tower fat and round, bricks blushing in the afternoon sun.

Gulls quarrel as they swoop overhead, white against blue. One lands on a nearby strut at Artemisia's eye-level. Its beak is big and hooked, the yellow of ripe lemons. Its strange eye swivels before it flings itself back into the sky, the vast span of its wings opening. She watches it sweep upward magnificently, tucking its talons into its undercarriage, imagining she too is propelled on wings up into the endless blue.

Merisi deposits her on the top of a wall, ordering a group of grubby-faced boys to move over, before he and Orazio scramble up beside her. From there she can see an empty space at the centre of the piazza with a circle of hurdles to hold back the crowd. In the middle is a stage, strewn with straw, holding a wooden structure like the one that suspends the angels in the Easter play. A choir of holy brothers is lined up nearby, singing psalms.

'Will it be a play?' she asks.

'In a way,' says her father, with an odd, knotted look.

Merisi laughs. 'You'll see.' He squeezes her shoulder.

8

'There's Reni! Over there in the stand.' He is pointing and waving to someone, shouting the man's name.

And they are on the move again, pushing through towards the side where rows of benches are banked and filled with seated people in colourful clothes.

A man is calling to them: 'Over here! I've kept you a place.' Artemisia has seen him once or twice at her father's studio. He is a painter too.

When they manage to reach him, up a set of steep steps, Artemisia overhears him say quietly, 'Isn't she a bit young for this kind of thing, Orazio?'

At that moment their conversation is drowned in a chant: '*Bring out the girl, bring out the girl, bring out the girl.*'

More join in, and more, stamping their feet until the entire piazza is thundering with noise.

They sit, she on her father's lap. A large woman squeezes herself in beside them and they all shuffle up. She is glistening with sweat and waves a fan at her face, spreading a strongly perfumed scent that makes Artemisia feel vaguely sick.

Suddenly the place falls silent save for the rumble of a cart entering the square. The holy brothers break into song once more. Artemisia stands to see the girl better. She is not a small girl like her, but a grown-up girl being led from the cart and onto the stage close to where they are seated.

She is very pretty but her costume is plain. Artemisia has only ever seen two plays and the players had worn gaudy outfits in both. They were all men or boys. She has never seen a girl player before, thought such a thing didn't exist, and it occurs to her that this may well be a pretty boy.

She (or he) is wearing a sensible dun-coloured dress and

is bare-headed, a skein of straight dark hair scraped up onto the top of her head. She seems to be murmuring quietly to herself in prayer and her brown eyes look mostly down at her small white hands, fingers threaded tightly together. Occasionally her gaze flicks up at her surroundings. A just-visible tic in her jaw says she is nervous. Artemisia supposes it must be the occasion, the multitude of people all looking her way. She tries to imagine herself in that position, skin bristling at the thought of so many eyes on her.

Gulls continue to circle above while the girl is walked to the centre of the stage beside a step. The holy brothers sing on, swaying in unison, the hems of their grey cassocks wafting gently as they move, rosaries swinging in time. A big man, bald with a bushy beard that looks as if his hair has slid from his head to his chin, approaches the girl.

She hands him a purse and he says, loudly enough for everyone to hear, 'Please forgive me,' then says something else quietly into her ear. Her eyes catch his briefly with what looks like real dread, making Artemisia wonder how it is possible to be so convincing with make-believe.

The girl gets to her knees and the man ties a blindfold over her eyes.

A lone voice from the back shouts something angry. The audience becomes restless and Artemisia is glad they are sitting safely in the seats. The woman beside her is breathing heavily and noisily. Artemisia puts her hand over her nose and mouth to block out the smell of her scent.

When the girl lies down on her front, head on the step like a pillow with both arms splayed out, Artemisia supposes she must be enacting the martyrdom of one of the saints. She racks her brain to work out which of the Virgin Martyrs she is. On her fingers she counts them off from the prayer drummed into her by Sister Ilaria: Dorothy, Justina, Agatha, Lucy, Agnes, Cecilia . . . She can't remember the others.

The axe moves in a whistling arc through the air.

It falls with a loud thump.

At once the girl's leg kicks violently up, flinging her dress almost over her shoulders as the pretend head rolls away. A spurt of red liquid springs up, raining onto the stage to form a gluey pool around her and all over her dun-coloured dress.

The crowd groans and snarls, shifting like rough water.

A warm splash lands on Artemisia's hand. When she looks it is not red but clear, someone's tear, or spit, or a splash of the sweat that is now trailing down her neighbour's face as she shouts and waves a fist.

'How do they do it?' she asks. 'How do they make it so real?'

The woman looks at her strangely. 'What do you mean, child?' Her cheeks wobble as she speaks.

'The play. The martyrdom. It looks so real.'

'Martyrdom?' The woman makes a kind of laugh. 'It's an *execution*, poppet.'

It is a moment before the woman's words sink in. This is not a play, not a boy pretending to be one of the Virgin Martyrs. Her belly hollows out. She is a real girl who is really dead on the platform, with real blood pumping on and on from where only moments ago her head was attached to her shoulders.

'But who is she? What did she do?' Artemisia's voice is small. Blood rushes in her ears.

'She is Beatrice Cenci and she murdered her father.' It is Merisi who tells her this.

Artemisia's hand flies to her throat. Her head swills. Heat drives up through her body. She sways, lids heavy, vaguely aware of a commotion, voices, her name, a sharp slap on her cheek, water poured into her mouth, before the world turns red then black . . .

The next she knows she is back at home, her mother's cool hand on her forehead. She is talking to Orazio who looms with Merisi, two shadowy shapes across the room. Her voice is snappish. She is annoyed. Artemisia's baby brother has begun to grumble.

'What can I say? You were right, my love. Always right, Pru. I shouldn't have taken her with us.' Her father stoops to kiss her mother's brow, making all the sharpness drop away. A damp cloth is pressed to Artemisia's head. She keeps her eyes shut, not ready to wake yet.

'That poor Beatrice. As if she hadn't suffered enough.'

'That's as may be, but murder can't go unpunished.'

Artemisia continues to drift in the safety of her mother's arms, half listening to their conversation as images flash through her mind: the fountain of blood, the rolling head, the girl's small white hands, like butterflies.

'This afternoon has inspired me. I'm going to paint a *Judith*,' Merisi is saying. 'Not in the usual way. I want to show her in the moment she decapitates the Assyrian.' Artemisia can hear the scratch of charcoal on rough paper. 'Get right to the truth of what it means to take a life.'

'All that violence,' her mother says. 'Is it necessary?'

'Who is Judith?' Artemisia asks, sitting up, her curiosity sparked.

They fuss over her: does her head hurt, is she dizzy, can she see clearly?

'But who's Judith?' she asks again.

'She was a very courageous woman from the Bible,' her mother says. 'You will learn about her when you are older.'

'Was she a murderer too, like Beatrice Cenci?' Artemisia notices a severe look pass from her mother to her father, as if to say: *See what you've started.*

'No, my love. She killed her enemy to save her people, the Lord's people. It is different.'

'But how is it different?'

'It just is.' Her father slams the conversation shut.

Merisi looks up from his drawing. This time, his wink makes Artemisia feel uneasy.

The Judith Fragment

He stumbles, the great Assyrian, Holofernes, a swill of wine spilling.

Canvas walls quiver as he rights himself.

'Sit,' says Judith.

Like an infant he obeys, lifting his arms so she can unbuckle his breastplate and sword.

They clatter to the floor.

Her silent prayer circulates.

'Save me, O Lord!'

He smells of horse and sweat and saddle oil.

She heaves the pitcher, replenishing his drink, tipping it into his waiting mouth.

She thinks of the children of besieged Bethulia, her city, bellies bloated, eyes sunken, awaiting a small sip of gritty water from the almost empty cistern.

The Assyrian camp is so near they can hear the men's heathen singing.

But their thirst is louder and the buzz of the flies . . . *[some text illegible]*

She draws off his boots and gives him a gentle backward shove, her bangles clanging like temple bells.

Falling into a sea of cushioned purple silk, he laughs, a filthy sound.

Grappling with wine-heavy lids, he loses the battle, slurring a few indecipherable words before his huge form slumps.

Judith seizes his sword, unsheathing it.

It was such a sword that widowed her.

Her husband's death rattles through her mind.

Daunted now, breath staunched, she ekes another prayer from deep within: 'Save me, O Lord!'

The blighted children howl, 'Save us!'

She grabs a fistful of enemy hair, coarse as brush, and swings the heavy weapon.

His black eyes pop open, confused, then spilling sudden panic.

Rage drives the sharp edge into his flesh easily, as if through liquid.

Blood spurts, scalding droplets on her skin.

A butcher's thud now, as blade meets bone.

'Save me, O Lord!'

All thought curbed, she hacks until the job is done, then swaddles the Assyrian's severed head, still warm.

Her bracelets chime once more as she thrusts the bundle, innocent as soiled linens, into her maid's waiting basket.

Questions squat in Abra's brown gaze.

Judith has lost her tongue.

The two women steal away, back to the gates of Bethulia.

The city is jubilant, while Judith picks blood from beneath her nails.

The children's laughter rings out.

Judith searches for her heart.

Finding, in its place, her fist, gripped for eternity to the hilt of her enemy's sword.

Anonymous fragment – trans. F. E. Lamenter

2. The Nightingale

Rome, March 1611. Twelve years later . . .

Two painters, a father and daughter, are deep in concentration. A large canvas holds court in the centre of the studio. It depicts Judith and her maidservant fleeing the Assyrian camp. Judith grips a half-visible sword in one fist. Her servant carries the severed head of Holofernes in a basket beneath her sky-blue arm. Both women look back and away into the night, as if in response to a sound.

Two models at the end of the studio, bathed in light from the window to their left, make a living approximation of the painting. The older of the two stifles a yawn. The other fidgets, eyes flickering. A melon substitutes the severed head.

The daughter, crouched on her haunches, deep in concentration, paints the imagined drips of gore that seep through the wicker. The head, the napkin it is wrapped in, stained with the blood of a slaughtered hen, and the basket, are all her work. Her father is putting the meticulous final details to the gauzy folds of the servant's white shawl.

Peace is shattered with the arrival of a small brown bird flying in through the open door. It ricochets back and forth, striking one wall then another, then a beam, then the underside of the roof. The models cry out as if a demon has entered, one turning to follow the panicked creature with her eyes, the other crouching, head in hands, as if it might peck out her brains.

Artemisia, her gore-tipped paintbrush held aloft, seems to recognize its fear, each collision causing her own body to jolt minutely.

Orazio slams down his palette with an exasperated grunt.

The bird skims the upper edge of the canvas, depositing a chalky white blot, bright against the dark ground of the painting, the painting that is late, the only commission Orazio has had in six months.

The studio assistant emits a guffaw of laughter from the back of the room.

Artemisia suppresses a snort.

A curse bursts from Orazio, loud and sudden as a shot, shocking the place into absolute stillness.

The bird flits up to perch under the roof.

Time is suspended for a moment as they wait for what will happen next, four pairs of wary eyes fixed on Orazio.

Orazio frowns, watching the white stain drool downward over the painstakingly rendered detail in the brooch on Judith's painted shoulder.

The bird takes flight once more. Orazio springs up, arm high, fingers snapping round the small form as if it is a *pallone* ball.

'NO!' Without thinking Artemisia kicks her father hard on the shin, causing his hand to open.

The models shrink back, clasping each other.

The bird escapes, darting towards the light of the closed window. It makes a thud as it meets the glass and drops stunned to the sill. Ignoring her father's order to stop,

Artemisia yanks the gauze shawl from the model's head, wafting it over the oblivious bird to gather it tenderly into her hand.

She glares at him as she stalks towards the door.

'Where do you think you're going?' Orazio rubs his smarting shin. He is battling the urge to grab his disobedient daughter by the scruff and retaliate, curbed only by the presence of witnesses.

She says nothing as she continues on out of the studio, the tiny creature cupped in her palm as if it is the sacrament. 'Fetch her back,' he barks at the assistant, who gives him an insolent look before following her out.

Orazio doesn't like the boy, doesn't like having a mincing *finocchio* about the place, around his sons, particularly since he discovered him locked in an embrace with the youth he sometimes uses as a model if he needs an angel. At least he doesn't pose a threat to his daughter's virtue. Orazio is supposed to be teaching him to paint as a favour to the Stiatessis. Giovanni Stiatessi is his oldest friend and is Piero's uncle, but the boy hasn't a jot of artistic ability. He does have an eye for colour, though, and a particular gift for milling pigments, so he is of some small use.

Orazio surveys the stain on the painting, worrying now about the client, who has already demanded a discount for late delivery. He can envisage the commission given instead to one of the young artists, brimming with talent and enthusiasm, who hang about the Piazza del Popolo touting for business. He knows they will undercut him. They don't have families to support.

Orazio's thoughts swirl. The light is fading. Time is running away. They are moving from this house in a few days to a cheaper district – saving money, always having to save money. He is calculating how long it will take to restore the damage the bird has wreaked, taking up a palette knife to scrape away the stain carefully. It is not as bad as he'd thought. The brooch is relatively unscathed. It is the chalky mark on the dark swathes of curtain behind that will need repairing.

He stands a moment to admire his work on Judith's red dress, the woven pattern in the brocade, the subtle changes of colour where the light catches the undulations and folds, the places where the material is pulled taut across the bodice, so the eye becomes aware of the invisible starched interfacing. Orazio reminds himself that he is known for his gift in painting fabrics.

His eye is drawn down to his daughter's work. She had fought him to allow her to paint the severed head, such an unsuitable subject for a girl. He had reasoned that no one would know. The painting would bear his name, after all. The head nestled in its basket seems, rather than dead, in a tormented sleep. Its skin is colourless as vellum, all its warmth seeping away through the wicker in trails of crimson ooze. He can feel the chill on those blue-grey lips. The napkin, trailing over the basket's edge, is exquisitely rendered. Pinkish smudges seep along the linen's weft where the women appear to have wiped their bloodied hands.

A shiver runs through him. The gruesome bundle seems to contain the very act itself that caused those bloody marks. And all concocted in his daughter's head. Why have none of his three sons shown such ability? She, at seventeen, is more accomplished even – it galls him to admit – than he, who has a lifetime of painting behind him. He fancies he can hear God's laughter.

Orazio comforts himself with the beauty of his brocade, a careful mix of madder lake, with a few grains of vermilion and enough earth-red ochre to dull any hint of garishness. He is pleased with the effect, very pleased. He takes up a fine brush and carefully begins to stipple a blackish green over the residue left by the bird's mess.

The bird is almost weightless in Artemisia's hands. She'd thought it would flap and scramble to escape but its talons are clasped around her thumb and it is absolutely still, except for the staccato tick of its tiny heart. She opens her fingers carefully. Its sharp little grip tightens, eye rotating.

How easily life can be doused – one moment a thing exists and the next it is gone. She feels sick at the thought of how nearly this small creature was crushed in her father's fist as if it were nothing more than a fly. But even a fly is a life. On occasion she has felt a pang of guilt, sent up a prayer for forgiveness, having slapped a mosquito between her palms, then felt silly for it.

All life is sacred – all God's creatures. Sister Ilaria, scourge of her childhood catechism classes, had labelled her overly sentimental for caring about things she herself deemed unimportant. 'God put all the creatures on this earth to labour for us and feed us, just as he created woman to serve man.'

'Why?'

'It is not for you to question, Artemisia, but simply to accept that it is so.'

The red-hot shock of the ferule across her open palm

ensured she never voiced such a query again, though it germinated in a mossy niche at the back of her mind: why is it so?

In the hot gasp of late afternoon Artemisia slips through the gate and into the small public garden behind the house, enjoying the thrill of freedom, no one to watch in case she should carelessly misplace her virtue. The condition of his only daughter's reputation is a constant preoccupation of her father. He seems to think her curious nature imperils it. But it is he who raised her as an artist, and without curiosity there is no art, or so she firmly believes.

She reaches up, lifting the bird high into the blossom-heavy branches of the Judas tree, an embarrassment of pink. It flits up, perching to sing, the audacity of its trills and whistles at odds with its ordinary buff plumage. She imagines its performance is a show of gratitude for her, when in truth she knows it is rejoicing in its liberty.

In the garden Piero watches her unseen as she gazes at the nightingale, entranced, inscrutable. Like the bird, she is not a beauty in the conventional sense, unlike the models who come and go in her father's studio with their coppery curls and painted pillowy flesh. Artemisia's smile is crooked, her hair wayward, her body spare and angular. Piero cannot say whence her magnetism comes but suspects it is generated by the belief she has in her own abilities. And it is no delusion: she could transform a dishcloth into a holy relic with her brush.

He is about to speak but she turns, placing a finger over her mouth, glancing back and up towards the bird, not wanting to disturb its song. He follows her to the shaded stone bench where an ancient dryad gurgles water into a little pond and the air is thick with the scent of spring.

'Your father wants you to go back in. Help him paint over the stain the bird made.'

She laughs, covering her mouth with her hand. 'It shat on his painting, Piero. Clever little bird.' Her once-white apron is smeared with crimson paint. 'He doesn't need my help. Just doesn't want me outside.' Her tone has soured.

'Just as well I'm here to preserve your honour.' He teases another cough of laughter from her.

The bird flies away as the bells ring for compline, a bellowing chorus marking the shift to evening. She scrutinizes Piero, as if working out how she will paint him. 'Why do you look so tired?'

'Out late last night.'

'Where?' She prods him with her elbow.

'Just around.'

Raising her eyebrows towards him briefly, she takes her sketchbook and a nub of chalk from her pocket, beginning to draw. She has no intention of obeying her irascible father and Piero is glad. It is this defiant spirit he so admires.

'Why so secretive?' she asks, after some time.

He shrugs.

'You were at the cardinal's palazzo, weren't you?'

He nods.

He has told her a little of the goings-on there, parties just for men, where youths dress in girls' clothes, so convincing you would never know what hung between their legs, and of the cardinal himself, who likes to watch them when they fall to drunken abandonment. He'd thought she might be shocked but she wasn't. She asked if he'd ever dressed up like that. He'd told her the opportunity hadn't arisen.

She draws in silence.

All at once the garden is invaded by gangs of whistling swifts, fleet as arrows. Piero watches them, dazzled by their agility, swooping and diving overhead.

Had it not been for his friendship with Artemisia, his stay in Rome would have been a great disappointment. His inadequacies as an artist were soon and starkly exposed, his ambition to earn his living as a painter dashed within days of his arrival. But meeting Artemisia had softened the blow.

Some believe that there exists for everyone in the world a perfect match, like a pair of gloves. Piero believes he has found his own lost glove in Artemisia. Uncomplicated by desires of the flesh, their friendship is instinctive – as if they are twins separated and reunited. For her there is nothing but her art, and his corporeal needs are well met elsewhere.

'Tell me about the evening. Did anything happen?' She doesn't look up from her drawing.

He knows what she means. 'As a matter of fact, yes.'

'Go on.' She looks up, now.

'I was shown something secret. I'm not supposed to say.'

'But you can tell *me*.'

'He has a marble statue that he keeps in a locked closet. It's older than the Colosseum.'

'Why? Why locked away?'

'It is of Hermaphroditus . . .'

She tilts her head, not understanding.

23

'You know . . .' He lowers his voice, though there is no one in earshot. 'The parts of a man *and* a woman.'

'You mean . . . ?' She puts one hand to her breast and the other in the fold of her lap.

He nods. 'Don't you know the story of the nymph who fell for the son of Hermes and Aphrodite? When he cast her off, she prayed to the gods that they never be separated. So she clung to his back and her body fused with his. It's from Ovid.'

'Girls are not told *those* stories. Apparently, they will corrupt us.' She returns to her drawing and they are silent for some time until she looks right at him saying: 'The parts of a man and a woman. I'd like to see that.'

He doesn't have the heart to tell her that the likelihood of her being given the chance to see the *Hermaphroditus* is infinitesimally small. She must already know it. 'The cardinal's looking for a sculptor to carve a couch for it to lie on.'

They both stare wordlessly into the surface of the pond a moment. Patterns of reflected light ripple its surface. 'Do you think one day I shall be commissioned to paint for him – people like him?'

'I do.' Piero hopes this is true.

She changes the subject. 'I'll miss this place. There's not even a balcony at the via della Croce, just a gloomy yard where the drain runs. It is a quarter of the size of this house *and* we will be sharing with Zita Medaglia and her children, whom I have never even met.' She slumps. 'Father says I will benefit from having another woman about the place. But really he wants her to . . .'

'Spy on you!'

'Exactly.' Despondency invades her tone. 'He wants to

keep me cooped up, doesn't trust me. Thinks I will ruin my reputation by "going about".'

'But you need inspiration. And how will you meet other painters, see their work, gain commissions, if you don't "go about"?'

'How indeed? Father wants me preserved, like a pickled egg, for some fat burgher, who counts his money every day and will expect a string of children to spoil.'

'You were not made for some fat burgher. You were made to paint. If I were your husband I would insist upon your freedom.' It is not the first time they have touched on this topic.

Piero has tried not to think about her inevitable marriage because it will certainly sound the death knell for their friendship.

'Imagine if you were to come to Florence. I could be in charge of arranging your multitudes of commissions.'

'It's a nice dream, Piero.' She gets up abruptly, walking back towards the studio.

The garden seems sapped of its colour when she is gone. He picks up her abandoned sketchbook. She has drawn the nightingale – no, not drawn, but embodied, as if there is some invisible conduit travelling from her eye to her heart, to her hand, to the paper. In just a few smudges the bird has sprung into existence, so much so he can almost hear its song once more.

He is reminded of another story from Ovid, can't quite remember how it goes, of a woman who is transformed into a nightingale. The memory leaves a bad feeling trailing in his mind.

Taking up the charcoal he attempts to copy her sketch. It

begins well but soon becomes flat and lifeless, serving to illustrate his friend's superior gifts. All Rome is abuzz with talk of the Bernini boy, who, at twelve years of age, is being touted as a genius for his sculpture. His talents have already caught the attention of the cardinal. His career is made before it has begun, for the cardinal seeks to amass the greatest collection of art in all Rome and, being the Pope's nephew, has the means to do so. All the has-beens in the city are scrambling to gain his attention. An averagely gifted painter like Orazio would kill for a commission. In Piero's opinion, Artemisia is every bit as skilled with a paintbrush as young Bernini is with a chisel, if only she were allowed to prove it so.

He rips his shameful sketch from the book, screwing it into a ball and tossing it away as he returns inside.

Orazio's temper seems to have abated. Artemisia says he wasn't always so disagreeable, but Piero finds that hard to believe. She is sitting at the table with him and the model, Fillide, still in the red dress, drinking wine. The melon, so recently standing in for a severed head, sits on a board, sliced in half, a knife stuck upright in its body.

'May I?' Piero points towards the fruit. Orazio word-lessly shunts it towards him. He slices it, aware of the other man's simmering disdain.

The melon's flesh is the colour of fresh trout. It releases its fragrant aroma and Artemisia takes a slice. A sticky trail runs down her wrist that she brings to her mouth to lick.

'Are you not going to cut some for me?' Fillide is smil-ing up at Piero from under her lashes, flirting pointlessly.

Artemisia rolls her eyes. Fillide is the kind of woman who must be desired by all, even by a boy who prefers

26

boys. Piero offers her a piece on the point of the knife, which she takes between the tips of her fingers to nibble delicately.

Turning back to Orazio, Fillide says, 'You've flattered me in your painting.' She speaks in a little girl's sing-song voice.

The stain on the painting is all but gone, the only evidence a glossy patch in the dark background. It will be invisible once it has dried, as if it was never there. He remembers Orazio's rage, so out of proportion to the damage.

'You've made me young again.' Fillide slurs slightly. Up close Piero can see the tangle of fine red veins on her cheeks and the lines around her eyes. It's true Orazio has flattered her. She is still undeniably striking but in his opinion her vanity mutes her beauty more than her age.

'Needs must. Judith was a young woman. Younger than you, Fillide.' Orazio's laugh is a kind of porcine grunt. He swigs his wine and refills their cups.

Piero can see his large paint-smudged hand massaging the woman's knee beneath the table. There is nothing of Artemisia in this uncouth man and it makes him wonder what her mother was like. Artemisia was twelve when she died.

When she'd told him of her mother's death she'd said only: 'Don't pity me, for it will make me hate you.'

She, too, has noticed her father's hand kneading Fillide's thigh, and swaps a raised eyebrow with Piero. He imagines for a moment how different her life would have been had she gone, after the death of her mother, into the household of his uncle, Giovanni Stiatessi and his aunt Porzia, here in Rome. The two women had been as close as sisters.

It was discussed at the time but Orazio had changed his mind.

Piero begins to scrape the freshly milled paint into a container, sealing it carefully so the air won't get to it, then wiping the residue from the mixing slab with a cloth soaked in turpentine.

'You'd better pack everything away for the move before you go,' says Orazio.

'It's a shame you are leaving this place.'

Orazio snaps back, something about how Piero has no inkling of what it is to support a family and pay the bills.

Artemisia lobs a look of disapproval at her father, hating the scorn he harbours for her friend. If she had the chance to choose between them, she knows which she would pick. But Heaven will fall in before she has such a chance.

She watches Piero a while. He has the slate-grey eyes of a northerner, rendered all the more striking by the coal-black curls and tawny skin inherited from his Algerian mother. It is no wonder he is so popular at the cardinal's palace.

Leaving the studio, she climbs the stairs to her bed-chamber, where she casts off her clothes and sponges down her body with cool water from the ewer, enjoying the freedom of her nakedness. She recalls her mother, even when she was very small, insisting that she dress and undress in the dark. It had to be achieved by wriggling out of one garment and into the other without exposing any of her body. 'A good woman never shows her flesh, not even to God,' she used to say, and 'The devil can see in the dark.'

When Artemisia had suggested that both God and the devil saw everything anyway, so what difference would it make, she'd told her daughter to take her immodest thoughts to confession and repent of them. Naturally this served only to arouse further her fascination with the human body.

She tries to picture the *Hermaphroditus*, to imagine the fusing of the two bodies, like limpet to rock. The world is so wide, so full of novelty, pressing her with a compulsion to witness it in its entirety. What she would give to paint it all.

She stands in the window from where the undulating rooftops of Rome spread into the distance, roseate against the darkening blue of the sky. Here and there the vast pale domes of the city's many churches rise up above the buildings. It is throbbing with life and art, and she is driven to take her place in it all, to see everything, to be seen. But every part of her – her body, her talent, her true self – must remain hidden from the world.

3. Via della Croce

Zita is in the upstairs parlour, feeding the baby, Luca. Her girls are making a terrible noise, chasing each other up and down the staircase. She calls, half-heartedly, for them to stop but they can't hear, or don't listen – that is the trouble with twins. If she disturbs the baby's feed to pull them into line, she'll only add his cries to the racket.

She feels Artemisia's eyes on her. She is a strange one, this girl Zita has been tasked to watch over. Quiet, with an unsettling way of staring – as if she can read a person's secrets. Zita supposes it might be because she is a painter. She is very unfeminine, her dress so plain and spotted with paint, her hair uncombed and unflattering. No concession to prettiness, not even a single lace edging, and she seems much older than seventeen. Zita worries because, if she is honest, though she is a married woman of twenty-four, she finds Artemisia a little intimidating. She fears she might fail to keep her in line. The girl doesn't even appear to be wearing a rosary.

She smiles, saying, 'This is a nice house.'

'Do you think so?' It is clear from Artemisia's tone that she doesn't think so and neither does Zita, really. She had only said it for something to say. In fact, the house is tall and dark and meanly proportioned, with the studio on the ground floor, opening onto the street, behind which is a kitchen leading to a small yard where Zita is sure she saw a rat in the drain. A rickety staircase winds up and up, through the back of the building, unlit and narrow, past two floors, two rooms on each, one smallish and one smaller. Its windows are on the front face close enough for the opposite neighbours to see right inside when the shutters are open. Zita's apartment – only a room really – is in the attic.

'You've sat for artists before?' Artemisia says.

'That's right.' Zita lists some of their names. Artemisia nods, as if she has heard of them, but says nothing in response.

Luca has not had his fill yet, so Zita latches his hungry mouth onto her other breast.

'Have you sat naked?'

The question makes Zita blush. 'I certainly have not. It would be sinful.' She touches a finger to her rosary.

Artemisia rolls her eyes. 'You're a pious one! We all sin.'

She is right: Zita sins every day in small ways – and sometimes in bigger ways, but the less she thinks of that the better. That is what confession is for.

'Where's your husband?'

Despite the unembellished manner in which the question is delivered, Zita is glad of a topic she feels comfortable with. 'He's travelling to the Americas.' She explains that she had waved goodbye to him on the dockside in January when Luca was not much bigger than a borlotti bean. His last words to the twins had been 'You look after your mother,' and they had all cried there on the dock. It was a trading voyage. He couldn't tell her when he would return, had said it would be 'Sometime after Christmas. Or maybe before – God willing.' She crosses herself.

She stops a moment, expecting Artemisia to say something, anything, ask a question about her husband – what is he like? Is he good-looking? What is he trading in the Americas? What is it like to be left for so long? – as any normal person would out of politeness.

But she doesn't say anything at all, so Zita continues, explaining that they had been staying with her sister in the countryside, while waiting for the Gentileschi family to move into this place. 'It's good I can come here because there's barely enough space at my sister's for her, her husband and their six children, let alone me and my three.' She laughs, not mentioning that she and her sister do not get on very well, that her sister disapproves of her sitting for artists.

If Artemisia considers her pious, what would she think of her sister, who says being a painter's model is as good as prostitution? Zita has given up trying to explain that it is not like that at all. 'My husband made the arrangements with your father – paid him nine months' rent up front, so here we are.' She shrugs with a smile. 'I do worry about him on the seas. You hear such terrible things . . . pray to Saint Christopher every day for his safety . . .'

Artemisia has stopped listening – the woman barely draws breath. Her thick country accent is startlingly at odds with her looks. She is breathtakingly beautiful, big bovine eyes, skin smooth and glowing as a sunken candle, hair burnished, her features conspiring to create perfect harmony. The baby's fat hand reaches up to clutch the small crucifix that swings from her neck. Artemisia itches to settle down and capture the scene, but there is unpacking to do and the Stiatessis will be here soon to see the new house.

'I'd like to paint you sometime,' she says, interrupting the woman's chatter about her husband and the Saint Christopher prayer card she'd secretly slipped into his pocket before he left. 'If you don't mind,' she adds, to sound less blunt.

'Of course. It's part of the arrangement – with your father.' She looks down at her baby. 'Right, little fellow. You've had your share. Would you mind holding him for a moment,' she points to a stack of luggage visible on the landing, 'while I get that lot up to my room?' Before Artemisia can think of an excuse, Zita has pressed the sleeping infant into her arms.

The child smells of sour milk. Artemisia stares at him, holding him away from her body, carefully, awkwardly, as if he might break. Zita's two raucous girls career into the room, shrieking with excitement. Artemisia's youngest brother, Marco, is in their wake, equally wild. The door bangs loudly, jolting the baby awake.

Balancing the infant in one hand, she catches Marco by the arm as the girls run back out and upstairs to their mother. 'Calm down.' He is puffing, out of breath. 'You're making enough racket to raise the devil.'

'It's not me, it's them.' He flails an arm, narrowly missing the infant's head.

'Mind the baby! Why don't you go and help your brothers unload the cart?'

'Why should I?' Marco's mouth draws tight and he throws his sister a defiant toss of the head.

'You wouldn't want me to tell Father you were misbehaving, would you?' Seeing him cower, Artemisia regrets resorting to such a threat. She would never dream of involving her father. He has ruled his children by fear, pitted them against each other, and they have all perfected the art of creeping carefully around him, particularly when he is in his cups.

She had noticed him surreptitiously drinking that morning when the cart was being loaded. He'd announced his intention to sacrifice strong drink for Lent but it's a mere two weeks since Ash Wednesday and he has already failed in that promise.

Artemisia remembers a time when he wasn't like this, before her mother died. She and her brothers have had to learn to keep a tight eye on the rise and fall of his unpredictable temper. Easter is not far off now, after which he will no longer feel the need to hide his drinking.

The baby spits a trail of opaque substance. She wipes it with his bib, trying to keep her disgust at bay, relieved to hand him back to his mother. 'Let's go downstairs together,' she says to her brother, 'and see what we can do to help.'

Her father is barking orders in the doorway, organizing the unloading of an enormous carton into the arms of her other two brothers.

'Where do you want it?' asks Francesco. He has grown muscular, suddenly, so his clothes are too small and a smudge of darkness has appeared on his upper lip that makes him seem a good deal older than his fourteen years.

'What's in it?' Orazio reads the label attached to the box. 'Artemisia's things. Take it up to the bedchamber on the second floor.'

'Is she to have that room to herself? Wouldn't it be better if she has the box bed' – Francesco points to the closet in the corner – 'and we boys have the room upstairs?'

'Yes, the upstairs room,' echoes Giulio, who is nine and always takes the lead from his older brother.

Artemisia is thinking of the dingy space on the second floor, with its keyhole-sized window. She would much rather the box bed, which Francesco is now complaining is too small for him and his brothers to share. On the ground floor she might have more chance to sneak out . . . and she could paint all night if inspiration arrived unexpectedly.

'I don't mind the box bed, if it's easier.' She is careful to hide any enthusiasm that might lead Orazio to think she is taking advantage.

'You see?' Francesco looks triumphant and ducks too late to avoid the sharp clip his father delivers. He has to stay himself not to cry out in pain. One day he will realize he has become the stronger man and retaliate – it won't be long. Artemisia imagines her brother landing a heavy punch on his jaw, her father staggering back.

'Artemisia is our asset.' Orazio's voice is a growl. Francesco gives her a sideways scowl and Giulio looks at his feet. 'When you prove you have the potential to bring something of value to our family' – he prods a finger in Artemisia's direction – 'then you might also gain the privilege to go with it.'

She turns her back, crouching, pretending to rub at a stubborn mark on the floor with a rag, resenting her father for creating this discord – divide and rule. It will serve only to fuel the mouldering jealousy her brothers feel for her.

She'd happily give her heart and kidneys to change places with them, to have their freedom, to go to school and learn to write, to loiter in the square and witness the world. Let *them* be imprisoned upstairs with Zita spying on them, only allowed out to go to mass or confession.

Orazio stands in the open doorway, looking up. 'All that bloody laundry is blocking the light.' He is referring to the rows of washing strung across the street like pennants. 'I don't know how we'll be able to see to paint.'

She takes the broom and, handing the dustpan to Marco, begins to sweep the floor. The dust curls up in eddies around their feet, motes swirling in the single ray of filtered sun that has made it into the room. Marco's jacket is a solid block of pure pea-green against the pale flagstones. She prefers the subdued quality of the light in this studio – it makes the colours true. 'I've been thinking of experimenting with using less light, a single source – lamplight. Like . . .'

'Don't start on about *him*.' Her father's mouth forms a bitter knot. She'd anticipated his response almost before she'd spoken and now regrets her comment. 'All anyone ever talks of is *him* and his novel approach to lighting. Nothing new about it any more – it was years ago. He's long gone, and good riddance.'

Artemisia is not so much a fool as to remind him that Merisi remains at the forefront of everyone's minds – Caravaggio, they call him, these days – because no painter since has achieved his brilliance. Not in Rome, anyway. She keeps her mouth shut. It is not the moment to further rile her father. She finds it hard to imagine they were such close friends once.

On the pretext of confession, she goes often to sit in the Cerasi chapel where her mother was laid to rest and gaze for hours at Merisi's painting of Saint Paul hanging there. The saint lies on his back, his head at the very front of the painting, arms outstretched, an expression of rapture over his foreshortened face. An enormous skewbald looms over him, casting an eye down, one hoof lifted, iron shoe visible. No angels mark the divine presence, only a spill of amber light. Saint Paul is not some distant icon: rather, he is a man one might encounter in the street who has fallen from his horse and needs a hand up. It makes Carraci's *Assumption*, hung close by, in all its gaudy brightness, look like some confection one might find on display in a cakemaker's shop.

As the final pieces of furniture are unloaded from the cart, the Stiatessis arrive: Piero, with his uncle and aunt, Giovanni and Porzia. Little Marco flings aside the dustpan, spilling its contents, and runs towards them. Giovanni crouches down drawing something from his pocket.

Marco squeals, 'Can I hold it?' and Giovanni delivers a grey-striped kitten into his small hands.

'There are two more.' Porzia peels back the cloth that covers her basket to reveal a pair of whiskered faces. 'We thought they'd make good mousers for you.' She casts her eyes round the space unable, despite her bright comments about the proportions of the studio and its proximity to the pigment dealer, to hide what she really thinks of the Gentileschis' new home – that it is several steps down in the world.

Artemisia shows Porzia round the house. They sit on her bed side by side as Zita and her children bang about upstairs. Porzia must sense Artemisia's despondency because she says: 'You do know you are always welcome to come and stay with us if you find . . .' She searches for a word, smoothing a palm over her black hair, severely parted with two plaits wound into a skein at her nape. It is the way Artemisia's mother used to wear her hair. Porzia and she looked so alike they were often mistaken for sisters. 'If you become too on top of one another here.' The warmth of her smile is like an embrace, but it comes with a swirl of sweet-sad memories.

The loss of her mother had brought about such a profound alteration in the pattern of Artemisia's life. There would be no more days passed in the Stiatessis' large kitchen, shelling beans from their velvety pockets, or rolling out pastry, secretly cutting off the ends to eat raw, or mixing sweet batter and squabbling over which of them would lick the spoon and listening to the women's easy chat.

They talked of female things: of mysterious remedies, powders and tinctures and plasters, that could cure any ailment – recipes their grandmothers had taught them to be passed down in secret. They talked of the irritating habits of their husbands, the untidiness of their children, the people they disapproved of, dropping their voices, or talking in code so the children couldn't understand quite what it was those whispered-about people had done wrong. And they talked of the women they knew whom God had taken in childbirth, crossing themselves solemnly as they said their names: *Laudomia, Marta, Clara*.

She remembers watching the swelling of her mother's belly, her ankles, her face, until she lumbered heavily about the house, one hand on the small of her back, her breath shallow. Each month she would wear a more capacious garment. Artemisia craved a glimpse of that curtained body, to understand its new form. She knew her fascination was wrong: the body is the site of shame. They all

38

had to pretend not to notice that their mother was changing shape.

As the baby grew, so fear germinated in Artemisia. She couldn't erase those whispered names from her head: *Laudomia, Marta, Clara*. 'Will God take you, like He took those other women?' she'd asked, knowing it was not the sort of thing you said, even to your mother, but the question had pressed so hard she couldn't contain it.

'Only if it is His will.' Her mother's fingers glanced from forehead to heart, from shoulder to shoulder. 'I have birthed three of you already without turning a hair, so there is no reason it shouldn't be the same with this one.' She smiled her pink smile, running her hand over her belly and then over Artemisia's head, drawing her into a hug.

Artemisia made a bargain with God: if He preserved her mother, she would give herself to Him entirely, body and soul, take the veil – become His bride.

It took her mother three days to die, three days of Porzia carefully blending powders into tinctures and administering them to her, while the baby's wet ruddy howls trailed through the house.

Artemisia felt herself drifting further from God's grace until she could no longer feel its warmth. God had failed her, as had the powders and remedies.

Porzia hadn't thought an artist's studio was a suitable environment for a girl to be raised. There had been discussions about Artemisia and baby Marco being absorbed into the large Stiatessi family, for a time, at least. Arrangements were made.

But Orazio must have had a change of heart. Artemisia did the rest of her growing up in the studio where she learned of other powders: precious minerals prised from the earth, like lead and tin and quartz, which, combined in a secret alchemy, releases the yellow of cowslips; rare new-world beetles, crushed, produce a crimson so rich it leaves fingers blood-stained for days; bones burned and suffocated make the blackest of blacks; dung layered over lead and vinegar and left three months to fester becomes lead-white, the finest touch of which can give sight to a painted eye; the *guado* plant from the east, when steeped and strained and settled eventually transforms into indigo blue, a hue that must be trapped beneath varnish or it will fade to a spectre.

These powders never failed her. She learned to make life out of them, so she no longer needed to rely on God.

Porzia stands, drawing her out of her memories. 'Coming downstairs?'

Returning to the studio, Orazio is ebullient. 'This man here' – he pats Giovanni firmly on the back – 'has arranged an invitation for me to visit the Palazzo Conscente and show the conte some of my work.'

'The conte is a man with a large collection of paintings.' Giovanni is absently rubbing his beard. He becomes more ursine as each year passes. 'I've been handling some legal details about his daughter's dowry, so I know how deep his pockets are.'

'Good news, then.' Artemisia hopes this might be the patron her father has been so desperately seeking.

'I'd say so,' replies Giovanni. 'The conte is a good connection to make.'

'You can show him the *Judith*.' She points to the painting that they had rushed so hard to finish, which now loiters, awaiting the man who commissioned it to return from abroad.

'And you will come with me,' her father says, nodding in her direction. 'You can show the conte what you are able to do with a sheet of paper and a piece of chalk. He has a new grandchild apparently – might be charmed by a likeness, which would be good for us all.'

Artemisia swaps a roll of the eyes with Piero, who is across the room quietly arranging all the pigment jars on a shelf. She doesn't relish the idea of being her father's performing monkey but at least she will gain a peek at the conte's famed collection of paintings.

4. Judith's Nipples

One thought crosses Orazio's mind as he takes in his surroundings at the Palazzo Conscente. Wealth may enable a
man to acquire beautiful things but good taste cannot be
bought. An elaborate gold clock ticks loudly, its sound
reverberating around the acres of marble – vivid pink and
veined in white, reminding him of the *mortadella di prato* of
his Tuscan childhood. Otherwise, the large, light-flooded
room is silent as a church, cocooned from the noises of
the city by thick walls on which are hung several paintings
of high quality.

The conte's son is making stilted conversation, apologizing for his father's lateness and for the fact that he hasn't
had time to change out of his riding outfit.

Even the riding outfit – a buff silk concoction teamed
with canary yellow stockings – puts the Gentileschis' best
clothes to shame, making Orazio very aware of the shab-
biness of his own suit and the small burn hole in his
breeches, which he strives to cover with his hand. Francesco's shirt hangs untidily beneath his jacket, which he has
grown out of, the fastenings straining over his chest. Artemisia has paint on her cuffs. He is somewhat annoyed that
Piero looks by far the smartest of them all. He wonders
where the boy came by the means to fit himself out so
well, supposes his uncle must help him.

'My father will be here soon.' The son smiles at Artemisia.

'You are also a painter, I understand?' He blushes and Orazio allows himself a flight of fancy, imagining the boy falling for his daughter and insisting on making her his wife. The Gentileschi money worries would be solved in one go. He is well aware of the absurdity of such a dream.

A servant offers them refreshments, some kind of fruit concoction in glass goblets so fragile Orazio is nervous his will shatter in his hand. Soon a young woman appears with an infant on her hip, who is introduced as the wife, putting paid to Orazio's fanciful dream.

Piero is drawn to the infant, like a bee to pollen, pulling silly faces to tease a smile out of it. The young mother is naturally delighted, much to Orazio's irritation: he had told Piero, in no uncertain terms, that he could join them only on the condition he remained in the background and kept his mouth shut. Artemisia, instead of paying polite attention to the child, has drifted off to the other end of the room and is gazing at one of the paintings. Orazio smiles obsequiously at the young father with a shrug. 'Can't help herself. Your father's collection is remarkable.'

He draws beside his daughter, chiding her for her bad manners under his breath. She barely notices him, is stupefied, staring at the painting. It is a picture he remembers well. Merisi painted it more than a decade ago: *Judith Slaying Holofernes*. He is as shocked by its violence now as he had been then. He remembers Merisi's insistence on painting the moment in which Judith decapitates the Assyrian. It has all the subtlety of a cosh to the head.

He'd forgotten Merisi had used Fillide to portray his Judith. A shame her breasts are not so pert these days. How young she is there, how horrified by the spurt of blood

43

projecting from the neck of her victim, as if she can't believe what she has done. It is a strange coincidence that he himself used Fillide for his own recent Judith, brought today for the conte's perusal. His is a more restrained and palatable scene, the severed head tucked away in its basket – more conventional, Merisi would have called it.

'Is this the work inspired by the Cenci execution?' asks Artemisia. He takes her wrist, pulling her firmly away, back to the young family. It is an image far too brutal, too erotic with its red ejaculation, wholly unsuitable for the eyes of a seventeen-year-old girl.

Orazio wonders how his daughter remembers the details of that day. She'd been so young. She'd passed out before the worst of the bloody business began, the Cenci boy drawn and quartered, guts and gore everywhere. Merisi had been transfixed, had had to be dragged away – always had a taste for the gruesome.

They linger some more, pretending polite adoration of the infant, until the door opens and the conte swings into the room with a booming apology for his lack of punctuality: 'An inescapable unplanned meeting.'

'Not at all. Not at all.' Orazio is fully aware of his place in the pecking order, given the conte is the Pope's banker. 'We have been making acquaintance with your charming family. What a delightful infant.' Orazio hates the servile tone that has crept into his voice but if a little grovelling can bring him a commission then it will have been worth it.

'I see my son has offered you something to drink.' He is a large man with the relaxed confidence that only great wealth can bring. He is friendly, open, talking about the beauty of the day, how lucky he is to have a view of the river. 'The light that reflects off the water has an ethereal quality that makes everything so much more beautiful. Wouldn't you agree?' He says this while looking directly at Artemisia, who is no great beauty and stubbornly refuses to respond to his flattery. Orazio can't help but think of the poor quality of the light in his gloomy new studio on the via della Croce. 'Now, let's get down to the important matters – your works.'

In silence the conte passes his eyes over the several canvases they have brought, standing before each one for some time, stepping close to inspect the brushwork, squinting slightly before standing back again and approaching once more armed with a magnifying glass.

Orazio is girded for disappointment, tells himself that the man has no taste, merely buys art to display his spending power, his opinion is irrelevant. The conte lingers a while at the *Judith* before moving on to a portrait of little Marco, of which Orazio is quite proud. But the conte returns his attention to the biblical scene, asking that it be moved further into the light, where he scrutinizes it through his magnifier once more.

Eventually he speaks. 'Now, this is extraordinarily good. I haven't seen work such as this since Merisi di Caravaggio passed on – God rest his soul.' He makes the sign of the cross. 'I am impressed.'

Orazio feels himself inflate with pride. The man has taste after all. He certainly has a fine collection of paintings. 'Without wanting to contradict someone with a discerning eye like yours, my work could never be compared to such a master.'

The conte dismisses the comment as the disingenuous babble it is. 'See here, how the head appears to sleep.' He is pointing, almost touching, the severed head nestled in its basket. 'The colour seems to drain from it before the eye, these drips here, so real I almost feel the blood would be left on my fingertip were I to dare touch it. And here – the napkin, the marks of the wiped blood. Truly marvellous.'

Orazio swallows. 'Do you see, I used Fillide Melandrone to sit for Judith, as did Merisi?' He points, hoping to draw the conte's attention away from the severed head towards the figure of Judith, awaiting praise for his meticulous working of the red brocade dress and the beautiful woman who wears it. 'Of course, she's not so young now.'

'Yes . . .' The conte pauses for a few moments, as if giving great thought to what he is about to pronounce. 'I hope you don't mind me saying.' He meets the artist's eyes plainly, making it clear he is going to say whatever it is whether Orazio minds it or not. 'I find your Judith devoid of something. She's somehow lacking in life. The dress is nicely done.' Orazio battles with his disappointment as the man leans in once more to inspect the fine brushwork. 'You are right to say it can't be compared to someone with the rare gifts of . . . There are dozens of Caravaggisti producing perfectly good work of this kind. But it is this' – he indicates once more the severed head in the blood-drenched basket – 'that is the true heart of your painting, where your talent truly blossoms.' He smiles broadly. 'This demonstrates your extraordinary gift, Signor Gentileschi.'

Orazio nods, simmering with profound indignation.

'How did you achieve this effect?' The conte is pointing at the stained napkin.

Orazio can feel his daughter's eyes boring through him.

Before he has the chance to respond with a lie, she interjects, 'That is *my* work.'

The conte jolts up, astonished, looking at her as if she is an apparition. 'Goodness!' He holds out his hand to take hers, planting a kiss on her glove. 'Those who spoke of your promise were not exaggerating. I didn't expect –'

Artemisia doesn't make a grovelling denial, simply thanks him. She knows how good she is.

'We were rather hoping you might allow Artemisia to sketch our grandson.' The conte is speaking directly to Orazio.

Artemisia takes it upon herself to respond before Orazio speaks for her. 'It would be my great pleasure.'

Piero, an undisguised smirk on his face, passes her the bag of equipment and they put their heads together to discuss the best light in which to set the portrait, while Orazio pretends to look at the works on the far wall.

Artemisia drags a small ornate chair into a pool of light where the mother and infant sit. She quashes her nerves with trivial conversation as she carefully adjusts the hang of the mother's dress and suggests she angle the infant a little more towards the window. The woman is young, seems about her own age, and radiates an all-encompassing delight in her offspring.

Artemisia begins to draw, but Merisi's *Judith* keeps catching her attention. The expression on that young Judith's face – as if she is surprised to see that she has severed her enemy's head, surprised her own hand is wielding the sword. The act itself, the beheading, recedes into darkness.

The tomato gush of blood loses in a competition with the brilliant white of Judith's chemise. The eye is instantly drawn to the bright fabric pulled tightly over her breasts, nipples startlingly erect. It is almost as if the artist had wanted to depict her arousal.

The thought makes Artemisia's face burn.

'The room is very warm,' she pretends, unwinding her shawl as she forces her eyes away from the painting and onto the carefully placed mother and child. The infant is fat and sweet as the *putti* on a church mural.

Piero passes her the box of chalks, from which she selects one in a dark, earthy red and sets to work in earnest. Her nape prickles with the conte's gaze as he stands behind watching her every stroke. The image takes shape easily and she has all but forgotten her annoyance at being brought here as a curiosity.

The idea that this commission might be hers tightens inside her like a stopper swelling in a bottle. The chalk seems to have taken on its own life, gliding over the page, a finger rubbed here and there to create density; a spot of white gives gloss to the infant's mouth; a line of it bleeds into the light behind.

Orazio glowers from afar, as if she has stolen something from him. She becomes distracted by the thought of how he will act when they leave – will he give way to his temper? She sneaks another glimpse at the Merisi, regretting it instantly, daunted by its quality. Her hands become silted with chalk and clumsy with sweat. She wipes them on her dress, taking a moment to compose herself.

Returning to the sketch, her fingers seem to have become disobedient. Normally she would abandon it, screw up the paper and throw it onto the fire. But she is supposed to be displaying the spontaneous gifts that the conte has heard talk of – proving her worth.

The noon bells ring. She is taking far too long. Her lines are now irretrievably clogged and the form she had created is flat and lifeless. All her confidence has drained away.

She stops. 'I'm – I'm sorry.'

The conte says something to the tune of never mind but she can hear the dismissal in his tone.

'I'm sorry,' she repeats, annoyed with herself at not being able to find anything else to say. Piero briefly touches her shoulder, a welcome gesture of solidarity, before he sets to putting away the materials.

'Can I see it?' asks the mother.

Artemisia wants to refuse but that would be a slight too far, so she hands it over, attempting the best smile she can muster. 'I haven't really captured him. He is such a beautiful child.' She only just prevents herself from further apology. The mother's expression is as flat as the sketch. She hands it back wordlessly.

'There was a moment when you had it.' The conte is smiling kindly, patronizing, making her shrivel. 'Did your nerves get the better of you?'

'I suppose they must have.' The infant is twitching, on the brink of hungry bawls. 'I could start again.' The mother is on her feet, though, and is moving to the door, the child now howling.

'Perhaps another day,' says the conte. But Artemisia knows he only means to be polite. She had her opportunity and squandered it.

Orazio is making his own unctuous apology now, talking

of the quality of the conte's art collection, what an impeccable eye he has. 'The very best of the very best.'

'That's as may be but I have a rival in Cardinal Borghese. From what I gather he is seeking to fill his new palazzo in the Monte Cavallo gardens with works from Rome's finest. The competition will drive up the price of art, no doubt.'

'Ah, yes, I have heard talk of the cardinal's growing collection.' Her father seems to shrink in stature as he rolls out his empty flattery. 'He will never be a true rival to you.'

It is time to leave this world to which they do not belong. The conte sees their party down the sweep of white marble steps to the exit. As they descend, Artemisia hangs on to the small hope that he will ask her to return, give her another chance.

They arrive at the vast brass-studded door, opened for them by a servant, her hopes dying as the conte bids them a friendly goodbye and the door is closed.

The boys hoist the pictures onto the tatty conveyance, more cart than carriage. Heart heavy and hard as a brick, she clambers into the cabin with her father while the boys sit up front. No one says a word. They lumber out of the gates into the busy street, a cacophony of city sounds after the peace of the Palazzo Conscente.

'What an awful man,' spits Orazio. 'Such vulgar taste. That grotesque chamber. What does *he* know about the art of painting? All those works on his walls – just *things* to him. Investments! Since when did bankers become the arbiters of taste?'

Artemisia is tempted to point out to him that the Medici family were bankers and are now the rulers of Florence with a collection to surpass any in the civilized world. But she is not fool enough to provoke him when he is in such ill humour. He turns to her. 'Don't go getting ideas about yourself. Conscente doesn't know what he is talking about.'

When the conte had given his opinion, Artemisia had the sensation of growing taller, branches thrusting up to the sky, roots penetrating deep into the earth. Now she feels small again, transparent and fragile. The hope she has secretly held to see her work hanging alongside the great masters one day, she a woman, is shattered – that sinful pride of hers.

They fall into their own private thoughts, her mood becoming increasingly crushed as the carriage trundles on.

After some time, her father adds: 'You proved yourself lacking in the end, didn't you?' There is a spark of glee behind his eyes.

Suddenly Artemisia imagines striking him with the flat of her hand, so vividly she can feel the pink burn on her palm.

5. Saint Agatha's Breasts

Zita's back aches. Pins and needles run through her arms. She has been posing as the Blessed Virgin all morning, draped in a blue robe with Luca splayed over her lap.

While Orazio and Artemisia work in silence and Piero quietly gives instructions to Francesco on the correct milling of pigments, Zita's mind drifts to another painting she has modelled for – a secret painting. It was a few evenings ago. Orazio was out with the older boys, and the children were all in bed, when Artemisia asked her if she would sit naked.

Zita had hesitated and Artemisia had said: 'You're not going to let your pretend piety get in the way, are you?' That had stung. 'Anyway, the woman I want to depict is from the Bible. Susanna, who was famed for the strength of her faith and virtue.'

'But what will your father say?'

'He doesn't need to know.' Artemisia looked at her with a conspiratorial smile.

Those words, *pretend piety*, continue to ring around her head. Perhaps it is true. All Zita knows is that life is easier if you try to obey God's laws. Artemisia seems to march to her own tune.

At last Orazio suggests they stop for a few minutes. She carefully places her sleeping infant on the couch and stretches, arms up, clenching and unclenching her fizzing hands and twisting her body until her spine makes an audible click. At the table she slices some hard cheese and the loaf that she and Piero had gone out to buy first thing.

'Anyone hungry?' She offers the plate around, then crouches to take a package surreptitiously from her basket in the corner. It contains a small round iced cake with a cherry planted on its top. Half turning her back she sinks her teeth into it.

'Where did you get *that*?' Francesco looks up from the mortar where he is pummelling azurite, pointing with a blue-stained finger.

'Get what?' She slips the confection behind her back, tongue darting out, lizard-like, to capture a granule of sugar stuck to her lip.

'The cake you're trying to hide.'

'I bought it at the bakery.' She holds it up brazenly.

Piero stabs her with a look and she instantly regrets her statement. He knows it is a lie.

Her conscience jabs – *pretend piety* – shame twisting through her. The baker had just opened his doors, billows of warm yeasty air luring them in. The tray of cakes, set out to cool, had whispered to her like a seduction with their scarlet cherries and sweet smell. One had slipped into her basket almost before she realized what she was doing.

She has felt unmoored since her husband's departure. Neither has she settled in under the Gentileschis' roof in the month she has been here. For a short while, with the knowledge of her secret prize, this trivial pastry, everything had felt less daunting, the whole world momentarily in her control. But now her mind swirls frantically on what might happen if Orazio discovers this misdemeanour. He would be justified in throwing a thief into the street.

'I don't know how you can eat that.' Francesco grimaces, his face twisting in disgust.

'It's just a cake.' It is turning to goo in her hot hand.

'You know why they call them Saint Agatha's Breasts?' He directs a cool stare at her.

She shrugs. Zita finds Francesco intimidating. She is not used to boys, never had a brother and, despite his youth, this one seems so full of confidence where she feels so lacking.

'You know in mass when the sacrament transforms into the Body of Christ?' She nods. 'Same thing happens with those cakes. In your mouth they actually become the saint's flesh.'

Zita drops the confection as if it has scalded her, immediately feeling a fool. Surely he is teasing her but she can't be sure, for he looks deadly serious. She is caught in a wave of remorse. The first time she'd stolen something – a favourite pair of lace gloves that belonged to a spiteful older cousin who baited her at every opportunity – her feeling of secret triumph had made the cousin's cruelty pale to nothing.

It became a habit for a time but had all been in her past until the cherry-topped cake had whispered to her from its tray. She will have to come clean about it at confession.

Francesco is going on, reminding her of the story of the martyred Saint Agatha, 'who had her breasts cut off when she refused to give herself to –'

'That's enough, Franco!' snaps Artemisia, who scoops up the fallen cake, putting it on a plate on the table. She turns to Zita, who can't take her eyes off the sticky mark on the floor. 'Don't listen to him. He's making fun of you.' Francesco throws his sister an irritated sneer, as if to say she's spoiled his game.

Piero, to mollify the situation, sends Francesco out into the yard with the pot of fish glue to wash the crushed granules of azurite. 'You'll need to rinse them at least three times.' Francesco sniffs the glue, his face crumpling in revulsion, muttering an oath under his breath as he leaves. Little Marco follows him out, like an orphaned gosling.

'Here.' Piero passes Zita a slice of bread. 'Franco was being mean. If I were you, I'd ignore him.' He looks at her as if he's wondering how she, a mother of three, could be so gullible.

Marco returns with the empty gluepot to be refilled. Piero slurps in a measure of the viscous liquid. 'It's heavy. Can you manage it?'

The child insists he can but as he walks away he stumbles, spilling some across the studio floor.

With menacing speed Orazio grabs his son by the scruff until his feet are almost off the ground. 'You stupid little cretin!' With his free hand he is attempting to undo the buckle of his belt.

Artemisia jumps in, placing a protective arm around her smallest brother. The little boy is grey with fear. Zita gathers her children close, making herself small, while Giulio slinks away to the far reaches of the studio.

Artemisia squares up to her father. 'No, you don't! Not him too. He's *six*.' She prises his fingers away from the child's collar. 'What would Mother have thought? She'd never have stood for it. Beating a small child for a mishap?' He removes his hand from Marco's scruff, stepping away with a loud intake of breath.

The atmosphere in the studio is brittle, everyone pretending to be busy. Orazio stands by the door, bruised from the chiding his daughter has given him, watching from the side of his eye as she refills the jar of glue and helps Marco take it out to the yard.

When she returns, she suggests to him that Marco might be better off going to stay with Porzia and Giovanni for a time. 'I'm sure they'd be delighted to have him.'

'I'm sure they would,' echoes Piero.

'I don't know what business it is of yours.' Orazio turns his anger on Piero. 'I won't have our family divided.'

'As you wish.' Artemisia shrugs. 'It was merely a suggestion. I thought it would give me more time to help you with your painting.' She turns away from him, continuing to clean up the spilled glue, sweeping it out into the drain with a brush.

'Now you come to mention it,' says Orazio, after some time, 'it might not be such a bad idea after all.'

'I think you're right.' She makes it sound as if it was his idea in the first place.

Zita is impressed at the way she has handled him, a man who strikes terror into all his children – all but his daughter. Even Francesco with all his bluster shrinks in the face of his father's temper. Artemisia seems to have been given the entire family's ration of courage. It is the thing that both bewilders her and makes her admire the girl – this refusal to be cowed.

*

Orazio takes a few breaths to calm himself, loosening his unwittingly clenched fists. The stink of fish glue clogs the air. He could do with a drink. Appraising the morning's work, he is dissatisfied. He has painted the curve of Zita's arm, her hand cupping her infant's foot, but his painted foot is hollow and insubstantial, floating above Zita's upturned hand rather than resting in it. He compares it to his daughter's preparatory drawing. She has depicted the weight of that small foot cradled in his mother's palm. Its flesh, the bones beneath, even the maternal emotion are apparent in her few chalk lines.

'I'm going out,' he says, mumbling that he needs some fresh air. His daughter looks infuriatingly pleased to be rid of him. She is becoming unruly – too clever for her own good and certainly too clever for most prospective husbands. Hopefully he will be able to find someone sufficiently dazzled by her talent to overlook her flaws – the sooner the better. 'And don't go tinkering with my work while I'm away.'

'Of course, Father.' He wonders then, in the face of the meek smile she gives him, if he'd been somehow mistaken about the insubordinate look he'd seen only moments before.

It is horribly bright out in the street, and hot. He wanders up towards his usual drinking place. It is further than it was from the old house and he emerges, sweaty and thirsty, from the narrow street into the open space of the piazza, saturated in midday sun. He drags a stool into the shade that hugs the walls of the tavern and sits quietly until the patron emerges from the dark interior with a jug of his usual local red. One day he will surprise the man and order something better. Not today, though.

The wine is young and sharp as vinegar. His head begins, at last, to swim pleasantly, his worries drifting off, and in a comfortable daze he watches a gaggle of pigeons pecking and dancing around a few fallen crumbs.

A shadow reaches over him, and looking up, he sees a young man whose face he recognizes but can't place.

'Would I be disturbing you if I were to sit here?' The man is smiling and would be quite presentable were it not for one of his eyes that appears, disconcertingly, to work independently of the other.

Orazio would rather not be disturbed but doesn't want to cause offence in case the young man happens to be somebody of influence. He is certainly dressed the part – the jacket is discreet but well-tailored and of expensive cloth, with, if his eyes do not deceive him, buttons of *real* silver. Scouring his mind for a name he notices the large ring, intaglio in carnelian with an embossed coat of arms, which would give Orazio a clue to the fellow's identity, if only he could see it properly. 'Not at all.' He tries to make it sound as if he means it.

The young man pulls up a seat. 'Orazio Gentileschi, isn't it? We met last year at the house of Giovanni Stiatessi.'

Orazio still can't bring a name to mind.

'Geronimo Modenese,' he says.

It all floods back. He is the son of a wealthy gem dealer who fancies himself as something of a collector – new money. He recalls having had a conversation about a commission that never went any further and, vaguely, that they had raised a glass to his imminent marriage. He was to wed the daughter of some minor Neapolitan nobleman, or perhaps the girl was from Puglia. He remembers thinking it was an ambitious match for a family who, Porzia had whispered to him, were cheesemongers from Udine a generation ago.

'Weren't you on the brink of matrimony?'

A cloud passes over Modenese's face. 'It was most ill-starred.' Orazio is preparing to commiserate the bride's untimely death when Modenese says, 'Surely you heard about it. My father's conviction.'

Abruptly, he does remember a fuss about some scandal: white sapphires passed off as diamonds, or something similar.

'Her family pulled out of the betrothal agreement, a month before the wedding.'

'How unfortunate.'

Modenese swiftly changes the subject, noticing that the carafe is empty and offering to replenish it, calls over the patron, waving the empty vessel. 'Fill this with Lacryma Christi, if it is cold. And something to eat . . .' He enters a long discussion about which of the cured meats, suspended like miniature corpses from the interior ceiling, are best, opting eventually for a plate of bresaola.

He turns to Orazio, lowering his voice: 'Thank heavens Lent is over and we can enjoy meat once more.'

The wine he has ordered is the most expensive the house has to offer. Orazio knows this because he can't afford it.

Modenese makes small-talk, asking after Stiatessi, whether they have seen one another recently. 'Isn't his young half-brother studying with you? I forget his name.'

'Piero, yes, he is. Very good eye for colour.' It is the only complimentary thing he can think to say about Piero.

'Quite the flamboyant character, from what I gather.'

Modenese meets his eye with a weighted look of condemnation.

'I wouldn't know what he gets up to away from my studio.'

Modenese moves the conversation on, saying he recently saw one of Orazio's works in church and how well it looked in its setting. 'A *Saint Francis*. Made a great impression on me.'

Orazio is particularly proud of that *Saint Francis*, completed some years ago. He is beginning to warm to this personable young man. The wine is slipping down nicely. It is cool and floral on the tongue, complementing the delicately flavoured bresaola cut fine as parchment.

'I hear your daughter's making quite a reputation for herself.'

'Artemisia!' Orazio's hackles rise. 'Her reputation is stainless, I'll have you know.'

'Oh, no.' Modenese is laughing now. 'I didn't mean that. I apologize if I insulted you. I meant her artistic gifts. It is said she has great promise.'

Orazio feels a little foolish for jumping so quickly to offence. 'Yes. She is a fine painter.' His pride for Artemisia's talent battles with his envy of it. 'I taught her all she knows, of course.'

'Indeed, so I have heard. I suppose she couldn't attend one of the schools – being of the fairer sex. To be exposed to . . .' He doesn't say it, but it is clear what he means: the nudity and the rough talk at the very least.

'I have only the one daughter and would protect her innocence with my life.' An idea is forming. 'And . . .' He hesitates, wondering if he is being a little unsubtle but decides better that than an opportunity lost. 'Are you courting anew?'

'Alas, no.' Modenese places a hand over his heart. 'Our family has been somewhat blighted – and until my father is able to clear his name, which he will –'

'I have no doubt in the slightest that he will,' agrees Orazio. They drink a little more and gossip about various artists as the sun creeps across the piazza.

'And what are you painting now?' Modenese finally asks.

'A *Madonna*.' He seizes his opportunity. 'Why don't you pay us a visit and take a look at her?'

'I should like that very much. I hope I will be able to see some of your daughter's work at the same time – to satisfy my curiosity. Meet her too if you felt it appropriate.'

'I'm sure that can be arranged.' Orazio feels quite uplifted as the young man slaps down several coins and casually calls to the patron to keep the change, before taking his leave.

Orazio remains a while, draining the carafe and considers sliding one of those coins into his sleeve. Modenese's tip is excessively generous, and the patron would be none the wiser.

He resists the temptation and orders a measure of grappa.

6. The Red Dress

The glue stench lingers on as Artemisia, taking advantage of her father's absence, delves through the boxes of clothing. They mostly contain costumes for painting that haven't yet been unpacked since the move.

'What are you looking for?' She starts, hadn't noticed Piero in the kitchen doorway, watching her.

'The red dress that Fillide wore for the *Judith*.' She pulls out a length of silk, appraising it and setting it aside on a pile of other fabrics and outfits.

'You know she was a famous courtesan once. Used to entertain a string of influential men.'

'She's come down in the world, then. I heard her leaving Father's room at dawn the other day and it wasn't the first time.'

'I suppose he has to get his comfort somewhere.' Piero picks up a feather that has drifted to the floor. 'Merisi was besotted with her. It's said she never let him touch her, but he would have done anything for her.'

'I don't understand.' It seems illogical to Artemisia.

'You don't know about men's desire.' Piero wears an amused look. 'The more you hate them the more they love you. When men want what they can't have, they are completely disarmed.'

She still doesn't fully understand how this could be. It seems perverse to her. 'You only have to look at how

Merisi portrayed her in his *Judith* to see he was besotted.'
She has thought about the painting at the Palazzo Conscente a great deal. During the wakeful nights in her
oppressive little bedchamber, she casts the image onto the
dark ceiling, every detail remembered.

'He painted her killing a man. Says something about
their relationship.' Piero lifts his eyebrows.

'It is an extraordinary work, a masterpiece, but . . .'

'But what?'

'There's something not quite right about it. I don't know
why he chose to structure it in that way.' She continues
rifling through the costumes, drawing out a diaphanous veil
woven through with gold thread. She shakes it out, seeing
how the gold catches the light, draping it over her head and
across her face, eyes peeping over the top. 'What do you
think? Would I make a good Salome?' She laughs, digging
up a pair of goose-feather wings, holding them to his back.

'I don't think *I*'d make much of an angel.'

'Oh, I don't know.'

'And don't change the subject.' He sets the wings aside.
'I want to know what you think is wrong with the way
Merisi painted his *Judith*.'

She stops rummaging to look directly at him. 'The eye
should surely be drawn to the dramatic focus of the subject, the action – the beheading. But it isn't. What you first
see are – well – Fillide's breasts.'

Piero snorts out a laugh.

'It is as if Merisi is saying we must judge women by
their bodies rather than their actions. And it is the act of
killing –' Piero is gaping at her. 'Why are you looking at
me like that?'

'Most people see a work by Merisi and assume it must be flawless. They wouldn't dare question it.'

'Do you suppose it is a sign that my critical faculties are maturing' – she is only half joking – 'that I've noticed the way men allow their lustful desires to interfere with the purity of their art?'

'You're quite something, Arti. Apparently, you know more than you think you do about men's desires.'

She looks at him. 'I watch. And I listen.'

'So how would *you* have painted the scene?'

'If only I had the chance. If Father had his way, I'd paint nothing but backgrounds and drapery and the odd portrait for the rest of my life.'

'But imagine you could.'

'I don't know.' With a sly smile, she adds, 'Yet,' and removes the veil with a flourish. 'Can you keep a secret?'

'You have to ask?'

'Where are the boys?'

'They said they were going up to the lake for a swim.'

'Good. I want to show you something.' From a stack of canvases leaning face to wall in a far corner of the studio, she slides one out. 'I've been working on this – *Susanna and the Elders*.'

The image is only roughly sketched out. A naked Zita seated in the foreground is the only area fully painted. One foot, tenderly pink as if a pair of too-tight shoes has recently been discarded, is dipped in a pool of water. Two vague looming shapes lean over a wall behind. Even undefined they crudely ogle the woman. They whisper to one another, judging, plotting, threatening, while she attempts to cover herself with an insubstantial wisp of cloth.

She scrutinizes Piero's expression as he inspects her painting in silence, her self-doubt gathering. She wishes he would say something. 'You mustn't tell anyone. If Father . . .' There is no need for her to outline the consequences of Orazio discovering that she has secretly been painting Zita without a stitch of clothing.

Piero still hasn't said anything.

'It's not finished,' she says unnecessarily.

He speaks at last. 'From life?'

'Of course from life.'

'How did you persuade her?' He nods in the direction of the kitchen, where Zita is singing tunelessly as she washes up.

'But . . .' She is reluctant to say it. 'But what do you *think*?'

'I think' – he grabs her with his gaze – 'it's better than anything your father has painted. You don't need *me* to tell you that.'

Relief makes her want to screech with glee. 'I have had so much difficulty with the composition. I don't want her to be just something for men to leer at. I wanted to make her discomfort absolutely clear – her fear.' She stops a moment, considering how to articulate her thoughts. 'But more than that I want to show *their* enjoyment' – she points to the two shadowy men – 'of her fear.'

Piero has never really thought of it like that. Aside from its armies of naked men, Rome is also bursting with images of undressed nymphs and dryads and Venuses all delighting in their nakedness – a celebration of female beauty, God's perfect creations.

'You *have* captured it. Her discomfort.' It is clear from

the ruffle of Zita's painted brow, in the awkward twist of her body and the placement of her hands, an attempt to make a barrier between herself and the two ominous shapes behind her. 'Her expression – you have it.'

'I told her to imagine she had seen a spider the size of a rat crawling down the wall behind her.' Piero laughs. Artemisia lowers her voice. 'She doesn't have much of an imagination.' She can hear Zita gathering the children for their afternoon rest and slides the painting back into its hiding place before they come through to get to the stairs. She doesn't want to make Zita feel self-conscious. 'There's a good deal still to do.'

'How did you persuade her to sit for you?' Piero whispers.

'Zita's a mix of contradictions.'

'That's certainly the case.' He makes an odd expression. 'That cake, earlier.'

'What about it?'

'She stole it.'

'Zita – no. She wouldn't. She's at confession every other day.'

'Perhaps she has much to confess.'

'Did you *see* her pinch it?'

'If I had, I'd have stopped her.'

'So perhaps she paid for it after all.'

'I was there, in the baker's.' He is shaking his head. 'She may look angelic but she's not as trustworthy as you think.'

'Well, *I* have nothing for her to steal.' She makes a cynical laugh. 'All I have is my talent.'

'And your virtue.' He makes a sarcastic snort.

'How could I forget my precious virtue?'

66

Zita parades the children through just as the mid-afternoon bells ring. She stops a moment, half turning away and, fingers to her rosary, silently mouths the angelus, her daughters doing the same, before they continue on to the stairs.

Artemisia nudges Piero. 'See?'

'I know what I saw,' he mouths, pointing to the remains of the cake, still on the table. 'Half of Rome stops to pray when the bells sound. It's force of habit more than piety.'

Artemisia stares at the sticky remains, puce icing sweaty, scarlet cherry askew. It strikes her that such a thing – this crude imitation of a breast – reduces all the horror of Saint Agatha's suffering to comedy.

'What if your father finds it?'

She thinks at first that he means the cake until she realizes he's talking about her painting. 'That's highly unlikely. He's too drunk to notice much, these days, and all this' – she indicates the stacks of old canvases and boxes of equipment pushed far into the corner under a drape – 'has barely been touched since we moved here.'

Opening another box Artemisia finds at last the red dress, pulling it out, holding it to the light. The colour is exactly as she remembered.

'And what do you intend to do with it, now you've found it?'

Zita reappears from the stairs, hovering.

Artemisia is aware that Zita feels duty-bound to keep an eye on her. 'Don't you want to put your feet up while the children are resting?'

'I don't think I should.'

'You've no need to worry about *Piero*.' Artemisia

67

deliberately doesn't look at her friend for fear laughter will get the better of her.

'I can assure you, her reputation's safe with me.' Piero makes a theatrical little bow.

Zita doesn't move, looking at him for some time as if trying to unknot a riddle in her head, before saying, 'You're one of *those*, aren't you?'

Artemisia holds her breath.

'In that case . . .' Zita turns and disappears into the stairs once more.

They listen to her departing footsteps and only when they hear the door at the very top click shut do they give way to their laughter.

She holds the red dress up to him, mimicking, 'You're one of *those*, aren't you?' causing another wave of mirth to carry them off.

'Why don't you try this on?' She is suddenly serious.

He removes his shirt. A floorboard creaks above. They wait for new footsteps on the stairs but the place falls back to quiet.

He slips the dress over his head and ties it at the side. It is sleeveless and low cut, exposing his shoulders and chest.

Without speaking she puts smears of pigment onto her palette, a semicircle of colour from pale to dark. Leading him towards the window, careful not to go too close where he would be visible from the street, she hauls the canvas screen across to hide them from view should anyone come in from the stairs or the door. He crouches to remove his boots, tossing them to one side.

She looks at him for some time in silence, taking in the

way the light falls in bright splashes over him. His body is lithe and lean, skin dark as bistre, muscles defined, veins and sinews bulging at the folds of his inner elbows.

Piero could not be described as a masculine man. He is young – only a couple of years older than her. But the dress brings his maleness to the surface: his jaw seems heavier, his throat more defined, the sprinkling of dark hairs on his chest coarser.

She drags over a stool. He positions himself delicately, ankles crossed, hands folded in his lap.

'Not like that. Sit as you normally do. Like a man.' She has in mind the *Hermaphroditus*. He splays his knees, a palm on each, leaning slightly forward, his elbows bent out to the sides, looking at her with the kind of disarming directness that would be unsettling in a stranger.

'That's it.' He has that confidence about him, now – the way men occupy the world as if it belongs to them.

She paints fast, sketching loosely in the malleable oils, mixing vermilion with the smallest touch of blue to sharpen it. Where the light hits it, the fabric is the saturated red of arterial blood, fading to deep crimson as it darkens into the shadows and disappearing into the gloom of the background.

She finally lays down her brush. Piero stands and walks round to her side of the easel, rendered speechless by the sight of himself, looking half whore, half cardinal, clad in crimson brocade.

'You don't like it.'

'You're wrong, I do.'

'It's just the bare bones.' She throws him his clothes. 'I have an idea. Give me the dress.' Feeling her impatience, he unpicks the laces, pulling the garment over his head. She takes it, tucking herself into the corner, removing the dress she is wearing and putting on the other. 'Can you do this?' She lifts her arm for him to fasten it and begins to search behind a stack of half-finished paintings, pulling out a pockmarked looking-glass.

Asking him to hold it up, she sits herself on the stool in an exact imitation of his pose. 'I want to make a pair, you and me, in the same dress, same stance.' She is flushed with emotion, quite breathless, catching him up in her excitement.

'*Anima gemella*,' he murmurs.

'Soul-mates. Yes.' She smiles at him and they are suspended in a moment of wordless understanding.

They hear the front door bang open. 'Where are you all?' Something crashes to the floor. Orazio is drunk.

'Here, Father.' Artemisia and Piero emerge from behind the screen. 'We were tidying some of the boxes. Zita and the children are resting upstairs and the boys went out, up to the lake for a swim.' Tension is making her voice reedy.

Orazio is holding on to the wall. An upended chair lies at his feet. His face is pink and slick with sweat and he is wheezing. He looks towards his daughter, blinking several times, seeming to take a while to bring her into focus. 'Get that dress off immediately!'

'Why?' She steps towards him. Piero tries to stop her but she shakes him off, stepping closer.

'The colour – it's shameless!'

'The clergy wear this colour.' She is spitting defiance. 'It's meant to signify the blood of martyrs.'

'Don't school me, young lady. You know *exactly* what I

mean.' His voice is slurred and might have seemed comical were the circumstances different. 'I won't have my daughter wearing a whore's dress.'

She steps closer still. '*Your* whore's dress, don't you mean?'

Piero tries to put himself between them but Orazio shoves him aside and flails a fist at his daughter, catching her with his ring, leaving a red welt beneath her eye. Pain sears through her cheekbone.

'What in hell's name is this . . .' Orazio is pointing to the painting of Piero with an expression of sheer disgust '. . . this aberration?'

'It's nothing to do with you.' She shows no emotion.

Orazio snatches up a large palette knife, brandishing it drunkenly. Artemisia lunges towards him, but Piero seizes her arm, dragging her away before Orazio can plunge it into her body. He lurches over to the painting, scraping manically at the wet oils, until it is reduced to a bloody smear.

'Get out!' he shouts at Piero. 'Get out from under my roof, you wretched filthy *finocchio*.' He is tripping over his words, staggering and waving the palette knife, making stabbing gestures towards Piero before he lurches forward. Piero and Artemisia take one arm each and jostle him into a chair, where he slumps helplessly. 'Get out,' he says again, and louder: 'GET OUT of my house and don't come back.'

Artemisia takes Piero's arm and they run round the corner into the narrow side alley. Leaning against the wall, her heartbeat settling, she says, 'I'm so sorry.'

'Sorry for what? *I* can leave. You have to live with him.'

'It may be hard to believe, but I pity him. I know it's

71

inexcusable, the way he speaks to you ...' She stops a moment. 'Will you go back to Florence?'

'I wish –'

'Don't.' She can't bear to hear all the things he wishes they could do together.

'I suppose I'll *have* to – go back with my tail between my legs, begging a position in my father's business. I was never going to become a painter, anyway.'

'I can't pretend you're wrong about that.' She says it lightly, teasing, trying to lift the atmosphere.

'Hopefully I'll make a better pigment dealer.'

'Of that I've no doubt.' She wraps her arms around him, drawing him close, resting her head on his shoulder. 'One day,' she breathes, 'when I've proved myself, and can earn my own keep with my painting, I shall come to Florence.'

They both know the likelihood of that is infinitesimally small. She will become someone's wife before long and their lives will follow separate paths.

'Go!' She gives him a little push on the chest. 'I can't be seen out in the street in this.' She is still wearing the crimson dress, her thin arms bare, her small breasts scarcely covered, her expression forlorn, a purple bruise swelling on her cheekbone.

His lips graze her cheek and he walks slowly away, down the via della Croce. She imagines tears stabbing at his eyelids as they do hers.

The Susanna Fragment

Bathing in the silence of her garden, cool water against the day's cloying heat, only the birds for company.

A sound, a growl, draws her look, with it a grip of fear.

Half hidden in the ivy are four male eyes, seeming to multiply until a thousand eyes swarm over her naked flesh.

She grabs a cloth, too small, barely covering her gaze-stung skin.

'Lie with us. No one will know,' they say, with jackal leers.

Her hot tears spill. 'I will not.'

She makes to leave but they stand in her way, a pack of two.

'We will say you did. Who will believe your word against ours when we are the makers of the law?'

She feels the punishment already: skin flayed, stones thrown, body headless, children motherless.

A prayer swills through her like fresh water. 'I will not.' She feels her feet firm on the earth, her tears staunched. 'I will be judged in the Lord's court.'

Anonymous fragment – trans. F. E. Lamenter

7. One Eye Looking at You

Orazio's tongue is dry and swollen. He levers his legs to the floor. Each small movement, each sound, sends a new jab of pain through his skull. Sound travels unimpeded through the papery partitions of the house – the chatter of the children, a squabble between his two older boys, the clump of footfall on the stairs, the liquid slap of a piss pot being emptied.

He sits awhile on the edge of the bed cradling his head, attempting to piece together the events of the previous day. Time has been pilfered from him. He is unable to recall how his shirt came to be smeared with what looks like blood. Wondering if he might have got himself involved in a fight, he searches his body for injuries, finding none. He scratches at the stain; it is paint. The faint smell of frying bacon emanates up the stairwell and into his room. His taste-buds flicker. He stands, wincing as the pain surges anew.

Opening the shutters, blinking in the brightness, he can't see what time of day it is because the accursed rows of laundry impede his view of the sun. The street below bustles with life. He is tempted to return to bed, to feign illness, but there is something, he can't quite remember what, some reason he must rise. He pieces together the fragments of yesterday, remembering first the delicate flavours of that white wine and fine-cut bresaola and then – of course – his encounter with Modenese. Modenese, who is visiting today at noon.

There is no time to wash. He hastily pulls on his best clothes. Dragging a comb through his beard, he notices, with a sinking feeling, that the hairs caught between the teeth are almost all white. He sniffs his armpits, dabbing on oil of citronella to mask the reek. He rubs his teeth with a cloth, chews on some aniseed. As he rushes downstairs the air fills with the clamour of bells. Urgency grabs him, but it is not the long peal of the midday chimes, just the short morning one, telling him he was mistaken – he has three hours before the arrival of his visitor. The stolen time has been returned to him.

The studio falls to silence as he enters. Zita and the little ones are in the kitchen, visible through the open door. His boys, halting an unfinished conversation, busy themselves cleaning brushes while Artemisia works on the *Madonna* with her back to him. He notices that she has added a sheer veil, threaded with gold, draped over the Virgin's head and hand – its transparency flawlessly described. She hasn't touched the figures, as he told her not to, but now they seem all the more lacking beside her fine work. He regrets not giving himself more time to adjust their features before Modenese's arrival.

Francesco looks up. 'Where's Piero? Did you send him on an errand?'

'He's not coming back.' Artemisia's tone is sharp.

Orazio is confused, wants to ask the reason, feeling certain that it has something to do with him.

'Why not?' says Giulio.

'Ask Father.' Artemisia launches a pointed look at Orazio.

He changes the subject. 'We have a potential client visiting at noon. Get Zita to help you into your best clothes,' he tells his daughter. 'We need to impress him.'

'Surely,' she says, under her breath, 'we should impress him with our paintings rather than my dress.'

His head is still throbbing horribly and he is desperate to wet his parched mouth. A faint sizzling sound comes from the kitchen and another delicious waft of bacon. 'Giulio, take a brush to the floor. Francesco, clear up all this.' He indicates the disarray of the pigment bench, still wondering about Piero's absence.

Artemisia continues dabbing at the *Madonna*. 'It won't take me three hours to make myself presentable. Let me finish this. What do you think?'

Unexpectedly, Orazio feels a sudden swelling of pride in his daughter's ability. 'I like it very much.'

'You don't mind the veil? I can paint it out if it doesn't please you. I thought it might invoke the idea of halo.'

Though she is excusing herself she wears an unapologetic look. Now that he is close he can see a raised welt on her cheekbone and a purple bruise. A sudden memory thrusts itself to the forefront of his mind, of his hand striking her. The welt was made by his ring.

Slowly an image emerges of her in that wretched dress. Fillide's dress, which he'd asked her to wear on the night before they left the house in the via Margutta. Without the under-shift it made her deliciously lewd and helped him achieve the necessary hardness to perform. He has had trouble with that recently. The wretched garment probably still has the stain of his seed on it.

Regret gushes into him. Artemisia wasn't to know the

76

dress's shameful history. The mark on her face is proof of his failings, as a man, as a father.

'What became of Piero?' He tries to ask the question lightly.

'Don't tell me you can't remember.' Artemisia's cold gaze is making him uneasy. 'He's going back to Florence. You're the one who sent him away.' She returns to the painting, delicately working shine into the highlights of the gold edging. 'We'll never find anyone as good as him to mill our paint.'

'I can take over,' says Francesco. 'I learned a lot from Piero.'

'You're a capable enough assistant,' Artemisia dismisses her brother, 'but you're far from ready to run a studio.'

'Reni's head apprentice is only a few months older than me,' counters Francesco, but no one is listening as he mutters about being worth more than sweeping floors and priming canvases.

Orazio hates to admit his daughter is right. 'I'm sure I can persuade Nicolò Bendino to come back. He was touting for work the other day.'

'Him?' She makes a face. 'He's bone idle.'

'At least he knows us – how we like to work.' He is trying to recall why he let Bendino go in the first place.

'He spoiled a consignment of pigment. All of it wasted,' says Francesco. 'Surely you can't have forgotten. You were angry enough at the time.'

'Are you sure?'

'If you can't remember that you must be drinking too much.' Artemisia is sharp.

Enough, Orazio thinks. Enough of his family's insolence.

The sooner Artemisia is married the better, before she ruins herself. Let her be another man's problem. Pips of hope tick through him as he thinks of Modenese. It would have been an over-ambitious match a few months ago but, given the circumstances, the Modenese family will likely be glad of a girl only a few rungs down and one with such unique talents. She might even be considered something of a prize.

'The veil is perfect. Truly beautiful work, Arti. You make me very proud.' He cracks his face into a smile. 'Very proud indeed. Now go up and dress yourself.'

He follows the smell of bacon into the kitchen where Zita looks up from the pan submissively, offering him a rasher on a slice of bread. 'If you don't mind my saying . . .' Zita blushes as she speaks to him, cow eyes cast down. Her timidity always surprises him. Usually women who look as she does have more than enough confidence. '. . . you are looking a little peaky this morning. Can I prepare you some powders?'

'No need. This should do the trick.' He folds the bacon into the bread and sinks his teeth into it. She pours him a cup of milk, which he drinks to line his queasy stomach. 'I have a visitor coming at noon. Go and help Artemisia get dressed. I want her looking her best. Do her hair. Rub a little rouge on her cheeks. Give her some colour – but not too much. And see if you can cover that mark on her face.' He scrutinizes her for signs that she knows how Artemisia came by the injury but it seems, from the bland look on Zita's face, that his daughter has held her tongue. 'We wouldn't want to give the wrong impression.'

'Is it a suitor?' Her eyes flash. It makes him a little sad

that beautiful Zita is saddled with a husband who is never at home, always abroad selling whatever it is he trades in. It seems such a waste.

'Potentially. But don't mention it to her. He is coming to look at our paintings. That is all she need know.' He presses a finger to his lips.

'I won't breathe a word.'

'Keep her upstairs. I'll send up one of the boys when we are ready for her.'

She rubs her hands together, seeming thrilled by the conspiracy. 'I hope she likes him. Is he handsome?'

'That's not for me to say.' He envisages Modenese's somewhat ordinary countenance. 'He is from a good family – and generous. Very generous.'

By the time Modenese arrives the studio is swept and tidied, looking the best it ever has, with the big doors open to the street so that the midday light filters in.

Orazio introduces the visitor to his sons and offers him a glass of wine. He had sent Francesco out for a good bottle, certain it would be worth it, and some fresh *ciambelle*. After a few trivialities, Modenese confesses to being impatient to see the *Madonna*. 'I paint a little myself, you know.'

'Ah!' Orazio keeps smiling. If he had a *scudo* for every time someone had told him they fancied themselves a painter, his money troubles would be over. 'Here she is!' He leads Modenese to the painting displayed on its easel. 'Unfinished, I must stress. There is still a great deal of work to be done on the figures.'

'Yes, I see. But it is clear she will be magnificent when

she is completed.' He takes a step closer to inspect the work. Orazio notices his shoes. They are spotless and made of particularly fine, supple leather, the sort he cannot afford. 'This work is outstanding.' Modenese indicates the transparent scarf. 'The gold detail is exquisite. And so delicate, not at all garish as painted gold can sometimes be.'

Orazio considers saying nothing, merely expressing his gratitude but changes his mind – after all, it is Artemisia he hopes to promote. 'That is my daughter's hand.'

'The famous Artemisia.'

'Would you like to see more of her work?'

'I should be honoured.' He places his hand on Orazio's shoulder, an encouragingly familiar gesture considering how little they know one another. 'Perhaps I could have the pleasure of meeting the artist herself?'

His eagerness is touching, even to Orazio. 'Of course. But first let me find you some examples of her painting.' He removes the covering from a stack of canvases leaning against the wall. 'There are portraits of her siblings here somewhere.' He draws out a couple, turning them to face the visitor.

'Oh, goodness! I hadn't expected –' Modenese has clasped his hand to his mouth. 'Is it prudent to allow your daughter to paint such an image? Such a tender age. The body of the woman.' He seems to be finding it difficult to get his words out.

Orazio, baffled, follows the man's eyeline to another painting – one he has never seen before. Zita – naked as the day she was born!

'Ah, no . . .' Orazio, shoving the drape over the offending

picture, glances ferociously towards the boys, wondering if they know anything about it. 'The *Susanna* is mine.'

'I'm so sorry. I didn't mean to suggest your daughter' – Modenese is clearly embarrassed, crushing his gloves in his fist – 'is anything other than chaste.'

'A perfectly understandable mistake.'

'Do let me see it.' Modenese, ignoring Orazio's protestations, pulls the canvas into a patch of light, squatting down to study it closely for some time.

'I must say,' he stands, rubbing his hands together, like a money-lender, 'this has the makings of a very fine painting. I might be interested in making you an offer.'

'I'm afraid it is already spoken for.' He slides the *Susanna* away, out of sight.

'Shame.' Modenese has turned his attention to the portraits, glancing at the two boys and back to the canvases depicting them. 'Your daughter has captured her brothers perfectly. You must be very proud of her. You have taught her well.'

Orazio mumbles a response to the compliment. He turns to his boys. 'Giulio, will you go up and ask your sister to join us?'

The moment Artemisia encounters Modenese she understands exactly her father's intentions. She had suspected the visitor might be a potential suitor when Zita had produced the curling iron and insisted on rouging her cheeks. She'd rubbed most of the pink grease off as they descended the stairs and can feel it sticky on her hands.

Modenese seems perfectly nice, if a little over-eager, oozing compliments. If he were a colour he would occupy that unremarkable hinterland between buff and brown. It is only his boss eye that marks him out.

'And you are the model,' he says to Zita, looking strangely self-conscious.

Zita offers him an unsmiling nod.

Artemisia notices an awkwardness between the two men, Orazio seeming so stiff and falsely bright and Modenese so unfathomably embarrassed, his eyes seeming to creep over Zita. She can see her secret painting's edge tucked away against the wall behind some of her portraits. It is not where she put it and she wonders if it has been exposed, wishing she had hidden it better. That would explain Modenese's discomfort.

'She makes a perfect Madonna, don't you think?' says Orazio.

Francesco's snort from the back of the room makes Artemisia suspect that perhaps *he* has seen the *Susanna*.

'I do.' Modenese is still looking at Zita, as if something is not quite right.

Orazio is waffling about the *Madonna*.

'I am wondering . . .' says Modenese, his look now fixed on Artemisia. She brings her fingers to her collar to make sure she is properly buttoned up. '. . . if you might do me the honour of painting a likeness of my sister.'

'The honour would be ours,' says Orazio, too quickly.

He should say she is very much in demand and glean a better fee – it is clear to Artemisia that Modenese can afford it.

Nonetheless, her heart quickens – her first commission. She can't help remembering the disastrous portrait of the

Conscente baby. What if her nerves get the better of her again?

'You could visit our house to do it. The afternoon light there is perfect for portraiture.'

'I shall be the judge of that.' She notices her father wince visibly at her bluntness. 'I'd prefer it if your sister were to sit for me here, where I can control the light to my liking.' She can already imagine going to his house. His mother would pick over her as if she were a chicken carcass, making her lose her concentration.

'If I could accompany her here – as chaperone – that might be acceptable.' He makes it sound as if the studio were a den of iniquity.

'Of course.' Orazio is folding his hands one over the other.

She is thinking what a prig this man seems, is tempted to say something crude just to see him blush. She must hold her tongue or he might rescind the commission. 'I would be delighted for you to accompany her.' She dips her head to the side in pretend docility.

Modenese approaches her. Orazio and Zita move to the opposite end of the studio on some pretext, leaving the two of them to converse alone. Artemisia wonders if the two men have already discussed her future, whether hands have been shaken, a matrimonial deal struck.

He talks with great seriousness about art, says he loves Carracci, of whom she is not particularly fond. She finds his work too cloyingly sweet. She doesn't say so, just nods as she tells him there is a Carracci in the chapel where her mother is buried. 'That one is lovely,' he says. 'But rather put in the shade by the magnificent work that

83

sits beside it.' This is better, she thinks, as he enthuses about the drama of Merisi's *Saint Paul*, that she too admires greatly.

'What happened here?' he asks, pointing to her face.

Not understanding, she brings her hand to her cheek, feeling the swelling, its tenderness. 'Oh! A silly accident. I managed to prod myself with the sharp end of a paint-brush.' She wonders how he would react if she told him the truth.

'One of the hazards of your profession.'

Realizing it is his attempt at a joke, she laughs politely. 'Fortunately, the hazards are few.'

He seems kind, and she knows kindness is the most important quality in a husband. She imagines his reaction were she to show him the picture of Piero in the red dress, feeling a return of yesterday's anger – her father defacing it beyond repair.

When he has gone, Zita whispers, 'He's not very hand-some.' She makes a face, cupping her hand to say, 'One eye looking *at* you. One eye looking *for* you.'

Artemisia snorts.

'So?' says Orazio. 'What did you think?'

'I couldn't be happier' – she watches the edges of her father's mouth twitch upward – 'to be given my first commission.'

'Yes, yes, but the man himself. What is your opinion?'

'He seems perfectly nice. I haven't really considered.' She pretends not to understand what he means.

'The family are very well-to-do. He's a generous man. Likes to throw his money around.'

84

'So, he won't rescind on my payment for the commission.' The idea of being paid for her work sinks in suddenly, lighting a spark in her.

Zita, in the corner, is suppressing giggles.

Showing signs of exasperation, Orazio is forced to make himself clear. 'Would you consider Modenese for a husband?'

'Goodness, the thought hadn't crossed my mind.' He makes it seem as if she has the choice when she is well aware the decision will be his.

'So?' He has all the eagerness of a beagle.

'At least he knows a good painting when he sees it. That is something, I suppose.'

8. The Visitors

The Modenese girl, Esmeralda, is plain as an onion: weak chin, big nose, protruding teeth. Zita thinks her dress, brocade – orange as hawkweed – would look a sight better worn by almost anyone else. And as for the brother, Artemisia's suitor, well, he is dull – dull *and* boss-eyed.

On first seeing Modenese, Zita had thought that if Artemisia married him, she would more than likely have crooked-eyed babies. Looking at the sister she fears it could be much, much worse. Zita is blessed with beautiful children. Her husband is a feast for the eyes. And he loves her. 'You know why I love you so much?' he'd often say, not waiting for her response. 'Because you're the prettiest and the stupidest little thing I have ever met.' And he's never laid a finger on her in anger, unlike some she could name.

Francesco, who is meant to be stretching canvases, is smirking and whispering with Nicolò Bendino, glancing over at her. Francesco, she has become used to in the weeks since she arrived at the via della Croce – she has glimpsed his soft underbelly. Nicolò, though, seems stitched through with spite. He has raisin eyes, a loose wet mouth and cheeks covered with an angry rash. He is certainly not an improvement on Piero, who was here one day and gone the next. Piero had always given Zita the horrible feeling that he would lead Artemisia into trouble and that *she* would be blamed for it. But Nicolò makes her uneasy in a different way.

Zita looks at Artemisia's painting. She has flattered Esmeralda, defined her chin and set her at an angle that makes her nose look smaller. Zita hadn't noticed until now how beautiful the girl's hands are, right at the centre of the canvas, the first thing you see. Her long fingers are threaded through a rosary made of semi-precious beads. It is a far cry from Zita's own wooden one, which she was given at her first communion and thought the most beautiful thing in the world. She knows better now. She remembers that the Modenese family are gem dealers and weighs up whether that might make him a better prospect. But no. Not even for the jewels could she look at that wonky eye every day.

'I have no intention of getting married to Modenese, or anyone else, for that matter,' Artemisia had said last night, when they were lying side by side on the bed. Zita had felt the girl, if not exactly friendly, warming to her.

'Oh, but you mustn't worry about the wedding night.' Zita was sure that was the problem. Artemisia wouldn't be the first to fear it. 'Once the embarrassment's done with, it's really quite . . .' She'd wanted to say it was the most intoxicating feeling in the world but it was enough to think it, let alone say it out loud. 'It's not so bad.'

'It's not *that*. I don't care about *that*. I just don't want a husband telling me what to do. I've enough of it already from Father.'

'But you want babies, surely?'

'Not really.'

'But why?'

Zita cannot fathom how any woman would not be as delighted as she is by that milky scent, a peach-soft head, a miniature hand. The thought alone makes her melt inside.

'Motherhood – marriage – would prevent me from painting.'

'How so?' Zita can understand Artemisia's passion for her art – after all she never seems to think about anything else – but every girl wants to get married. It's what girls are made for. 'Look at Modenese,' she'd said. 'I mean, he may not look like much, but he wants your hand and he's commissioned a painting from you.'

'A *portrait*. He's commissioned a portrait. I don't think you understand. I'd rather die than paint portraits for the rest of my life. I want to paint subjects that – Oh, it doesn't matter.'

Zita has an idea of the kinds of things Artemisia wants to paint if the *Susanna* is anything to go by. The kind of things that turn her father to rage.

'But if your father wants you to marry him, how can you refuse?' Zita realized then the truth of Artemisia's fate: ugly babies and a dull, squint-eyed husband. 'I suppose you will get all the jewellery you want.'

'How little you understand me,' she had said, making Zita feel further away than ever from friendship. 'Don't you worry about me. I won't have him. I'll put him off me.' Zita had caught her sly smile before she left the room.

Luca has begun to cry. Zita picks him up, taking him into the kitchen to settle him into a feed. She is unable to drag her eyes away from the quickening of his hot little cheek and the jagged curve of his eyelashes, the shine of his dark eye looking up at her as if she is his whole world – and she is. She might die of love. But she can't help thinking that soon he won't need her any more – not like this. She felt it with her girls, the wrench of separation as they threw off babyhood, like their outgrown shoes, and turned their fascination elsewhere.

Zita is at her happiest when she is with child, the sacred mystery unfolding in her body. The thought makes her yearn for another, already, before this one is even weaned. But with her husband away for she doesn't know how long . . . Her heart sinks. Luca's mouth unclasps, swollen with sucking, his head lolling.

As Zita returns to the studio, Esmeralda's face lights up. 'What a beautiful child! May I?' She holds open her arms and Zita delivers him into her chinless embrace.

Artemisia seems annoyed by the interruption. 'I suppose we should take a pause.' She looks directly at Modenese, with a roll of her eyes. 'Babies!'

He flinches, as if flicked by a whip. His sister is staring at Artemisia, open-mouthed, catching flies.

Artemisia meets Zita's eye with a briefly raised brow and Zita forces down the laughter that wants to push its way up her throat.

Modenese is gazing at the portrait, saying how pleased he is. He should be pleased, Zita thinks. Artemisia has made a silk purse out of his sow's-ear sister.

Just as they settle back to the painting, they are interrupted again. This time by two men, one old, the other young, striding into the studio as if the place belongs to them. The older man leans against the pigment bench, smoking a pipe, looking at them fixedly down a beaky nose. Smoke swirls into the room. He is most unattractive, with his thinning pate, his cheeks and nose the same raw puce of his cape – unlike his friend. Zita cannot quite drag her eyes away from *him*.

'Orazio about?' he says, looking around the studio.

'He's out, I'm afraid. Who shall I say called for him?' Artemisia holds her paintbrush as if it is a weapon. She is trying to sound polite but Zita can tell she's annoyed at being interrupted again. *She* can't imagine being annoyed by this man, who is so tall and elegant in his indigo jacket, tailored in the latest style, with his cascade of inky hair and his shirt unlaced so a tempting sliver of chest is visible. His almost-green eyes fix hungrily on Zita, casting up and down her body. Her insides contract.

Removing his cap with a flourish, he turns to Artemisia. 'You must be Orazio's daughter.' He runs a look over her too, before moving round to take in the painting. 'This is good.' He sounds as if he means it.

Artemisia gives him a haughty glare and briefly introduces the Modenese siblings. Beside this disarmingly attractive man, Modenese looks even less appealing. 'And you are?'

'Agostino Tassi.' He makes a small bow, extending a gloved hand. Artemisia ignores the gesture and he slowly withdraws his arm. 'And this is Furiere Quorli.' The older man nods wordlessly. 'I'm a friend of your father. Where might we find him?'

'He's up at the Piazza del Popolo,' says Francesco.

As they depart Zita notices a line of dark paint smeared across the older man's cape where he had been leaning against the bench. She is about to run after them and offer to scrub it with turpentine – it would make a good excuse to catch the eye of his younger companion again.

But Artemisia, who has also seen the stain, grabs her hand. 'Let them go. I need to concentrate on this.' She waves an arm towards the portrait on her easel.

Zita wonders how it is possible for her to be so impervious to a man like that as to have barely noticed him. For her, his absence has drained the room of life.

9. Master of Illusion

'I don't know what passed between the two of you.' Giovanni Stiatessi turns to look Orazio directly in the eye as they walk slowly around the perimeter of the piazza.

They wait to allow a line of nuns to pass, walking briskly towards the church, grey habits fluttering to give them the appearance of collared doves. 'But Piero says he will not be returning to your studio. He seemed awfully upset, refused to tell me what happened. I hope he didn't do something to slight you – or Artemisia.'

'No, no. It was nothing like that. Your nephew is a delightful young man.' Orazio tries not to sound disingenuous. 'He and Artemisia became good friends, nothing underhand, I'm sure.' Sure, Orazio is thinking, because that boy would sooner defile a stone pillar than a woman. 'I must be honest, though, Giovanni.' He slides his arm through the crook of the other man's elbow. 'Piero has much in his favour, but he will not make a painter. I had to be frank with him. Perhaps that was the cause of his upset – the truth can be hard to accept.' It is not exactly a lie. Orazio *had* discussed the matter with Piero, some time ago. In fact, the boy had taken the blunt assessment of his prospects as an artist with surprising equanimity.

Giovanni wipes his hand over his hair, pitch-black and as lush as his beard. The result of an easy life: a notary's income, an equable wife, obedient children. Orazio's hair is thinning and stripped of its colour.

'Better he know the truth now, than waste his youth pursuing a dream he will never achieve,' says Giovanni, as they push through a crowd milling around a dice game. 'Porzia is enjoying having your little Marco to stay.'

Orazio's remorse surges back as he remembers how close he was to beating the child. Though it pains him to admit it, Artemisia was right. He resolves to check his temper in future.

They skirt round a cart piled with wheels of hard cheese. While two lads unload, another has sliced a measure of it for a purchaser to taste. The whiff catches. 'Why is it hard cheese smells so foul, yet tastes so good?' Giovanni is fond of pointing out the small contradictions of life. Which makes it all the more strange, Orazio thinks, that a man with such an enquiring mind does not appear to have noticed his nephew's fondness for perversity.

Orazio's mind has wandered back to the studio. Two or three sittings should give his daughter and Modenese enough time to grow on each other.

Giovanni is still musing about cheese: 'Strange, really, that blue cheese hasn't half the stink of pecorino . . .'

Orazio continues pretending to listen. He can't get the *Susanna* out of his head, doesn't know whether to be angry with Artemisia or to revel in the brilliance of her work. He curses God silently, once more, for bestowing all his family's talent on his daughter.

'Damn!' mutters Giovanni. 'It's that *awful* cousin of mine over there' – he points towards the south side of the piazza – 'with Agostino Tassi.'

Orazio hasn't seen Tassi for some years, remembers that he still owes the man a sum of money.

'I'm going before he sees me.' Giovanni slinks away.

Orazio calls after his friend: 'Come to the house, bring Porzia. We haven't eaten together since the move.' He considers slinking off too but he sees that Tassi has spotted him, is waving, striding over.

'Agostino Tassi. Where have you been?' Orazio slaps him on the back. 'How long is it? Must be at least three years.'

'You owe me four *scudi*, if I remember rightly.' Tassi prods him with a laugh. 'But I'm prepared to let it go.'

Orazio remembers him as rather callow but the confident man standing before him has the sheen of someone doing well for himself.

'Have you time to sit and have a drink with me? I'm very keen to introduce you to a friend of mine.' Tassi glances towards his companion, still several paces away and lowers his voice. 'A very well-connected friend. So, mind your French, if you know what I mean.'

Tassi introduces the man as 'Furiere Quorli'. Orazio, impressed to learn that the man is a papal orderly, makes a deferent greeting. The three of them walk towards one of the grand taverns on the shaded side of the piazza. A cascade of bougainvillaea tumbles down its front wall, making it appear to blush. Orazio's usual haunt sits in the glare on the opposite side.

Quorli removes his cape. It is spirited away as they are shown to the best table in the house, laid with thick starched napkins, a candle in a silver holder and glass drinking vessels. Quorli picks one up, appraising it, flicking it with his nail, making it ring. Food and drink appear as if by magic, silently delivered by discreet waiting staff. Between sips of wine Quorli sucks at a pipe with umber-stained lips. Tassi, charming as ever, explains to Quorli that he and Orazio had worked together several years ago on some frescos at the Palazzo Quirinale.

'I am familiar with those decorations. The cardinal is particularly fond of them.'

'Cardinal Borghese?' Orazio is beginning to allow himself the belief that this meeting might turn into a commission. He nurses his drink trying to resist the urge to swill it back and refill his glass.

'Yes. The cardinal is keen to have something similar in his new project. His garden loggia is just built and –'

'I've heard of it.' Orazio's eagerness has caused him to interrupt rudely but Quorli seems not to mind.

'He has charged me to oversee a decorative scheme for the ceiling on the theme of music.' The pipe has gone out. He taps the bowl vigorously, tipping the ash out onto the table and, taking a pouch from his breast pocket, presses in a pinch of new tobacco. Orazio holds the candle for him to light it. It fizzles and glows as Quorli sucks. He doesn't particularly like the smell of the smoke but at least it keeps the mosquitoes away.

Meanwhile Tassi is describing the cardinal's loggia. 'I've been working for several months on the ceiling perspectives.'

'Of course, yes. You, my friend, are the master of architectural illusion.' Agostino seems to swell visibly with Orazio's overblown compliment.

'He's the best in Rome – no doubt,' says Quorli. 'And we wondered,' Orazio is almost breathless with anticipation, 'if you might be the one to populate it with painted figures – you know, musicians, singers and suchlike.'

'It would be a great honour.' Orazio is doing his best to contain his glee. With this and the hoped-for Modenese match it seems his run of bad luck is over. Nervous optimism flares through him as the two men outline the details of the planned works.

'The fee is a little tight,' says Quorli, gouging a small dent in Orazio's confidence, 'but if the result pleases the cardinal, then he has promised more work, greater schemes in the interior of his new palazzo. Would that be acceptable?'

Orazio would like to ask how tight, to bargain up a little for pride's sake, but he finds himself saying, 'Yes, absolutely.' Even if he works for a pittance, he tells himself, taking a gulp of wine, it will be worth it for the connections – an introduction to Cardinal Borghese and his deep pockets.

'And, naturally, I will need to see some of your recent work before we finalize the deal, as it were.' Two coils of smoke emerge from Quorli's nostrils, giving him the appearance of a demon in a play.

'Yes, I understand.'

Tassi has an arm around his shoulder, squeezing. 'I'm sure you have plenty to show us at your studio.'

Orazio describes the *Madonna*, resolving to flesh out the figures before their visit.

Quorli is nodding. 'Anything else?'

His expectant expression forces a lie from Orazio before he has time to think: 'And I have the beginnings of a *Susanna*.' He recites a silent prayer, glad that he resisted the impulse to destroy the canvas.

'Painted from life?' Quorli is sporting a lecherous

expression and describes a female form in the air with both hands.

'You like to paint from life, don't you, Orazio?' says Tassi, and the two men share a grunt of laughter. 'Don't all the Caravaggisti?'

Orazio's hackles rise. 'I wouldn't know.' He resents being lumped together, yet again, with Merisi's imitators.

'Of course you wouldn't!' Tassi's hand claps down on his back. 'Orazio's far from one of that lot of common daubers,' he says to Quorli. 'I for one am looking forward to seeing this *Susanna*.'

The older man begins to talk with some enthusiasm about a *Cleopatra* he has recently seen and it dawns on Orazio that he might have gained more commissions had he painted more women without their clothes.

'Why did you move from the via Margutta?' asks Tassi. 'I must confess to having been exceedingly jealous of your situation there, next to that pretty garden.'

'The garden *was* charming, but it was very noisy.' Orazio hopes he sounds convincing. 'And I wanted more space so that we could have a married companion for my daughter – you know, to keep an eye. She's reached that age. With no woman in the house and only brothers . . .' His voice trails off.

Quorli mumbles something about a daughter's chastity being the most precious of a father's possessions.

'Your daughter was at the studio when we passed by,' says Tassi. 'I see you're making her earn her keep. She's become a woman since I last saw her.'

'Girls have a tendency to do that.' Quorli seems pleased with his little joke.

97

'She has her father's talent.' Orazio's pride bristles at Tassi's compliment. 'What age is she, now?'

'Seventeen.'

'You'll be wanting to find her a husband. And your boys? Do they paint too?'

'They're learning.' He isn't about to admit that his boys haven't a shred of artistic ability.

'Ha! I understand. It's your daughter who has the natural skills.' Quorli has seen right through him. 'That must be a source of annoyance.'

'It is not for me to question the Lord's plan.' Orazio drains his glass. The other two men leave theirs half finished as they rise from the table and make their way to the door.

'What's this?' Quorli says, as his cape is returned to him, pointing out a dark smear on the fabric. 'It was pristine when I gave it to you.'

'I believe, signore' – the waiting boy is visibly cowed – 'that the mark was already there.'

'Are you telling me I am wrong?'

'No, signore – I don't know.' The boy's eyes are fixed on the floor.

'It looks like gravy, to me. Do you think it looks like gravy?' He sniffs it and holds it up for his two companions. 'Smell it. Does it smell fatty to you?'

Orazio does as he is asked. It is unmistakably paint, but he dissembles, 'Impossible to say.' He feels a little guilty in the knowledge that the boy will likely have his wages docked. But it is not worth contradicting Quorli and getting on his wrong side.

'Doesn't smell of gravy. More like paint,' says Tassi,

with disarming frankness. 'You must have brushed against something at the studio.'

Quorli huffs. The owner has arrived, asking what is wrong. 'Your boy has ruined my cape.'

He displays the offending stain, drawing a lengthy apology and an assurance that the boy will be duly punished. 'Leave it with me. I'll have it cleaned.'

Quorli merely flings the garment over his shoulder and exits. Orazio notices Tassi discreetly explaining to the owner that Quorli was mistaken, and that the boy is not at fault.

The sun reflecting off the pale cobbles is blindingly bright after the dim interior. They make arrangements for the studio visit. Just as they are parting a pungent floral aroma hails the approach of two young women, models Orazio has seen about the place. Their two pairs of eyes settle greedily on Tassi, who offers a smile – his teeth are startlingly white and straight.

The women walk on, heads huddled in a whisper.

Tassi exhales a long low whistle.

'*Madonna!*' mutters Quorli. 'I'd offer up my right arm for the chance to give one of those beauties a poke.'

As he walks away Orazio can't help remembering the Conte di Conscente's dismissive comments about his work. A measure of doubt corrupts his pleasure at having gained the commission. Perhaps he is no longer capable of the standards the cardinal will expect.

Has he lost his touch? Why is it that as his daughter's talents burgeon his own seem to wither?

He pushes the thought away.

10. The *Hermaphroditus*

Artemisia asks Esmeralda if she would like to see her portrait, resisting the impulse to continue making tiny alterations.

'Is it finished?' The girl looks relieved. She had been fidgeting all afternoon, clearly battling profound boredom while Artemisia tried to prise half-decent paint out of Nicolò Bendino. The consistency had been gritty and difficult to handle, the colours lacking intensity. When she had asked him to mill it more finely, his eyes had narrowed and he'd turned his back, not even trying to hide his resentment at being told what to do by a woman.

'I think so.' She is not quite satisfied but wonders if she ever will be.

'It certainly looks finished to me,' Orazio says briskly, turning to Modenese. 'My daughter is a perfectionist. Would carry on for another month, given half a chance.'

She watches the girl's expression as the painting takes its effect on her. Esmeralda brings up her hand to cover her mouth, pupils expanding. 'Is that really me?'

The others crowd round the easel making appreciative noises – even the scowling Bendino seems impressed.

Modenese seems delighted too, pointing out little details to his sister, the fine brushwork in the rosary and the light catching the birdcage half visible in the background, the spotted wing of the goldfinch inside it, the flash of yellow flight-feather, its jewel-red poll a bright splash. The real birdcage suspended at the end of the studio is empty.

Satisfied as she ever will be, she begins to clear away her things, removing her apron and wiping her palette. Really, she would like to continue working, put the finishing touches on the *Madonna*, but she will have to wait until the visitors have gone.

Since her father had a change of heart and asked her to work on the figures, she has been itching to get on with it. 'Bring them to life, Arti,' he'd said, surprising her. But his mood has been strangely ebullient these last couple of days, something to do with Agostino Tassi and a 'prospect' that he refuses to elaborate on 'for fear of cursing it'.

When she has finished cleaning her brushes, she turns back to the room, realizing with a sinking feeling that everyone has slipped away and left her alone with the awkwardly hovering Modenese. She understands exactly what is happening. There is a hubbub of chatter from the kitchen. She can hear her father's big brass voice and her brothers' chatter.

Panic hisses through her as Modenese approaches. Pictures depicting the enduring dullness of a life with him, or anyone like him, spool through her head. She will be the painted goldfinch in its cage. He pats his jacket, fumbling in his pockets. Her breath stutters.

He is speaking, talking of his three houses. She is supposed to be impressed. 'I wouldn't expect you to stop painting. I understand how important your art is to you. Indeed, it is the very thing –'

'But you don't know me. You don't know the things I like, the ideas, the things that spark my fascination.' She is thinking of Piero, how they could talk for hours – the ease of it all, the laughter.

'I understand the prospect of marriage is daunting' – his manically swivelling eye betrays his nervousness – 'but we will learn about each other over time. Why don't you tell me what those things are that spark your fascination?' He lowers himself onto one of the stools, suggesting she sit too.

She leans in quite close, speaking quietly. 'I want to know the world.'

He seems not to comprehend.

'Are you familiar with the tale from Ovid – of Hermaphroditus?' She recounts, in animated detail, the story of the nymph who wraps herself round the body of the man she loves until they become a single creature, both man and woman. His rapt fascination slides into dismay, then revulsion as she tells him of the secret sculpture hidden in the cardinal's closet and her burning desire to lay her eyes on it.

'Didn't he ask you? He was supposed to. He showed me the ring.' Orazio is agitated. 'Why didn't he ask you?'

'He must have changed his mind. I've no idea why.' She regards her father with a deadpan air. 'Perhaps I don't please him.'

She fingers the purse in her pocket – her earnings. Eleven *scudi*, more than she has ever held in her hand at one time. A memory surfaces, of her hot little six-year-old palm closing round those two small coins from Merisi. She longs to write to Piero and tell him. He would be so proud of her. She imagines how he would laugh to hear of her strategies to repel poor Modenese. But she can neither read nor write – skills unnecessary for a girl. 'It is possible that he had a change of heart about marrying a woman with a profession.'

Orazio makes a kind of throat-clearing sound, indicating his dissatisfaction.

She moves away from him, treading carefully in case his mood turns. Setting the unfinished *Madonna* on the easel and tying her apron, she begins to smear new colours onto her palette. 'Where's Bendino? I'll be needing this lead-white milled more finely.'

Bendino slinks out from the shadows and she wonders if he's been listening to their conversation. Was he hidden there when she spoke with Modenese? Her skin prickles unpleasantly.

'Is my work not to your satisfaction?' He addresses her father rather than her, but Orazio mumbles something about doing as she asks before ducking out of the door into the afternoon.

Bendino's mouth crimps in disapproval.

She calls Zita down to sit for her but her girls are restless and keep interrupting, so she suggests Francesco and Giulio leave their studio duties and take them up to the lake for a couple of hours.

Peace descends.

Artemisia becomes wholly absorbed in capturing the way the light falls on the smooth undulations of Zita's face, the only sounds the rhythmic whet from the pigment bench and the quiet hum of a circulating fly. Zita twitches and swats at the insect.

'Don't move a muscle,' Artemisia says. The fly has

landed on the Virgin's blue shawl. Responding to the urgent grab of inspiration, she rummages for her finest three-hair brush. Drawing its tip over the ooze of black on her palette, she carefully paints the insect into the image. A passing glance and it will read as a pin – only on closer inspection will the fly emerge.

Artemisia's thoughts trail off. To her it is a moment of superficial humour in a serious subject – a miniature rebellion. Sister Ilaria's staccato voice sounds in her head: *In the Bible flies represent all that is bad*. Artemisia had dared suggest that even flies were God's creatures, which had resulted in the usual stinging punishment. *I sometimes wonder if there is any hope for you at all*.

Her father will more than likely paint it out.

The light is fading and the colours in the room have altered.

'That'll be all,' she says to Bendino. 'Thank you. The mill was so much better this time. Look at the fine detail I achieved with it.' He casts a cursory glance towards the canvas, shrugs and slips out to the kitchen.

'A piece of work, that one,' comments Zita, once he's out of earshot.

They begin to tidy the studio.

After some time, Zita says, 'Do you think Signor Tassi will visit again, since your father is to do some work with him?' This is not the first time she has mentioned Tassi, with that bright look in her eye, a child gazing at a confectioner's stall.

'I don't know. I suppose he'll have to come at some point. The commission isn't finalized yet and he'll want to see Father's work. Or if not him then that Quorli fellow.'

'I don't like the look of that one . . .' Zita screws up her beautiful face, '. . . but Tassi.' She blushes.

Artemisia laughs. 'You like him.' She is remembering Tassi with his swagger and confidence, and his unsettling stare – the pair of them wiping their eyes all over her. 'And you a married woman.'

Zita pretends to busy herself, smothering a grin.

'I saw the way he looked at you – as if he wanted to eat you.'

'Did he?' Zita sounds breathless.

'That is not supposed to be a good thing.' Artemisia wonders how Zita, so utterly lacking in guile, has managed to get through life unscathed.

11. The Lake

Towards the end of the day, Artemisia is sitting on the front step, watching life go by. Spotting her girlhood friend Lisabetta ambling past with her new husband, she waves. Her friend's expression lights up as she returns the gesture, but the husband takes her elbow, like a boat's rudder, guiding her away. She throws Artemisia a wistful backward glance before disappearing from view among the evening walkers.

The almost-encounter shrouds Artemisia in loneliness. Piero is gone and all the girls she grew up with are married or betrothed, some even already mothers. For the first time she is thankful for Zita. Despite her role as Orazio's spy and the gulf that separates their temperaments, Zita only ever means well.

Her thoughts are disturbed by a woman, her hair a wild cloud, clothes filthy, marching down the street shouting unintelligibly. A knot of sparrows pecking at the cobbles, alarmed by the noise, scatter, taking to the air, bobbing and skimming up, up, weightless as they vanish.

Artemisia imagines sprouting wings, following them up and away, over the piazza and on past the city walls, across the vineyards and into the hills beyond. There she would perch in a tall cypress and take in the city at sunset, the glistening ribbon of river, boats gathered at its banks, the vast domes rising from the jumble of rooftops, where filaments of smoke coil skyward, like lost souls. She could watch as evening's alchemy transforms the city to gold, listening to the pitchy clatter of the compline bells and the distant calls of the hawkers in the piazza far below. How beautiful it must be up there. She has the sensation that her life is shrinking, that she is shrinking. Soon she will be a doll in a doll's house, painting miniature scenes with pretend paints.

'You can't sit out there on display like that.' Zita has returned. 'People will think –'

'What will people think? That I'm for sale?' Artemisia stands too fast, feeling giddy after sitting in the bright sun and the heat.

'I'm a bit worried about the children,' says Zita. 'Don't you think the boys have been gone too long?'

Artemisia sees a shadow of concern in the other woman's eyes. They *have* been a while.

'Do you think something's happened to them?' Zita begins to fret.

'I hope they haven't come to any harm.' Artemisia is certain the girls are safe with her brothers and feels a little wicked exploiting Zita's credulity. But her need to escape these four walls is too much to resist.

Zita's face blanches, concern turning to panic. 'We must go and get them.' She is already manoeuvring Luca into a shawl slung to her back, hustling Artemisia on. 'Hurry, there's no time to lose. I should never have let them take my girls. They're too young.'

Luca's small black head bobs as they run. They push past the throngs in the street, cobbles still hot underfoot, puffing their way up the steep hill past the white edifice of the Trinità dei Monte and on through the avenue of trees behind the Villa Medici where the houses thin out towards the Porta Pinciana.

Once beyond the city gates and in the hillside vineyards beyond, they run along row after row of vines, on and on. Artemisia relishes the sensation of liberty, spreading her arms out to catch the air beneath them as if she might lift away from the ground.

Zita curses her. 'How can you laugh at such a time? My girls might be dead for all you know.'

Eventually, gasping for breath, they arrive at a vast weeping willow beside the lake, a secluded spot from where, hidden in its dome of leaves, they can see a group of youths have collected on an old wooden pier.

'Don't look!' Zita covers her eyes with her shawl.

Artemisia pretends to cast her gaze away, while surreptitiously absorbing the scene. The naked youths take turns to jump, curling themselves tightly, arms gripped around knees, exploding into the water with peals of glee.

'There they are,' cries Zita, pointing. 'Thank the Good Lord.' She crosses herself several times, muttering a prayer. The children are sitting away from the pier, on the gritty sand that slopes gently down to the water, building castles with the help of Francesco and Giulio.

'Sssh.' Artemisia draws Zita back into the tree's green atrium. 'Don't let them see us. We can surprise them.' She wants a moment more to watch the divers.

'But we must get them home before compline.'

'Let's not spoil their fun just yet.' She squats on a stump, looking through a gap in the foliage towards the pier. Rome is full of undressed bodies, white marble pietàs, ill-proportioned Adams and Eves, angels – hundreds of splendid painted angels. But this is different. These boys larking about, their shrieks raucous in the air, are teeming with life.

Pretending to look at a family of coots, fuzzy-headed babies dipping at the edge of the water, Artemisia takes in the sight of the boys' bodies. They are slender and gangling, the strange protrusions emerging from their crotches like the stamens of lilies. In the grip of fascination, she watches the way their muscles move, how their spines articulate, the rows of bones protruding, like creatures beneath their skin, how their limbs attach to their torsos, sinews stretching tight. She observes every detail, the shapes they make in motion, the way the water paints shining highlights on their curves and ridges, the way their shoulder blades seem like half-formed wings, their calves angular, thighs long and lean, and the slick dark hair they shake, like dogs, as they emerge from the water, forming crystal crowns that glitter in the last of the sun.

In this moment she is free.

But she can sense Zita's impatience, drawing her back to her cage. She twitches, huffs, rubs her nose, adjusts her scarf. Having seen her girls are safe she must be anxious at having brought her charge out into the forbidden world. She will be thinking of Orazio's wrath. Artemisia feels guilty for drawing Zita into her own break for freedom; it was selfish of her. And with that thought her moment of joy pops, like a bubble, and is gone.

She shouts to her brothers, waving.

'You shouldn't be out here.' Francesco is striding towards them, swiping sand from his clothes.

'You should have brought the children back hours ago. Zita was worried.'

'There's no harm in them playing here.' He squints at the low sun. 'It's not *that* late.'

Zita is brushing her girls down. Their arms are pink and highlights have gilded their hair. Artemisia heaves one of them onto her hip. 'We had so much fun, Arti. You should have come with us.'

'I was working. Another time.' She cannot bring herself to say that it is a lie, that there will never be a time when she can come to a place like this, take off her clothes and slide into the silver embrace of the water. She can't bear to be the one to tell her that it is her fate, too – the fate of all girls who grow up. 'Now, where are your shoes? I can't carry you all the way home.'

They trudge back, dragging the exhausted children. The route that had seemed so short in the other direction stretches out interminably. A blister is forming on her heel, more tender with each step. Francesco and Giulio each take one of Zita's girls on their backs, their thin, weary limbs hanging limply.

The bells chime just as they turn into the via della Croce where the shouting woman is still marching up and down, a pair of boys taunting her from the corner.

The studio is empty, no sign of Orazio. They all breathe a collective sigh of relief. Zita heats some milk for the little ones and puts them to bed, while Artemisia sits beside the window with her chalks, trying to capture those diving boys while they are still alive in her mind.

When Zita returns she tucks away her sketchbook, but

a loose sheet of paper falls to the floor from between its pages.

'What's this?' Zita picks it up. 'Doesn't look like your work.'

'It's not. Just a drawing of me as a child.'

'Strange picture.' She holds it at arm's length, dipping her head to the side, squinting.

Artemisia slips it back into place, remembering when she first found it tucked into the sleeve of her outdoor coat. It was a secret, drawn when she was hiding in the shadows beneath the stairs to eavesdrop on her father and his friends, who came at night to drink and talk.

They often spoke of the models they painted, the women who passed through the studio, seeming to Artemisia like exotic birds, strange and wild in their dazzling plumage. 'If Fillide only had the breasts of Bianca and the hair of Fausta, we would have perfection.'

Orazio and his friends would squabble for hours about petty matters until, one by one, they would peel away and stagger into the street, leaving just Merisi, always the last to leave.

The pair of them would get into long and involved discussions about who was the greatest of the great masters, discussing their various merits and flaws. She would listen entranced as they described a world to which she had no admission and works of art in distant places that she could only dream of one day seeing.

Merisi caught her just once. Her belly shrank, fearing exposure, but he briefly ran a finger over his lips to indicate his silence. He took up a leaf of paper and, there and then, set to drawing her. He made the occasional glance her way and back to the paper, manipulating a piece of charcoal in nimble fingers, as if performing a card trick. Her father never even realized.

She found the drawing the following day. Waiting until she was alone, she unrolled it to find the entire surface of the paper was covered in shades of black, in some places densely layered, an absolute absence of light, in others a thinner darkness, warmer, like faded funeral hangings. In only a few areas did the white paper remain visible, the curve of a cheek, the line of a limb, the glimmer in the orb of an eye. It was undeniably her, in her shadowy lair at the base of the stairs.

The treasured drawing made her understand something she overheard Merisi say sometime later: *Painters insist upon flooding everything with light, when it is the darkness that makes the form of things emerge, invests them with life.*

Zita hears Orazio return: the slam of the door downstairs, the sound of laughter and voices trickling up the stairwell. Artemisia is deep in her own world, looking out of the window into the darkness. Zita goes out to the landing, leaning over the banisters, sure it is Signor Tassi's indigo coat she can see flung over a chair below.

Desire makes itself known deep in the root of her. She has already had to say twelve Ave Marias as penance for stealing the cake, many more for posing naked. The priest had questioned her, asked if she had taken pleasure in her body. She had said that she kept her thoughts as much as she could on the lesson of Susanna. 'And what was the lesson, my child?' he'd asked.

'That God will protect you if you resist the ills of lust,' she'd replied.

'Keep that lesson in mind,' was the last thing the priest had said.

She attempts to calculate what kind of penance she will have to pay for the lustful thoughts about Signor Tassi that crowd her head. She has tried to resist but her spirit is weak. Perhaps she can go at a different time or to a different booth, make her confession to another priest. Those words of Artemisia's – *pretend piety* – taunt her. God will know.

Laughter trickles up from below. 'Lord, forgive my weakness,' she whispers, as she creeps down one flight. She still can't make out what the men are discussing.

'Are you going downstairs?' Artemisia calls to her. 'Can you bring up something to eat? I'm ravenous.'

She has her excuse so walks quietly on down, waiting at the bottom, listening, watching. Tassi and his horrid friend are there with Orazio, standing in a circle of light around the *Madonna*. The two visitors are inspecting the picture, making the occasional comment. Tassi has his back to her. His hands gesticulate as he talks quietly. Her gut contracts as she imagines those hands on her, in her private places.

'Where did you find this model?' he is saying. 'She is exquisite. Looks familiar.'

Zita has to suppress a delighted gasp.

Orazio explains: 'She lives here on the upper floor.'

'Ah, yes, the married companion for your daughter,' says Quorli. 'Didn't we see her here before?' His tone makes Zita's flesh crawl.

'You have really found your form, Orazio,' Tassi is

saying. 'I thought you'd lost your way rather for a while, but this – this is simply beautiful.' Quorli grunts in agreement. 'The figures are so strikingly depicted, so filled with life. How did you achieve such emotion? It vibrates with maternal love.'

'I have been developing my style,' Orazio replies.

Zita is shocked by his outright lie. There is a cowed awkwardness about his posture, making him seem unfamiliar. She has only ever felt intimidated by Orazio. Now she sees weakness.

Zita takes a breath and emerges from the darkness. 'Excuse me.' She explains she is fetching some supper to take upstairs.

'Here she is – the *Madonna*.' It is Quorli who says this, grabbing the lamp and holding it up to her as if she is a painting. He is red-faced and sweating, eyes running up and down her body. Zita is used to men with that look.

She remembers when she first became aware of it, a friend of her father who invited her to sit on his knee: big hands and hungry stare. Her mother had hustled her away. 'When men look at you in that way, they only want one thing and it is a sin to let them have it.' Zita didn't learn until she was older what that thing was.

'Would you bring us something to drink while you're in the kitchen?' asks Orazio.

Tassi is smiling at her. She hardly dares glance his way, as if he is too bright and she might turn blind.

She can feel both pairs of eyes following her as she crosses the room and picks up a candle to take to the kitchen.

'Let me find more works for you to look at.' Orazio is sorting through some canvases.

'Didn't you say you had the beginnings of a *Susanna*?' Panic surges through Zita: she is sure the picture is stashed not far from where Orazio is looking. And how do they know about it?

'I can't seem to lay my hands on it,' he is saying. 'With the move everything is in disarray.'

She remembers, with a flood of relief, that Artemisia had taken it upstairs.

'That's a shame,' says Quorli. 'I should have liked to see it but it's not necessary. On the strength of this *Madonna*, it's safe to say the commission is yours.'

Once in the kitchen, Zita leans against the cool wall remembering the lesson of Susanna. 'God rewards those who resist lust,' she whispers, gathering her thoughts, searching for the good wine, putting a few things to eat on a tray. She drags a stool to the high shelf to reach the rarely used glasses. Men like that will want to drink from glass, she is sure. Taking them down carefully, one at a time, she places them on the tray. But her sleeve drags over one, knocking it so it smashes onto the floor.

'What was that?' Orazio is in the doorway already.

Her heart jabbers. 'I'm sorry . . . so sorry.'

'It's only a glass.' He is not angry. Why is he not angry?

She is on her knees with the brush, sweeping the shards into a pan, still saying she is sorry, while he is reaching up for a replacement.

'Come and join us for a drink.' He has picked up the tray. 'No need to look so timid. I won't eat you.'

The wine is rich and makes Zita light-headed.

'What do you think of it?' Tassi is addressing her. She thinks he means the wine, not immediately understanding

that he wants to know what she thinks of the *Madonna*.
'Hasn't Orazio captured you perfectly?'

'I think . . .' They are waiting to hear what she has to say.
Orazio must be aware that she knows most of the work is
Artemisia's. She glances towards him.

'What do you think, Zita?' he says.

She doesn't want to say he has captured her perfectly
and add a lie to her list of sins. 'I like it a lot.'

'She likes it *a lot*!' Quorli is making fun of her, imitating
her accent, sweeping his arm towards her. 'The voice of
wisdom, gentlemen!'

But Tassi puts a hand on her nape, warm and enclosing,
palpating his fingers gently. 'The *Madonna* is very beautiful.
But not quite as beautiful as you are in the flesh.'

She feels as if she might melt into a puddle of wax on
the floor.

'What happened?' Tassi is pointing to her hand. It is
bleeding. A spot has dripped onto her apron, is spreading
into the fibres of the linen.

'I went and broke a glass, didn't I?'

'Here!' He takes a napkin from the tray, gently wrapping
it around her hand.

Orazio is looking at her as if he can see what she's thinking, giving her the urgent impulse to escape.

'If you'd please excuse me. Arti will be wondering what's
become of me.'

'Off you go, then,' says Orazio.

Zita makes for the staircase, wondering if she should
tell Artemisia that her father is pretending her work is his.
Envisaging the fuss she will make, Zita decides that what
Artemisia doesn't know can't hurt her.

12. The Monte Cavallo Gardens

Cardinal Borghese's garden on the Quirinal Hill is an unfinished Eden, as if God has abandoned his masterpiece half done. The brightness of the sun renders the colours vivid – rockroses, yellow as egg-yolk, nestle in mossy crannies while spots of rich purple mark the edges where bellflowers have self-seeded. Artemisia almost expects to see a serpent shifting through the undergrowth to lead her into temptation. But where there should be birdsong, the air is filled with hammering and the rumble of carts removing rubble.

A towering palazzo casts a sharp-edged shadow across a geometric pattern of clipped yew, intricate as Calabrian brocade. It frames a waterless fountain – a marble sea nymph, clutching a monstrous gape-mouthed fish, designed to drool into a basin set beneath. A stonemason chips away at the nymph's twin on the opposite side of the ornamental garden, where more yew bushes patiently anticipate the shears.

To one side lies a row of caryatids awaiting erection along the incomplete stone balustrade, beyond which the ground falls steeply. Brambles and nettles have taken hold there, and ivy cascades wildly. Each branch, each bud, is bursting with abundant life. She imagines this beautiful chaos tamed as surely it will be. These wild late-April greens are so beautiful Artemisia would like to take each one, mill it and stash it before it disappears.

'What are they?' Zita is pointing to the caryatids.

'They are what remains of the ruins of an ancient thermal baths that were destroyed to accommodate the new casino,' says Orazio. 'Shame, really. It was a beautiful spot. Quite wild.' Artemisia meets her father's gaze in a rare moment of understanding, as if they share a single thought of sorrow at the destruction.

Orazio guides them towards a garden loggia. Inside a scaffold is visible, a complicated structure of ladders and platforms. A large table stands at its base, where half a dozen lads are drawing and milling colours, Francesco and Nicolò Bendino among them. They chat and joke easily with each other as they work. On seeing the two women, they stop to stare. Bendino says something inaudible and they all laugh until Orazio barks for them to get back to work.

Quorli appears from the interior to greet them. 'Brought these two beauties to see the work in progress, have you, Orazio?' Artemisia watches his eyes skim briefly over her to languish on Zita, as if she is a cheap cut of meat. It makes her like him even less and Zita more. Zita is still a poor substitute for Piero but she is sweet and kind and harmless. Artemisia thinks that she might even grow to care for her.

They follow Quorli into the interior, their eyes drawn immediately upward.

'Well I never!' Zita is gaping at the ceiling in wonder.

At the far end it is a flat surface of unadorned plaster, but directly above it seems to come alive, arching ever upward, in a dizzying series of pillars and balconies and galleries, to a summit that opens into a circle of painted sky. Artemisia is speechless. All this – this extraordinary deception in paint – must be Tassi's work. She understands now why he is so sought after and feels a new respect for the man.

Outlines of figures are just visible behind the painted balustrades, some leaning over to gaze down, some singing, others playing instruments. Even at this early stage Artemisia can see their proportions are off.

'Couldn't I help you with them?' she suggests. 'There is so much still to do.'

'Don't be silly.' Orazio already seems irritated, so she doesn't press. 'Can't have you up on the scaffold. What would people say?'

She would like to tell him that once they have seen what she is capable of they won't say anything. But she knows words are useless here, among these men.

'Hoy there,' comes a voice from above. She watches Zita's face light up as Agostino Tassi appears out of the gloom, swinging down the ladder, jumping to the floor, covered in a constellation of coloured drips.

'Impressed with our little project?' He removes his spattered overall, flinging it to one side before greeting them both with kisses on the backs of their hands. Zita appears unable to drag her gaze from where his shirt has stuck to his damp skin. Artemisia is struck by his tilted feline eyes, but finds little to stir her in his handsomeness. Though his looks could never be described as bland, everything is too correctly placed for him to be of artistic interest to her.

'The illusion is so very convincing,' Artemisia says. 'Father tells me you are the best painter of perspective in Rome.'

'Well, I wouldn't want to contradict him.' He is smiling, enjoying the compliment.

'Could I go up – inspect it more closely?' She is itching to see how it is done.

'That's the spirit!' Tassi is laughing and she can't tell if he is mocking her or not.

'Absolutely not,' says Orazio. 'And I must get back to work. Now you've seen it, Francesco will walk you home.'

Tassi whispers something to Quorli, glancing at the two women. Quorli nods.

'Perhaps you would like to see inside the palazzo before you go. The view of the city from the cardinal's private apartments is spectacular,' says Quorli.

'But the cardinal –' begins Orazio, a frown forming.

'He's away. It can't do any harm.' Tassi gives Orazio a reassuring pat on the shoulder.

Artemisia notices a hierarchy between the three of them, her father at the lowest point. It makes her want to be better than him, better than them all.

'He need never know,' says Quorli. 'I have the run of the palazzo.' He holds up a large ring of keys, smug as if they could unlock the gates to Heaven itself.

'I have too much to do.' Orazio points towards the drawing table. 'Have to oversee Bendino. I'm not pleased with his work.'

'There's no need for you to come.' Tassi's tone oozes, like soft cheese in the sun. 'We shall take care of these two as if they were our own daughters, won't we, Cosimo?'

Quorli seems to smirk slightly as he nods in agreement.

'No. No, I shall join you.' Orazio's tone is clipped, his reticence clear. Artemisia wonders what is going on between the three of them. This is so unlike the father who rules their household with a fist of iron.

Tassi takes Artemisia's arm, leading the way back across the ornamental garden towards the far wing of the building. The hammering has stopped, the stonemasons sitting in the shade, unwrapping napkins of sausage and bread. Their little group walks in silence, feet crunching on the gravel. Inside an arched entrance a wide gallery is lined with niches, each one housing a sculpted figure. The smooth marble underfoot seeps cool through the thin soles of her shoes. Tassi's hand is hot on her arm and she wishes there was a way to ask him to remove it without causing offence.

Instead she asks him about the painting of the loggia ceiling, quizzing him about the artifice of space and height.

'It's a mathematical method that uses light and shade and lines of perspective to trick the eye.' He becomes animated as he explains, letting go of her arm to gesture with his hands, describing the various apparatus he uses, a special frame to divide the view into squares. 'It could be anything. I usually paint architecture, but it could be a person, an object, a piece of fruit, anything. The frame allows you to understand distortion, the foreshortening, truly to see what is before your eyes rather than what you suppose you see.' He glances her way. 'But you do it instinctively. I've seen you work. Seen the way you look at things.'

She assumes he is flattering her for the sake of it. He can't have understood this just from watching her paint Esmeralda Modenese for a few brief moments. 'I prefer to trust my gaze.'

'You see' – he takes her arm again, squeezing too

tightly – 'instinctive. But it takes a good deal of practice and a certain eye to create *that* level of illusion' – he waves in the direction of the garden loggia – 'and there are particular techniques that can be taught.'

'I should like to learn.' She feels she has judged the man unfairly. The way he talks so passionately about his art has cast him in a new light.

'I could teach you.'

'I don't think so.' Her father has drawn up beside them and must have been listening to their conversation.

She says nothing, knowing if she tries to persuade him it will push him further away.

It is Tassi who says, 'I'm surprised at you, Orazio. You've taught her so much – her talent springs from you – and a lesson in perspective would only serve to complete what you have begun.'

She senses her father puffing up with the praise, yet still he hesitates. 'I wouldn't want to put you to the trouble, Tassi – a busy man like you.'

'Trouble? No. It would be a pleasure – to nurture the next generation.' Tassi goes on: 'Imagine the painter she could be, how it would reflect on you – on your studio.'

Artemisia finds herself holding her breath until she hears her father's words: 'I don't see why not. As long as Zita chaperones you. Wouldn't want people casting aspersions.'

She grabs his hand. 'Thank you, Father. You won't regret it, I promise you.'

'Rest assured,' says Tassi. 'I will take the greatest care of your daughter.'

They come to a halt at a door at the far end of the gallery.

'This leads to the cardinal's private apartments,' Quorli says, with reverence. He takes his ring of keys and, after trying several, finds the one that fits.

The door swings open to reveal a wide oval staircase, which coils up, like the inside of a snail's shell, to a cupola at the top. Artemisia takes Zita's hand as they mount all the way up, to find another locked door.

'Here we are.' Quorli is out of breath from the climb, as he unlocks it. 'The inner sanctum.'

The room beyond appears to be some kind of study, its walls lined with books and curiosities. Artemisia's eye is drawn to an array of small bronze figurines. Thinking of the cardinal's secret collection, she inspects the panelling for signs of a concealed opening.

'You can go in.' Quorli gives her a little push. 'Look at the view.'

Zita pulls her over to the window, exclaiming about the cityscape, but Artemisia deftly extricates herself to take in the room, searching for an insight into the man who commissions most of the art in Rome.

A high-backed red leather chair is pulled out from a table, as if its occupant has just left his spot for a moment and will be returning. The surface of the table is scattered with papers weighted down with carved objects, an ink-pot, a jar of quills. A rosary lies abandoned, half concealed beneath a book; beside it a small cross is set with rubies. A half-drunk glass of wine sits on a leaf of vellum, a curve of crimson staining the pale surface. An uneasy sensation creeps over her, that they are trespassing, that the cardinal might burst in and find them there.

A thick Turkish carpet muffles their steps. She notices

Quorli, when he thinks no one is watching, tip the dead ash from his pipe and tread it into the pile with his foot. A small act of deliberate carelessness that indicates a certain disdain for the man who lines his pockets. He sees her watching.

Zita perches on the edge of the chair, running her fingers over the contents of the desk. 'Don't touch anything,' snaps Quorli, and the hand is withdrawn.

Artemisia looks out of the window. The city rolls away steeply in a seemingly endless vista of miniature buildings, people small as fleas in the streets, the Colosseum shrunk to the size of her thumbnail, and far into the distance the hazy purple hills. She feels lightheaded, imagining herself falling, and steps abruptly back.

Tassi, his hand hovering at Zita's waist, is pointing out a painted frieze, a scene of plump cherubs gallivanting in a fluff of clouds.

'I wonder,' says Quorli to Artemisia, 'if you might like to see one of the cardinal's treasures.'

Anticipation catches her like a hooked fish.

He opens an adjacent door. It is dark within, heavy drapes leaking only slivers of light. She expects him to sweep back the hangings but he takes her by surprise, pushing her against the wall, pressing himself up to her. He has a sharp unpleasant smell, like rancid cheese. 'I know what you want.' He rummages at her skirts.

'What are you doing?' She slaps his hand away and gives him a firm shove. As he staggers backward, she dashes out into the corridor, heart thudding, ashamed at her own foolishness.

He laughs. 'Nothing ventured.'

She can hear Orazio calling for her.

'Perhaps you'd like to show my father the cardinal's treasures,' she says, loudly enough for them all to hear.

Quorli tries to hide his scowl.

'I wish there was the time,' Orazio is saying, coming out onto the landing, taking her hand proprietorially as they make their way back to the loggia. She makes no mention of Quorli's attempted fumble. It would only ignite her father's temper and potentially jeopardize his commission.

13. A Lesson in Perspective

Tassi arrives, shiny boots snapping on the studio flag-stones. Zita has rouged her cheeks and is wearing the lace collar she saves for church but now he is here, she can hardly look at him. He is all courtesy, bowing and greeting the pair of them as if they were Borghese princesses. Artemisia is businesslike, her hair scraped back, and is armoured tightly in a vast and filthy painter's apron. Artemisia is a puzzle to Zita.

He places a large leather case on the table. 'My bag of tricks.'

Zita wipes her damp palms on her skirts.

They watch and Artemisia asks questions, as he unpacks his case. He removes several lengths of polished wood, a skein of silk thread and some drawing materials, placing everything methodically on the bench. The lengths of wood fit together, forming a frame, which he sets on a stand. Then, squinting in concentration, he strings the thread through evenly spaced holes in the frame, making a mesh of horizontal and vertical lines. 'This divides the scene into sections, so you stop looking at the whole and take each part on its own.' He speaks like an adult explaining something to an infant.

'I understand the principle.' Artemisia sounds indignant.

She sets up an easel, clipping a sheet of paper to a board. He does the same. Zita watches him minutely.

Feeling ignored, she retreats to a chair. The two artists are so deep in conversation it is almost as if they have forgotten anyone else is there. Zita would like to say something, remind him of her presence, ask a question, but she can't think of anything intelligent to ask. She doesn't want Tassi to think her stupid. She clears her throat. They seem not to notice.

Tassi describes the vanishing point, indicating how the view through the open kitchen door shrinks away, how the lines of the beams and skirting boards appear to run closer the further away they are. 'Imagine a point beyond the far wall of the kitchen where they disappear into one another.' He sketches it out demonstrating how to exaggerate the lines of perspective to trick the eye.

To Zita, it sounds like magic.

Artemisia, as she sharpens a stick of graphite with a small blade, says, 'I learned about the vanishing point as a child. What I want to know is whether it is possible to create two vanishing points in a single drawing.'

Tassi says: 'If it was possible, one of the great painters would have discovered it. I've never come across such a thing.'

'Just because *you* haven't seen it, it doesn't mean it hasn't been done.' She begins to describe how it might be achieved.

Zita can't believe Artemisia's rudeness and is glad of it because it will make him like her less but he doesn't seem offended, is staring at her as if she is something he has never seen before.

'I suggest you focus on mastering a single point first.' He is smiling.

She laughs. 'Trying to walk before I can crawl.'

'I like your ambition.'

Zita sees the smile Artemisia is trying to hide. She thinks it is a compliment, clearly, but Zita knows ambition is not a quality that is becoming in a woman. Perhaps he is being sarcastic.

'You don't find it unfeminine?' says Artemisia.

'Who cares about femininity?' He makes a small derisive snort. 'Talent is rare. It should be nurtured.'

So, he is not being sarcastic. Zita feels jealousy pecking at her.

The pair of them draw in silence.

'Let me see what you've done,' Tassi says, after a time, walking over to stand beside Artemisia, placing a hand at the base of her spine.

She steps aside, with a glance at Tassi that could freeze Hell. His lip curls minutely and a little muscle in his jaw flexes. All Zita can think is that she wouldn't have stepped aside – no. She imagines leaning her body into his embrace, feeling those arms holding her, the strength of him.

They return to their silent drawing. Zita can see the intensity of their focus as if they are pulled by a magnet, something beyond the scope of her understanding. She has been completely forgotten, as if she is invisible. She can hear her girls rolling out pastry in the kitchen, chattering quietly for once, and is thankful the baby is asleep.

She staves off her boredom by sending her mind back to the cardinal's rooms and all the beautiful objects there – things lying about the like of which she could never imagine even so much as holding in her hands.

She hadn't been able to help herself. The cross was so

very pretty, its crimson eye winking at her as it caught the light. It had found its way into her sleeve, almost without her awareness. She is burning with shame now. What will she do? She can't confess to having stolen something from the cardinal – and not something trivial, like a cake or a ribbon, but a jewelled cross belonging to a man of God.

She can feel the Lord's judgement, painful as a whipping. What has she done? She must return it. But how?

She forces her mind away from the cross, from her guilt, making herself watch the passers-by out of the window and thinking of ways she might inveigle herself into Tassi's company. She could stop to greet him when he is with the other artists sharing an evening drink in the square, linger a little in the hope that he invites her to join him. She allows the fantasy to unfurl, her eyelids becoming heavy.

His words repeat in Artemisia's head: *I like your ambition.* Only Piero has ever said this to her. Everyone else – her father, Porzia, Sister Ilaria, even Francesco – has implied, if they haven't said it, that her ambition is better either hidden or driven into submission. *Talent is rare. It should be nurtured.* The compliment continues to ring through her, making her swell.

She carefully draws the web of lines, looking and drawing, looking and drawing, her world reduced to that small frame divided up into its smaller squares.

Eventually he announces that their time is up and scrutinizes her drawing for some time through narrowed eyes, eventually saying: 'Impressive.'

'Thank you,' she says formally, with a nod. But inside

she is thrilled by that single word, storing it up with his other compliments. They make her feel her dreams are within touching distance. An image springs to mind of the fresco on the ceiling of the Pope's chapel: God's hand reaching out towards Adam, the tips of their fingers almost touching. She was taken to see it once.

She allows herself to envisage people – collectors and painters – appraising her work. The imagined crowd stands speechless before some future creation of hers, a seed yet ungerminated in her mind. She can see the impact of her work in their faces. They are impressed, not because they see the work of a woman and find it good but because they see the work of a painter and find it good.

'So much for your chaperone,' says Tassi, pointing with a grin towards Zita, who is fast asleep in her chair, snoring. 'We could have got up to all sorts of things. I might have ravished you.' He seems pleased with his joke.

Artemisia casts him her most scathing look.

'Zita? Wakey-wakey.' He prods her and she jerks up out of her sleep, looking about confused, wiping a string of drool from her chin. Tassi is laughing.

Zita looks mortified. 'I wasn't snoring, was I?'

'No,' Artemisia says, to spare her even more embarrassment.

Despite his compliments, she is glad when he has packed up his things and gone.

14. New Moon through Glass

Orazio's back aches from painting for hours at such an awkward angle. The light is almost gone and he is alone underneath Tassi's magnificent soaring deceit. All Bendino's drawings had been wrong, the perspective awry. No matter how many times he explained that their proportions needed to compensate for being observed from far below, the talentless boy couldn't seem to understand.

Orazio has had to adjust them but is still not satisfied, and neither is Quorli. That afternoon he had hauled himself all the way up the ladder, puffing and wheezing, to view the work. 'I was expecting them to have . . . well, to have more power in them, frankly,' he'd said. Orazio had assured him that they would when they were finished, though in truth, given his recent form, he doubts whether he is able to deliver what is required.

Only a few weeks ago all had seemed so full of hope. He had this commission and Artemisia was on the brink of a betrothal. Modenese had been gracious but abstruse, explaining that his father had other ideas for him, his hands were tied, but Orazio knew it was an excuse.

Aside from completing this commission, finding a match for his daughter is now his foremost concern. He needs a wealthy son-in-law, and she needs a firm hand. The euphoric feeling, the feeling of his future being secured, his problems solved, has dissipated, leaving only an ominous sense of failure.

His hand is shaking as he squints in the half-light to add detail to a face. What he would give for a slug of strong grappa now. The flask he keeps in his pocket is empty. He imagines the blazing trail it would make down his gullet and the glorious swimming feeling it would bring, rendering his worries small. He can barely see what he is doing. His hand wobbles, leaving a dark smudge. He curses under his breath and, deciding to call it a day, begins to gather his things.

Just as he is about to climb down he hears the grind of footsteps on gravel and the patter of voices: Quorli and Tassi. He stays absolutely still, doesn't want to have to face them, not now.

As they approach he begins to make out a few words. His ears prick at his own name. They settle on a bench right below him. 'He's not as good as I thought he'd be.' It is Quorli who says this, taking a deep suck on his pipe and exhaling with a long sigh.

The smoke rises, flooding Orazio's nostrils, intensifying his craving for a drink.

'Frankly, he's been a disappointment all round. I expected greater things . . . That *Madonna* he showed us was a wonder. You wouldn't think it was painted by the same hand . . .'

'Are you considering someone else?'

'There's no one any good who'd do it for as little as I'm paying him. All the budget is spent on *you*.'

'But *I'm* worth the fee.'

Orazio hears one man give the other a jovial punch followed by another slew of laughter and then quiet, only the fizzle of Quorli's pipe.

Tassi breaks the silence: 'I like the man. Give him a chance. His work's not finished yet. I know he's capable of something spectacular – I wouldn't have recommended him otherwise.'

Orazio could jump down and hug Tassi for his kindness. 'I'm not convinced.'

An insect thrums loudly, landing on Orazio's face. He brushes it away, and a white cat tiptoes silently along the very lip of the scaffold, an exercise in agility. He can hear the trickle of cups being filled with liquid. He would exchange his soul for a drink in this moment.

'I was hoping he'd be a candidate for all the work the cardinal is commissioning for his new pavilion outside the city. You should see the plans, Tassi. It dwarfs this place in its ambition.'

A sense of urgency grips Orazio, to be better, to prove his worth. A vision comes to him of his own decline into decrepitude, a forgotten man. He must tease his abilities from wherever they are hiding. Perhaps, in the meantime, he should ask Artemisia to help him on the quiet. Get rid of Bendino. That might make the difference.

'There will be work for me, I assume,' Tassi is saying.

'Naturally. Far too much for you alone. This is why I mention it. I'm hoping you don't have any commissions that will take you away from Rome.' Quorli goes on to describe the cardinal's plans to raze the vineyards beyond the city walls on the high land to the north-east. It is to be a summer retreat, an escape from the heat of the city, with extensive gardens, fountains and the villa designed to take advantage of the cool breezes. 'There is a large pond up there, which will be dug out to form an ornamental lake.'

Orazio knows the place. He used to walk there with Prudenzia when they were newlywed, when he was bursting with promise and ambition. The thought of Prudenzia makes him ache with sadness. Five years has done little to dull the pain. His life has slowly disintegrated since she departed, as if there is some relationship between the decomposition of her mortal remains and his own life's trajectory. Tears needle the backs of his eyes. The two men talk on, replenishing their drinks, their discussion loosening, descending inevitably to matters of the flesh.

'What about that woman – the daughter's companion?' says Quorli. 'I'd like to give *her* one. *And* she'd be grateful.'

'A beauty.'

'Stupid as a nanny-goat. But those tits make up for it. Husband's away by all accounts.'

The cat takes a leap, landing with a soft thud on the ground.

'Who's there?' It is Tassi, an edge to his voice. 'Is someone there?'

Orazio holds his breath.

'Just a cat.' The animal pads across the gravel, slipping into the undergrowth, out of sight.

The vespers bells begin to ring, loud in the darkness. Orazio shivers. The air has taken on a chill and his coat is down at the bottom. He wraps his arms around his torso, trying to generate a little warmth.

'And the daughter. She's an odd creature. Not very feminine.'

'I find her quite intriguing. So curious about things, so keen to learn. An interesting mind . . . and her ability is impressive. She's not like most women, is she?'

'You mean she hasn't fallen instantly for your charms.' Quorli snorts. 'Seems a frigid thing to me.'

'Give me half an hour alone with her and, I guarantee you, I'll have her warmed up well and good.'

Orazio's rage makes itself known, a knot tightening in the pit of his gut. Bastards.

'You've already had her alone. Didn't you give her a drawing lesson the other day?'

'Orazio was very keen for me to show her my techniques.' They both erupt into a bout of crude laughter. 'But the companion wouldn't leave her side.'

'He'd never be stupid enough to leave her alone with *you*,' says Quorli, still sputtering. 'The nanny-goat watches over the daughter's virtue.'

'But if I did conceive to find myself alone with her, I wager you I'd find a way in.'

'Thirty *scudi* says you can't.'

Orazio hears the two men shake on their bet. Thirty *scudi* is a vast sum – more than he's ever been paid for a painting. An idea pushes itself towards the front of his mind, an idea that might turn everything good again. It is not Tassi who is the villain here – didn't he jump to Orazio's defence only moments before? And that crude talk – well, men will be men.

Tassi may not have Modenese's wealth, but he is a man with connections, a man with prospects, talent and an attachment to a noble family. If Artemisia were married to him it would benefit them all. And Tassi is from their world. He understands the artistic temperament – he might even consider it an asset in Artemisia. Orazio is astonished the thought hadn't occurred to him before – it seems so obvious now.

The two men move to stroll around the garden, once more out of earshot. The sounds of the city rise up: a trickle of festive music from somewhere, the occasional rattle of laughter, raised voices, a barking dog. A jasmine climbing up the loggia releases its sweet evening fragrance. Out here, the world seems at peace.

Framed in a small circular window at the apex of the roof, Orazio has a view of the moon, a sharp silver curve rising above a row of pines. He looks away sharply, remembering Prudenzia's warning: 'Never look at a new moon through glass.' What was it? Seven years' bad luck? Some other kind of curse? He used to tease her about her superstitions: never set the bread upside down, never put a hat on the bed, never bring feathers into the house. Yet he can hear his dead wife's whisper – *bad luck* – or is it the breeze?

He shakes his head. *Pull yourself together*.

Creeping down the ladder and avoiding the gravel, he sidles silently round to the gate, opening it and clanging it shut, as if he has just arrived.

'Who goes there?' shouts Quorli.

'It's me, Orazio. I forgot my coat.' He heads over to the two men. 'What are you up to?'

'Nothing much. You?'

'I've been thinking. I'm unhappy with the work I've done so far.' He gestures towards the loggia. 'I'm going to employ someone else to do the sketches – someone better than Bendino.' He cannot bring himself to say that this person will be his daughter. He fears their ridicule.

'Good,' says Quorli. He gives Orazio a patronizing cuff on the back of the head. 'Now, we must be off. The cardinal's on the warpath. He's missing some trinket or other

136

and thinks his servants are stealing from him. Don't want him wondering what we're doing here so late.'

They leave together, walking down the hill until Quorli breaks away, leaving Orazio alone with Tassi. It is an opportunity to broach the subject that has been pressing at him.

'You have established quite a name for yourself since we first worked together.' Orazio makes his tone light. 'And you're still a young man. Are you in the market for a bride?'

'To be completely honest, I enjoy my freedom . . .' They walk on. 'But if the right woman fell into my path, then you never know.'

'I was wondering.' Orazio searches for the right way to put it. 'I'd like to see my daughter settled.'

'Artemisia?' Tassi stops, turning to meet Orazio's eye with his unerring gaze. 'She's an extraordinary young woman, your daughter.' Something in his tone makes Orazio realize his offer is about to be refused. 'Truth be told, I had thought I might be able to claim someone . . . someone from one of the . . .' Tassi looks askance, clearly struggling to find a way to avoid causing offence. 'A wife who might take me up in the world. You know how things are for us painters. So unpredictable. Feast and famine. Marriage could be an opportunity for me. And with my connection to the Marchesa di Tassi . . .' He pauses, seeming a little embarrassed. 'I don't like to make too much of it but as the marchesa's adopted son, I might just be in a position to catch a girl with . . . well . . . You know what I mean?'

'I see.' Orazio tries his best to hide his disappointment.

'Please don't get me wrong. I admire Artemisia – would be honoured to help her develop her work. I'd be glad to continue teaching her . . . wouldn't expect a fee.'

'That's very generous of you.' Orazio has a sinking sensation, as if his entire body is collapsing in on itself. He is tired, tired of being headed off at every pass.

They walk in silence until they reach the piazza Santa Trinità. The air is high with merriment. A group of drunken youths have gathered around the water pump and are splashing each other, laughing wildly. He thinks he spots his two older boys among them, half hiding, probably afraid he will clip them round their ears and insist they go home, embarrassing them in front of their friends. Not tonight – he is too deflated and pretends he hasn't seen them.

Tassi suggests they stop for a drink. Orazio craves a drink more than ever, but the idea of sitting with Agostino Tassi, with all his bluster and confidence, is more than he can take. He makes an excuse and walks on, towards Fillide's apartments near the river.

He stops to buy a measure of wine, unable to resist drinking it there in the street, like a vagrant. His head is drifting pleasantly as he arrives, calling her name below the window. She leans out, hissing for him to keep it down. 'You can't come up. I'm entertaining.'

He sits in a quiet spot by the river, draining the carafe. The surface of the water is scribbled with patterns of moonlight as faint strains of a late mass float through the air from the Pope's chapel. He recognizes the composition as one of Palestrina's, a chant of exquisite perfection, the delicate melding of voices, the thrum of the basses, building, moving through the middle tones up and up to the indescribably glorious sound of the boy sopranos soaring heavenward.

He is overwhelmed by the extraordinary beauty of it all, this world God has created, his own minuscule part in it. For the first time in years Orazio finds himself praying fervently, sincerely, begging for guidance. At that moment a snippet of conversation drifts up to him from one of the river boats, clear as a bell: 'Give him a chance.'

Remembering instantly that Tassi had used those precise words in his defence a mere hour before, Orazio is struck by a certainty. It must be a sign. The Lord has answered his prayers. *Give him a chance*. Marriage is a sacrament, after all and he has no doubt now that he has Heavenly approval to match Agostino Tassi with his daughter.

He expels a drunken belch as his mind folds and unfolds this idea and how to achieve it. Tassi may have made his refusal plain, but there is something else, another way, that might make him open to persuasion.

15. The Swallow

The Stiatessis are taking Artemisia and Zita to San Giovanni in Laterano, far in the southernmost reaches of Rome where the city gives way to smallholdings. A eucharist is to be held to celebrate the unveiling of a new set of statues of the apostles.

Their party – with the Stiatessis' daughter and her children – is packed tight as salted anchovies in the carriage, rattling uncomfortably over the cobbles. Artemisia can see crowds gathering, milling about the front of the basilica in their finest dress.

Marco is heavy on her lap, half asleep from the motion of the carriage, his head tucked into her shoulder. She is glad to be reunited with her little brother, who seems to be thriving under Porzia's care. Orazio had said he was too busy working to join them today. She knew they were all relieved.

Zita sits beside her, clearly agitated, hands tightly gripped together in her lap, knuckles blanched, her shoulders clenched to her ears. 'Is something wrong?' whispers Artemisia.

'It's just . . . it's just . . .' Zita seems unable to finish her sentence and sits staring at her bitten nails for some time, before cupping a hand over her mouth to say, almost inaudibly, 'I can't go to confession. Not today.'

'Why not?' Artemisia has noticed Zita avoiding Sunday mass lately. Luca had had a fever, then it was one of the girls and then it was something else. Artemisia doesn't know why but assumes that this time it must have something to do with the events of the previous evening.

Her father had stayed out late and she had been woken in the night by noises coming from Zita's apartment: conversation, laughter, heavy footfall. When she'd finally managed to drop off, her pillow pressed over her ears, she was jolted awake by a shattering crash.

Furious, she hauled herself out of bed, calling from the landing, 'What's going on up there?'

'Oh, look, Agostino, we've roused the other one.' To her dismay she could see the odious Quorli swaying at the top of the stairs, very much the worse for wear.

'What are you doing here?' She employed her most officious tone. 'I think you had better leave.'

'Come on, time to go.' Tassi appeared then, also clearly inebriated, making a deep exaggerated bow as they passed her on the landing. She was tempted to kick their ankles.

Rushing up, she found Zita on the floor, too drunk to stand, with the shards of a broken flagon scattered around her.

'What happened? Did they hurt you?'

''S nuffin' ter worry about,' she slurred. 'Jus' couldn' get them to go.'

'Well, they've gone now. What were they doing here, anyway?'

Come morning, Zita had refused to speak about it. As far as Artemisia was concerned it was none of her business what Zita got up to in her own apartment, but she didn't relish the idea of those two becoming regular upstairs visitors at the via della Croce.

'Did I tell you that Piero will be returning to Rome for a few weeks in the autumn?' Porzia is saying. 'He wrote and asked that I be sure to send you his special regards. He was keen to have news of you.'

Artemisia's heart lightens to hear this, but it falls heavy once more when she remembers that she will quite likely be married off by autumn. She won't be able to see Piero except under formal conditions.

Her father had recently proposed Tassi as a suitor. She'd firmly told him no, that Tassi wasn't for her. She admires his talent and was certainly flattered by his appraisal of her work but as a husband – she would find his arrogance insufferable. She had been surprised that her father had accepted her refusal without ado. They both knew he could make life very difficult for her if she refused his wishes. But that had been the end of it.

The more she thought about it, the more she realized that her father had been in an unusually good mood in recent weeks. She supposed it had to do with the success of the figures in the fresco he was working on. He'd triumphantly announced: 'We've brought those dead shapes to life, Artemisia.' He had asked her to draw out a new set of cartoons in the studio rather than on site. He hadn't wanted her working alongside the men and she was glad to avoid Quorli, with his wandering hands and lecherous eye.

'We make quite the team, you and I,' he had said, almost lovingly. It was good to see him so full of plans for the cardinal's new summer pavilion and all the work it would bring. It made her feel safe, even content. Perhaps he would forget about the need to find her a husband.

The carriage draws to a halt and they all pile out, though when she turns back Zita is still slumped on the bench, pale and waxy. 'You look awful.'

'I'm . . . I'm . . .' Zita's voice is small and weak '. . . not feeling up to it.'

'Must we get you home to bed?' Artemisia feels the pull between duty to Zita and her desire to see the sculptures.

'No, no. I can wait here.' She folds her arms over her chest, huddling further into the corner, looking deathly. 'Please. I don't want to make a fuss. I will join you when I feel better.'

When they return after mass they find Zita munching sugared almonds that she must have bought from one of the hawkers. They all clamber into the carriage and are about to pull away when a face appears in the open window. 'Are you heading north? I don't suppose you have room for a stray?'

Artemisia's heart sinks. It is a hot day, there is so little room in the carriage, and Tassi is not a small man.

'I don't see why not,' says Porzia, brightly. 'Move up, girls.' The carriage lists under Tassi's weight as he steps inside, ducking his head under the door with a grin. He slides into the seat beside Artemisia. On her other side Zita blushes into her bag of almonds.

'It's very kind of you. My companions were in a rush and I . . .' He launches into a convoluted excuse as to why he hasn't a horse to convey him home. Artemisia is not really listening. With everyone departing mass at once, the carriage is barely moving. The proximity of this large man sitting beside her in such a cramped space, his leg pressed against hers, the heat radiating from his body, is suffocating.

The queue of vehicles eventually grinds to a halt. They wait. Tassi is holding forth loudly. Artemisia can bear it no longer. 'I'm going to walk. Need the fresh air.' Before she can be persuaded otherwise, she opens the door and jumps down onto the road.

Feeling the most glorious sense of liberation, she begins to march briskly in the direction of home.

Almost as soon as Artemisia has jumped from the carriage Tassi follows her out.

The door slams, leaving Zita sinking into disappointment. She'd been enjoying his presence, his familiar manner, the way he had dipped his hand into her bag of sweets with a wink, saying, 'My favourite.' She felt he was not talking about the almonds at all. When he is not with Quorli he is a different man altogether.

She scratches at her neckline where her coarse sackcloth under-shift is grating at her skin. She had worn it to punish herself. She reddens, remembering the previous night. Things had almost gone too far.

'Zita!' Porzia jolts her from her thoughts. 'Have you lost your senses? You can't leave him to walk alone with Artemisia.' She opens the door, giving Zita a pointed glare and a nod.

Zita shoves the almonds into her pocket before climbing down onto the dusty verge. She can see the pair of them already quite far ahead. Tassi has caught up with Artemisia, his white hat-feather bobbing above the heads of the thinning crowds.

Zita scrambles in their wake, half running, half walking, catching up enough for threads of their conversation to trail back to her. A stitch begins to form in her side. She hears Artemisia tell him, politely enough, that she'd rather walk alone, that she has things she wants to think about in peace.

'I can't leave you unescorted.' He seems genuinely worried about her safety. Even at a distance Zita can hear the concern in his voice. He places a hand on Artemisia's forearm. She shakes it off.

The familiar spark of jealousy reignites in Zita. *How could he prefer plain, unfeminine Artemisia, with her dirty nails and rat's-tail hair, over me?* He seems to have barely noticed her beauty, which is the single thing anyone ever notices about her. *Perhaps my behaviour last night has put him off me.*

She had been in such a state this morning, panicked about revealing her sins to the priest. She had been so easily persuaded to invite Tassi and Quorli up to her rooms. But it is not just her wayward behaviour, drinking with those two. She has got herself into a muddle.

If she lets herself think about it for too long, she becomes panicky. Her mind seethes with thoughts of Hell and she tells herself she must replace the stolen cross. But try as she might, she can't think of a way to achieve this. She doesn't even know any more what made her take it. It isn't having the thing that brings pleasure. No, it is the sense, however small, of a victory over the owner. It is only fair that she wins sometimes, too.

The figures ahead turn off the road into a lane running through a vineyard, which Zita supposes must be a short-cut. A sense of unease creeps over her – it is so quiet.

They pass a man with a dog on a chain. It barks viciously, straining at its collar, fangs springing from black gums.

'Control that animal.' Tassi's tone is sharp with authority. Zita slinks behind the vines, still unseen.

'You're trespassing,' says the man. 'This is private property.'

'I'm aware of that. It's my brother's land. So, stand aside.'

The man hauls his dog out of the path and they continue on.

Zita hears Artemisia ask if it really is his brother's land. He laughs, 'Of course not. I don't have a brother.'

He lies with ease, Zita thinks, as if it is nothing at all.

They walk further.

The light is starting to fade into the gloaming, shadows lengthening into monsters. Swallows flit overhead, hunting insects, fork-tailed darts against the sky. Underfoot is gritty earth now, not a proper path at all and the vines are all around, too high to see over.

Zita staggers after them, her best slippers now covered with filth. She can still hear the dog barking behind. The stitch in her side is so bad she has to stop, doubling over, waiting for the pain to subside. A hawk wheels silently above, wing feathers like fingertips. She watches it for a moment as it climbs. Then it dives with terrifying speed, scattering the swallows, grabbing a straggler in mid-air, swooping away with it in its talons.

She continues, half running to keep the pair in sight and manages to catch up, in earshot again.

Artemisia says: 'Where in Heaven's name are we?' Worry makes her voice sound hollow. Zita, too, can sense that something is wrong. There are no buildings in sight, no spires or domes, only endless row upon row of vines.

Artemisia crouches down, pulling her shoe off and shaking out what must be a stone. He crouches beside her, whispering something that Zita can't quite catch. Then they are on the ground, Artemisia lying under him.

Zita's eyes well up. Of course he'd prefer Artemisia, the brilliant artist, he an artist himself. The sight of them together is torment but neither can she tear her gaze away.

Suddenly she understands that what she is seeing is not what she'd thought. Artemisia is struggling, grunting, flailing, trying to push him off. He has her pinned to the ground by her shoulders. 'You know what you want, you little tease.'

Zita flies towards them, shouting as loudly as she can, flapping her arms: 'Get off her. Leave her alone.'

He jumps up, his eyes meeting hers, stopping her in her tracks. He looms, a great black shadow with the low sun behind him, fists clenched. 'Might have known you'd ruin our fun.'

Artemisia is sitting up. Her shift is torn at the front and she has dirt on her face. 'Zita! Thank Heaven you're here.' If she is upset, she is not letting it show. 'Now leave us be, Tassi.' She is firm.

'You don't really want me to go, do you?' His voice is smooth again, as if nothing wrong has happened. 'We were just starting to enjoy ourselves.' He is looking at them, smiling, as he swipes his hair off his forehead. Zita is repulsed, all her pent-up desire for him drained away in an instant.

Artemisia steps calmly towards him. His face opens into

147

a satisfied smile. When she slaps him hard across the cheek, he is clearly shocked. Zita wants to cheer. His hand darts up to the red mark she has left, his expression boiling with rage, making Zita fear he will retaliate.

'What are you waiting for? Go!' Artemisia is quite calm – how so, Zita doesn't know.

He stands a moment longer, seeming to wonder if there is any means by which his pride can be salvaged, before turning and striding back in the direction they came. 'Prick-tease,' he mutters, with a black look, as he passes.

Once his footsteps have faded Artemisia heaves a loud sigh of relief, brushing the dirt off her dress. Then she bursts, inexplicably, into a gust of crazed laughter.

'What's so funny?' What could she possibly find amusing about the situation? Her virtue was almost stolen from her, the worst possible thing for a girl – worse than death.

When she finally stops laughing, she looks up, pink-cheeked. 'Apparently Father was right about my needing a chaperone. You know, I've resented your presence but now I see why I need you.' She links her arm through Zita's. 'I had an instinct Tassi wasn't quite right. But I didn't expect . . .'

'What an idiot I've been, to think that man was . . .' Zita isn't sure *what* she thought Tassi was. 'I didn't see beyond his looks.' When she considers the fantasies she, a married woman, entertained about him, she thinks Artemisia may not be the only one to have had a narrow escape.

'And to think Father suggested him as a suitor.' She makes a grimace. 'Don't mention this to him, will you?' Artemisia has fixed her with a determined look.

Zita is about to question this when Artemisia interrupts

her: 'He'll only punish me for putting myself in the way of harm.'

They march in silence uphill, just the sound of their breath puffing with the effort of the climb. Zita is still rattled, playing the incident over and over in her head, thinking of what might have happened. Once at the top, she is relieved to see buildings and the spire of Santa Maria Maggiore. She mutters a prayer of thanks, able now to imagine getting home safely, finding her children there, with the boys. The fullness in her breasts tells her Luca will be wanting a feed.

'Look.' Artemisia is pointing at the sky. It is striated a silvery pink, and a last bright sliver of sun peeps over the horizon. She opens her arms as if to embrace the sight, the colours reflecting onto her white dress so the dirty smudges can hardly be seen. 'Isn't it wondrous?'

They stand for some time without speaking until the sun has altogether gone. Impatience prods at Zita. The under-shift is itching horribly and she is anxious to get home before dark but Artemisia seems unperturbed that it is past sunset. Eventually she meets Zita's gaze. 'Promise you won't leave me alone with him again.'

'I promise' – Zita is solemn, as if reciting a vow – 'on my children's lives, I will never leave you alone with that man again.'

'You don't need to promise on your children's lives.' Artemisia takes her hand, as if they are real friends. 'Your word is good enough for me.'

Hearing this makes her guilt spring up once more. What would Artemisia think if she knew she was a thief? A thief, and a liar.

16. A Silver *Scudo*

There is a new spring in Orazio's step as he strides through almost empty streets towards the studio from the Monte Cavallo gardens. The frescos are coming along and Quorli is finally content. He has even dropped one or two hints about further commissions.

As he turns into the via della Croce he is surprised to see Quorli loitering outside the studio, wearing a preposterous pointed hat festooned with large silk flowers. He looks like something out of carnival.

'Ah, there you are,' Quorli calls. 'I was about to give up.'

'What brings you here?' Orazio is remembering that he hasn't anything to drink in the house, or certainly nothing good enough to serve to Quorli. 'I'm afraid I haven't a drop of anything to offer you.'

'Never mind that. I'm here on a matter of business.'

Orazio feels a tight sense of anticipation in his chest – resolving to negotiate a proper fee for himself this time. He opens the door, welcoming his visitor into the shadowy interior. It is cool and dark with the shutters closed.

'Who's upstairs?' Quorli points to the ceiling, from which a thumping sound is emanating. 'Not your charming daughter and her companion?'

'It's my older boys. They stayed behind to look after the little ones. My daughter and her companion are at the mass at San Giovanni.'

'You didn't let them go alone – those two lovelies?'

'No, of course not. They went with the Stiatessis.'

Quorli makes a sour face. 'My cousin and I are not close.'

Orazio wonders what the bad blood could be between them but doesn't ask, just says, in a noncommittal way, 'I've known Giovanni a long time.'

Quorli sucks his teeth. 'The wife's a little temptress.'

This is certainly not the impression he has ever had of Porzia. 'She was like a sister to my wife.'

Quorli makes a kind of unintelligible grunt and begins to fill his pipe. 'Got something I can light this with?'

Orazio ignites a taper from the kitchen hearth, returning with his hand cupped round the flame. Quorli inhales deeply. The smoke gets into Orazio's eyes, making them sting.

'The reason I'm here is that it's my wife's saint's day soon and I promised her a painting. Generous, I know.' He emits a crude spit of laughter. 'But she's upset with me and I want to get on her right side again.'

'I have the *Madonna*.' Orazio points to the painting on an easel across the studio and opens the shutters to light it. 'You know the one.'

'Lovely . . .' he murmurs. 'It's charming, this, but' – two streams of pale blue vapour pour from his nostrils – 'actually, I was rather keen to see that *Susanna*, if I may?'

It strikes Orazio that a painting of a naked woman being ogled by two men isn't the kind of thing that would placate most wives, no matter the moral lesson it contains. Besides, he suspects that Artemisia has painted over it as it disappeared from the studio weeks ago.

'I'm sorry to say the *Susanna*'s no longer . . . Let me see what else I can show you.' He looks through the stack of canvases against the wall behind them. 'I've the beginnings of . . .'

To his astonishment, the *Susanna* is there and apparently finished. 'Ah, here she is!' He half draws it out to where he can see it properly, struck yet again by the quality of his daughter's work, until he notices that one of the lecherous men is unmistakably a portrait of Quorli. Cursing Artemisia inwardly, he shoves the canvas back into the shadows. 'I'm not entirely happy with her yet. She needs more work.'

Quorli is on his feet now, approaching. His curiosity has been aroused and he half shoves the other man out of the way. Despite Orazio's polite protestations, Quorli picks up the canvas and props it up in the light.

'I see why you were trying to hide it, you sly old dog.' He leers at Orazio. 'Didn't want me looking at your daughter's companion in her birthday suit? She your fancy woman?' He is smirking.

'Sadly not.' To Orazio's relief it seems that the sight of naked flesh has grabbed all of Quorli's attention. 'Now how about the *Madonna*? Surely a more suitable subject as a gift for your wife.'

'What's this?'

Orazio's gut clenches.

'Have you depicted *me*?' He peers at the male figure.

'What makes you think that?' Orazio tries to keep his tone light as he makes an attempt to slide the canvas away but Quorli has a grip on it.

He is inspecting the picture minutely. 'Bloody cheek.'

A few drops of his spit land on Orazio's face.

Orazio begins to form a grovelling apology until he sees that the man is grinning.

'What a dark horse you are, Gentileschi. I'd never have imagined you harboured such a wicked sense of humour.'

Orazio manages a huff of pretend amusement. 'You like it? I feared you might be insulted.'

'Insulted?' Quorli slaps him firmly on the back. 'On the contrary, I'm flattered. Didn't know you had it in you. Now I see why you didn't think it suitable for the wife. Tempted to take it anyway to hang in my study.'

Relief emboldens Orazio. 'You could take this *and* the *Madonna*. And, of course, I hope you'll find work for me on the cardinal's new summer house.'

By the time he is ready to depart, Orazio has pocketed a deposit for both paintings. If he can just persuade Tassi to wed his daughter his future will seem less unsure. He can picture it now, a sun-drenched landscape, free from the relentless concerns that have hounded him lately.

Her father looks at her dirt-smudged dress and dishevelled hair. 'What happened to you?'

'Nothing. I tripped over. I'm not hurt.' Artemisia meets Zita's eye, wiping her finger across her lips as they follow Orazio into the kitchen. Her brothers barely look up from their card game.

'I sold two paintings this afternoon.'

Artemisia thought her father seemed unusually cheerful. 'Which ones? The *Madonna*?'

'Your *Susanna*.' He looks at her with alarming directness.

'My what?' Immediately annoyed with herself for failing to return it safely upstairs, she tries to assess whether the spark in her father's eye is the precursor to anger or glee.

'You know what I'm talking about.'

Artemisia can see the colour drain from Zita's face. She will have to be bold. 'What of my *Susanna*?'

The place falls silent, awaiting an explosion.

Orazio throws a silver *scudo* onto the table. 'It's sold.' He seems very pleased with himself.

Artemisia glances at the coin and back at her father. 'Where's the rest?' Despite a flash of elation – her painting, sold! – she maintains her frosty expression.

'The other eleven will be paid on delivery.'

'That's a good price.'

'It is.'

'Who's paying it?'

'Furiere Quorli. He also bought the *Madonna*.' Orazio rubs his hands together.

'Quorli? But . . .' She is perplexed, thought she'd caught the Furiere's features with precision.

Her father says nothing for a moment.

'He was amused by it.'

'Amused?' She is revolted at the idea of that vile man finding enjoyment from the sight of himself depicted leering at a terrified naked woman. She glances at Zita, who doesn't appear to share her concern. She has turned back to her child, is cooing, teasing a gummy smile from him. 'I suppose he had something to say about my choice of subject.'

'Well, as you come to mention it . . .' Orazio appears to be weighing up what exactly he is going to say '. . . he believes the work is painted by me.'

154

Rage catapults her to her feet and over to him. The candles quiver. 'How dare you pass off my work as yours? How could you sink so low?' Her arms are flailing.

He grabs her wrists. 'You should count yourself lucky I sought to protect your virtue, my girl.' His face is ruddy, yellow teeth bared. 'Painting something like that.'

She catches a glimpse of her brother, expecting to see a smirk on Francesco's face but finding instead only concern. He has his fists clenched, ready to defend her. He is not a little boy any more.

'My virtue is my business,' she spits.

But she is well aware that this is not the case: her virtue is the whole family's business. They will all suffer the shame if she loses it, and she had a narrow escape in the vineyard only a couple of hours ago.

'You should be glad I made the sale and that I am prepared to share the proceeds. Most fathers would send their daughters to a nunnery for less . . . painting Zita naked. A disgrace.'

'Send me to a nunnery?' She is emboldened by Francesco's silent support. 'Whose work could you pass off as your own then? You'd lose all the new commissions you keep boasting of, since you are incapable of painting anything of worth these days.'

'You . . . you . . .' He is trembling, still has a tight hold of her wrists. She can smell stale drink on his breath. 'Ungrateful bitch!'

Artemisia holds her breath, waiting for the strike, remembering the slap she gave Tassi. She sees the look of desperation glance over her father's face.

He lets go of her, sinking onto the bench, and the

tension drains from the room. In that moment she recognizes that this has nothing to do with her virtue, or the potential loss of it, but about the fact that she, at seventeen, has surpassed him as a painter. Pity grips her with surprising force.

'I *am* grateful, Father – very grateful.' She picks up the coin. It is cool and hard in her palm, solid proof of her worth.

Orazio is trying to pour himself a drink but is shaking so much he spills wine onto the table. Artemisia eases the bottle from his hand and pours him a modest measure.

'More.' He points to the rim.

'I think you've had enough.' She sounds like her mother.

He slumps, defeated, looking at her with hangdog eyes, and takes a gulp of the drink. She cuts him some cheese and a slice of bread, which she butters and sprinkles salt on, as he likes it. 'Here. Eat something. When was the last time you ate?'

He shrugs, eating obediently while the boys continue their card game in silence.

A knock at the outer door interrupts the hush. Francesco goes to see who it is, returning with a letter. Orazio rips it open, squinting to read it.

Artemisia wonders if his eyesight is fading and whether this might be the cause of his diminishing ability. But she knows in her heart that she is merely seeking excuses for him. It is not his ability that is waning but hers that is waxing.

After a few moments, he announces, almost triumphantly: 'Signor Tassi is coming the day after tomorrow to give you another lesson in perspective.'

She looks at him, speechless.

'I counsel you not to mention that the *Susanna* is your work. It wouldn't do to confuse things.'

She feels like a lobster in a pot of heating water. The *Susanna* is the last thing on her mind. 'I think I've learned all I can from him. I don't need another lesson.' She tries to sound measured and casual, but a hint of worry threads itself through her tone.

'You will do as I say.' Orazio is back to his usual belligerent self. 'He's offered to waive his fee. I can't tell him his generosity is no longer wanted. It would be an unforgivable insult. Do you not understand what a privilege it is to learn from someone like Agostino Tassi?'

Artemisia holds her tongue, turning the silver *scudo* over and over in her hand, as he mutters about all the work he stands to lose if Tassi is offended.

Zita shoots her a meaningful look, as if to ask why she is not speaking out.

Artemisia ignores her. She stands, desperate to get out of the room. 'Let's put the little ones to bed.'

But Zita cannot prevent herself from blurting: 'Signor Tassi can't come here.'

'Are you forgetting this is *my* house?' Orazio whips his head round to Zita, who recoils.

Artemisia cannot let her spill the events of this afternoon and complicate things further. She grabs Zita's arm and drags her upstairs.

17. The Cross

'Where's your brother?' Orazio calls up to Francesco, who is at the top of the scaffold filling in details on the ceiling with gold leaf.

'No idea. Isn't he down there? He was working at the bench last I saw of him.'

'I turn my back . . .' Orazio's irritation burgeons. 'There's no time for skiving. Giulio!' he shouts. 'Where the hell are you?'

'He went out there.' One of Tassi's assistants is pointing towards the palazzo.

'What for? He has no reason to go there.' Orazio doesn't want the boy snooping about where he's not allowed, getting himself accused of trespassing.

'How should I know?'

Ignoring the assistant's insolence Orazio strides across the garden, spotting the dark head of his middle son above a clipped yew hedge. He calls, but the head disappears. There is no sign of him. He wonders for an instant if he was mistaken, until a movement snags the corner of his eye: the wretched child dashing back towards the loggia.

Orazio breaks into a run, shouting for him to stop. But Giulio continues, flashing a guilt-filled look back at his father, tearing past the loggia and down the steep slope towards the wild undergrowth at the far end of the gardens. Orazio loses his footing and skids down, half on his backside, to where the boy is cornered against a wall beside an impenetrable thicket of brambles.

'What are you hiding from me?' Orazio's elbow is burning from a graze and his hip is throbbing horribly, making his anger flare.

'Nothing.' The boy cowers.

Orazio waits for his son to come clean.

Silence rings. Even the birds have stopped singing.

He hears the small chinking sound of something meeting the earth. His eyes glance down to where an object has fallen behind Giulio's foot, blinking in the sun. 'Pick that up.'

The boy is terrified, seems unable to move. He repeats the order and Giulio crouches to recuperate the trinket. 'Show me.'

'It wasn't me. I didn't take it. I was only putting it back.' His pinched little fear-scrawled face looks up as he opens his hand.

In his son's grubby palm is the cardinal's ruby crucifix. He recalls an enquiry about its disappearance and one of the cardinal's servants having been accused. 'If *you* didn't take it then how exactly did it come to be in your possession?' He takes a sharp breath.

'I . . . I . . .' Giulio's chin quivers. 'I can't say. I made a promise.'

'You made a promise? Do you understand the gravity of this?' Orazio cannot stop himself ranting at the boy, who now has a fat tear running down his cheek, clearing a path through the grime.

'Stop crying, for pity's sake. You're nine years old. Soft as a girl. This is not some gewgaw made of glass from a market stall – it is the cardinal's most precious crucifix. I wouldn't doubt it was blessed by His Holiness himself.' He is shaking. 'You know what they do to thieves? Chop their hands off.' He snatches the cross. 'I didn't raise my children to be pocket-pickers. If this gets out, I could lose everything. Did you think of *that* when you stole it, you little crook? Did you not think you might bring shame on your whole family?'

'But it wasn't me.' Orazio notices a dark wet patch spreading over the front of Giulio's breeches.

He looks up at his father through long tear-drenched lashes and Orazio is struck by the extent to which the boy resembles his mother. How might their lives have been different if she had lived? He might have avoided raising a wilful daughter who behaves like a boy and a boy who's spineless as a ball of mozzarella.

His son's woeful expression induces a splinter of tenderness, making him wonder if the child is perhaps telling the truth. 'I'll think of something.' He scuffs Giulio's hair. 'But you must tell me everything.'

'Zita asked me to leave it somewhere near the palazzo for someone to find it. She gave me this for my trouble.' He pulls a small copper coin from his pocket.

'Zita? *She* stole it?'

Giulio makes a small shrug. 'I don't know how she came by it.'

'Light-fingered little mare. And to try to draw you into it. You haven't told anyone about this, have you?'

Giulio shakes his head.

Orazio's mind is stirring. 'Don't tell a soul. Not even your brother. Understand?'

Giulio crosses his heart with the words 'Hope to die.'

18. A Nosebleed

A sparrow is perched on the washing line, chattering happily. Artemisia recalls the nightingale rescued from her father's grip, the tick of its tiny heart and its heavenly serenade to liberty from the branches of the Judas tree.

She misses the songbirds that congregated in the garden by the old house. But she has grown fond of the ordinary chirp of the sparrows, content with fallen crumbs in the via della Croce. A pair has built a nest under the eaves. She has seen them flitting back and forth and can sometimes hear the insistent cries of their hatchlings. Soon they will fledge. Life out there is bursting forth, every crevice teeming with it, while she sits inside waiting and waiting for her chance to escape.

The day is becoming hot, so she opens her bedroom door in an attempt to create a cool current of air, loosening the ties on her dress.

Zita clatters up and down with the laundry and the children, finally settling into a chair with her sewing. 'I'm grateful to you, Zita.' Artemisia touches the other woman lightly on the shoulder. She is tense as a bow string. 'For staying so vigilant.'

'It's nothing,' Zita mumbles, without looking up from her mending.

She has been sulking since they'd argued on the previous evening. Zita had tried to persuade her to tell her father about the incident in the vineyard. 'He won't let Tassi come if he knows what happened.' She had become unusually vehement and Artemisia had lost her patience.

'Look,' she had said later, attempting to placate her, 'we don't have to answer the door. We can stay upstairs and pretend we didn't hear him. Father will never know any better.'

From the window Artemisia spots him turning into the via della Croce with his usual swagger. She ducks out of sight. 'He's coming.'

Zita hustles the girls up into her apartment, bribing them with sweets not to make a peep. They think it is a game.

It is not a game.

Zita returns and settles down to feed the baby. Seeking a distraction, Artemisia picks up her sketchbook to draw them. The room is quiet enough to make all the soft noises loud: the scrape of the chalk against paper, the sucking of the infant and the distant discord of a neighbour practising a viol.

A beam creaks.

His knock on the door sounds up through the layers of the house.

Silence.

He knocks again, his voice reaching through the open window: 'Anybody home? Signorina Gentileschi?'

Silence.

She can hear the tap of her heart.

He thumps the door hard now and tries the latch.

It opens, scraping against the studio flagstones.

A spark of alarm catches in her. She locked the door when her brothers left.

She meets Zita's gaze with a question, miming the turning of a key.

The other woman shakes her head, fear scribbled over her features.

They hear footsteps.

Zita is lead-white, her eyes darting nervously as she tucks an exposed breast into her shift as if Tassi is already in the room and able to see her.

'Hello?' The kitchen door bangs.

And silence.

For a moment Artemisia allows herself to believe he has gone. Then they hear boots mounting the stairs. He must have nails hammered into the soles. They clack loudly against the wooden treads. He stops on the landing below, opening and closing the doors, calling again.

Artemisia closes her eyes, holding her breath, as if she might make herself vanish.

He begins to climb the next flight, clack, clack, clack.

The sparrow is singing again, full of joy.

She tries to imagine flinging herself from the window, wings opening, carrying her up and up, away, but can only see herself plummet, her head smashing on the cobbles.

The door flies open, thudding back on its hinges and he swings in on a sickly waft of musk.

'What are you doing here?' Artemisia exclaims, as if he is unexpected, as if they hadn't listened to his every step up through the house.

'You shouldn't be here, signore.' Zita is nervy.

Without responding he takes one long stride towards Artemisia, plucking her sketchbook from her hand. 'I was of the understanding that I was to give you a lesson. Did your father forget to mention it?' He peruses the sketch for a while.

Artemisia hitches up the collar of her shift.

'Charming,' he says, turning her drawing towards her as if she has never seen it. 'Nothing touches the heart quite so much as a mother and child.'

She feels small seated with him towering over her, so she stands, but still feels small. He, with his great bulk, his height, his broadness, has made the room shrink. She wishes she'd not loosened her dress earlier. Her fingers go to her very top button, snapping it firmly shut.

'Leave us alone,' he says to Zita.

Artemisia glances towards her, confident in the knowledge that she will not do as he says. Zita doesn't meet her eye, is fussing with Luca, whose little hand is clutching an escaped frond of her hair.

'Please may I have my sketchbook back. I have not finished.' Her voice is thin and reedy despite the effort she makes to keep the tension out of it. She doesn't want to give him the satisfaction of knowing she is afraid.

But she *is* afraid.

He leans in the doorway to her bedroom, silently flipping through her sketches.

'Please will you leave,' she says firmly.

Together Zita and she will herd him to the door and down the stairs and out into the street.

But that is not what happens.

Zita hauls herself to her feet, Luca on her hip. 'I'm sorry,' she mutters, as she slinks from the room, saying something about needing to change Luca's napkin.

'Zita! Where are you going?' Artemisia is struck cold to

the bone. His eyes are on her, penetrating, seeing the fear that she is no longer able to hide.

She swallows.

Her throat is dry.

He smiles.

He is close enough for her to smell the tang of sweat beneath the musk.

'Zita!' She can only manage a croak now.

'Zita wouldn't want to ruin our fun again, would she?' He slides a hand around the back of her neck, rubbing, gripping. 'You're so tense. Why are you so tense?'

She tries to wriggle free, but he has his other hand around her arm. 'Let go.' She sounds pathetically feeble and hates herself for it. 'Please . . .'

'You are a most fascinating young woman.' He is leering. 'Some of your sketches are very . . . How should I put it? Unconventional.'

'Show me which you mean.' If she keeps him in conversation, she might feel more in control.

He removes his hand from her neck but keeps hold of her arm, shuffling through the pages with his free hand.

'These, for example.' It is the page of naked diving boys.

'There are a thousand such images on the walls and ceilings of Rome.' Her confidence builds.

'But none of them by a woman.'

'Isn't it the duty of an artist to question convention?'

He regards her with a long stare that seems to question her sanity. 'Don't you have a care for your reputation?'

'If *you* had a care for my reputation, you wouldn't be up here in my private rooms.'

'Fair point.'

A thread of hope tacks itself through her, as he lets go of her arm. 'Besides, they are only bodies. A painter must have an understanding of anatomy.'

He makes a scornful snort.

'You think I'm ridiculous.' Her confidence swells as she begins to believe she might be able to talk her way out of the situation that only moments ago had seemed horribly inevitable.

'Not ridiculous, no. Overly curious, perhaps.'

'I *am* curious. Curiosity is what makes me an artist. I want to be able to see everything forbidden to me. I want to understand it all, even things considered . . .'

'Considered what?'

She can show him how unfeminine she is. 'Perverse.'

She feels the power of her words as he takes a sharp step away from her. 'Things like what?'

'Things like the cardinal's *Hermaphroditus*. I know of it, but I want to see it, to draw it, to capture it, to understand it.'

Glaring defiantly at her adversary she remembers how Modenese's expression had crowded with disgust the instant she mentioned the *Hermaphroditus*. Tassi's expression, though, is not one of shock or revulsion but of something else, something she can't decipher.

The horrible realization is driven into her that the control she had felt so sure of only moments ago was a mere illusion. How could she have been such a fool as to believe she could manipulate him – the master of deception?

'The cardinal's *Hermaphroditus*?' His look is hungry. Panic ignites suddenly in her, catching, burning. 'You are *that* kind of girl.' He runs the tip of his tongue along the edge of his teeth.

Her heart throbs.

Where is Zita?

All her life it has been hammered into her, by her father, by her mother, by her confessor, by Sister Ilaria, the irrevocable fact that a man will reject any girl whose virtue is questionable. She berates herself inwardly. What a fool she has been not to understand that what is abhorrent to one man might arouse desire in another. She has been ambushed by her own ignorance and now she is a fowl waiting to be plucked.

'I must find Zita.' She skirts his large form, making for the door, shouting for her friend. Where is she?

He holds her fast from behind, his forearm across her chest. 'Zita won't save you – not this time.' He kicks the door to the landing shut and rams the pin into the latch with his free hand.

'She will.' But she feels the residue of hope drain away. 'She promised.'

'Promises made by women like her are about as much use as a sieve for carrying water.' He keeps his arm firmly clutched round her as he softly strokes her cheek. She attempts to squirm out of his grip. 'You are a strange little thing. I've never come across anyone quite like you.' His breath is warm on her skin.

She feels sick.

He pushes her into the bedroom, flinging her towards the bed but she clasps the bedpost tight as she can, desperate to keep upright.

She remembers being told once that if a dog is attacking you, you must remain on your feet. If it gets you on the ground you will be savaged. From the corner of her eye she is aware of the paring knife she uses to sharpen her graphite sticks. It is there, sitting on the table, but she can't reach it without letting go of the bedpost.

She dares not let go.

She hears the thud as this door too shuts and then the click of its lock.

He grips one hand firmly to the stiff lip of her bodice; the other unlaces his hose. 'I could fall for you.' He looks amused.

'Let me go.' She tries to reach his hand with her mouth to bite it but he's too quick and too strong. He pitches her down with such force her grip is lost and her head bangs hard against the headboard.

Stars fly on a black sky.

She feels herself slipping away but is determined to fight.

He has both her wrists in a single fist and with the other hand flings up her skirts. She kicks out wildly but he pushes his knee between her legs. She forces them together. He prises them apart. 'I like it more when you resist – you dirty little whore.'

'No!' she screams, struggling. 'No! Zita! Help!'

With a searing pain he is in her and is pressing a handkerchief over her nose and mouth to stop her cries. She tries again to bite him. Reaching blindly she grabs his thing, half in her half out, digging her nails as hard as she can into the skin. He winces loudly, seizing her hand, ramming it up behind her head, wrenching her shoulder almost from its socket, thrusting on and on.

She can't catch a breath.

Her lungs scream for want of air.

She loses consciousness.

She falls, limp as a rag.

She is up in the rafters looking down on her lifeless form beneath his manic grunting and pumping. The handkerchief is covered with blood. She has a nosebleed. It is all over the pillow. Like a massacre.

She floats.

Her body is empty, down there on the bed.

She has reached a place where he cannot touch her.

She is free – no pain, no fear, no torment.

He makes several heaving thrusts and with a groan, releases his huge hand from her face.

With a great heave, her ribcage expands, like a set of bellows, pulling her back into her body, back to the pain, back to the agony between her legs and the hot trickle of his deposit on her thigh. But not back to the fear.

'I got rather carried away,' he says, as if it is nothing, like someone who's drunk too much at a wedding.

She leaps from the bed, grabbing her knife, brandishing it. It looks absurdly small in the face of his vastness, but she knows its edge is sharp.

He opens his jacket, 'Here I am,' taunting her. 'Come on!'

She calculates her next move. If she steps near enough to plunge the blade into him, he will, sure as day is day, seize her wrist, prise the weapon from her hand and turn it on her.

She can taste blood in her mouth, like copper.

With all the force she can gather she throws the knife like a dart, aiming for his torso.

It breaks the skin and glances off. He jumps back as if stung by a wasp.

The knife skitters over the floor, spinning into the far corner.

His fingers touch his chest. He holds them up, inspecting them. 'You've cut me, you bitch.' He is laughing. 'What a wild thing you are.'

She looks around for a heavy object, aware that the fire iron is behind her, inching back towards it while keeping her eyes on him.

'For one who seems to care so little for your reputation you defended it vigorously. Or did you seek to arouse me with resistance? You certainly succeeded.'

The truth slams into her. Her honour, the honour of her family has, in a few sordid painful moments, been spent, and she will be blamed.

It occurs to her, in another abrupt realization, that she will be compelled to marry this monster. It is the only means by which the Gentileschis' good reputation can be restored.

She reaches back, fingers meeting the unyielding contours of the fire iron. It is heavy enough to cave his head in. She imagines her defence. And then she remembers Beatrice Cenci laying her head on the block, the spurt of blood, bright as tomato juice. She was a victim too.

Her thoughts whir as she recalibrates her plan.

'No one is ever to know of this.' Her tone is as rigid as the object in her hand. 'Especially not my father.'

'I'm more than happy to keep our little tryst a secret.' He seems pleased, tilting his head back at an angle, looking down at her, wondering, perhaps, if she really means it.

She *does* mean it.

'To call it a . . . a –' she can't say the word out loud, even through gritted teeth '– such a thing, implies I was a willing party.' Rage is swelling in her breast, as if a great vengeful monster will burst out of her and rip his head from his body.

She takes several deep trembling breaths to calm herself but finds she is awash with sudden despair. 'I wish you'd killed me.' Her voice is almost a whisper. 'Then, at least, you would be punished.'

'You'll come round.' He smiles. 'I'm sure.' He does up his hose. Then he bends down and kisses her lips. She can smell the musk on his clothes. It reminds her of incense, of mass. 'You are *mine* now.'

He lets the door slam as he leaves.

She wipes the wet of his kiss away. 'I am not yours,' she says, to the empty room. Pain assaults her now, a deep, inner agony, the bridge of her nose smarting, her wrists aching where he held her down, her shoulder throbbing and tender. She sits immobile on the floor staring at the bed – a battlefield.

The covers have slid off and lie rumpled by the skirting board, revealing the impossible white of the linen sheets. At one side they have become untucked, a frayed edge exposed, uncovering the stuffed contours of the mattress beneath. Trails of blood run over it, along it. Her blood.

She touches her nose, feeling where it is caking around her nostrils. So much of it – smears on her skin, spots on her dress, spatters on the floor. It is not one red: where a beam of sun collides into the bed, it is shocking crimson, here and there it fades to rust, elsewhere dark as the purple flesh of plump cherries, and where it slips into the shadows, it is black as treacle.

She sees her head there, where it was, right at the edge of the bed with him above, all his force bearing down on her, hands, arms, with the strength of two men. 'No,' the imagined woman shrieks, her imagined eyes rolling back towards her glossed with terror.

Artemisia gasps, looking away, only to see in the corner his blood-drenched handkerchief. Wherever she turns, he will be there. This will be there, indelible spots of her own blood blotting her future.

She will never be free.

You are mine now.

She shuts her eyes but scenes flash through her mind: his snarl, his vast form, his hand, his handkerchief. He is thrusting into her. She is struggling for breath again and again, dying each time anew.

I will never be yours.

She finds herself shaking uncontrollably and suddenly retches up a mouthful of bile. It makes a little yellow pool on the floor, shockingly bright. The bitterness invades her mouth, as if she will never taste anything else ever again.

The door bangs open.

She expects Zita but it is her brother, short of breath and bristling. 'Where is he?'

'Who?' She uses all her remaining strength to gather herself together.

'What in Hell's name happened?' Horrified, Francesco crouches beside her, hands hovering, afraid to touch her even lightly, for fear of wreaking more damage. 'Did *he* do this to you?'

'I tripped and banged myself. Had a nosebleed.' She wants to weep, rant, rage but she hauls herself to her feet, wiping her face on her sleeve, and smearing the pool of bile underfoot so he can't see it.

The pain persists. She wants to wash herself, immerse her entire body in water, in white spirit, in lye, scrub every inch of her skin until it is raw.

Her brother's bewildered gaze flicks between her and the bed.

She forces a small laugh up from the dregs of her being. 'I didn't know I had so much blood in me.'

He crosses himself. 'I thought . . . I thought . . .'

She paints on a pink smile. 'It's not what it looks like . . . Just a nosebleed, Franco.'

He returns with a real smile. 'Thank God.'

He soaks a napkin in water from the washbasin and gently dabs at her nose. 'Lucky it's not broken.' Her brother's touch is so gentle, so loving, his kindness so sweet, she could cry, fall into his arms, allow him to hold her, lose herself entirely.

Instead, she manages to spit out another laugh. 'I'll look a fright.'

She digs around to find a splinter of advantage in her situation. With her virtue gone, she has nothing more to lose – there is freedom in that. It is a consolation so small as to be almost invisible to the human eye.

She sluices her mouth with water, but the bitter taste persists.

'You go down,' she says, 'while I change my clothes.'

'Are you sure you're all right?' A stitch catches in his brow.

'No need to worry, really, Franco.' She strokes his shoulder.

When he has gone, she stands paralysed, staring at the bed for some time. Images loop through her head once more. She is floating watching herself, him, the handkerchief, the struggle for breath, and then she is Beatrice Cenci, her head rolling away, releasing a fountain of blood.

No!

Forcing herself to transform what she sees, she imagines herself wiping a painted canvas with spirit. She can feel the rough cloth in her fingers. Her senses sting from the harsh vapours. The colours and shapes smear into one another, losing their clarity.

And she paints a new scene.

It is not *her* struggling form lying there on the bed, not *her* eyes pivoting in terror, but *his*. The terror is in *his* eyes now, the blood is *his*, *his* great muscular arms struggling uselessly, grabbing at the collar of a woman standing over him. No. Two women. Their four arms stronger, holding him still. She has one fist tight round his ear, pulling back his head to expose his throat.

Her small blade is now the size of a sword, vast, heavy and razor sharp, like Judith's. Blood sprays, spotting the women. It is warm on her skin and she can feel, too, the way the steel slides through his skin as easily as a knife through dough, traversing muscle, hacking through gristle and bone.

PART II

You will find the spirit of Caesar in this soul of a woman.

Artemisia Gentileschi

19. The Handkerchief

Zita moves slowly. The air is thick and foetid in the narrow streets, heat radiating off the cobbles. The market vendors slump by their stalls waving fans, their produce wilting faster than it can be sold. Luca is a dead weight, mewling on her hip. She stops to buy milk. It is warm as blood and will be half curdled by the time she gets home.

As she reaches the door she can already hear her girls quarrelling. The atmosphere inside is more oppressive even than in the streets. No one greets her. Orazio broods in a corner and the boys loll about, their work abandoned. Giulio leaves the kitchen as she enters without meeting her eye. He has been avoiding her – doesn't want to explain about the cross. She doesn't need *him* to tell her. She knows what became of it.

Her moment of weakness has cost her dear. How she regrets giving such a delicate mission to Giulio, who is so young. It was her mistake. She unpacks the shopping and opens the back door, hoping for a whisper of air, but the stink of the drain is worse than the heat.

Artemisia bursts in with nothing but a black look for Zita as she pours herself a drink from the ewer. Swilling it back, she slams her cup down and leaves the kitchen. Zita follows her out, standing in the doorway, watching as she takes a lump of pigment from a jar and sets it on the mortar, grinding it with force.

She has barely said a word to Zita in the days since Tassi came, and goes about with a manic fervour, the only one of them who seems unaffected by the oppressive weather. Zita can feel the force of her hatred in her silence. She can't blame her, wishes she could explain why she left her alone with that man, but she is knotted in a tangle of secrets and lies and remorse.

When she had returned that day, she had found Francesco alone in the studio and asked him what happened, where Tassi was. 'Haven't seen him,' he'd said. 'She's upstairs changing. Had a nosebleed.'

'He hit her?'

'What are you talking about? It was an accident.'

She'd found Artemisia on the landing with a bundle of linens in her arms. Zita could see the bloodstains. 'Did you have a nosebleed? Francesco said –'

'What does it look like?' Artemisia hissed, holding out the bloody bundle.

'Did he . . . ?'

'He didn't do anything.' She began to go downstairs, turning back to say, 'Can't you stop interfering and leave me alone?'

Zita had looked into Artemisia's room. It was spotless. The bed was freshly made and the floor pristine, still slightly damp as if it had just been mopped. She searched for signs of what might have happened but found nothing. *He didn't do anything*. Perhaps it was true.

Orazio had cornered her, probing her for information, as she'd known he would. 'How did the lesson go?' She had nothing to tell him – she wasn't there. He became impatient. 'She must have told you something. Women talk to each other, don't they?' Her response was a two-shouldered shrug. Artemisia is not like most women.

Francesco joins his sister at the pigment bench. They are whispering. He takes over the grinding while she adds the oil drop by drop. They discuss whether the consistency is right while Orazio watches.

'What are you working on?' he asks.

'That's my business.' Scooping the colour into a bowl, she makes for the stairs. She has been painting with furious intensity in the small second-floor parlour, away from her father.

Zita retreats back into the kitchen.

Sometime later she hears the boys leave, no doubt glad to get away from the heavy atmosphere. She is desperate to escape, longs for her husband to return and rescue her, but it is months before he's due home.

Orazio is banging about in the studio. She peeps out to see what he is doing. He appears to be searching for something, looking behind the stacks of old canvases, tipping out the contents of boxes, lying on the floor to peer under the work bench.

A knock at the door disturbs him. Zita retreats into the shadows. It is Porzia. 'Are you alone?' she says, before he has even made a greeting. It is clear by the strain on her face that something is wrong.

'What is it?' Orazio has picked up on her worry.

'It's about Artemisia.'

Orazio offers her a drink and Zita makes to retreat further behind the kitchen door, relieved when Porzia refuses. 'Gio heard a rumour.' Porzia is pulling a ring on and off her finger. 'I thought you ought to know. I'm her godmother, feel a responsibility for her.' She glances at Orazio, who nods for her to continue. 'People are saying that Quorli made a wager with Tassi that he couldn't seduce Artemisia.'

'Oh, that!' Orazio huffs out a laugh, seeming relieved. 'Just men's talk. Nothing to worry about.'

'But no!' Porzia is distraught, her voice shrill. 'There's more. Gio said he heard Tassi was bragging about it, tipped a purse out in the tavern. Said he was buying the drinks as he'd won thirty *scudi* off the Furiere for seducing a painter's daughter.' Porzia seems now to be struggling to make things seem better than they are because, if Zita understands correctly, what has just been said is that Tassi has ruined Artemisia for a bet. It is hard to find a positive note to that.

'Gio said we should establish the truth first, but I thought you should know. You can't let those two go around saying those things. They dishonour you with such scurrilous lies.'

The two of them stand in silence for a moment, the word 'dishonour' circling in the air. They both know, as does Zita, that when there is dishonour no good comes of it.

'Tassi said he won the bet?' Orazio is unreadable.

'I believe so.'

'Didn't hear it first-hand, then?'

She shakes her head. 'Still, rumours like that . . .' Porzia continues worrying absently at her ring.

'I'd better talk to her.' Orazio makes for the stairs.

Porzia follows him into the dark stairwell saying something about it being women's business.

*

Orazio forces the door open. Artemisia hurriedly covers her picture as they enter and greets Porzia warmly, ignoring him.

Porzia seems shocked at the sight of her and goes to take her hands but draws back on seeing that she is covered in paint. Orazio sees her as Porzia must. She has grown thin and looks sallow, smudges, dark as charcoal, ringing her eyes. Her cuffs are stained and there is a smear of dark umber on her face, where she must have swiped back a stray lock of hair with dirty fingers.

'There's something I want to talk about,' he says.

'I'm busy with this.' Her answer is clipped.

'It's important, sweetheart.' The endearment leaves a taste of deceit in his mouth. 'It's about Signor Tassi and your lesson the other day.'

She exhales a defeated sigh. 'I've told you already. There's nothing to say.'

Porzia turns to him, speaking quietly. 'Why don't you give us a moment, Orazio?'

He leaves the room, can hear the quiet mumble of their conversation and resists pressing his ear to the door. He'll know soon enough.

He finds Zita and her brats in the kitchen, glad that she straight away hustles them up to bed. Once alone, he searches for the bottle of grappa he couldn't find earlier. He's convinced someone is hiding it from him deliberately. One of his children.

He finds it eventually, in a corner half concealed behind some pots. Pouring himself a slug, he swallows it in one and pops an olive from a bowl on the table into his mouth. It is bitter and he cracks his tooth on the stone, pain stabbing up through his jaw. He curses loudly and drinks more grappa, straight from the bottle this time.

Slumped at the table, he waits. It seems like an age. What can they be talking about up there? The front door slams, announcing the boys' return.

'What are you doing sitting in the dark?' Francesco is standing over him. 'Giulio, pass the tinder box.'

Giulio, in the doorway, not wanting to approach, tosses it to his brother who catches it in one hand and crouches over to work up a spark.

Soon the kitchen is filled with a flickering glow.

'What's going on? There's something going on.' Francesco has a challenge in his voice.

'It's your sister.' Orazio begins to explain what's being said about Tassi.

'When was this? Was it when she had the nosebleed?'

'What are you talking about?' Orazio doesn't know anything about a nosebleed.

'If she didn't tell you, she obviously doesn't want you to know.'

'For God's sake, Franco. I'm the head of this household.' He looks around for his middle son, to ask him if he knows anything but Giulio has sniffed the bad atmosphere and slipped away.

How has he lost control of the goings-on in his own house – all the things they are keeping from him?

They can hear the two women descending the stairs. Porzia is saying, 'Are you sure you don't want me to stay?'

'Quite sure.' Artemisia sounds brusque and confident. 'I can deal with this.'

His daughter appears, wearing a bludgeon of a stare.

'Artemisia, sweetheart.'

'Artemisia, sweetheart,' she mimics. 'If I am so dear to you, then why did you put me in the way of that vile man?' She sniffs sharply with undisguised disdain.

'We can solve this.' His optimism sprouts fragile shoots. 'Since he has seduced you, he must accept your hand.' Orazio hopes to God that Porzia hasn't told her the details, that her virtue was the subject of a bet, or she'll never come round. And the rest is worse, much worse. If she should learn that he, her own father . . . The thought causes fingers of guilt to compress his throat.

She makes a noise, a kind of cynical laugh, frilled with hysteria, and he wonders for an instant if she is losing her mind. It would explain her recent behaviour. 'Seduced?' She folds forward, so he can't see her face. Her shoulders are shaking. She is making a strange sound. He can't tell if she is crying or laughing.

She stops suddenly to look up, her mouth tight, eyes dry. 'Is that what you call seduction, Father? You lend it such a pretty ring of romance.' Her sarcasm is barbed.

He wonders now, if he's been mistaken, if perhaps the wager he overheard Quorli challenge Tassi with was something different, something benign. Perhaps they make wagers all the time. Perhaps it *was* all drunken bravado after all. 'Tell me, be honest with me . . . please, Arti.'

She shakes her head, looking down at the floor.

A silence envelops them, thick and black as tar.

Then she speaks, fast and angry. 'You really want the truth? Your marvellous Agostino Tassi, the man you want me to marry' – she opens her arms and offers him a smile, crooked with scorn – 'he raped me.'

The instant Artemisia has uttered the words, she regrets it. Now it is said it cannot be unsaid. *He raped me.* The fact of it will take on its own momentum, over which she will have no control. *He raped me.* Those words will stalk her down the years.

She is light-headed, as if her blood has been let. Francesco has leaped to her side and has his arm around her, is guiding her to the bench to sit. 'The *bastard.*' His voice spills hot rage.

Orazio is wringing his hands and wears a crumpled expression as if he is the injured party. He thinks he is, she realizes. She is his property, after all.

'He has dishonoured you, dishonoured our family.' Her father speaks slowly, as if he can't quite make sense of what he's saying, 'But it will be made right, my darling girl.' He leans over to stroke her hair. She ducks away from his touch. 'I will make sure of it.'

Those scenes start to play in her head again: his hands, his snarl, her blood. Her heart thumps. There is a bottle of grappa on the table. She pours some into a cup, almost to the rim.

The smell alone makes her want to retch but she flings it down her throat. It scalds a trail deep into her belly. Her head begins to drift almost immediately, blurring the sharp edges of her inescapable situation.

Zita has crept into the room, is hovering by the door.

'Did *you* know about it too?' Orazio springs to his feet, looming over her. Zita is cowering as if he might thump her – and he might.

'About what?' Zita's voice is almost inaudible.

'About the fact that Agostino Tassi raped me when *you* left us alone together.' Artemisia tries to keep her rage at bay, as if she is talking of something that happened to someone else.

Zita claps a hand over her mouth theatrically, muttering, '*Maria Madre di Dio*,' and crossing herself several times. 'He raped you?' Artemisia expects her to burst into tears but instead she stands straight, meeting Orazio's gaze dead on. '*You* did this.'

Something, a fleeting look that Artemisia can't interpret, passes between Zita and Orazio.

He turns back to Artemisia. 'Are you sure . . . absolutely sure' – her father's doubt is clear from his tone – 'it happened as you say, that you were unwilling?'

'You don't believe me. I might have expected as much.' Those images return but she forces them away. 'Who asks for that? I was beaten, suffocated.' Don't cry, she tells herself. Don't cry. Upstairs with her painting, with her fury, she feels strong, but here in the face of her father she has the sensation of shrinking back to girlhood.

Some grappa has spilled. She takes a cloth, rubbing and rubbing at it, as if she can rub the images from her head. Francesco places his hand tenderly over hers to stop her.

'I thought I had died. I thought he had killed me.' Her voice cracks, the pain of her own words almost too much to bear. 'But since you doubt me, I will show you.' She pulls up her sleeves, thrusting her wrists towards her father. 'See the bruises where he held me down.' But the marks have already faded to ochre and in this light they are almost invisible.

Her father looks at her bared arms and then back to her. He is not convinced. She musters her strength once more, thinking quickly. 'Zita, go upstairs and fetch my embroidery bag.'

The kitchen falls to silence while they wait for Zita to return, each of them avoiding the other's gaze. Zita reappears, breathless from rushing, proffering the bag. From it Artemisia produces a crumpled square of linen the colour of rust, which she hands to Father.

'What is this?' He looks puzzled.

'Read the initials, in the corner.'

He peers at the lettering. 'AT . . .' Artemisia watches his face as understanding alights. 'Agostino Tassi. This is your *blood*?'

She nods stonily. 'So much blood, enough to soak every thread of that handkerchief and more, much, much more – just ask Franco.' She turns to her brother. 'You saw the sheets, didn't you? So badly stained I had to throw them away.'

'A nosebleed, you said. How could I not have seen that it was more than that?' Francesco has a hand on his forehead, eyes brimming with pain.

'Don't blame yourself.' She strokes his hair. 'We all know whose fault it was.' Her father flinches under her bitter glare.

'Shame on you, Father.' Francesco seems invested with an air of confidence that was lacking only moments before, a new thread of authority running through his voice. She has never seen him stand up to Orazio in this way.

Orazio, conversely, is diminished, crouching, crumbling. 'Please believe me, it wasn't my intention for him to take your sister against her will. All I hoped for was a happy courtship.' He drops his face into his hands, remaining like that for several moments, before looking up pleadingly, facing the room. 'I will make it right if it's my last act on earth. He will make an honest woman of you.' He stands then. 'Franco, come with me. We shall confront him together, force him to do the honourable thing.'

Zita looks horrified. 'You can't . . .'

'He can,' Artemisia says heavily. She has been running through the outcomes in her head and there are only four possible conclusions: death, a nunnery, a brothel or marriage to Tassi.

Francesco kisses her cheek before they leave, saying, 'He'll pay for this. I'll make sure of it.'

But she knows that it is she who will pay.

Once they have gone, Zita hovers, guilt printed through her.

'Leave me alone.' Artemisia doesn't try to disguise her antipathy, pushing Zita away, like an unwanted animal.

But, instead of doing as she asks, Zita drops to her knees in supplication, squeezing her hands and apologizing over and over again. 'I beg you, forgive me. I beg you . . . Your father made me.' They stare at each other a moment. 'You see, I stole the cardinal's ruby cross from his private apartments.'

'I don't know why you think your thieving habits have anything to do with me.' Zita looks terrified and Artemisia is glad. 'Piero warned me about you. Said you couldn't be trusted.' She is flooded, suddenly, with a longing for her friend to return, feeling his absence with a painful intensity.

As words continue to spill out of Zita, Artemisia isn't

listening, is thinking of Piero. 'Your father found out. Said if I didn't do as he told me, he would hand me over to the authorities.'

She has Artemisia's attention now. 'My father *threatened* you?'

'He said, if I tried to deny it, I would have the truth screwed out of me by the Sybille, have all my fingers broken – lose the use of my hands.' She is speaking between wet sobs. 'He said the punishment for thieving something that precious is to have a hand chopped off.' She is holding her arm up, her opposite hand gripped around her wrist, her face horror-struck, as if imagining that punishment being meted out.

'I still don't understand what this has to do with me.'

'I tried . . . I tried to stop it – told him about what happened in the vineyard.' She coughs out a defeated whimper. 'But still he told me I must leave Tassi alone with you.'

Artemisia can hardly believe her ears. She'd blamed her father but had no inkling of the extent of his ill-doing. 'My own father. Why would he have wanted . . .' As she asks herself the question, understanding alights. 'He *planned* this. Wanted a reason to force Tassi into a match.'

'I went straight to fetch Franco, so he could . . .' She is still holding her hand up, wrist gripped.

Artemisia is remembering her brother arriving too late, out of breath, alarmed to find her covered with blood. So, Zita sent him.

'I thought . . . I thought . . . I didn't think . . .' Zita is struggling to make sense. 'A nosebleed, Franco said. I shouldn't've believed him. I should've known.'

'I didn't want you to know. Didn't want anyone to know.'

Zita looks suddenly, inexplicably, terrified and fingers the small silver crucifix she wears. 'You won't tell him, will you? If he finds out I've told you about the cross he'll . . .' Her mouth is moving but no words are coming out.

'Won't say a thing.' As the realization sinks in, Artemisia feels suddenly unstable, as if the world has tipped off its axis. 'This house is built on deceit – deceit and secrets.'

'You must refuse to marry him.' Zita puffs up with false hope.

'I've no choice. It won't be long before the whole city knows I'm spoiled goods and that Tassi is the one I let ruin me.'

'You can paint.' Zita's golden eyes are round and dewy with hope. 'You've already sold two paintings.'

'Three. The *Madonna* may be signed by him but we all know whose work it is.' She takes Zita's hand. It is hot, her palm clammy. 'Who will buy a painting from a . . .' The word sticks in her craw. 'They'll call me a whore. And how else will I keep myself from starving?'

'You could sit for painters, like I do.' Zita seems determined to find a way to make things right but there is no happy solution.

Artemisia takes in the sight of her. Even in this dim light, in her dirty apron, face stained with tears, she looks as if she should be accompanied by a choir of angels. 'If I had your beauty, then, perhaps. But you have a husband who pays your rent and makes you respectable.'

Artemisia steels herself to face the stark reality of having to submit to that man day after day. She thinks of the painting taking shape upstairs, a furious expression of her own truth, of her own experience.

He may gain the rights to her body but he will never claim her talent, her thoughts, her mind. She will paint. She will paint the truth. She will paint her *self*.

20. Still-Life

Tassi answers the door wearing nothing but his breeches. He is unshaven, dark curls tumbling all about his face and chest, like a satyr.

'Orazio! Franco!' They have taken him by surprise. A woman's voice calls from inside, asking who it is. 'Nobody,' he yells back.

Orazio greets him perfunctorily. Stony-faced, he has girded himself for Tassi to resist, prepared a series of threats, has a sharp little poniard tucked discreetly into his belt. He hopes he won't need to use it.

'Is something the matter?' Tassi invites them in, excusing himself, telling them to make themselves comfortable while he gets dressed, disappearing into the bedroom.

His apartments are on the top floor of a grand stone building. He has a row of large north-facing windows that have a view over a small piazza with a fountain at its heart. It is a vast and beautiful room, an ideal place to paint. Or it would be, were every surface not covered with detritus. A long table houses the dregs of a previous meal. Cheeses on a board emit a pungent stink. Fruit flies hover over a half-eaten bowl of grapes. Clothes are draped, or have been flung, over the chairs – even woollen winter coats, which must have languished there for months.

His painting things are at the far end. A palette contains a landscape of dried-out pigment, collecting dust, with other painters' tools: brushes, a magnifier, a pile of smeared rags, a perspective instrument. A corner table is arranged as a still-life, with a few artfully placed bottles and books, a skull perched atop, a wrinkled apple.

Paintings and drawings haphazardly line every inch of wall, some framed and properly hung, others merely tacked to the plaster. Curious objects are scattered about: a piece of Roman pilaster, a small headless bronze, a tangled rosary, all covered with a film of grime. The whole place is at odds with the man himself, who is always so well put together, the walking embodiment of the clean precision of his work.

Tassi reappears, now wearing a shirt, his hair slicked back. The woman lurks behind him rubbing her eyes with her fists. He hustles her out of the door without making an introduction. Francesco's eyes drag after her. She is that sort of woman.

He suggests they take a seat, removing the garments from the chairs, flinging them aside. 'You must excuse the state of the place. My maid had to leave and I haven't had time to find another. You know how busy I've been with work. Barely a moment to lay my head down.' He smiles his impossibly beguiling smile. 'I don't suppose you know of someone, do you?'

'What? A maid?' Orazio is a little thrown by Tassi's friendliness but, of course, he reminds himself, Tassi doesn't yet know the reason for their visit. 'I can ask around. Zita might know of someone.'

'Ah, your beautiful Zita! Is she well?'

'She is not *my* Zita.'

'Ha, no, of course.' His tone is unusually apologetic,

which gives Orazio a measure of confidence for the confrontation ahead.

Tassi rummages in a cupboard, producing some wine and three dusty beakers, which he wipes on the tails of his shirt. Orazio is glad; he had been wondering if he could face this meeting without a drink.

Tassi cuts some pieces of cheese and flaps a napkin over the bowl of grapes to get rid of the flies. 'Now, to what do I owe the honour of a visit at this hour?' He takes a bite of cheese, savouring it a moment, eyes shut, mumbling about how good it is, pushing the plate towards Francesco, whose fury is barely contained.

Orazio has never seen such anger in his eldest son, had had to prevent him from taking matters into his own hands. On the way over he'd said he would 'beat the reprobate to a pulp' for bringing dishonour to his sister. Francesco is strapping enough for fourteen but would certainly come off worst in a fight with Tassi, who is intimidatingly well-built.

Besides, Orazio prefers diplomacy – though it had been hard to convince the boy that this situation might prove to be an opportunity rather than a disadvantage.

'I have come to discuss my daughter.' He watches Tassi, who doesn't move a muscle. 'Artemisia,' he adds unnecessarily.

'I see.' Tassi looks less cheerful.

'Have you anything you would like to confess – to tell me?'

'About your daughter – I don't think so. Only that she has a remarkable talent.' He takes a sip of his drink, wiping his mouth with the back of his hand. 'Shame she's a girl.'

'Am I going to have to say it for you?' Orazio tamps down his irritation, knows Tassi is trying to play him.

'I really can't think –'

'You deflowered her, and in doing so have tarnished the name of my family.' He thumps his fist onto the table to emphasize his point. 'I demand reparation.' He pauses, and when Tassi doesn't immediately respond, adds, 'Or I will have you charged with the crime.'

He is ready to whip out the bloodied handkerchief as proof. There is no need.

Orazio watches as a wry grin takes over his adversary's face.

'Guilty as charged!' Not one hint of shame clouds Tassi's features. 'I will gladly marry her if that is your wish.'

Orazio is wrong-footed by the man's willingness, eagerness even, to make amends. He had prepared himself for resistance, for Tassi to remind him of his connections, that he's after a better match.

'It *is* my wish.' He scrutinizes the other man to be sure this is not some kind of ruse, Quorli appearing from behind an arras laughing at the joke. 'She will come to you without a dowry.'

'Just as I would expect.' Tassi is holding out his hand so they can shake on the agreement. Orazio still half imagines he will bring his thumb to his nose just as his own hand reaches out.

But no – they shake on it. Tassi's palm is dry and firm, and he removes a ring from his little finger – a large green stone, jade or agate perhaps, bearing his initials in intaglio. 'To give to my bride-to-be.'

Orazio takes it. 'I shall be glad to be able to call you my

son.' He is still reeling slightly in disbelief that the negotiation has been so straightforward. 'We will want to seal the match as soon as is possible.'

'Yes, yes. I am due to leave Rome for a time in a few days.' He looks pleased with himself. 'A pending Medici commission in Florence. The wedding can take place soon after I return in the autumn. If it so suits you.'

Tassi had mentioned the Medici commission before – it had inspired no little envy in Orazio. Once his daughter is wed to a man with connections, perhaps a Medici commission will find its way to him. Orazio feels triumphant. Though he wishes Francesco wouldn't scowl at the man, now they have come to an accommodation. He'll come round. They'll all come round in time.

'I should like to pay a visit to her – my future bride – if I may.' Tassi looks solemn. 'Formalize our betrothal. Get down on my knee and ask her properly, as it were. Tell her all about the life she has to look forward to.'

21. A Betrothal

Artemisia strives to mix the right shade of pigment for the blood in her painting's foreground. She is repelled now, when she remembers Merisi's *Judith* at the Palazzo Conscente – those sickeningly pert breasts and the bright spurt of blood, much too bright, a single scarlet fan: the colour of joy and strawberries. A decapitation is messier, dirtier, darker, more violent. It is not the colour for *her* painting.

The finished image already exists in her head, deeply etched there, the vision that had come to her in the aftermath of Tassi's violation. She had only needed her brothers and Zita to sit in for the trio of figures – Zita as Judith brandishing a broom for a sword, Francesco the supine Holofernes, Giulio as the maidservant – so she could sketch out the proportions. Otherwise, it is all pouring out from a deep untapped reservoir within her.

Zita is fussing about, tidying up after her children, distracting her.

Artemisia stops, dissatisfied with the effect, unable to quite replicate the dense, coagulating colours that swirl in her mind's eye. The three figures are almost there – Judith, wielding her weapon with a dispassionate look, the maidservant businesslike, her fist, large, almost as large as her face, pressing the figure of the condemned man firmly to the bed. His fist, even larger, reaches up to clutch her collar in a hopeless attempt to resist.

Where Merisi had given his Holofernes a sudden shocked howl, a fleeting moment of fatal insight, as the sword slices with swift efficiency through the flesh of his neck, in Artemisia's the blade hacks away messily, painfully, with excruciating slowness. There will be no swift end for her Holofernes – no, he wears the desperate terror of a long and painful death. It cannot be easy to cut through a man's neck with a sword. Even a fowl's decapitation needs the brute force of a cleaver.

As she cleans her brushes Francesco comes to tell her of Tassi's arrival. 'He's down there,' he points to the floor, 'talking with Father.' Her brother is tense, pent-up anger making his jaw twitch.

She takes the stairs slowly, like a condemned woman approaching the block. As she emerges from the dark of the stairwell she sees, first, her father's sickeningly victorious expression. His eyes then flick over her clothes, registering his annoyance that she hasn't bothered even to remove her painting overall, or comb her hair, which sits in wild coils, giving her the air of a Medusa.

Tassi is beside him. Scenes flash before her eyes: his snarl, his force. She feels faint, unable to breathe, but forces her mind onto the painting upstairs, drawing strength from it, meeting his eyes. They are poison green, flecked with ochre. Many women have fallen for those eyes. Not her. She knows there is nothing behind them.

'Good afternoon, Signor Tassi. I understand you have come to ask for my hand in marriage.' Her voice is a flat grey, absent of emotion.

He smiles. Women will have liked that smile too.

Orazio fusses about, pouring wine, proposing a toast.

She refuses to meet either man's eye as they raise their glasses. It is bad luck, but she doesn't care – she is already neck deep in misfortune.

Now she must participate in this artifice. She allows him to take her hand, noticing that the red paint has got beneath her nails, as if she has been butchering meat.

'An artist's hands,' he says. 'You are not wearing my ring. I hope you received it. Perhaps it was too big and you have it on a chain about –'

'I did receive it. Thank you.' She would like to tell him she'd rather chop her own finger off than wear a ring bearing his initials but instead offers him a rigid, disingenuous smile.

'I will have another made for you if you prefer. We will visit the goldsmith together. You can choose the stone.'

'A plain band will suffice. It won't get in the way when I'm painting.' He looks disappointed by her response. She supposes he would rather she lied and indulged him in the fantasy of a real courtship.

'Would you do me the honour of becoming my wife?'

She nods a mumbled assent.

'You are mine now,' Tassi says, with a return of that smile. Has he forgotten those were the words he said after raping her? Perhaps it is deliberate. She feels sick, only just about maintains her composure.

'Now I can call you my son.' Her father seems to burst with joy as he shakes Tassi's hand. It is only she who notices the withering look Tassi gives him.

He visits the via della Croce several times after that, sometimes with Quorli, sometimes alone, as if he has the right to come and go as he pleases. She is hauled away from her painting to sit with him, while her father blathers merrily and Zita lurks, watching him, unable to hide her loathing.

He tells Artemisia he wants to see her as much as possible before leaving for Florence, boasting about his Medici commission. She counts down the days until he goes, when she will at least be able to concentrate on her *Judith* and pretend she is free.

On the day before his departure, though, he arrives downstairs, calling, as usual. But no one answers him. She knows Zita is at confession, she'd told her so. But where are the others? They must all have gone out while she was absorbed in her painting. Now the betrothal is sealed, they have forgotten about protecting her virtue.

She can hear him calling her name and mounting the stairs, just as before. Her heart slides into her throat, panic firing through her.

There is nowhere to hide.

He is on the landing now.

She has to face him alone sometime and draws on her resolve. He has already taken all there is to take from her. She looks at his painted double, shrieking in fear, holding that image in her mind as she covers the picture and calls, 'I'm in here.' She wants it to be on her own terms.

The door swings open. His scent reaches her before he has stepped into the room and with it comes a wave of nausea. She inhales deeply, steadying herself, quashing the memories, the gasping for breath, the pain, forcing them into a coffer in a deep and inaccessible crevice.

He stands before her in that indigo jacket, the cuff of which she can still feel pressed over the skin of her face.

Don't think of that.

The recollection spins away and instead she considers how she might recreate that colour: a base of smalt with a little dense peach-stone black and a grain of crimson to add the warmth. A two-day-old bruise – that is the hue. If she reduces the world to colour, she can manage it.

'What is this you are working on now?' He indicates, with a nudge of his head, towards her shrouded painting.

'It's a *Judith*.' She is deliberately vague, aware he will assume it depicts the two women fleeing the Assyrian camp rather than the killing itself. She feels the thrill of her secret conquest, knowing that she has overcome him with her brush, imagining his reaction were he to see himself slaughtered on the bed. 'Before you ask, it is not yet ready to show.'

'A courageous woman – Judith. I should very much like to see it when you see fit. You know how I admire your work.'

'There's no need for flattery. Your opinion of my work is meaningless to me.'

He is staring at her. She has seen that hungry look before. Alarm screeches silently up her spine. She *must* find a way to take charge. 'On second thoughts' – she makes herself smile – 'I don't see why you shouldn't see it.' Her voice is light, unlike her heart.

All his attention is now directed towards the easel. She has gained a small advantage. She carefully removes the cover and watches as he recognizes himself in the throes of terror on that painted bed. He is trying to speak but seems unable, all the force drained out of him. He is lost for words.

He reminds her a little of her father, in the way he is disarmed by her refusal to show fear. She learned the lesson young that you cannot fight a bully. The way to deal with one is to behave in the manner they least expect.

This has nothing to do with desire, she realizes. It is about power.

He picks her up, suddenly, sweeping her off her feet and into his arms. She has no choice but to submit. If she struggles it will be worse. He places her on the small couch in the corner. She is thankful he hasn't taken her into the bedroom, doesn't think she could cope with being returned to the site of the violation.

Don't think about that.

He is speaking, saying things, things about his desire. 'I've never encountered a woman like you.' She isn't listening. His smell makes her stomach churn. He shakes off the bruise-coloured jacket and leans in to place his dry lips on the corner of her mouth. His nostrils flare, pupils expanding as his desire ignites.

He fumbles with his laces, disobedient fingers unable to loosen them, wrenching, snapping them with a curse under his breath.

She quashes the impulse to struggle. *I like it more when you resist.* That is what he said, so she will not resist. He can have her body. Her body is not her.

She lies back and stares towards the window, where she can see rows of drying laundry waving in the breeze. Its gentle back-and-forth motion, its startling whiteness and the moving patterns of light and shade lull her, drawing her away, out of her flesh, up, up into the endless sky.

He kneels above her, flaccid, an embarrassed flush

working its way up through the thicket of chest hair and blotching onto his throat and cheeks.

He takes a breast in one of his hands, kneading as if it is a lump of dough. It is not her breast. With his other hand he is trying to caress some life into his inert prick. He rubs desperately, burning with humiliation. She flits about in the air as the light dances around her, only half aware of what is taking place in the room, and her empty body.

'This has never happened to me before.' He slouches onto the edge of the couch, defeated.

She supposes he would like her to say that it doesn't matter, to stroke his bruised pride. She knows enough about the fragility of men's vanity. Another lesson from her father. 'Perhaps it is violence that arouses you.'

He winces. There is that look again.

'You were no better than an animal. Imagine if your mother had seen you brutalize me in that way, how ashamed she would be of you – her son.'

He inhales shakily and she knows she has touched on his deepest weakness. Men surely don't want their mothers to know of the beasts hidden inside them.

He makes a sudden grunt, jumping up to punch at the wall, releasing a cry of pain. A fragment of plaster is dislodged and falls, scattering powder over the floorboards.

He pulls on his clothes, staring at the canvas, his blighted expression persisting.

'You still haven't given me your opinion.'

'I think . . . I think . . .' He seems to pull himself together slightly, detach himself from the figure on the painted bed. 'I am honoured that a woman of your talent has agreed to be mine.'

She moves close to him so she can whisper, 'I might have agreed to wed you, but I will *never* be yours.'

His bravado has deserted him entirely and he appears not fully to understand, head tipped in a question, as if the rules have been changed and he was not informed. He begins to say something, then seems to change his mind.

'I'd like to get back to my work, now.' She is firm but polite. 'Excuse me if I don't see you out.'

He looks utterly crushed as he leaves.

She feels inert as a slab of granite.

22. Carmine Red

That man – Zita will not say his name, or even think it – visited several times before he left for Florence. Artemisia never for a moment lost her composure. Zita spat in the drinks she prepared him and served them with a pretend smile – a petty revenge that makes her feel better.

She stood guard but once he came when the house was empty. Artemisia didn't protest or say a word about what had happened when he was alone with her. Zita knows anyway. He came to take what is his – or what will be his as soon as their vows are exchanged before a priest. They are to be wed in the autumn. 'Perhaps a fever will claim me before then,' Artemisia had said, with a broken laugh.

They all stifle in the house, where the atmosphere crackles, like the air before a storm. Artemisia says little and Francesco smoulders with hostility. Giulio has sided with his brother, whom he has always looked up to. They have taken to dallying in the street outside the studio, as if to be on hand to protect their sister, should she need it. All the sibling rivalry has dried up, Orazio's children united against him.

Francesco has taken up smoking. He must think it makes him appear older, but it doesn't. He looks like a boy with a pipe. Orazio drinks heavily, his rages replaced with miserable self-pity. Zita hasn't an ounce of sympathy for him. He sits wilting in a shadowy corner, silently, doing nothing, as if he has become a ghost.

The knowledge that all the misfortune in the house began with her is a heavy weight on Zita's back. She curses her light fingers. Had she not stolen the cross, Orazio would have had nothing against her, nothing to stop her remaining in the room when that man visited, and Artemisia would never have had her virtue stolen. That first dishonest act gave rise to what followed.

She has finally confessed, but a hundred thousand Ave Marias won't lift the burden of her shame. *Father, I have sinned. I have stolen a valuable object.* She didn't dare be more specific. *You must return it, my child,* her confessor had said, *and make your amends to its owner.* She can't return what is not in her possession. She doesn't know what has become of it, assumes it is still in Orazio's possession.

She had asked Giulio how it came to fall into Orazio's hands. 'It wasn't my fault,' he'd said. 'He dragged it out of me.' His mouth was drawn tight and in the nervy flicker of his eyes she could see the dregs of the fear he must have felt at the time. 'I don't blame you, Giu-giu. You couldn't help it. I know that.' She often finds Orazio terrifying, but to a nine-year-old he must be like an ogre.

Zita harbours a belief that if she can only find and return the cross God will forgive her and make everything right again. She has searched for it everywhere, save Orazio's bedroom, which he keeps locked, but it is nowhere to be found. She hopes against hope that Orazio found a way to return it. If that is so she wonders whether, if it is returned by someone other than her, her sin is less readily absolved, given she has no way to ask its owner's forgiveness. She is in a terrible muddle with it all.

Artemisia shuts out the world, painting all day, every

day, as if her life depends on it. Zita cannot reach her and is glad of the children's relentless needs, the meals to prepare, the tantrums to calm, the lullabies to sing, the bumps and bruises to kiss better. These small things keep her from sinking to misery too.

Orazio talks from time to time, through a stupor of drunkenness, of the coming wedding but nobody is listening. And Artemisia says she doesn't care how or where it takes place.

Zita longs more than ever for her husband's return. He will give her another baby to love, make life straightforward again. But there has been no word from him in months and, anyway, he is not due back until the end of the year. She is stuck here as much as the rest of them.

A small package arrives from Florence. Artemisia assumes it is yet another gift from Tassi. He has sent several: a pair of pearl earrings, though her ears are not pierced, a Venetian glass vessel that arrived broken, a length of elaborate silk for the kind of dress she loathes to wear. How little he knows her if he believes she will be persuaded to forgive him with useless expensive things.

Before he left, he told her he had never felt for any woman the way he feels for her. He spoke of love. She wanted to laugh in his face. Even she, who knows so little of such matters, is aware that his so-called love springs from her antipathy. Each gift he sends reminds her of what lies ahead: all her artistic ability, her inspiration, draining away as she is subsumed by the inevitable crush of motherhood and marriage to a man she loathes.

She leaves the latest packet unopened for several days.

She paints.

When she is not painting, she goes about as she pleases. Occasionally her father tries to stop her. 'What will people think?' he says. She doesn't reply, though she is tempted to ask him what people would think if she told them of his part in her situation. He locks the door to keep her in but she takes advantage of his inebriation to steal the key and let herself out.

She walks the city alone, absorbing its sights, feeding her imagination: an expression on a face, the distortion of shadows, the way the city falls into an instant of stasis when the prayer bells ring, the grey-blue quiver of dusk. She stashes away these impressions, to recreate later.

Out one morning, she sees Nicolò Bendino loitering near the studio, beady eyes on her, filled with silent venom. He didn't take his dismissal well, is the type to harbour a grievance. On this occasion, she bids him good day. He pretends not to hear.

She walks down to the riverbank where the laundry women take their washing, stopping to watch. They smack their linens against the slick flat stones with muscular forearms, releasing a rainbow mist of droplets. They sing and laugh while they work. They have a female camaraderie of which Artemisia understands little. It makes her feel sorry for Zita, who yearns for company, for another woman to gossip with. But Artemisia has no talent for talking about who said what of whom.

On her way home she passes a cloth dealer's, stopping to watch as the bolts of bright fabric are unrolled for a customer to peruse. The brocades and velvets, the spools of thread and the reels of ribbon are displayed in an enthralling array of colour. Everything she sees is stored for the future.

Walking by a butcher's, where rows of cured ham and sausage hang like garlands, she stops to buy some meat for the table. An open door gives onto a yard, from where she can hear a terrified squealing. Two men are slaughtering a hog. She finds herself captivated by the manner in which the blood gushes out when the throat is cut. She is suddenly lightheaded, the vivid red splashes on the butchers' white aprons making her unsteady, as if she has looked at the sun and can no longer see.

'Signorina?' A man's voice jolts her attention from the scene. 'Are you ailing? Do you need to sit down?' She cannot respond. He brings a stool and gives her a drink of cool water. 'You shouldn't be watching that.'

She finds her voice to thank him. He tells her she looks better. 'The colour's returned to your cheeks.'

'I don't know what came over me.'

'Can I send for someone to collect you?'

She says it won't be necessary.

As she walks away, she can hear him discussing her: 'That's Gentileschi's daughter . . .' She moves on out of earshot, doesn't want to hear him say she's spoiled goods, and isn't it fortunate that a man as upright and successful as Tassi has stooped to marry her? She knows that is what's said about her. She doesn't care.

Goods can be spoiled only once and there is freedom in that knowledge. It turns out that this precious virtue of hers, so closely guarded for so long, is not missed at all. She spots Bendino again, leaning on the wall opposite the butcher's, pretending not to see her as she passes, and she wonders if he has been following her.

On her return, the studio is dead. She doesn't at first see Orazio in his chair, sleeping, head dropped to one side, mouth hanging open. A string of drool catches the light, as if he has been dining on pearls. She watches him for a moment. Something is wrong. He is pale, his skin sallow, and he is so still, too still, no rise and fall in his ribs, no sign of breath on his lips.

Her mind clamours, her chest tightening. But she cannot deny the spark of relief that flickers to life deep within her, catching hold. What kind of daughter feels relief in such a moment? Where is her grief?

She doesn't know what to do, who to call for help. She could run to the Stiatessis', call Zita down from upstairs, seek out a neighbour. Someone will know what to do.

She does nothing, seems to slip out of her body, looking at herself, looking at him.

Time is suspended.

She tries to call for Zita but cannot make any sound.

She is caught in a welter of contradictions and impulses: to capture him in charcoal, to pray for his soul, to weep hot tears of grief.

She moves closer. His skin is creased as a walnut and splotched with liver spots. His hands are huge and knotted, his ring fused to his finger. She touches her face, below her eye, where there is still a raised white scar. She can smell the drink on him. She imagines how life will be without him, wonders whether she will be able to extract herself from her promise of marriage, shocked that she is thinking of herself rather than of him in this moment.

She notices then the very slight movement of breath in his ribcage and feels he has tricked her for appearing dead when he was only sleeping. A vague memory drifts to her from the distant past, she in the safety of her mother's embrace, hearing Merisi's voice: *Get to the truth of what it means to take a life.* She has a momentary vision of stuffing her father's mouth and nose with painters' rags, holding them in place until the life is gone from him.

She recoils in horror that she is able even to contemplate such a thing.

Orazio grunts, his eyes bursting open.

Startled, she jumps back.

His look snaps onto her. 'What are you doing? Trying to steal from my pocket?'

'No.' She steps away further in case he lashes out. 'I thought you were . . .' She can't tell him she thought he was dead. She wonders, with a stab of self-reproach, whether it was wishful thinking. She does not really wish he was dead – only that he was different. But perhaps if he was not the man he is, she would not be herself either.

Grasping at the table, he levers himself up with a groan and disappears into the dark mouth of the stairs, laboured steps plodding up. She hears him collapse heavily onto his bed with a *whump*.

Sitting in his chair, she simmers with a strange fear as she tries to tame her thoughts, tries not to think of the terrible thing she imagined herself doing. The slaughtered animal asserts itself in her mind again, with the chilling sound of its cries, leading her to the blood-soaked Beatrice Cenci hurtling towards her from the past. *Let her see what becomes of girls who disobey their fathers*. She must not look away from the dark.

Her painting is pulling her up from the chair with a force she cannot resist. She removes its cover, a thrill rising through her as she sees her own work. The figures emerging from the blackness, the light spilling over them from a single direction, she, the viewer, its source. Her mind reels back to that sketch of her as a child crouched eavesdropping in the shadows of the stairwell, and then to other images, other paintings: the *Saint Paul* in the chapel where her mother lies, his body prone, head to the foreground. Her own depiction of Holofernes is an echo of this, and she understands that she has absorbed the lessons of the master. She can see with absolute clarity the way in which works of art – all art – speak to each other down the years. Her painting is part of that conversation.

But the colour of the blood isn't quite true.

At the bench, still half dazed, she mixes paints, bringing back to mind the scene from the butcher's, unable to find the pigment to recreate what she saw. Admitting defeat, she notices a splash of colour has defaced the package from Florence that still awaits her attention.

On impulse, she opens it. Layers of wrapping unfold to reveal not some valuable, useless charm, as she expects, but a stoppered jar, wound with twine and sealed with wax.

She turns it over in her hands. It has a pleasing weight and shape, but it is no ornament, just a plain clay container. She rummages in the wrapping and a note flutters to the floor. She can't make sense of the short scrawl but she knows the signature. It is not from Tassi as she'd assumed, but Piero.

Picking off the wax seal, she prises away the twine and draws out the stopper. The unmistakable mineral scent of pigment fills her nostrils. Dipping a finger inside, it emerges carmine red. Excited now, she tips a measure onto the mortar adding drip by drip a little linseed oil, working it in for some time until the powder and oil combine into a paste. As she mills it, the colour enriches, deepens, takes on a sheen.

Applying the colour to her canvas, she has the sense that by some invisible force Piero knows what she has been searching for. Though he is far away, she feels he is close, watching her as her work takes shape, as if the two of them are attached to the wheel of fortune by a single unbreakable thread.

She layers the colour on, delicately, mixing it, adding darker tones in places and highlights in others. She cannot shake off Merisi's voice: *Get to the truth of what it means to take a life*. Understanding seeps slowly into her as she works, that while she has fixated on finding the perfect colour, she hasn't grasped that what her painting needed was for her truly to confront *that* feeling, the murderous impulse locked in every human soul – *the truth of what it means*.

Now the painting slowly unfolds into life, blood exploding from Holofernes' neck, spilling over the scene. She can hear the puff of the painted women's breath, can smell their sweat, sense their courage, can hear their victim's anguished screech, can smell the fear, his fear, his horror, the maid's horror, Judith's horror, and then her relief, and then the inner bristle of her triumph.

Artemisia lays down her brush. It is finished.

23. Bone Black

Four months later . . .

Summer has crept by and slunk into autumn, the street corners already silted with leaves blown in on cool winds. Orazio can feel winter on its way. In a month it will be Advent, and before that, in ten days, his daughter will be wed. What sweet relief that will be.

She no longer makes any pretences for him, avoiding him as much as possible and refusing to help him with his work. The painting she had been working on for months with such disturbing intensity, now stands finished in the studio, like an open sore. He moves it to a shadowy corner, for fear people will see it from the street.

On first recognizing the likeness of her husband-to-be in the blood-drenched Holofernes, he was chilled – chilled yet spellbound by the force of her talent. The work is a glorious monstrosity that taunts him, an unremitting reminder of his own inadequacies. It forces him to recognize that where Artemisia embraces audacity, abandoning herself entirely to her art, he cares too much about the opinions of others.

He lays out his preliminary drawings for the cardinal's latest project. He has been up to the site on several occasions. The summer pavilion is fast taking shape, and on Tassi's return they are to begin work on the frescos. In the meantime his life is in stasis, waiting, his daughter still unmarried, his new work still sketches on rolls of paper, his finances still finely balanced. He has negotiated a proper payment with Quorli, won't be taken for a fool, not this time.

He ponders his design: garlands of flowers and fat putti hovering in a friendly sky. But his putti are ungainly, their winged bodies grotesque rather than charming.

Artemisia bursts in from the stairway. 'What's this doing over here?' She moves her painting back to the window.

'I was worried the colours might fade in the light.'

'Do you think I'm stupid?' Her look shrivels him. 'How will it sell if no one sees it?'

'People will talk. They will wonder why you have painted Tassi's likeness so, so . . . Oh, you know what I mean.' He is attempting to be diplomatic about the horrific portrayal of Tassi in the throes of being slaughtered like an Epiphany hog. His foremost worry is that if Tassi should learn of it he might reconsider his decision to wed her. The betrothal is a promise to be kept, but this could well be considered grounds to retract. Orazio doesn't want things to become malicious.

'If you see the figure as Tassi, it was not my intention. I pluck faces from my mind. Any similarities are coincidental.' Her mouth twists.

'What about Quorli's likeness appearing in your *Susanna*? That was coincidental too, I suppose?' He is remembering the man's unexpected amusement on seeing himself portrayed and waits for her to harangue him for passing off her work as his own. But she merely turns her back to tidy the jars of pigment, adjusting their labels to face the front.

'You surely don't want to cause offence?'

'Quorli wasn't offended – he paid handsomely for my *Susanna*.' She rubs her fingers together, like a usurer.

'You must be able to see that this is different.' He is unsure how to put it without lighting her fuse. She has changed beyond recognition, has hardened and sharpened, meeting him with a constant crushing disdain. There is nothing left of his spirited daughter. The knowledge of the part he played in her transformation brings with it a real physical pain, the screw of a blade into his heart.

'Tassi might be back any day and were he to see himself as the victim of such brutality . . .' He tiptoes around her, softening his tone. 'Have you considered altering the face?' It sounds like a desperate plea.

'He's seen it already – months ago.' She gives him an impenetrable look. 'It was still unfinished, but he got the general idea.' She is half smiling, as if laughing inwardly at the memory.

'And he knew it was *your* work?' Orazio is trying to understand why she would expose herself in such a way to her intended.

'Of course. Anyone with even half an eye can tell my work from yours. Perhaps Quorli was taken in, but Tassi at least can judge a painting. Quorli's nothing more than the cardinal's agent – the sort to assess a picture by the price.'

Orazio is taken aback. She is absolutely right, but he can't fathom how she has understood this when she knows so little of Quorli.

He can feel her growing beyond him, out of his reach, which makes him unsure of himself. A nagging fear returns that he will lose her altogether once she is married, making his breath catch.

He casts an eye over his clumsy cherubs, burying his pride to ask for her help. 'I don't know if I can do it without you.'

She gives him a withering look. 'You should see yourself, Father. Anyone would think you were a vagrant. You haven't seen a barber in God only knows how many months, your clothes are filthy, you smell of piss.' He blanches at her crude turn of phrase, wants to admonish her but is at a loss for words. 'You are dead drunk half the time. Even Fillide's cast you aside, and she's –'

'She's what?' He mounts a half-hearted defence of his one-time mistress. It's true, she no longer visits. She's found more fertile fields to sow.

'Oh, never mind.' Artemisia changes tack. 'Where's your self-respect? If you drank less, you might find you could draw properly.' She points to his sketches.

Her words sting, but she is right. He glances down at his clothes. They are grubby and threadbare. He notices a line of black grime around his cuffs. He hadn't realized until this moment quite the extent to which he has been obliterating reality with drink. He is about to make excuses, tell her that he has been too busy but that is a lie. 'I'll stop, Arti – stop the drinking.'

She glances up at him, embossed with doubt.

'I mean it – I do.' He *does* mean it.

She returns to her tidying while he stares at the drawings on the bench. His ugly cavorting cherubs seem to laugh at him.

A knock interrupts the quiet and the door opens to

reveal Giovanni. Piero is with him. Artemisia rushes over to them with an animated joy he hasn't seen in her for months, embracing the boy without a care for modesty, welcoming them, pulling up chairs for them to sit, going to fetch refreshments from the kitchen.

'Where have you been?' Giovanni asks. Orazio notices the way the other man's eye travels over his shabby clothes and unkempt beard, registering worry. 'Why have you been hiding yourself away? Porzia is protesting that you never visit us any more.' He is jocular and warm, and Orazio realizes he has missed his old friend.

'Now, I'm aware you parted on bad terms with Piero' – his nephew is loitering slightly behind him – 'but so much water has passed under the bridge that I didn't think you'd object to him visiting with me. He and Artemisia were as close as cousins until . . .' he meets Orazio's eye with a questioning look '. . . until whatever happened, happened. It would be a shame for them not to have the chance to see one another before she is wed.'

Orazio can only remember the anger he had felt at the boy, telling him to leave and never come back. He can't even recall what exactly had provoked him. He has such gaps in his memory. It was something, he begins to remember, to do with his attempts to protect Artemisia's reputation. Giovanni is right about water having passed under the bridge. He smiles. 'As you say, soon she will be married.'

'And what is this?' He has seen Artemisia's painting. 'So, this is the reason we haven't seen you. You've been working, clearly. It's so bold, so unflinching. So unlike your usual work. It's no wonder you're gaining all these commissions for the cardinal if you are producing pieces of this calibre.'

Orazio glances towards the kitchen. The door is ajar, and Artemisia appears not to have heard. He is dithering about whether to come clean, when Piero, who has also been giving close scrutiny to the picture, says, 'This looks more like Arti's brushwork.' Orazio might have known the sharp-eyed boy would recognize her hand.

'Surely not.' Giovanni is looking at Orazio, awaiting a response.

Orazio considers lying but he wouldn't get it past Giovanni, with his lawyer's nose for the truth. 'No, Piero's right. It's Arti's piece. She's considering making changes, particularly to the male figure – the features.'

'I don't know why she would.' He has stepped back to take another look. 'I'd say the features are perfect. Wouldn't you agree, Piero?'

Strangely, he seems not to have recognized Tassi in the half-decapitated man writhing in his own blood. Orazio considers that perhaps he had imagined the likeness. After all, Artemisia had said it was not her intention and one bearded man looks much like another, particularly when screeching in pain.

Piero is agreeing with his uncle, nodding and talking, something about the quality of the colour, but Orazio is trying to remember who once said to him, 'People see what they want to see.' Who was it? He racks his mind, frustrated by the voids in his memory, dark and empty as bone-black pigment.

'I'll go and help Arti,' says Piero, disappearing into the kitchen.

'Ask her to bring us some wine,' Orazio calls after him.

It is coming back to him now, Fillide's dress and that appalling painting of the boy wearing it.

Piero closes the kitchen door. Artemisia smiles. She looks different, harder, sadder. She is thin too, her cuffs bagging at her wrists, her head seeming too heavy for her neck. Something has happened in this house.

'I'm so glad you're back in Rome.' She doesn't seem glad. She seems brittle and gloomy. He wonders if it is her impending marriage. Their friendship will have no space to breathe once Tassi's ring is on her finger.

'I've missed you.' He would like to embrace her but can't surmount the invisible barrier between them. 'You received the carmine pigment?'

'It was exactly the colour . . . How did you know?'

'I thought it was particularly fine. And red. It reminded me of the dress – remember?'

She smiles briefly but the awkwardness continues to prevail.

'So, you are to be married?'

'Yes. In less than a week – apparently.' She sounds forcedly bright. 'He's a painter. I'll be able to continue my work. Probably.'

'I'm glad.' He is not glad. Not at all. Piero has never been able to imagine Artemisia belonging to a husband, not even a painter. 'My uncle tells me he's very successful – Medici commissions.'

'It's Father who cares about such things.' She turns away, closing the conversation and opens a cupboard, half disappearing into it, reappearing with a loaf and some other victuals. 'He paints illusions. Very well. Very precise. But there's no emotion in his work.'

'Your father's asked for wine.'

She looks at him with a distant intensity. 'Has he? He promised only minutes ago he would stop the drinking.' She shrugs, pointing to a bottle on the shelf. He reaches for it, pulling out the stopper, sniffing it. It smells unpleasant and mildewy.

'It's not very good.'

'Father won't care.'

'What's the matter, Arti? You don't seem yourself.'

She sits heavily, elbows on the table, chin resting on her hands. 'If you want the truth, I *hate* the man I am being made to wed.' She stresses the word 'hate' with a grimace.

'I thought . . .' He'd supposed she was happy, at least, to be able to continue her work after marriage even if that work will be limited to 'appropriate' subjects. 'Are you reconciled to it?'

'Reconciled, I don't know about that. But I have no choice.' She looks up at him. 'The murdered man in my painting is a depiction of him. That might give you an idea of the extent of my loathing. You did see it, didn't you – my painting?' Her eyes flash momentarily, recounting this act of defiance, but all he can see is sadness – profound sadness. It is unimaginable to him that this artist of such great vision will have her wings clipped so brutally because she was born a woman. He thinks of all the works she will not paint – it seems like sacrilege.

'I'm so sorry . . .' He places a hand gingerly on her back but she shrugs him off.

'Don't pity me.' She wipes her hands over her face.

'How could I pity someone who has the ability to produce a work like that?' He forces her to look at him properly. 'It's magnificent.' Ordinary language feels insufficient to describe the effect, a mix of horror and wonder, her painting had had on him. 'You do know how good it is, don't you?'

Now her smile is genuine. 'It's the best thing I've ever done. Piero' – she grabs his hand, squeezing it tight – 'it was . . .' She seems about to say something, looks momentarily haunted. 'It just came out of me.' The smile has returned but Piero is disturbed by that fleeting look.

'I'd like to show it to someone. Would you mind?'

'Who?'

'Just a friend.'

'Just a friend? It's clear, from the grin you're failing to smother, that this person is more than "just a friend".'

'I'd forgotten how impossible it is to hide anything from you.'

'That's because you're transparent as gauze.'

Now all the tension is gone and she is the defiant, candid Artemisia he remembers. How small his world has been without her in it.

'My friend might know of a buyer.'

'A buyer! But it's not finished. I can't show it to a buyer unfinished.'

'It looks finished to me.'

'No. I haven't quite captured . . . There's something lacking in it. I need more time.'

'My friend understands painting.' Piero knows the difficulty Artemisia has in considering a piece of work finished – it was ever thus. 'Please let me show him.'

Before she has a chance to respond Orazio interrupts them, asking what's taking so long. He snatches the bottle from Piero's hand.

'It's smells off,' Piero says.

'I'll be the judge of that.' He tips out a large measure, glugging it back, smacking his lips. 'Perfectly all right.'

Artemisia watches his back as he departs, her face dark. 'Bring your friend here later. Father's usually out in the early evening.'

24. Five Gold *Scudi*

Artemisia is surprised to discover that Piero's 'friend' is a seminarian. She had been expecting someone older, a dealer, wearing a suit of showy brocade, fingers weighted with rings – certainly not the serious young priest regarding her with a pair of hooded brown eyes and a mouth he might have stolen from a cupid.

A man of the cloth he may be, but it is abundantly clear he is not penniless. His cassock is tailored in expensive fabric, his cuffs are of fine lace, but it is the cross around his neck that betrays the fact that he belongs to no ordinary family. It is gold, set with precious stones. It makes her think, for a moment, of the stolen ruby cross that caused so much trouble, wondering if it made its way back to the cardinal's closet. Zita hasn't mentioned it again. If Orazio still has it, he's probably forgotten where he put it.

Faced with this young priest, she is nervous that he might disapprove of her Judith's bloodthirsty brazenness. Perhaps this was a mistake. She tries to indicate as much to Piero, glad that she'd thought to cover the canvas before they arrived, but he blithely continues introducing his friend.

He calls him simply Carlo, without specifying a family name, which ignites Artemisia's curiosity. He takes her hand, a kiss hovering over its back. He smiles. His teeth are small and even. 'Piero tells me you have created a magnificent *Judith*. I'd very much like to see it.' He speaks with precision, as if each word has been carefully chosen. 'My mother might be interested in such a work.'

'Your mother? I should warn you –' Hesitation clips her words.

Piero interrupts: 'Carlo knows what it is.' He places a reassuring hand on her shoulder. 'I've described it to you, haven't I?'

The intensity of the look the two men exchange confirms to Artemisia that they are lovers. 'Where do you know one another from?' She attempts to make her query seem mere politeness, but really her curiosity has been lit. She wants to judge this stranger worthy of her friend.

'My family are Florentine too,' says Carlo, which still doesn't explain how his path might have crossed with that of an ordinary pigment dealer's son, even if they do hail from the same city. 'But we met here in Rome, didn't we?'

'At Cardinal Borghese's.' Piero is wearing a mischievous look and Artemisia is thrown back into his descriptions of the cardinal's parties, a whole secret world of enthralling wildness from which she is excluded.

'Is this it?' Piero is pointing to the covered painting.

She nods, feeling the last dregs of her confidence drain away, fearing that she has been deluding herself about the quality of her work, that all the compliments were merely to indulge her. The awful incident with the failed drawing at the Palazzo Conscente returns to her, like a bag of broken glass in her gut. Perhaps she is nothing more than a curiosity – an ape making colourful daubs with a paintbrush for people's amusement. She reminds herself of her earnings from paintings sold, of the coins, stashed carefully away, to shore her up against misfortune. But this work is different. It is personal. It is her revenge.

'Well, are you going to show us?' Piero has the cloth cover between thumb and forefinger.

'It's far from a masterpiece,' she says.

'False modesty doesn't suit you.' Piero has misinterpreted her genuine apprehension. He removes the cloth.

Carlo looks in silence at the canvas for several long minutes. Not so much as a flicker of interest registers in those dark eyes, the cupid's mouth immobile.

She wants to sink into the floor, disappear altogether, run into the street, vomit in the gutter.

After what seems a thousand agonizing hours, Piero says, 'Do you like it?'

'I do.' Carlo is giving little away with his expression but then he turns his gaze directly on her. 'You certainly haven't shied from the brutality of the scene. It takes courage to paint the bare truth.' He still doesn't smile. 'And you are the sole artist? Your father didn't –'

She interrupts on a surge of indignation: 'My father had nothing to do with it. Every stroke of it is mine.'

'Ah, now I have a glimpse of the passion that generated such a scene.' He looks amused. 'Will this ensure you don't sell it to someone else?'

Taking her hand, he tips five gold *scudi* into it. She tries to hide her astonishment. If this is the deposit then he must consider the painting, *her* painting, to be worth an enormous sum.

She gives him a businesslike nod, pretending nonchalance. 'This ought to be sufficient.'

They shake on the deal. His palm is cool and smooth as polished stone.

Piero sees him to the door, where they speak in hushed whispers, and returns beaming. 'I knew it. This is just the beginning for you.'

Artemisia doesn't want to ruin his enjoyment by reminding him that Tassi will be the one to decide whether this is her beginning. 'Who *is* Carlo?'

'His father was . . . his brother *is* the Grand Duke of Tuscany.' He takes both her hands.

'He's a Medici?' She doesn't believe him. 'No?'

'Yes.' He must see the doubt she is trying to hide. 'What is it?'

'I wish I could run away. Go somewhere that no one can find me.' A leaden feeling descends over her. There is nowhere she can run to, nowhere her father or Tassi won't be able to find her.

They fall into a long hug, both unaware of the door opening until it is too late.

They break apart abruptly, the image of guilty lovers.

Orazio is in the doorway – with Tassi.

'What's in Hell's name's going on?' Tassi's tone is proprietorial. 'I return from my travels to be greeted by this?'

'It's not how it appears, Agostino.' Artemisia won't be cowed. 'This is Piero Stiatessi. He's Giovanni's nephew.' She looks to her father for confirmation but Orazio is mute. 'We are as good as cousins.' She offers Tassi an ameliorating smile, her head tilted in a plea.

He regards her in a smouldering silence, with the scorn of a man whose pride has been dented. Noticing he has a knife in a sheath attached to his belt, she keeps gibbering about how she was almost raised in the Stiatessis' household, trying to prevent a full conflagration.

'As good as cousins?' His tone is clipped. 'You either *are* cousins or you are *not.*'

'Father, tell him.'

'The Stiatessis . . . close . . . yes . . . very . . .' Orazio cannot seem to get his words in a straight line and she realizes that he is dead drunk, propping himself up on the door, barely able to stand.

'So, they are *not* cousins.' Tassi is scrutinizing Piero. 'Haven't I seen you somewhere before?'

'I delivered a consignment of pigments to your apartments yesterday.' Piero is quite calm.

'A delivery boy!' Contempt is scrawled over Tassi's features.

Artemisia can't help but spring to Piero's defence. 'As a matter of fact, he is a dealer in the finest pigments.'

'They *were* of good quality, as it happens.' He makes a little snort of concession. 'Rather expensive, if I remember rightly.'

'I only deal in the best.' She is impressed at Piero's poise in the face of Tassi, who is doing his utmost to intimidate him, standing legs akimbo, a hand resting on the hilt of his knife.

'I can assure you I pose you no threat, signore.' Piero steps towards him. 'Nor am I any threat to Artemisia's reputation.' They are a similar height but Tassi is much broader, much stronger. 'I was merely comforting her because she was upset.'

The atmosphere shifts, the veneer of politeness slipping. The two men stare at each other, eyes level and close, very close, their foreheads almost touching. Piero's fists furl. Artemisia wills him not to throw the first blow – Tassi could swipe out that blade and kill him with a single strike. She knows first-hand what the brute is capable of.

Stepping between them, pushing hard on each of their breasts, she forces them apart. 'Piero, you should leave. I can deal with this.'

'I don't think –' he starts.

'I mean it.' She makes herself sound firm and leads Piero to the exit. His body is stiff, mouth clenched in a snarl. She can't stomach the idea of him risking himself on her account. 'I can manage.' He resists but she shoves him into the street and slams the door.

When Artemisia turns back to the room, her father has collapsed into a chair in a daze, leaving her to face Tassi alone.

They stare at each other in silence for a long moment. His face is set, rigid and unsmiling.

A pulse of fear throbs in her temple.

She is tired, tired of fear, tired of intimidation. If she is to be married to this man, she must begin as she means to go on. A lifetime of battling. Orazio has taught her that if he senses even a splinter of her weakness she will have lost.

She can see her painting behind him, Judith's arms so strong, her resolve unfailing, her courage infinite. Remembering his reaction on seeing himself under Judith's blade, Artemisia invokes the spirit of her creation. She draws herself to her fullest height.

He seems to shrink back slightly and glances behind, following her eye line. He must catch sight of his painted self because when he turns back to her the colour has fallen from his face.

She injects all the authority she can find into her voice: 'First, Agostino, do not insult me by coming into my house armed.' He glances down at his belt. She gives him a firm nod and he obediently removes the weapon, setting it to one side.

Encouraged, she continues: 'And, second, never presume to insult a guest of mine by making wild and unfounded accusations against them.'

He has the look of a hound awaiting a beating. 'I'm sorry.' He steps towards her, reaching out a hand to stroke her cheek, mumbling an apology.

His fingers are abrasive.

She can smell the drink on his breath. He is almost as far gone as her father, only he has a better capacity for disguising it.

'I have enough to do with one drunkard in my life.' She nods disdainfully towards Orazio, who shifts, seeming about to mount a defence but apparently changes his mind, dropping back into his stupor. 'Please tell me I will not be married to one too.'

'I'm sorry, I truly am. I'm a passionate man. Sometimes I can't control my emotions. I promise –'

She cuts him off. 'You shouldn't make promises unless you are sure you can keep them.' She is boiling with hatred for this wretched creature who will be her husband in a matter of days and even more so for her father who has forced this situation on her.

'You're right. I'm hopeless and I'm nothing without your guidance.' He lunges forward to kiss her on the mouth, but she manoeuvres herself so he meets her cheek instead.

'Are you forgetting yourself? Father doesn't want to witness your base cravings.'

He staggers back, away from her, to fully confront the painting cast in the glow of the lamp. 'So much blood.' He rubs at his neck. 'It's finished?'

'I've sold it.' Pride leaks into her voice. She can feel the outline of the five gold *scudi* tucked inside her skirts and has the sense that she is growing, until she is vast and he small, so small she could tread on him, grind him into the ground with her heel.

He turns. '*Sold* it?'

She nods.

'To whom?' There is a challenge in his tone.

'Carlo di Medici, for his mother.' She can't stem her elation. 'Think of it. *My* work will hang in the Palazzo Pitti.'

His features darken.

Orazio coughs, half roused.

Tassi's breath stutters, apparently attempting to measure his response. 'You will have to change it – alter the man's face. I won't allow a portrait of me' – he is shaking now – 'in such a demeaning position. To be hung in the Palazzo Pitti. Never!'

'I will not be told how to finish my own work.' Her firmness, so potent only moments ago, seems to have lost its effect on him. She feels the threads of her control snapping one by one as he stares at her, breathing heavily.

She assesses her means of escape.

He stands between her and the door.

His knife is on the table, within his reach.

She can hear voices in the street. Her brothers are

loitering, smoking with a group of friends, in their habitual place a mere twenty paces from the door.

'I WON'T HAVE IT!' Tassi's face is purple.

Fear gushes back into her.

Watching him, she sidles close enough to the door to fling it open and call for help, should she need to.

'What's going on?' Orazio scoops himself out of his torpor.

'Nothing, Father. Signor Tassi is leaving. That is all.'

Before she can prevent it, Tassi lifts the painting from its stand and marches out of the door, one side of the canvas dragging against the latch.

Artemisia is momentarily paralysed, looking on in horror as she sees the paint scrape away, as if it is her own flesh gouged out.

Coming to her senses she calls for her brothers to help, running out into the street, chasing after him, shouting, arms windmilling. But it is too late. He has gone, slipped into one of the many dark alleyways leading off the via della Croce. 'Somebody stop him. He's a thief. For pity's sake, HELP ME!'

A few people have halted to stare at the mad woman shouting to the empty street. She turns on them. 'What are you staring at?'

Somebody laughs.

Suddenly exhausted, she sits, deflating onto the cobbles, drawing more laughter. Someone calls her a lunatic.

'Leave me be.' Her voice is shrill.

Her brothers pull her up and lead her back inside.

She is beyond feeling. Tassi has stolen her soul. 'I can't marry him,' she says, but no one hears.

25. A Cuckoo

Artemisia can tell, though Piero hasn't said it in as many words, that he dreads her wedding day as much as she. They languish in the studio by the hearth, a pall hanging over them. Before Orazio left this morning, he said nothing about Piero visiting. She supposes he feels it doesn't matter, as she will be off his hands by the end of the week.

She will not talk about her wedding.

'I still find it hard to believe he would do such a thing.' Piero is talking about the theft of her painting, outrage hissing in his voice.

'Couldn't you paint another?' Zita means well with her question.

'It's not like that.' She tries, unsuccessfully, to hide her impatience. 'You've been around painters for years. You must know.'

Zita mutters to herself, 'It was a curse, a gruesome scene like that hanging in the house.'

Artemisia is about to turn on her when the street door bangs open bringing with it a gust of icy air. The fire flares. They all look round to see Orazio with Giovanni Stiatessi.

Something is clearly wrong. Giovanni is chalk-white and Orazio looks as he did when Artemisia's mother died, like a man under an evil spell.

'What's happened?' Artemisia asks.

He extends an arm towards her. He is quaking. 'I have bad news, but I give you my word I will make it right.'

She steps away so his touch can't reach her, remembering how he made such a promise before. Piero slips his hand into hers – a welcome gesture of solidarity.

Orazio seems unable to spit out the words and it is Giovanni who says it in the end: 'Tassi already has a wife.'

Zita gasps, mouth gaping as she crosses herself.

Piero catches Artemisia's eye. A thrill sparks in her breast, all her pent-up unease evaporating, a picture of another future unrolling in her mind.

Orazio continues his rant: 'And him the adopted son of the Marchesa di Tassi. I'd have thought he was raised to behave with honour.'

'Is that what he told you?' Giovanni turns sharply towards him. 'It's not true, Orazio.'

Piero, Zita and Artemisia watch agog, as if the two men are enacting a drama.

'He served the Tassi family as a page for six months – that's all.'

'No!' Orazio refuses to believe him. 'I heard it from his own mouth that the marchesa counted him a son.'

'I'm afraid he lied to you.' Giovanni smoothes his beard in a manner suggesting apprehension. 'Agostino Domenico is Tassi's real name. He's the son of a furrier from Perugia.'

'Why didn't you tell me?'

'I assumed you knew. You've worked with him, know him so much better than I do.'

Orazio's face colours, as if all the blood in his body is flooding to his head. Then he explodes: 'The man's a fraud!

He'll get what's coming. He's ruined my daughter, dishonoured *me* . . . the son of a *furrier*, for pity's sake! The man's an impostor. Tainted the Gentileschi name. All those people who came to celebrate the betrothal.' His arms flail. 'I've been had by an *accursed cuckoo*.'

He stops abruptly. None of them know what to say. Artemisia presses her lips tight for fear they will betray her with a flicker of joy.

After some time, his voice drops. 'A wife! *Bigamy!* What will they all say?'

Artemisia steps forward. 'Why does it matter what they say? Who cares? Not me. Certainly not me.' Now she is thinking of her painting, the painting she must ensure is returned to her, the painting that is sold, and the five gold *scudi* she will have to reimburse if Tassi will not give it back.

A seed of doubt begins to germinate in her. Perhaps her work will be contaminated by her reputation – a fallen woman. Perhaps Carlo di Medici will rescind his offer. Her future, so clear only a moment ago, is losing its sharpness.

Giovanni is attempting to calm her father. 'The best decisions are not made in anger.'

'But he forced her – violently,' blurts Orazio. 'The man is a rapist!'

The room falls to a silence so intense it might suffocate them all.

'How *dare* you?' Artemisia takes a breath to compose herself. 'You promised never to speak of it. You gave me your word.'

'Is this true?' Giovanni is looking at her with grim pity. Orazio has covered his face with his hands – the coward.

'It is.' Her voice is shaking. She musters her self-possession. 'But I didn't want it spoken of – ever.'

Giovanni reaches for her hand, but she shakes her head, her grip tightening round Piero's fingers. 'We can challenge this, Artemisia, challenge it legally – clear your name.'

'No. I won't have that.' She is as impermeable as polished marble.

'He must be punished. Rape, attempted bigamy – these are serious offences.' Giovanni has his notary's bit between the teeth.

'He's right.' Orazio looks at his daughter now. 'It's a matter of honour.'

'Whose honour? Yours or mine?' She is doing all she can to keep her temper under control, fearing if she doesn't the entire structure of all their lives will be crushed beneath it.

'I myself will testify to your good character. I will do everything it takes to ensure the . . .' Giovanni's voice constricts as he withholds the curse that sits on the brim of his tongue '. . . *the villain* pays for what he has done.'

Piero holds her hand tighter, a silent source of strength.

Artemisia meets Giovanni's gaze steadily. 'I know you mean well. You have been like an uncle to me – you and Porzia, such dear friends to our family for as long as I remember. For that I am – we are all – so grateful. But I don't want this matter pursued.'

'What *do* you want, then?' By his tone, Orazio seems to have turned his ire on his daughter. 'We will never find you a husband. Does it mean nothing to you if we, your family, are disgraced?'

She is aware that his questions are rhetorical, that she is

not meant to have a say in this, but she answers him anyway. 'What I want,' she flicks a brief glance to the man at her side, the only person who truly knows who she is, 'what I want' – she takes a breath – 'is to paint . . . to paint the truth.'

'Never mind the truth.' Orazio swipes an arm through the air dismissively, as if to imply that her desire to paint is the reason for all his problems. 'The Gentileschi name has been abused and must be put right in a court of law.'

'Was the abuse against you, Father, or me? It was *my* body he violated.' She already knows her father's answer. The inescapable truth is that she belongs to him. Her talent is his, her body is his, her dishonour is his.

'I should never have given you such a loose rein. I have created a – a –' He is unable to spit it out.

'*What* have you created?' She is strangely calm. 'A monster? Is that what you were going to say? No, Father, all you have created is a woman with a mind of her own. Perhaps that seems monstrous to you.'

'I should have sent you into the care of Porzia and Giovanni, a proper family with a woman at its heart – a real woman.'

She would ask him if he thinks she is not a real woman but can't stand the idea of yet another blazing family row. 'I'm exhausted,' she says and, wishing Piero a silent goodbye, retreats towards the stairs.

'I suggest we sleep on it,' Giovanni says, ever sensible. 'I'll make some investigations, and we can plan what path to take tomorrow when we're all thinking straight.'

She hears them leave as she reaches the landing. Shutting herself in, she stands at the window, wallowing in the blessed quiet as she gazes out into the blue gloom of the autumn dusk.

She can sense her freedom so close. Tassi has a wife. Her wings unfold painfully, old muscles, never used. Her quills fan out, opening slowly, spreading, lifting her up into the air, floating, catching the breeze, carrying her through the dense blanket of cloud to another place.

Beneath her a carpet of wildflowers has sprung to miraculous life: daisies with citrus eyes, poppies of scarlet parchment, jostling for space with towering foxgloves, pink as pomegranate, and leggy fronds of bright verbena. Bees heavy with pollen drone over the blooms, armies of ants marching up their stems, snails curled into their petals.

Here the colours are infinite – the possibilities are infinite.

26. A Bonfire

Piero sits quietly in the carriage.

His uncle is talking on and on about Artemisia's situation. 'That wretched man ... I'll make sure he's put behind bars. Poor, poor girl.'

How Artemisia would hate this pity. Piero is remembering the elation that crossed her features when she realized her wedding would be called off.

'I'll ensure Tassi is properly punished.'

'It's not what she wants. She made that clear. She'll be dragged through the mud.'

'She's too young to know what's best for her. Without legal restitution, her reputation will be lost for ever. No one will wed her.'

'Has it occurred to you that she may not care about that?'

'Don't be naïve, Piero.'

Piero holds back an infuriated retort.

'Listen, you may not believe it,' continues his uncle, 'but I only want what's best for her. You and she, both, are young and idealistic. One day you'll understand.'

Piero holds his tongue. He knows there's no point in trying to make Giovanni see things differently. It's true he means well, but Piero's tempted to point out that great harm has often unwittingly been done in the name of good intention.

'What if *I* were to offer to marry her?' He says it without thinking but it makes complete sense. 'We understand each other, could make each other happy.' His uncle's silence is pointed. 'You've often said it would be good for me to marry.'

'Yes, but . . . Orazio would never allow it. You've no prospects to speak of and he wouldn't be able to offer enough of a dowry to give the two of you any kind of stability.' His tone suggests he thinks it an appalling idea. 'And she's –'

'She's what?' Piero's tone is defensive.

'Unsuitable.'

'Weren't *you* thought an unsuitable match for Aunt Porzia?' His frustration pours out now. 'Didn't she turn down some nobleman in favour of you and upset her entire family? Look how happy you've been.'

'That's completely different. Anyway, once Tassi's been tried, Artemisia's prospects will be transformed. She's not the one for you.' He pauses in thought. 'You should find yourself a nice respectable girl in Florence who won't mind you –'

'Won't mind me what?' Piero doesn't hide his annoyance. He knows exactly what his uncle means but wants to hear him say it.

'Who won't mind you *carrying on*.'

Piero drops it. He is tired of his uncle treating him like a child.

They sit in a sullen silence. The carriage comes to a halt. A procession has congested the streets and people are shouting and cursing, everyone frustrated by the delay. It is almost dusk, and outside Piero can see a line of choirboys, each one holding a candle in cupped hands, like a row of glow worms.

'What's this about Tassi stealing Artemisia's painting?' says Giovanni, after some time. 'Do you know anything?'

'Tassi was upset because her depiction of Holofernes resembled him.'

'I didn't notice that.' Giovanni's voice softens. 'It's quite something. Trust Artemisia to depict such a scene.' There is admiration in his tone.

'It's a masterpiece.' An image of the painting unfolds in Piero's mind. 'She sold it to the Medicis – through a contact of mine.' Carlo had been beside himself with excitement about the purchase, had hardly spoken of anything else.

'A contact of yours? How did you manage to negotiate such a deal?'

'I am friends with Carlo di Medici.'

He looks surprised. 'How so?'

'Met him at the cardinal's –'

'Actually' – his uncle holds a hand in the air – 'I'd rather not know.'

They say nothing for a while in the stationary carriage, while Piero cogitates on his friend's predicament. He feels powerless to help her but then realizes that Tassi's apartment, where he had recently delivered some pigments, is not far from here. He could at least make an attempt to recover her painting.

'I think I'll walk back,' he says. 'Clear my head.'

Jumping out, he weaves through the crowds with a renewed sense of purpose. He is encouraged to see light emanating from the top windows of Tassi's building. He enters, marching up the five flights, waiting on the landing to catch his breath and steeling himself for a confrontation. He wonders if it is folly to challenge this man alone – but he is here now.

Courage gathered, he knocks on the door. Tassi appears almost immediately, seeming wrong-footed to see him, as if expecting someone else.

'The pigment dealer,' he says, with a sneer. 'What are *you* doing here? I haven't made an order.'

'Please could I come in, Signor Tassi?' Piero removes his cap out of politeness. 'There's something I'd like to discuss with you.'

'It needs to be quick. I'm awaiting a guest.'

Through the open door Piero can see that the place is in a state of complete disorder. He scans the room for Artemisia's painting. A studio is set up – an easel with a half-finished still-life, a jumble of jars and brushes, canvases stacked haphazardly against a table.

He steps forward but Tassi blocks his way, thrumming his fingers impatiently against the edge of the door. 'So, what is it, then?'

Clearly the man doesn't intend to invite him over the threshold. 'I've come to collect Signorina Gentileschi's *Judith*. I understand you have it in your possession.' He notices a chest spilling over with clothes, as if being either packed or unpacked, and wonders if Tassi is planning to go somewhere. He hopes so. If the wretch disappears, legal proceedings cannot be set in motion.

Tassi runs his eyes up and down Piero's body, his mouth set in a scowl. 'Why are *you* running errands for her? She is not your business.'

'She doesn't know I'm here.' He makes himself sound

affable, though it is far from how he is feeling. If he had a blade he would be tempted to plunge it into Tassi's black heart.

'Artemisia will be my wife soon, so the painting is as good as mine already.' Piero realizes that Tassi is completely unaware his secret has been uncovered – he still believes his bigamous wedding is to go ahead. He resists the temptation to confront the man about his deceit. He had forgotten quite how big Tassi is. Only tact will retrieve the painting. Tassi's mouth forms into an unfriendly smile. 'This will be her home and she will be reunited with her picture in good time.'

A look of affection passes fleetingly over Tassi's features as he says this, puzzling Piero. If he didn't know better, he might suspect the wretch genuinely cared for Artemisia. His hostility stinks of jealousy. But remembering the violence Tassi has perpetrated, he dismisses the thought.

He takes a small but definite step forward, refusing to be intimidated, wishing he'd been less rash in his decision to come here alone and unarmed. 'The painting is sold. Carlo di Medici has already made a down-payment.'

If Piero thought the mention of the illustrious Medici name would impress Tassi, he was wrong. He doesn't turn a hair as he says, 'Carlo di Medici? Isn't he the milksop younger son, who's being groomed for the *Church*?' He stresses the word as if he means something by it.

Piero knows that this isn't the moment to defend his lover, despite the needling comment. 'So, if you let me have the work, I shall deliver it to its new owner.' He tries to sound light, as if he is doing Tassi a favour. 'It is a handsome sum he's offered. Make quite a dowry.' Tassi will surely be tempted by the money, given he believes it will end up in his own pockets.

'Fancy yourself an art dealer now, do you?'

'I merely made the introduction. There's nothing in it for me.'

Tassi regards him with suspicion, as if it is inconceivable to him that a person would willingly perform a service for nothing. 'I no longer have the painting.'

He can hear footfall on the stairs. A young man appears. 'Oh, you have company.' He gives Piero the once-over.

'Here is my visitor, so I'm afraid I will have to bid you goodbye, Signor . . . Signor . . . I'm sorry, I don't recall your name.'

'Stiatessi,' says Piero, through his teeth. Tassi knows perfectly well who he is.

Tassi makes another insincere smile and, almost as an afterthought, adds, 'I'm afraid the picture you seek found its way mistakenly into a consignment of old clutter that was destined for the bonfire. Such a shame.'

'A bonfire?' Piero is thrown. It was the last thing he expected.

'Yes.' He makes a vaguely rueful shrug. 'Terrible mistake. Great shame, considering . . . It was my servant, you see. I ensured he was beaten for it. I will make it up to my betrothed.' He places the flat of his hand on Piero's chest and gives him a little push. His tone sharpens. 'But it has nothing to do with you. Do I make myself clear?'

Piero has no choice but to leave.

27. The Pearls

The door bangs downstairs. Artemisia drags herself out of bed into the frigid morning air. She peers out of the window, curious to know who is coming or going at this early hour. The sky is leaden and waterlogged. She can see Giovanni Stiatessi below, striding purposefully away down the via della Croce.

She immediately understands that he has been and gone already – her future decided in her absence. She shoves her slippers on and rushes downstairs. Orazio is in the studio, sober for once. Artemisia's intention had been to confront him, ask him why he didn't call her down to hear what Giovanni had to say, but he looks so gaunt and shrunken with worry, she fears that a show of resentment might break him.

She draws on a smile. 'Was that Giovanni I saw just now, departing?'

'Goodness, that man is a good friend to us, Arti. He told me he'd been up most of the night working out the best way to approach this business with your . . . your . . .' he clears his throat '. . . with Tassi.' He looks ashamed, or she hopes it is shame that is giving him his cowed air.

'And what did the pair of you decide?' Her tone is barbed, so she tempers it. 'What do you think is the best plan?'

'He thinks, if we make a formal accusation, we can win. It will mean –'

'I know what it will mean.' She is perfectly well aware that it will be an ordeal for her, and a public one at that. She doesn't need to hear him say it. 'Is there any other way? Can we not simply forget about it all?' She knows it is futile, that the family honour is at stake. Her father made that abundantly clear last night.

He is shaking his head, solemn as a funeral attendant. 'You know that's not possible, Arti . . .' He leaves something unsaid. She wonders if it is an apology, then laughs inwardly at herself for entertaining such an unlikelihood. Apologies from him are as rare as miracles. 'Giovanni says it will be nothing. You will make your statement. Tassi won't dare contradict it under oath and then he will be rightly punished.'

She doesn't want to think about it.

She can hear her brothers in the kitchen talking easily among themselves. She envies them the simplicity of their lives. One day each of them will encounter a girl who takes their fancy and they will marry. They will be either happy or unhappy but it will at least have been their own decision. She wonders fleetingly whether, given the choice, she would sacrifice her talents if it meant she could have been born a boy, dismissing the notion instantly. She *is* her art and being female is the price she has paid.

The early bells ring and Orazio creaks to his feet, taking his woollen cloak down from the peg. 'I'm going to talk to Quorli, see if he can help us with all this.'

'What do you think *he* can do?' As far as she's been able to tell, Quorli is the sort of man who helps only himself. She remembers his attempted fumble in the cardinal's rooms. The man is a disgrace.

'He has a good deal of influence. It will help to have him on our side.'

He makes it sound like a war. It *is* a war of sorts, she supposes, the men taking up their positions and she caught in the crossfire.

Once he has gone, she joins her brothers. Francesco is reading a pamphlet. She looks over his shoulder, but can't decipher the text, a chip of the old resentment catching in her that she was never taught to read or write as her brothers were – even little Marco knows his letters.

'Cheer up, Arti.' Giulio offers her a pastry. She hasn't any appetite.

They hear someone entering the studio. 'I'll see who it is.' Francesco stands in the doorway. 'What do you think *you*'re doing coming here?'

Artemisia knows exactly who has arrived.

She can see him standing in the entrance holding a small leather box, very carefully, as if it is full to the brim with liquid.

She gets to her feet. Despite herself, she is curious to hear what he has to say. 'Let me deal with this.' The knowledge that she no longer belongs to him emboldens her, but still her heart quickens with apprehension.

'Stay near,' she whispers to Francesco, who nods and stands to one side, like a guard.

'Why are you here?' she asks bluntly, assuming this must be an attempt to salvage his reputation.

'I wanted to make amends – apologize for removing your painting.' Tassi holds the box towards her, opening it, taking out a string of pearls, each one as big as a molar, and the string, long – long enough to hang a man. His eyes are dewy and remorseful. 'I was upset – should have shown more restraint.' The pearls dangle from his hand. She wonders if they are counterfeit like him.

'I'd prefer to have my painting returned.' Her response is cool. He appears so far removed from the brute who accosted her, it is almost impossible to reconcile him with that man. He is like a shape-shifter. But she knows that monster lurks somewhere and mustn't be provoked.

'I'm afraid it's impossible.' He looks down at his gift. 'I no longer have it.'

'Who has it, then?'

'There was an accident. Not exactly an accident – more of a mistake. I was upset.' He seems strangely distressed.

'What's the extent of the damage?' Thorny tendrils sprout inside her but she clips them, telling herself that a damaged painting can always be restored. 'Why didn't you bring it with you?'

'It's . . .' He still holds the necklace in front of him, like an altar boy presenting the sacrament. She watches him carefully. 'I'm afraid it's beyond repair. It was burned.'

'Burned?' She snaps, launching herself at him, beating her fists on his chest wildly, cursing him and scratching at his face.

He doesn't react, stands motionless – a man of wood.

Now she has started she can't stop, has lost all sense of herself, and carries on punching and flailing, like a creature possessed, on and on until she is spent.

Then, as an afterthought, she rips the pearls from his hands, flinging them to the floor.

The string breaks and they spill like hail.

Her heart is thudding. Her fists throb.

She comes to her senses, breath catching in her throat, and steps away, suddenly afraid of his reaction, glancing towards her brother, who has moved closer, in readiness.

But Tassi is immobile, just stares at the pearls scattered over the flagstones.

'My painting was *sold*.' Her voice is shaking. 'I doubt you could even afford to recompense me for its true value.' Her heart gutters as the full reality of the situation sinks in – the thought of having to tell Carlo di Medici what has become of the painting he bought, of having to return the five gold *scudi*, of losing the kind of opportunity that only comes once in a lifetime. 'It was priceless.'

'It was a mistake. I'm so sorry.'

'Sorry for *what*? For destroying my work or for neglecting to tell me you already have a wife?'

He blanches, making a small backward movement, his façade falling away, expression distraught.

'You didn't know that I knew.' She emits a sour cough of laughter. He is nothing to her now. He cannot touch her. 'The truth is, I'm glad. It means I won't be subjected to a life with you.'

He stares at her, mouth opening, seeming on the brink of uttering something but instead shakes his head and removes his hat, crushing it in his fist. She hears its peacock feather snap.

Then he moves minutely towards her, arms outstretched. To the side of her eye she is aware of Francesco priming himself. She doubts she will need his help. The axis of power has shifted and Tassi knows it.

Her brother continues to fix him with a bruising glare.

Tassi reaches out for her hands but she places them

firmly on her hips. 'Please let me explain,' he beseeches. His voice is small and thin. He bows his head, as if to collect himself.

She can see where his pate is thinning and there is dandruff on his indigo shoulders. When he looks up, his expression is desperate, eyes damp. It is quite a performance. 'My intention was never, never . . . to . . .' he stops, gives a small cough, then continues '. . . never to do you harm.'

She doesn't speak but her expression makes her disbelief clear.

'I mean it.' A tear falls down his cheek. It disgusts her. 'I can't stop thinking of you . . . always. I can't explain . . . I've never . . .' He is unable to articulate his feelings.

He is almost as convincing as one of his perspectives – so convincing he appears to have fooled even himself.

He doesn't fool her.

He pulls out a handkerchief and blows his nose. She notices, with a jolt, it has the same embroidered initials as its blood-soaked twin still cached among her things – testimony to his violence. She pushes down the images that spring into her head.

'When were you planning to tell me that you were married?' She doesn't take pains to hide her scorn. 'At the altar, or were you bent on bigamy from the start?'

He seems startled to hear the word 'bigamy', as if he had denied to himself what it really was. 'I *was* married, it's true, when I was too young to know better, but I have been estranged from the woman –'

'*The woman?* Don't you mean your *wife*?' For all his grovelling, she sees the flash of cruelty in those poison green eyes and feels a wash of relief that she is free of him. But she is not free. She will have to testify against him. 'It will be nothing,' Giovanni had said. It won't be 'nothing' to her. She shrivels thinking of the public humiliation.

Hatred knots painfully in her chest.

'I haven't seen my wife for almost a . . . a decade.' Tassi stumbles over his words. 'She . . . she left me for another, and I sought her out but couldn't find her. I thought . . .' his shoulders slump '. . . I truly believed she had died. But when I was in Florence recently, she reappeared wanting money. She had learned of my success and sought to gain from it.' He grabs Artemisia's sleeve with both hands, like a dogged infant. 'You *must* believe me. I wish she were dead so I could be free.'

'You wish she were *dead*? Listen to yourself. That's appalling.' It is plain to her that this poor woman is no more to him than an object standing in his path. If he is seeking to repair his reputation and avoid trouble, he is not making a very good fist of it. 'And please remove your hands from me.'

He does as he is told, pressing them together, wringing them out. 'I didn't mean . . . What I mean is I wish, I wish – I long to be free to wed you.'

'Well, you are not and, besides, you make a great assumption in thinking that I would be willing to take you. To be clear, I'd rather live my life a ruined woman than marry you.' She has heard enough. 'You'd better leave. If my father finds you here, he'll have you skinned alive. And pick these up before someone trips and breaks their neck.' She points to the scattered pearls.

He crouches down to scoop them into his big hands

and, with interminable slowness, he pulls himself back to his feet, replacing his cap. The broken feather sits at an odd angle, making him seem like a clown. Looking at her imploringly, he makes to begin a new plea.

'I've heard enough.' She nods towards Francesco.

He takes Tassi by the arm. 'Time to go.' As an afterthought, he adds: 'Next time we see you, it will be in court.'

Tassi turns, his old haughtiness emerging from behind the veneer of humility. 'What are you talking about?'

'You didn't think we were going to let you dishonour my sister, smear the Gentileschi name and get away with it, did you? The wheels of the law are already turning. Now go back to the pit you came out of.' Francesco pushes him towards the door. He stumbles slightly on the step. And he is gone.

When Francesco turns back to Artemisia he looks distraught. 'I shouldn't have told him, should I? He's going to disappear, isn't he?'

'I hope so.' She hopes he is gone for good. People make themselves disappear all the time, don't they? She is thinking of Tassi's estranged wife, who disappeared for almost a decade.

Part of her smoulders with the desire to be one of those disappeared people, to slip away into the shadows. But the other part, the artist, burns far stronger and it is a force that insists upon her being seen.

'Don't tell Father. He'll kill me for letting it out.' She can see Francesco's fear, the same fear she has often felt in the face of their father's wrath – not any more. The irony strikes her that Francesco could knock Orazio senseless with a single swing of his fist, yet he still wears the panic of the small boy he once was.

'I won't.' She touches a hand to her heart. She realizes that she and Francesco never really talked or shared their confidences. They never even talked about the death of their mother. Artemisia has no idea of the secrets he might be carrying. They never quite trusted each other, were raised like that. This house is a pit of secrets.

'It won't be long before you can go your own way,' she adds. 'He won't have a hold over you for ever.'

Francesco looks doubtful.

'You can always count on me, you know.'

He smiles. 'I'm supposed to be the one to say that to you.'

She had been so envious of him, being a boy but now she sees the burden he carries. He must always be strong, always be the one to hold things together. It makes her feel protective of him.

'I mean it.'

He nods. Nothing more needs saying.

'Did you see those pearls? Hideous.'

'Does he think you're some ancient dowager?' He is smirking.

'They were probably fake, like him.'

'Did you see his face when it dawned on him?'

They can't help the laughter bursting out of them. She has never felt closer to her brother.

28. The Filthy Dog

Orazio approaches Quorli's house, kicking at his hired horse, trying to raise it from its torpid pace. He had rented the animal, not because it was too far to walk but because he felt it might lend him a more thriving air. It does give him a view over the precipitous walls, where he can see a row of cypresses, dark elongated shapes stark against a sky dreary as a painter's rag.

The property is certainly well protected. A vast door is set into an arch, strapped with iron, better suited to a fortress. Orazio waits before it, gathering himself as he runs through what he will say to Quorli. He wonders whether he and Tassi have been laughing for months about the idiot who was duped into giving away his daughter under false pretences. It is early, early enough for Quorli still to be at home. Orazio had barely slept a wink the previous night, his mind turning over and over the predicament he has found himself in.

He tugs on the bell pull, hearing the chime echo faintly within, then, several moments later, the clack of hard-soled boots on flagstones. The door creaks open and a servant, wearing an expensive wool livery and a frosty expression, appears, asking what he wants.

'I'm here to see Furiere Quorli.'

'Is he expecting you?' The servant makes no attempt to disguise his derision. He is intimidatingly tall and muscular – looks as if he might once have been a soldier.

Orazio explains that he has come to discuss a matter of importance relating to the frescos Quorli has commissioned him to paint. He feels that the servant, knowing he is a painter and working for his employer, might be a little more willing to admit him.

'You'd better come in. The Furiere doesn't normally receive calls before noon but since you say it is important . . .' It is manifestly clear from his tone that the servant doubts it is important at all.

As Orazio rides through the arch into the courtyard, he notices the man cast a critical eye over his horse and regrets hiring it now, because the creature is an ancient, broken-winded hack. A large dog barks, tugging on its tether, drool spilling from pink jaws. 'Quiet, Cesare!' orders the servant, and the animal obeys, crouching, ready. 'Who shall I say you are?'

Orazio dismounts, giving his name and the servant thaws a little, seeming to recognize it, pointing wordlessly to a patch of shade with a hitching post and a water trough for the horse. He evidently isn't sufficiently impressed by the Gentileschi name to invite him to wait inside, leaving him instead loitering in the courtyard under the bloodshot eye of the guard dog.

The house, though not excessively large, is very appealing, symmetrical, with a central door beneath a portico, flanked by large windows. To one side an arch of evergreen vegetation leads to the gardens, through which he can see a stone fountain.

He paces, rubbing his hands together to generate a little warmth, irritated by the charm of the place. The babbling of the water is giving him the urge to urinate. He is just considering relieving himself in a dank corner when the servant returns to escort him inside. 'Furiere Quorli says he can spare a quarter-hour. Wait here.'

The hall is large and light, with a staircase sweeping up to a balustraded gallery. On a central table there is a display of small bronzes. One catches his eye, a winged figure. It is Icarus. It would be, he thinks, as if it has been placed there to show him a lesson about his own life. His bladder prods.

A door is thrown open and a beribboned girl runs out in pursuit of a white dog, barely bigger than a rat. She stops momentarily to toss a breathless apology Orazio's way, before chasing the creature into a corridor, leaving peals of laughter in her wake. He supposes she must be one of Quorli's children, or grandchildren, recalling the man's vulgar comments about daughters.

She has left the door open. He shifts along to peer inside, seeing the remains of what appears to be a family breakfast, and an aproned maid shuffling about clearing dishes. Paintings line the walls – he notices a Carracci and what appears to be a Reni and, beside it, his own *Madonna*. The sight of his work displayed so prominently gives him a little boost. The *Susanna* is nowhere to be seen. He assumes it must be in Quorli's private rooms. Another picture at the very far end, not hung but propped up on a chair, catches his eye. He starts, recognizing his daughter's monstrous stolen *Judith*.

'Gentileschi!'

He turns abruptly, guiltily, feeling like a child caught with his fingers in the jam, to find Quorli standing behind him.

'Sorry, did I startle you?' Quorli firmly shuts the door.

'No . . . no . . .' Orazio wonders how long the man has been standing there. 'I was admiring your collection.'

'To what do I owe the pleasure?' From Quorli's impatient tone, pleasure couldn't be further from his mind. 'My servant informed me you needed to discuss the designs for the frescos.'

'Not exactly.' Orazio hesitates, his bladder increasingly uncomfortable. 'It is a matter of some delicacy.' He finds he has stooped into a deferential bow, chastising himself inwardly for appearing so subservient. 'Involving Tassi.'

Quorli is tapping his foot. 'Well, what is it? I'm very short of time.' His mouth snaps in and out of an unpleasant smile.

'As I'm sure you are aware, Tassi was recently betrothed to my daughter.'

Tap, tap, goes Quorli's foot, as he makes a noncommittal 'Hmm.'

Orazio takes a breath. 'I have discovered that Tassi is already married.'

'No!' Quorli makes a great guffaw. 'The filthy dog!'

He is taken aback by the man's response, trivializing such a grave situation. 'I was . . . I wondered if you might be able to shed some light on the matter.'

'It's Tassi's business. His private life is nothing to do with me. We have a professional connection – that is all.'

'I was hoping . . . y-y-you' – he stumbles over his words – 'could help me.' As Orazio says it, he sees there is nothing Quorli can do and he regrets horribly his decision to come here, knows he should have sought Giovanni's counsel before acting.

Somehow he had hoped against hope that Quorli

might be able to tell him it wasn't true, or that Tassi was a widower, or given him some other perfectly reasonable explanation.

'I don't know what you think *I* can do.' Amusement continues to play over Quorli's mouth. 'I understand that this is a question of honour, but I can hardly unmarry them. You'd need His Holiness for that' – he suppresses a snort – 'and only if the union hasn't been consummated. I wouldn't know.'

'I didn't mean . . . I mean . . . I thought you might . . .' Quorli's foot-tapping has started up once more and Orazio senses he is on the brink of being dismissed.

What he wants to say is that he would like Quorli's support in bringing a legal suit against Tassi but just as he is seeking a way to form the request Quorli says: 'If you *will* let your daughter run about in that manner, it's hardly surprising she's been ruined. Wayward daughters, bane of a father's life.'

Orazio's anger sparks and he has to restrain himself from striking the man. 'The fault doesn't lie with Artemisia but with Tassi.' His voice is shaking.

'That's a matter of opinion. I *have* heard rumours about her.' His eyes are twinkling, mocking. 'And Agostino is a handsome devil. I'm sure he is very hard to resist.'

'My daughter is not like that.' He has a heavy sensation in his gut. 'Agostino Tassi forced himself on her.'

'As I said, it's a matter of opinion.' All the pretend cordiality has drained from Quorli's expression. 'The thing is' – he begins to usher Orazio in the direction of the door – 'if you and Agostino are at odds, I'm afraid I will have to find someone else to work with him on the frescos.' He gives Orazio a condescending pat on the shoulder. 'I'm sure you understand my predicament.'

Panic needles him, and he hopes his desperation doesn't show. 'That's just as well. I'm burdened with commissions – was wondering how I would make time.' He will not demean himself by begging for work. 'And I am arranging a more suitable match for Artemisia.' He manages something that looks like a smile but the other man can see through his false bravado if his raised eyebrow is anything to go by.

'Well, I'm glad things are resolved.' Quorli moves him further towards the exit.

'There is one more thing.' Orazio is determined not to leave entirely empty-handed. 'My daughter's *Judith*. You have it.' He points to the closed inner door. 'Tassi took it without permission, and it will have to be paid for.' He sounds firm.

'A *Judith*? I've no idea what you're talking about.'

'I saw it, with my own eyes.' Orazio's voice rises.

'You must be mistaken.' Quorli claps his hands and the rigid-faced servant appears as if from nowhere. 'Signor Gentileschi is leaving. Would you see him out?'

Orazio begins to protest, the last of his restraint shattering as he accuses Quorli of theft and worse. The servant takes him by the arm and manhandles him out into the yard where it has begun to drizzle. He relieves his bladder in a corner before mounting the old hack and plodding back across the gloomy city. Having returned the horse to the stables, he stops at the tavern for a much-needed drink before returning home.

He has barely got through the door when Giovanni

appears. He does not look happy. 'Thank God you're back. I've been looking everywhere for you. The bastard's scarpered.'

'Who, Tassi?'

'Yes, of course Tassi. As you know, I reported the offence to the judge's office first thing this morning. I've just had word that they sent an official to his apartment to ask some preliminary questions, but he wasn't there.'

'So, he wasn't at home.' Orazio shrugs. 'He'll be back.'

'No. The porter said he'd left in a hurry, with luggage, saying he didn't know when he'd be returning.' Giovanni sinks onto the corner of the workbench with a sigh bereft of his usual optimism. 'I'm so sorry, Orazio.'

'Did the porter say where he was going? We must get after him.' Orazio makes for the door urgently. 'You have good horses, don't you? We haven't a moment to spare.'

Giovanni puts out a hand to stop his friend. 'It's no good. We don't know where he went. It's getting late. He could be anywhere by now.'

Orazio inwardly curses the hours he wasted this morning. 'How did he find out? Do you think someone from the judge's office warned him?' Orazio would like to pull the loose tongue from the perpetrator's mouth with his own hands.

'I don't see how they would have been able to. They sent someone round there immediately and he was already gone.' Giovanni meets the other man's agitated gaze. 'Now's not the time to worry about that.'

'What's happened?' It is his daughter, standing in the kitchen doorway. She has a daunting spark in her eye.

'I'm afraid Tassi left the city to avoid being questioned.'

'Oh, well,' she says, seeming entirely unconcerned, returning to the kitchen where he can hear her whispering with her brother.

'I must go,' says Giovanni. 'You ask around for clues as to Tassi's destination. I'll send word to Florence to see if he turns up there, but if he does it might be wise to wait for him to return of his own accord. If we try to intervene while he's outside Roman jurisdiction, he's likely to disappear again.'

'Why would he come back if he knows he'll face charges?' Despondence trickles into Orazio, like sand through an hourglass. He is beginning to wonder if he'll ever clear his daughter's name.

'A fool returns to his folly, as a dog to its vomit.' Giovanni makes a face. 'He has the cardinal's favour here in Rome. The lure of the fame *that* could bring him will be too strong to resist. He has commissions here to fulfil. You mark my words, he'll be back.'

In the kitchen Orazio stands on a stool to reach the grappa from the high shelf.

Artemisia gives him a withering look, pointing to the bottle with a sharp finger. 'I thought this was going to stop.'

Her tone is surprisingly soft, but still he feels the judgement beneath it and has to prevent himself from countering that it is none of her business. 'Quorli was most unhelpful,' he says instead, jumping to the floor, bottle in hand. 'And your painting . . . your *Judith*. I saw it in his house.'

'You must have been mistaken. My *Judith* was destroyed. Tell him, Franco.'

'He said he'd burned it.'

'Burned it?' He is about to tell his daughter of his

260

absolute certainty that it was her painting he saw only that morning, but stops himself. He wouldn't put it past her to cause a furore and try to confront Quorli. He can't risk causing more trouble. 'When did he say that? When did you see him?'

'Earlier?' Francesco shrinks back slightly and Orazio wonders what he is afraid of.

'You saw him earlier? You should have told me.'

'We're telling you now.'

'Did he say anything about leaving Rome – where he was going?'

'Not a thing.' Francesco shrugs.

'You didn't tell him about my petition – the legal proceedings?'

Artemisia gives him a contemptuous look. 'Do you think we're stupid?'

Orazio removes the stopper from the bottle but Artemisia gently prises it from his grip, sniffing it with a grimace. 'I don't know how you can drink this stuff. It smells worse than turpentine.'

Only his shame stops him wresting it from her hands. His whole being is crying out for the blessed befuddlement it could bring him, all his worries disappearing into the air, like steam from a pan. All he can do is watch as she opens the back door and pours it into the kitchen drain, making him wonder when his daughter became his keeper.

29. Saint Lucy's Eyes

Orazio's bedchamber smells of beeswax polish and dust. At last it has been left unlocked. Zita can hear the rumble of his voice downstairs as she tiptoes across the floor to the bed. She crouches, running her hand beneath the mattress, under the pillows. A bottle on its side collects dust in a dark corner. She rummages in the coffer where he keeps his trinkets, and in the chest where he stores his clothes. The ruby cross is nowhere to be found.

A floorboard creaks outside. She turns, heart in mouth, to see the door opening. Its hinges whine. She swallows, looking round for a place to hide, all the hairs on her arms rising. Her mind runs wild, seeking an explanation for her presence in Orazio's bedchamber – the place she is not allowed, not even to clean.

The door falls open to reveal Artemisia.

Relief floods through her.

'What are you doing? If he finds you in here . . .' She doesn't need to say it: Zita is well aware of what would happen were Orazio to find her going through his private things.

'I was looking for the cardinal's cross.'

'Oh, that!' Zita follows Artemisia out onto the landing. 'Why?'

'I want to give it back,' she says, under her breath. 'Get it off my conscience.'

'I shouldn't worry about it. The cardinal's probably not even noticed – must have dozens like it.'

'But . . .' Zita can't find a way to explain that she wants to atone properly for the sin.

'How were you going to return it, anyway?'

'I don't know.' Zita hadn't really thought of what she would do once it was found.

'I wouldn't bother. Let it be Father's problem.' Artemisia seems not to understand Zita's predicament: that while Orazio has the cross in his possession, he has the means to threaten her. Though it was months ago that he confronted her with it, she still wakes in the night sweating. She dreams of the Sybille's knotted strings tightening, breaking her fingers and, worse, a chopper whacking off her hand at the wrist, blood everywhere, like in that horrible painting.

'We'll be late for mass.' They go downstairs, where the others are milling by the door, putting on their coats and hats.

Zita worries at her rosary as she walks. She hasn't even thought of pilfering anything since. It was a lesson learned, at least.

The sky begins to spit as they reach the piazza, and they see a figure running towards them. It is Piero, his face dashed with trouble. 'What's wrong?' Artemisia holds back, while the rest of the family continue towards the church.

He slips something to her. 'From Carlo. He wants you to keep it.'

Zita stands a few steps away, pretending not to listen, and can see Artemisia weighing a purse in her palm.

People pass, looking sideways at them. Word is out

about Artemisia's shame. 'I don't know how you can stay in that house,' a woman in the market had said to Zita the other day. 'Den of sin.' She had pretended not to hear.

Zita hears Artemisia say: 'All of it? No. I can't.' She tries to give the purse back to Piero but he won't take it.

'He insisted upon it, says you've lost enough as it is. But that's not why I'm here. I've come to say goodbye.'

'Goodbye?' Artemisia looks dejected. Zita knows how close the two of them are and has come round to him, even though he's one of *those*.

'I have to leave Rome,' he is saying. 'My father's ailing – need to keep an eye on the business – look after Mother.' Zita catches the two of them weaving fingers briefly, like secret lovers. 'Don't know when I'll be back. Didn't want to leave without saying goodbye.'

'Is it serious – your father?'

He responds with a distressed expression and a shake of the head before disappearing into the crowds.

'What was all that about?' Zita pretends she is hearing it for the first time, when Artemisia explains that Piero is leaving. She points to the purse, unable to resist asking, 'What's that for?'

'This?' Artemisia swings it like a pendulum, before tucking it away in her jacket. 'I asked Piero to return the down-payment for the *Judith* but the buyer wouldn't accept it. Apparently he said I'd faced enough misfortune.'

'Well, that's the truth.'

'I'll be able to pay you properly to pose for me.' Artemisia has barely put brush to canvas in months – this is a good sign, thinks Zita. 'I want to paint a Saint Lucy.'

'Which one is she?' Zita runs through the saints in her

head: Agnes, burned; Catherine, breaking wheel; Dorothy, decapitated; Justina, the sword . . . 'I can't remember.'

'Eyes.'

'Oh, yes.'

'She gouged her eyes out, so she no longer had to see men's lustful looks.' Artemisia has the intense air about her that she gets when she has an idea. 'I think I want my Lucy mid-act – one eye out.'

'I don't know why you still want to paint things like that.' Zita is thinking of the other picture, all that blood getting into her nightmares. She is secretly glad it was stolen so she doesn't have to look at it any more.

She is not sure she wants to be depicted with one eye, dripping scarlet tears. But she needs the money. Her husband has yet to send word of his return, and she can feel the beginnings of worry stirring. 'I once saw a painting of Saint Lucy. She was very beautiful.' She remembers quite clearly the golden-haired girl gazing straight out of the picture, holding out her hand – two eyes on her palm, like sweets.

'I'm not interested in depicting pretty falsehoods. I want people to see it and imagine how it must have felt – the truth of a young girl like that digging her own eyes out.' Artemisia laughs. 'You should see your face, Zita. You *are* funny.'

All through mass Artemisia was feeling the wrench of Piero's departure and still is as they leave the church. The family group moves slowly through the packed streets. When the crowd thins Francesco strides ahead and Giulio runs behind him with the girls, one holding each of his hands, turning out of sight into the via della Croce.

As Artemisia turns the corner she hears Francesco yelling, 'What in Hell's name?'

He is rushing back to her. 'Don't look at it, Arti. You don't need to see that.'

'At what?' Something is happening. A small ball of fear tightens in her stomach.

'What is it?' She shakes off his grip. 'Let me see.'

Following the trajectory of her father and brothers' silent stares, she looks up to see vast black dripping letters scrawled over the front wall of their house.

'What does *casa puttana* mean, Mama?' asks one of the girls.

'Whorehouse,' says Artemisia, under her breath, realizing, like a sharp jab to the gut, that their house has been defaced because of her: her disgrace for all to see.

They stand united in a suspended moment of disbelief, staring at the words, until Orazio roars: 'Whoever did this is a dead man.'

People have begun to gather, pointing and jeering.

Orazio growls at them – 'Which one of you bastards?' – provoking a hail of laughter and booing.

Francesco curses them, ripping off his jacket, priming himself for a fight. Artemisia pulls him away.

Zita appears with a basin of foaming water and a stiff-bristled brush. Artemisia snatches the brush, dunking it in the liquid. The lye stings her eyes as she scrubs at the paint, thick and viscous as tar.

Thoughts burn their way through her. How selfish she has been not to understand the impact of her personal disgrace on her whole family. It's a wonder they don't all resent her. Francesco and Giulio join in the scrubbing, the three siblings silent, the sound of their brushes drowning the taunts of the gathered throng. Her arm aches with the effort but the black paint refuses to shift.

Her hands blister and swell from the lye, but she can't stop scouring until Francesco finally forces her, prising the brush from her fingers. 'Enough now, Arti. It's no good. We'll have to paint over it, but not now – when they've all gone.'

'Everyone will see it.' Artemisia's protest is futile. Enough people have seen it already for all of Rome to know of it by vespers.

They might well be able to remove the words, strip them off with spirit, paint over them, cover them with a layer of render, but the true stain is indelible.

Once inside, they close the shutters and sit in silence while Zita prepares something to eat.

Artemisia is the first to speak: 'What will we do? We can't hide in here for ever.'

Orazio gives a long, pensive sigh, and she knows, from his apologetic expression, that she is not going to like what he is about to say. 'The best thing for us all.' He wavers, folding and unfolding his hands. 'The best thing might be for you to take the veil.'

Her world seems so flimsy it might collapse in on itself, like a tissue-paper house, crushed, with her inside. Her brothers, Zita, the girls, are all looking at their feet. Little Luca clangs a fork repeatedly on the table: clack, clack, clack.

'Never.'

PART III

As long as I live I will have control over my being.

Artemisia Gentileschi

A Song for the Virgin Martyrs

. . .

And sainted CECILIA, *fingers fine as feathers,*
Lute cradled to white breast.
Heart ringing praise, voice clear as the lark.
Fine neck struck thrice
Three days she lives
Three days she sings
And still she sings.
And immaculate, eyeless LUCY, seeing in infinite clarity, THE
   LORD.
And peerless DOROTHY, proffering blessed fruits, as her head
   rolls.
And CATHERINE, voice chiming the word of THE LORD
The salvation of a hundred-hundred, heathens.
Suffered she the agony of evil instruments: the breaking wheel
Flawless body unyielding,
Spotless mind resisting
Girded by faith, her goodness shining . . . **[some text missing]**
And perfect AGATHA, stretched and whipped, her breasts . . .
   [text illegible]
. . . *AGNES, docile as the lamb,*
dragged naked to the house of sin.
Each man blinded, who sought to defile her.
Her prayer so pure as to make her hair spin forth as flax
To cover her nakedness.

Mirror of purity
Bound to the stake,
Untouched by flame.
Untouched by evil.

**Anonymous fragment, c. fourteenth century – trans.
F. E. Lamenter**

30. Shame

Six months later . . .

The apartment in the Borgo Santo Spirito is poky and drab, three half-derelict rooms, all looking out over a knacker's yard with the grim view of penned animals, swivel-eyed with fear, awaiting their fate. Orazio cannot help but feel a kinship with them. Down a set of rickety wooden steps at the back is an old warehouse, dilapidated and freezing cold, which they have set up as a studio space.

There are few advantages to the gloomy upper rooms. Yet they are close to the Stiatessis' house, which looks down on them from a little way up the slope with an air of embarrassment about the proximity of its down-at-heel neighbour. Heat from the bread ovens of the bakery below spreads up through the building, meaning less expenditure on winter firewood, though now the warmer weather has arrived, the place can become unbearably hot. At least the scent of freshly baked bread masks the pervasive stench of rot.

And it is a relief after the abuse of via della Croce, the neighbours making comments and threats, the local shop-keepers increasingly reluctant to serve them and Artemisia had only to sit in view of a window for someone to shout a crude slur. So now they are here, on the other side of the river. Once again living in a place half the size of the last, costing a third as much, where the neighbours don't know them.

A loud hammering starts up and soon a few bricks in the opposite wall spill to the floor, sending a cloud of grit and dust into the room.

The sweaty face of a builder appears through the hole. 'These walls are thicker than I thought. Taken me longer. It'll cost more.'

Orazio sighs. 'Just get on with it.' He is totting up in his head what he has spent from his dwindling savings this month. They are making a door between the adjacent room that Zita has taken on her own, since her husband's delayed return. Orazio doesn't know how she is paying for it – doesn't want to.

The builder gives him a new price. He haggles it down, not much but every little helps. His commissions have all but dried up, though Giovanni has asked him and Artemisia to paint portraits of his grandchildren. Out of pity, he suspects.

He tells himself that when Tassi returns he will be able to clear the family name and everything will change for the better. But he has been telling himself this for months now and Tassi has disappeared without a trace. Even Quorli couldn't say what has become of him. When Orazio paid a second visit to his house a couple of months ago he hadn't been admitted beyond the outer gate, had been obliged to send a message in with the hatchet-faced servant. Now Quorli is gone – succumbed to a winter fever.

The interminable banging starts up again, forcing Orazio to retreat to the studio, where his children are hard at work whitewashing the walls. He watches them unseen for a while. They laugh and chat easily with each other, falling into a heavy silence when they notice his presence. Little Marco, wielding a vast brush, is covered from head to toe with paint. A drool of white falls from the bristles to the floor. He looks at his father, cowed, apologizing, apprehension stamped over his face. His fear makes Orazio sad.

He smiles, saying a little paint on the floor doesn't matter, while knowing they are, all of them, with their sideways glances, remembering the many occasions when he lost his temper over less. He comments on what a good job they are doing, what a great improvement it is, but still his youngest son looks wary. It is his own doing. Since he has brought his drinking under control he has been able to see the damage he has done.

Every moment of weakness, when the cravings get their claws into him, he reminds himself of the destruction he has wreaked on his family. So much of his past has gone, disappeared into a vat of darkness. He only needs to feel the coldness of his offspring, their caution around him, the sense of being held at arms' length, shut out, to be reminded of his failure as a father.

Artemisia is the coldest of them all. She paints alone now, working on her own projects, never discussing ideas with him as she might have done once. The distant, formal tone she takes breaks his heart. He has tried to unburden himself in the confession box, but each time he begins to articulate the extent of his shame he feels the whole fabric of his being threatening to unravel altogether.

A row of canvases is propped up against the back wall, his daughter's works, all incomplete, like ghosts. On one she has attempted a new version of her stolen *Judith*, her

275

frustration visible in the scrawl of dark paint obliterating half of the image. He understands. It is hard, if not impossible, to recapture the moment of inspiration that brings a work to life.

Anger builds inside him as he remembers the brief exchange he had with Quorli's widow after the funeral. 'I don't know why you feel you have a claim to the work. My husband obtained it legally. There is paperwork to prove it.' She'd said she would return it 'for a sum' – an astronomical sum, as it turned out, one he would never be able to raise.

He looks over his daughter's sketches. No sweet nymphs or cherubs for Artemisia, but a roll call of Virgin Martyrs, all unfinished: Saint Lucy drips gore from one eye, Saint Dorothy stares up from beneath inky lashes proffering her basket of fruit, a knife-stabbed red apple to the fore, and Saint Agnes is half strangled by her hair. They will never be commissioned. No one wants to see the saints like that. Even her self-portraits look out at the viewer grimly, as if they have glimpsed the void.

'Listen,' says Artemisia, holding a finger to her lips. They all stop what they are doing. A thin thread of music, barely audible, suspends them in a moment of ecstasy. The mass from the Vatican chapel is something they were unable to hear from the via della Croce.

'Oy!' comes a shout, snapping the thread of song. 'I'm looking for Signor Gentileschi.' A messenger, waving a letter.

'You have found him.' Orazio feels a faint frisson of optimism. He has all but given up hoping for news that Tassi has been apprehended.

He rips it open to find a curt missive from Guido Reni – whom he once considered a dear friend and colleague – informing him that he will no longer have need of Giulio as a studio apprentice, rescinding on a commitment made a year ago. *You know how these things are, Orazio. I have to consider my pupils. It's a matter of appearances. I hope you will understand.*

He screws the paper into a ball and flings it away. His coffin is more nails than wood, these days.

Artemisia picks up the crumpled letter, though she already knows it holds yet another piece of bad news. She can feel her father's stare as she tries to make sense of the jumbled words. 'What does it say? Tell me!'

Giulio had been so looking forward to his apprenticeship. A pallet on Reni's studio floor would be luxury compared to the place they've found themselves in, where the gaps in the windows cause neck-cricking draughts and rats the size of cats run behind the walls. They come so close at night she has the sense that they are scuffing the inside of her skull.

She is hollow with the knowledge that the deprivation they find themselves in is because of her.

She considers how their lives might have taken another path, had she been more obedient. Had she charmed Modenese she might be living in a puce-rendered villa now, marble floors sleek as ice, great coffin-sized vats filled with cut flowers. She might be becoming fat with child, eating sugared fancies in the afternoons with her new mother-in-law and painting all the dull wives of her husband's friends with a pretend smile smeared over her face. At least her family would not have to skulk about, mired in her disgrace.

But she knows that she could never have accepted such a destiny. And even this life is better than that other fate – the one so narrowly avoided: a life spent as Tassi's wife.

Packing up her portfolio of drawings she prepares to accompany her father on a visit to a potential client who wants a likeness of his wife. He is new to Rome but no doubt he will hear of the Gentileschis' shame and politely turn them down, no matter how much they undercut the other painters in consideration.

They walk in silence, the bridge bathed in sun as they cross the river. But the weather turns in an instant, the bright March sky now a boiling bruise, stealing away the warmth and light. Rain begins to fall in big gobs, soaking through her coat, and somewhere she hears, whispering from the past, her mother's voice: *Don't go out in the rain, Arti love, you'll catch your death.* Would she welcome joining her mother in death? Some would say such thoughts come from the devil and must be resisted with prayer. Artemisia wishes it were that easy.

They plod past the turning to the via della Croce, going further round to avoid having to walk past the old house. She wonders if dark smudges are pushing through the three layers of paint they had needed to cover those words. The rain comes in gusts now. She holds her bag over her head, though it provides little protection.

Up ahead she sees her girlhood friend, Lisabetta, with her sister Gianna. They both lumber behind vast bellies. How fortunate that they will have babies of the same age and be able to raise them together. Artemisia lifts her hand in greeting. They skirt her and her father as if they are leprous, Lisabetta's eyes swiftly slanting down and away. The sister mutters something inaudible with a scowl – Gianna was always full of sanctimony. She has become used to this, but from old friends, it smarts.

Would she exchange her life for theirs? The answer is no.

The cobbles in the piazza, slick and dark, are spotted with fallen almond blossom that has gathered in wet drifts. The rain thins to a fine mizzle and the sun forces a few rays through a break in the clouds, gilding the far rooftops, making the scene like a painted backdrop. A distant shadow moves fast towards them, transforming, as it nears, into a flock of starlings. They land on the wet ground in a chaos of oily black, moving, flitting, gossiping, taking off once more into the air, each bird seeming part of some secret unifying harmony.

Artemisia is so drawn to the birds, now whistling away into the distance, that she doesn't notice Giovanni running towards them, shouting and waving, until he is upon them. He wears a grimace. Artemisia girds herself for more bad news.

'Thank God I've found you. Been everywhere. Have you heard?'

She sees that what she'd initially thought a grimace is in fact a jubilant grin.

'He's back. He's been arrested.'

Orazio bursts into life, clapping his hands with a cheer, and the two men slam into an embrace, moving in a circle as if they are dancing. She watches them, heavy, as if her veins are clogged with lead. Their elation has nothing to do with her.

'And what's more,' says Giovanni, now with one hand

on each of Orazio's shoulders, gazing into his eyes like a lover, 'his wife has died.' He seems, suddenly, to grasp the unseemliness of his glee, as he crosses himself and douses his laughter.

Orazio says nothing for some time, appearing to concentrate on a scrap of paper blowing across the ground, a ruffle on his brow. A slow smile breaks over his face and he looks towards her.

She knows exactly what he is thinking. Dread expands inside her, as the wheel of her fate, so long in suspension, cranks into motion once more.

'No,' she says quietly, and then again, louder: 'No!'

But the men aren't listening.

31. God is Wrong

Brick dust is everywhere. Zita's eyes are gritty and Luca is rasping. She pulls him onto her lap to replace his grubby shift with a clean one that she knows will be filthy within half an hour.

His ribcage labours to drag air into his small lungs. She buttons him into a woollen jacket and opens the window, hoping to clear the air, glad that the doorway between her room and the Gentileschis' apartment is now knocked through. They will no longer have to take three flights of stairs, go out of one front door and in through another, climb a further three flights, to go between them. A large sheet of canvas has been temporarily hung over the opening until the door is fitted. More hammering and clouds of sawdust to look forward to. But she's worried about Luca, who was already wheezy from the damp before the building work even began.

The girls are in the corner, quiet for once, with their sewing. She stokes the fire and sets a pot over it to heat some water. Once it is steaming, she pours it into a bowl with a handful of thyme and, covering Luca's head with a cloth, coaxes his face over the steam.

She rubs his thin back, watching as one of the cats skulks round the edge of the room with a mouse in her jaws. She had tried to prevent the girls bringing them when they moved but is now glad they did. The place is rife with vermin.

'Am I disturbing you?' Artemisia is peeping round the canvas hanging. 'I have to get away from Father.' She looks pale and troubled. 'Can I stay with you?'

Zita is wondering if she means she wants to stay for the night and how she will make space in her already cramped quarters. But something is wrong. 'What is it?'

Artemisia is shaking her head, pacing back and forth. 'They've arrested Tassi. Father's renewed the petition against him.' She directs a blighted gaze at the other woman. 'Zita, I don't think I can cope with a trial. I will be picked apart in public. If we think things are bad now, they will be a thousand-fold worse.' She inhales sharply. 'I don't know if I have the strength any more.' Zita hardly recognizes this Artemisia, has never seen her daunted by anything. 'Father's trying to make me accept Tassi's hand after all – wants me to go to the Corte Savella where he's being held and tell him so.' She looks spent. 'It's that or testify. I don't know which is worse.'

Zita doesn't understand. 'But he's not free to marry . . .'

'His wife died.' There is a long silence before Artemisia adds, 'Conveniently,' her tone barbed. Zita doesn't know what to think of that word. Does she mean she thinks he killed his wife? Surely she doesn't think that. But she is remembering how he was that day in the vineyard, how he turned into a monster before her eyes.

She removes the cloth from Luca's head and wipes the condensation off his face. His breathing sounds better, at least.

'What will you do?' Zita is trying to put herself in her friend's position. 'Perhaps it wouldn't be so bad, a trial –'

Artemisia claps out her response before Zita has a

chance to finish. 'For God's sake! Of course it will be *so* bad. I will be made publicly to prove that I was –' She stops short of saying the word, glancing at the girls in the corner. They have halted their needlework and are listening avidly. 'You must know what that entails.' With a fixed stare she circles the fingers of one hand, around the fingers of the other, holding them up, crushing them tightly until their tips turn purple. 'I'll have to prove my testimony is true.'

Zita feels suddenly sick, remembering the threats Orazio made to her. She can see the ruby cross dangling from his fingers: *You know what they'll do if you deny it?* She imagines the knotted strings of the Sybille wrapped round Artemisia's fingers, pulled tighter and tighter again, and then more until they break.

'Only if Tassi denies it,' Zita says. '*I* will tell them the truth . . .' Her words trail away before she adds, 'He won't deny it. He wouldn't dare.'

'Why would Tassi come clean if it meant he'd be convicted?' Artemisia slumps onto a stool, her skirts spreading around her. She has grown even thinner, her collarbones sticking out. 'I haven't been able to paint. Lost my touch.' She looks at her open palms as if searching for something. 'It's as if my hands refuse to express what is in my head.'

Zita has seen all of Artemisia's failed attempts in the studio, watched her, at the end of a long day's work, furiously scrape every last smudge of paint off her canvas, like a woman possessed. Then she sits staring at nothing for hours on end.

'Wouldn't it be easier just to marry him?' Catching Artemisia's blistering look, she adds, 'If he can prove to you that he's learned his lesson. People can change.' Zita is thinking of all the saints who were once sinners.

Artemisia shakes her head. 'You make everything seem so simple, Zita.'

Artemisia broods in silence while Zita begins to prepare supper, chopping onions, her eyes smarting.

Eventually Artemisia says, 'I'm to choose between one hell or another. Doesn't it make you furious that women have so few choices?' She looks worn with despair.

Zita has never really thought of the disadvantages of being a woman, of which Artemisia speaks often, only the advantages, the lack of responsibility, God's gift of being able to bear children. Too many things to choose between might confuse her, make her fretful. 'It's how God made woman – from Adam's rib, to be his helpmeet.'

'Then God is wrong!' Artemisia's blasphemy cracks loudly in the air, like the snap of a harness breaking, bringing with it the runaway horse, the carriage crashing into the ditch, the passengers flung asunder, the broken skulls.

The girls stare from the corner, in shock.

'You mustn't say that. Not even think it.' Zita is appalled.

'I can say what I like.'

Zita doesn't know how to reply, knows no good will come of challenging the quick-witted Artemisia.

They hear the street door bang, followed by the sound of booted feet mounting the stairs, more than one pair.

'Are you expecting anyone?' Artemisia looks tense, as tense as Zita feels. Something is not quite right.

'Perhaps it's Porzia.' Zita doesn't know why she says this. It is clearly not Porzia unless she is wearing two pairs of hobnailed boots.

Neither woman moves, not even when a sharp rap sounds out and a male voice: 'Open up!'

'Aren't you going to let them in?' asks one of the girls, who has run to the door and opened it before Zita has the chance to stop her.

Two men step inside, taking in the mean surroundings. One brushes a smear of dust from his breeches. 'Is this the dwelling of Signora Zita Medaglia?'

Zita stands too quickly, feeling faint, holding the back of the chair to stop herself falling.

'Who wants her?' Artemisia steps towards them so they can't come further into the room.

'We have an order from the judge to bring her to the Tor di Nona.'

The floor gives way beneath Zita. Everything goes black for a moment and when she comes round she is propped up by the arm of one of the men.

'What business has the judge with Signora Medaglia?' Artemisia meets the larger of them dead in the eyes.

'She is to be questioned about her involvement in a crime.'

Dread brings Zita to her senses with a jolt. This is Orazio's doing. Why would he tell the authorities about the stolen cross after all this time?

'What sort of crime?' Artemisia's tone is commanding, forcing them to listen to her.

'It concerns a violation. More than that I am not at liberty to say.'

'It wasn't . . . I didn't . . .' Zita pleads, trying to wriggle out of the man's contracting grip, cursing the impulse that made her take that cross, feeling all her sins catching her up.

Luca, sensing his mother's upset, begins to wail.

'The judge will find no wrongdoing in Signora Medaglia.' Artemisia puts her arm around Zita's shoulders, saying quietly, 'You have no choice but to go with them. I'll look after the children. It'll only be for an hour or so, I'm sure. You'll be back by compline.'

Zita knows it will not be an hour or so. It is already almost dark. She bolsters herself for a night in the Tor di Nona, an image setting itself in her mind of the heads on stakes that sit above the entrance.

The girls look frightened, not understanding what is happening and Luca's bawling has become more urgent. Artemisia picks him up, attempting to soothe him as Zita is led out and down the stairs, alarm flapping about her head.

Orazio is standing beside the street door, seeming to understand what is going on without being told. As Zita is led past, he leans in close to her and whispers, 'Don't forget.' She knows, from his tone, it is a threat. He gives her a cold smile and makes the shape of a cross in the air with his finger as she is pulled away, half tripping on the steps.

Luca is inconsolable. Strings of mucus are trailing down his face. His body is hot and heavy in Artemisia's arms. She has no idea how to stop him wailing. Balancing him on her hip, she pours a cup of milk for him. He knocks it from her hand. It sloshes over her skirts. At a loss, she tells the girls to put their night things into a bag. Their pale forlorn little faces look at her for answers.

They walk the short way up the slope to the Stiatessis' house. Porzia answers the door, immediately understanding that something is very wrong, inviting them in without wanting an explanation. Taking Luca, she magically pacifies him until he nestles his head into her shoulder. Then she sends the girls into the kitchen, calling for the maid to give them something to eat.

'They came for Zita . . .' Porzia's face registers increasing concern as Artemisia explains what has occurred.

'I feared this might happen. I saw your father's latest petition against Tassi before it was submitted to the judge.' The maid carefully extracts the sleeping Luca from Porzia's arms.

'You saw his petition. He showed it to you?' Artemisia is furious at having been left in the dark and doesn't fully understand. 'And what's Father's petition got to do with Zita?'

'He didn't show it to me. I *came across* it among Giovanni's papers.' She raises her brow. 'In it your father says what happened to you was as a result of Zita's complicity. Is that true? It can't be.'

'It's not true. Father forced Zita to leave me alone with Tassi.'

'Forced? How so?' Porzia looks in equal parts horrified and puzzled. 'I know Zita's not the sharpest of women but surely . . . I mean, she was engaged as your chaperone. She would have known not to leave you alone. I don't understand.'

'He threatened her with . . .' Artemisia realizes she can't risk exposing Zita's theft, not even to Porzia. 'You know what he's like.'

She is glad when Giovanni appears before Porzia has a chance to press the point. 'What's the commotion?'

They explain about Zita's arrest. 'We have to do something,' Artemisia says. 'Get her released.'

Giovanni is already shrugging on his coat. 'I'll go straight there. Where have they taken her?'

'The Tor di Nona.'

'Goodness knows why they're holding her *there*.' He makes a grimace. 'It's unlikely I'll be able to secure her release tonight but at least I can find out what's behind this.' He puts his hat on, pulling it down over his ears. 'I don't know why Tassi should have the comparative luxury of the Corte Savella and she . . .' He doesn't bother to finish. They all know it is a question of connections and Tassi still has many.

Porzia tugs a large woollen shawl from a peg and takes a cushion from a chair, shoving them into her husband's arms. 'And she'll need victuals, clean water.' Artemisia abrades herself silently for not being the one to think of Zita's basic comforts.

When he has gone Porzia says, 'What on God's earth did your father think he was doing implicating poor Zita?' She closes the door and wipes a palm slowly over her brow. 'That man! Sometimes I despair.' Lightly touching Artemisia's sleeve, she adds, with a sigh, 'Why would he do this?'

Artemisia has no answer. All she can think is that incidental damage is nothing to him. She, Artemisia, is incidental damage too.

'He wants me to wed Tassi' – her voice falters – 'now he is free.' The reality of what her father is asking of her sinks in and with it comes a wave of panic. 'Wants me to go to the Corte Savella and accept his hand.'

'I know. He came to discuss the matter with us earlier.'

288

Porzia looks at Artemisia with her steady dark eyes. 'I wonder if it might not be the easier path to take.'

'Marry him? Surely you can't mean . . .' Artemisia's voice comes out strange and high-pitched, like the voice of another. 'Not you too.'

Porzia can no longer meet her eye. What had seemed so intolerable when Zita suggested it barely an hour ago, now seems unavoidable. The hall clock ticks loudly, the sound inside her head marking time's march towards the inevitable. The air feels thin. She opens the window, leaning out to fill her lungs with several fast, deep breaths.

Porzia smooths a stray curl away from Artemisia's face. Her fingers are cool. Artemisia has a fleeting memory of her mother combing her hair and feels choked by the gesture.

She shivers. Porzia draws her inside and shuts the window.

They are silent for a few moments, until Porzia breaks the spell. 'It wouldn't hurt to visit Tassi. Find out what he has to say. See if he's contrite.'

Artemisia is paralysed by her predicament. For all the talk of it being her choice, all the gentle coaxing, she suspects the decision will be made for her ultimately. 'I don't know.' She wants to shout, rant, vent her anger, but she is utterly exhausted – her body has given up resistance before her mind.

Porzia continues, as if Artemisia has already agreed to go. 'Giovanni and I will come with you. Best if your father stays well away from Tassi, since he is bringing the charge.' She takes both of Artemisia's hands in her own. 'What about it?' She enfolds her in her arms. Her shoulder smells faintly of lavender.

Artemisia breaks abruptly away. 'All right.' Her response is barely audible.

She is well aware that if she accepts Tassi's hand, her family's problems will melt away, instantly forgotten. She will be the sacrifice, though no one will see it so. The clock ticks on. She controls the impulse to smash it to the floor, stop dead its relentless march.

'Let's fetch Francesco for moral support, and we'll be ready to go as soon as Giovanni gets back.'

'Go there now? But it's so late.'

'The sooner the better. Don't you think?'

Artemisia doesn't know what she thinks any more, so submits to Porzia's tender control.

32. Corte Savella

The evening is mild and it is not far. They cross the bridge. The Tor di Nona is a dark shape against the dusk. Aware of the swell of water beneath them with its deadly hidden currents, Artemisia can't quite erase the image from her mind of poor Zita terrified, crouched in the corner of a cell.

She hears the wet slap as a vessel glides by, a raucous song rising from it. A half-dozen or so birds sit on the water, bobbing, grey in the gloom. One takes flight and the others follow. She might once have imagined joining them, soaring upward into the evening, but now they leave her with an empty feeling, as if even the idea of freedom has been rendered unimaginable to her.

'She's comfortable at least,' Giovanni is explaining in response to Porzia's questions about Zita's welfare. 'I'll have a word with the judge's office first thing tomorrow, but the gaoler seems to think she's to be held at least until the trial begins. I'll offer a bond. That might get her back home.'

It hangs in the air, unsaid, that all the charges will be dropped the minute Artemisia does as everyone wants. Everyone's fate depends on her.

Francesco whispers, 'It'll be all right,' though they both know this is not true.

They continue in silence towards the Corte Savella.

She can picture her father's face as they left, his undisguised pleasure to learn she intended to succumb to his will. Rather than look at him, she cast her eyes about their lodgings. One of the two cheap tallow candles spat and died, gloom descending over the place. What light was left caught on a damp patch of ancient panelling, laced with worm. The ceiling sagged low and the collection of dilapidated furniture looked forlorn. Artemisia felt a gush of resolve to get away from that miserable room and face her future, whatever it may hold.

The Corte Savella is a sheer edifice in pink brick, with small, high, barred windows. A man is lighting torches in sconces along the walls as they arrive. Francesco rings the bell, and after some time a small, starched porter opens up, asking what their business is. When Giovanni tells him, he ushers them in, unlocking an inner door. They shuffle inside and wait in an empty hall while a servant is dispatched to inform the head gaoler. The place is cavernous and sounds echo through the air: footsteps ring back and forth, and the occasional strange human noise, a cry or a shout or a bout of laughter, and the metallic jangle of a door being unlocked, followed by a heavy slam.

Now she is here and forced to wait, Artemisia's resolve begins to chip away. Francesco seems to intuit her mood as he puts his arm round her, making her feel minutely stronger.

The gaoler arrives, swinging a large ring of keys like a church censer. He leads them up a flight of stone steps and then, beyond another locked door, a further flight of wooden ones. They wait again, this time in a plain room brightly lit by several candles and torches, furnished with a table and a few chairs. A mildewy scent lingers, as if the floor has been mopped with rancid water. The windows are too high to look out of, just squares of darkening sky visible, divided evenly by the black stripes of their bars.

The thud of footsteps announces the prisoner's arrival. A guard, one of a pair, half shoves him into the room, where he staggers, almost falling. Porzia slips her arm through Artemisia's.

Tassi's skin is grey and he is painfully thin, cuffs bagging at his bony wrists. An angry pustule throbs on his neck and the bloodshot whites of his eyes are the colour of mustard in the candlelight. A stench emanates from him, so strong Artemisia blenches, disgust registering on her face in an unbidden reflex. He coughs and, without thinking, they all take a simultaneous step back, as if he is plague-ridden.

There is almost nothing left of the swaggering Tassi she remembers. She knows his vanity must make him hate the fact that he is filthy dirty, from the wild thicket of hair down to the encrusted toe peeping out of the hole in his shoe.

Lord save me, the voice in her head says, *if I must tie myself to this creature for eternity*. She reminds herself of the alternative – the other evil – pins and needles running down her arms at the thought of the Sybille. She can hear the snap of her bones, can imagine her hands deformed and useless, unable to wield a paintbrush. She clasps them together in a fist so tightly that her knuckles click.

Tassi attempts a smile, his chapped lips stretched to splitting, teeth mouldy. 'See how the mighty have fallen.' There is a dash of the old arrogance in his tone. 'I am so glad you have come, Artemisia. I have been dreaming of this moment – the opportunity to beg your forgiveness.'

'You don't deserve her forgiveness.' Francesco steps towards him, spitting on the floor at his feet. Tassi shrinks back.

'I'll see to this.' Giovanni pulls Francesco away with some force, muttering that he'll only make the situation worse, before approaching the prisoner himself. 'We have matters to discuss, Signor Tassi.' He is completely in control of himself, calm, his tone plain and unyielding, authoritative. 'I understand that your wife has passed away.'

'Alas, this is true.' Tassi makes a pathetic attempt to cross himself with his conjoined hands. Artemisia can see the sores where the steel cuffs have bitten into his skin.

'You have my commiserations,' says Giovanni, with a courtesy the man doesn't merit.

Artemisia remembers how he spoke of his wife, with a shocking absence of feeling, and how he had denied her existence altogether, was intent on bigamy. The misery he shows is for himself, not his poor wife, whose death seems to her suspiciously opportune. She feels a wave of nausea.

Giovanni continues: 'This means you are now free to fulfil your obligation to Signorina Gentileschi.'

Tassi smiles once more. A white scum has gathered at the corners of his mouth which he licks away with the point of his tongue. She recoils. 'I was hoping to persuade you of that fact. I have no greater wish than to fulfil my obligation to the lady.' He is looking at her rather than Giovanni.

Giovanni continues: 'We are all in agreement that this is the best course of action. I speak on behalf of Signor Gentileschi.'

Tassi makes another attempt to cross himself. 'I am

mortified at the disservice I have done to my fellow painter – my dear, dear friend and colleague.'

Artemisia is tempted to step forward and remind him of the truth that he and the odious Quorli held Orazio in utter disdain. But why should she defend her father?

'Given the circumstances, Signorina Gentileschi comes with no dowry.'

'I understand . . . I am quite able to provide well for her without.' He begins to list his outstanding commissions and the clients who have promised him work.

'Once the details are settled, in writing, then . . .' Giovanni pauses as if he wants to draw out the moment. Tassi hangs on his words. '. . . Signor Gentileschi has been persuaded that he will consider all amends made. Charges will be dropped.'

'I can't describe to you my gratitude. To be given a *tabula rasa*, after, after . . .'

'After your appalling behaviour.' It is Francesco again. Artemisia glances at him, acknowledging his support.

'Yes.' Tassi hunches over in apparent shame, a real tear now sliding down his face. 'My appalling behaviour. I trust that you will convey my word to Signor Gentileschi that I will treat his daughter with the utmost respect. She will be cared for as if she is made from cut glass.'

'Who's *she*? I have a name.'

Porzia says quietly, 'Come now.' A sign that it is better to remain silent, like a good girl. She wants to roar out her objections. Why would she want to be talked about as if she isn't here, treated as a thing fashioned in lifeless glass when she is flesh and blood?

'Of course, Artemisia. I'm sorry.' His pitiful expression,

the tears, the hope in his eyes make her want to retch. 'Will you accept my hand?' He drops to his knees.

Her acceptance sticks in her throat and she has difficulty finding her breath. Porzia gives her a smile of encouragement.

'I promise to earn your trust.' His desperation has every sign of authenticity, but she doesn't believe him, not for a moment. 'Let me prove to you that I am worthy.'

She nods vaguely, her words barely audible: 'I accept.' At once the tension releases from the room. She supposes they had all been praying she wouldn't change her mind and cause everyone more trouble, force the trial to go ahead after all. 'But . . .' There is something in Tassi's overblown display of regret that she doesn't trust. She finds her voice. 'How can I be sure, after all your lies, that you are truly free to wed?'

'I have a notary's statement – signed and sealed.' Something slips over his expression, something cruel and pleased with itself, gone almost before she has registered it. Her instincts flare and the image assaults her of his snarl, his big hand, the handkerchief over her face. Only it is not her but another woman gasping for breath.

Giovanni is saying something about having seen the document accounting for the first Signora Tassi's death and Porzia adds, with a smile, 'Shall we leave them alone to talk things over, dearest?'

Artemisia feels panic rising through her now, like milk on the boil, wants to cling to them, prevent them from leaving but they are already halfway out of the door.

'We'll be just outside. Take your time, dear.' Porzia is wearing a forced smile. 'Coming, Franco?'

'I'm staying.' Francesco, her faithful sentry, has positioned himself by the door near the two guards, who are slouched against the wall looking as if they would rather be elsewhere. Giovanni tries to persuade him to wait outside with them but he won't be moved.

Tassi is sitting now, staring forlornly at his cuffed hands resting on the table.

Artemisia doesn't sit but stands over his miserable form, reminded of the time she first let him see the *Judith*. 'Look what's become of you.' Contempt has whetted her tone.

He turns his eyes up to her. 'You are magnificent. Truly magnificent.'

'I will never forgive you.' He looks confused. Rage presses at her breastbone, painful as heartburn. 'You mean nothing to me. I will only ever tolerate you. And if I am to be your wife' – her voice breaks as she utters the word – 'I want your promise that you will never prevent me from painting whatever subject I choose.' As she says it, she knows that any promise made like this is built on sand. 'I will have it put in writing. You will sign it.' He still looks puzzled, as if he'd been expecting her to talk of something else. 'You know me well enough to be aware that my work is all that matters to me.'

'Say you will forgive me.' He is pleading. 'Let me hear you say it.'

She says nothing.

'I will return your painting to you.'

'How so?' It is her turn for confusion. 'You destroyed it, burned it.'

'It was a lie.' His gaze sinks. 'Quorli took it from me in lieu of a debt.'

'Not destroyed?' Her breath shortens, as hope grabs her in its embrace.

'Not destroyed.' A smile flickers over his cracked lips.

'But Quorli is dead.'

'I will obtain it from his widow. You have my word.'

Her heart swells at the thought of seeing her *Judith* once more. He is watching her carefully.

Still she says nothing.

He believes he has won. His pupils enlarge. 'Imagine what we will be together – our two talents united. We will conquer all of Europe with our art.'

Something in his look makes her falter. She saw it before when he'd talked of his wife's death, the cruel-edged conceit, the sense of being able to force the world to fit his plan.

Her spine bristles.

A warning.

She glances towards her brother, and then back to Tassi. 'I can't accept your offer.'

He makes a sound like a cough, seeming stunned in disbelief.

In her mind's eye she can see the consequences of her refusal as a trail of devastation, but still she doesn't waver.

'But you *must.*' His tone is charged with suppressed, indignant fury, and she knows she is right to refuse this man, no matter what the decision means.

His mouth is drawn tight like a miser's purse, those eyes flashing. He gets to his feet, managing to spit, 'Can't you do something?' in the direction of Francesco. 'Pull her into line.'

Francesco responds with his own angry outburst. 'My sister will do as she pleases.'

'You have no right . . .' He is seething.

'I have every right.' She is surprised that she sounds so calm.

'Get your bitch of a sister in order.' The full force of his contempt, contempt for them all, has burst through his surface.

He lurches towards her.

She jumps away, out of his reach.

The guards grab him, shoving him roughly out of the room.

He shouts back, 'You'll pay for this, you whore.'

The others rush in.

Giovanni and Porzia say nothing but their expressions speak volumes, faces stitched with worry and confusion. Only Francesco is glad. But only Francesco saw the real Tassi emerge.

'Can't we change your mind?' Porzia sounds like a mother trying to coax a reluctant infant to eat.

'You know what this means?' Giovanni says.

Her response is firm: 'Yes.' She does know – only too well. Francesco and Porzia each put an arm around her and they leave the room, go back down the stairs, into the dark street, the bolts of the door snapping into place behind them.

Walking through the dark, she grips her hands tightly together once more to ease the phantom throbbing in her fingers and hums to erase the crack of breaking bone.

She has made her choice and must live with the consequences.

33. Tor di Nona

Zita's throat is sore from shouting. When she first arrived she'd banged and banged against the door until her knuckles were raw, crying out for someone to come and tell her what was happening. At one point the guard had unlocked her cell and she'd leaped up in the belief she was to be released. 'Visitor,' the guard had said, leering aggressively at her. 'Shouldn't allow it, but since he's a man of the law I'll make an exception.'

She had foolishly thought Giovanni Stiatessi would secure her release. He'd said he would do his best and left her a package of victuals but three days have passed now and she is still in the cell, wondering desperately what will become of her.

She has spent her days worrying about her children, eking out her water and saying endless prayers on her rosary, thankful it had been in her pocket when they came for her. It is her sole source of comfort, the only thing preventing her from losing her mind in terror.

She has no appetite but forces herself to eat. The cheese has developed a white bloom and irritates the painful canker developing inside her cheek. The bread is like sawdust. A cockroach scurries across the floor. She casts aside her rations.

Her hips ache from lying on the thin pallet and her ankles are itchy with bites from its flea-infested straw stuffing. She is glad of the cushion that muffles the click and crackle of the insects scuttling through its filling.

The brick walls are chilled with damp, but at least she has a window. Well, it is more of a slit, high up by the ceiling, which casts a slender rectangle of light on the opposite wall. She waits for what will happen next, trying to stem her trepidation, cursing the day she ever agreed to move in with the Gentileschi family.

She worries constantly about Luca's congested chest, and her girls. They had seen her carted off by strangers. She has a picture in her head of their faces, pinched with fear. What must they think? She forces her mind to the small things for which she is grateful: the window, the blanket, the cushion, the victuals, her rosary. *Are you punishing me for my sins?* she asks the Lord. *I will do anything to show you I repent.* She pleads for the return of her husband, for her family to be back together, fending off desolation with the click, click, click of the wooden beads.

She watches the hours creep past in the sliver of light crawling along the wall of her cell and listens for the bells marking time through the days. If she manages to sleep, she is barely aware of it, unless a nightmare grabs her by the throat.

On the third day, the door is opened, bolts shooting back, and she is bundled out. A guard hustles her along a corridor and down a narrow flight of stairs. Several times she asks where she is being taken, what will happen, only to be told she will find out soon enough. She is pushed into a room where a young man in black is sitting at a desk, writing in a ledger. He gapes at her from under his cap, not noticing the ink drip from his pen onto the floor.

She is told to sit at the table and wait. The room is large, with a row of chairs along one wall and a heavy desk on a dais, behind which a carving of a dragon under a crowned eagle is hung. She glances upward to the high painted ceiling, where God looks down on her from a cloud.

Despite the size of the chamber, it is warm from the vast hearth behind her where a fire blazes. Her guard whispers something to the scribe and they glance at her, smirking. She feels a flush spread over her skin and looks at the table, alone with her muddle of thoughts and dread.

The fire cracks and spits at her back, and the scribe's pen scratches on and on. She disturbs her ulcer with her tongue and scratches at her ankles. When the bells next ring she mutters the angelus, fingering her beads in her lap, noticing the scribe does the same. She is worried now because the disruption has made her forget which bells they are, what time of day it is. If she loses track of time, she may lose herself altogether.

And then they come, two men, one portly and grizzled, wearing at least a pound of gold chain on his breast, from which a large crucifix is suspended. The other, younger, mean-mouthed, with a carefully curled moustache, walks slightly behind. His chain and cross are silver rather than gold. Both are robed in purple with white, lace-edged surplices beneath, so she knows they are bishops. A couple of young men, who must be servants of some kind, follow them in with yet another man, an orderly, she thinks.

The scribe stands, removing his cap and making a deep bow. His hair is thinning, several strands trained over his pate, like boot black.

The orderly nudges her in the back, quite hard. 'Stand in the presence of their lordships.'

She gets to her feet with a stumbled apology, dipping in a curtsey. Her hands are shaking so much she has to ram them out of sight into the waist of her skirts. They all cast their eyes over her, not a smile between them.

'Are you Signora Zita, wife of Stefano Medaglia of Rome?'

She nods.

'Speak up, so their lordships can hear you!' The orderly has a long face and big square horse teeth.

'I am Signora Zita, yes.' She wishes she could stop the tremor in her voice.

'There's no need to be afraid,' booms the moustachioed lord, smiling at her and tilting his head, like a kindly uncle. 'We merely want to ask you a few questions.' He pats her upper arm. They don't go to the dais as she expects but settle opposite her at the table, into a pair of upholstered chairs. There, the portly one fixes her with old-man eyes, opaque as dirty windows.

A Bible is pressed into her hands. It is bound in tooled leather inlaid with gilt and is heavier than it looks. They tell her to swear on it that she will tell the truth, which she does.

'Make sure you record every word,' the orderly commands the scribe, who closes one ledger and opens another, writing something at the top of the page.

'Do you know why you are here, Signora Zita?' The moustache dances as he speaks and beads of his spit land on the table.

She swallows. Her throat is dry as sand. 'I do not know

why I have been brought here, or why I am being questioned, my lord.' She doesn't know which of them to look at as she answers, the one questioning or the other, who, she assumes, with his gold chain, is the more senior of the two, so her gaze wavers back and forth from one to the other.

They ask her more questions about her living circumstances and how she came to make acquaintance with Orazio Gentileschi. She answers, saying that she had been Signor Orazio's neighbour in the via Margutta. As her husband was going away he had arranged with Signor Orazio, for her to live upstairs from them when they moved to the via della Croce, 'to act as companion to his daughter. Signorina Artemisia's mother was dead, you see, and she only had brothers . . .'

Now she has started, it all gushes out of her. '. . . and since my husband was to be away for the better part of a year – well, it has turned out to be longer than that, hasn't it? – he said I'd be better to move in there with my children. My husband had said, since I would be acting as companion to Signorina Artemisia, that he should pay a smaller sum for my board and lodging.'

Her ankles are itching horribly and she can't resist reaching down for a scratch, drawing a disgusted, withering look from the orderly. She'd like to remind him that fleas will bite anyone, even His Holiness. 'In the end they settled on a rent of twelve *scudi* to include firewood and that I would cook the evening meals for the family. Signorina Artemisia is not much of a cook, see. She likes to –'

She must have gone on too long as the moustached one interrupts her. 'And your husband, where is he now?'

'He's not come back.' She feels suddenly afraid that she will never be reunited with him, that he has gone for ever. 'Not yet.'

'I see.'

A lump is forming in her throat and she wonders when they will bring up the matter of the stolen cross.

A servant enters holding a tray with a pitcher and some drinking vessels, everything silver. He pours out a drink for each of the lords and she must be staring because the old portly one, who still hasn't said a word, asks her if she is thirsty.

'I am,' she says, 'parched,' and begins to tell them about eking out her clean water for fear of the flux.

He holds up a hand as if to indicate she has said enough and tells the orderly to give her his cup, which the man does. His face seems to say a cup like that is far too good for the likes of her. It is engraved silver but gold inside.

She takes a careful sip first, as if drinking from the communion chalice. The water is cool and tastes fresh and slightly metallic. She drains the cup and the orderly is told to refill it. He is clearly annoyed at being asked to do a servant's work for a prisoner, slitting his eyes at her.

The moustached one returns to his questions: did they pass between one apartment and another in the house, and what were the names of all those living there, and did Artemisia come and go as she pleased?

Zita has stopped shaking. She feels so much better after the water.

He asks about whether a fellow named Francesco also frequented the house or studio. Zita tells them the only Francesco she knows is Artemisia's eldest brother. He

insists he doesn't mean Francesco Gentileschi but someone else. She racks her brain, vaguely remembering talk of
an ugly type with long black hair whom she saw once or
twice at the via Margutta. 'Maybe you mean the Francesco
Orazio sometimes used as a model, but not recently.'

'Yes, him. Did they talk about him? Did he visit them at
the via della Croce?'

'As far as I know he wasn't welcome there. Signor Orazio
didn't seem to trust him. I never saw him there.'

'Who *did* you see there? What men did Signor Orazio
associate with?'

'There were lots of men who visited the studio, friends
of Signor Orazio and patrons . . .'

'Can you name any of them?'

'There was Signor Modenese who wanted a portrait of
his sister, and there was Nicolò Bendino who was the
studio assistant for a time after Piero Stiatessi was sent
away . . .' He quizzes her on whether Artemisia was close
with any of these men. 'Not as far as I know. But Piero
and she were friends, until he left.'

'What sort of friends?'

'They were very close.'

'Were they intimate?'

She sees now, what he means, feels like she's been led
into a trap. 'Oh, no, not like that. He wasn't the sort . . .'
She is staggering over her words now, wondering how she
can describe what sort Piero was. She can't say *that*, not to
these men. 'They were like brother and sister.'

'Brother and sister?' He seems not to believe her, paus-
ing, lifting his brow, but moves on: 'And were there
others – other men?'

'There was the painter Signor Tassi, of course, and Furiere Quorli.' The older lord leans forward in his seat with a wheeze. 'Signor Orazio was working with them, on a garden loggia at Cardinal Borghese's palazzo on the Quirinal Hill.' She regrets, now, mentioning the cardinal, remembering Orazio's silent threat, his fingers making the shape of a cross in the air, his cold smile. Panic bubbles up in her.

But they don't ask her about that. They ask if the two men 'aforementioned' were ever in the house in the absence of Signor Orazio.

When she answers that they were, 'particularly Signor Tassi, several times,' the moustached one meets the eye of the scribe, who nods, as if to reassure him that he's getting it all down.

She continues to answer questions about Tassi and Quorli and whether Artemisia ever encountered either man when out of the house. Zita tells them about how Tassi had joined them on their way back from San Giovanni in Laterano. She doesn't recount the incident in the vineyard. The Bible sits on the table, like an accusation. An omission is not quite a lie, she tells herself, thumbing her rosary.

'Did the said Signor Tassi ever visit you in your apartments?'

'He did, yes.' Shame creeps over her at the memory, how her head had spun so. 'With Furiere Quorli.'

'So, would you say you were friendly with Signor Tassi?'

'No . . .'

'Am I understanding this correctly? He was not a friend of yours, yet he visited you in your home. Why would that be?' His voice is still soft but a steely gleam has appeared in his eyes that is making her guts shrivel.

'At first he seemed . . . Well, I thought . . .'

'How did he seem at first?'

'Nice. He seemed nice at first.'

'So, Signor Tassi, whom you thought was "nice", visited you in your home. I'd say that was very amicable. But you still maintain that he was no friend of yours?'

'No.' She is becoming tangled in the questions, can't tell quite how she is meant to answer.

'So, he *was* your friend?'

'No, I mean . . . I don't know.'

He sighs impatiently. 'If you can't tell us whether the man was your friend or not . . .' he pauses, making a faint huff of impatience '. . . perhaps you can tell us whether he was ever in the house when Signorina Artemisia was painting.'

'Oh, yes, he was.' Relieved that he has changed tack, she continues blithely, telling of the drawing lesson and also when he and Quorli first came to the studio. 'Signorina Artemisia was making a likeness of Signor Modenese's sister, who was plain as a toad, and then another time he came in alone, upstairs while Arti . . . Signorina Artemisia was drawing a portrait of my son –' She stops abruptly.

'Take your time, my dear,' says the old one. But his kindness doesn't soothe her any more, not now she has realized that she has said too much and will have to tell a lie.

The Bible watches her from the table.

The fire blazes on her back, too hot, making her face burn, and beads of sweat are forming on her forehead. She wipes them away with her sleeve.

'Upstairs, you said. And what happened then?' Her interrogator suddenly seems not kind at all, his gaze cold, his tone harsh.

She clutches her rosary tightly, until the beads dig into the flesh of her fingers. 'I left them together.'

'Alone?'

She nods, soothed slightly at having been able to avoid a lie.

The scribe's pen continues to scratch.

'Were you not supposed to be the chaperone to Signorina Artemisia?'

'I was, yes . . .' she falters. They both stare at her with the intensity of a pair of mousers.

'It might be construed, then, that you intended for the couple to be left alone, indeed that you *arranged* for this to be so. One might think that you procured the young lady for –'

'No . . . no! That is not what I said at all. You are twisting my words.' Her heart is hammering. 'I . . . I had to attend to my son, you see, who was sickening for something.' There it is: her lie. She holds her breath, glancing up at the painted ceiling, where God is sitting among the clouds, looking down at her in judgement.

And now he is asking whether she had seen the pair alone on other occasions, pushing her and pushing her, and she is getting hotter and hotter, feeling her cheeks burning, so hot she fears she will pass out.

The words burst out of her: 'After that time, before he left for Florence, Signor Tassi visited again and again, and they were alone in her bedchamber.' She stops but, knowing they will suggest it was her fault they were left alone together, adds: 'It was when I was at confession.'

But that is not enough. He keeps prodding her for more, the moustache rising and falling, spit showering, on and on. 'Were you aware of whether they knew each other carnally?'

'I don't know.' She can feel tears pricking at her eyes as she shakes her head, repeating, 'I don't know.'

'Did she not confide to you about it – you, her *companion*?'

She is sobbing now, tears and snot running down her face.

'That's enough,' says the old one.

'We have what we need,' says the other.

The scribe is blotting his ledger and the two lords have begun to leave the room without as much as a glance her way. There is not a single word uttered as to what will become of her.

34. The Truth

Artemisia is the first of the family to be questioned. They come, three of them, two judges – ecclesiastic – and a clerk with a squint, to the tawdry rooms on the Borgo Santo Spirito. Her father greets them obsequiously. She tells him to leave, which he does slowly and reluctantly.

She invites the men to take a place at the table. One, the most smartly dressed, takes out a handkerchief and wipes the seat before he sits. He has the pale hair and supercilious expression of a northerner. The other is so nondescript she wonders if she would ever recognize him again.

Her father is listening at the door. She can hear the rasp of his breath and keeps her voice low so he can't hear. He thinks it is his business, doesn't seem aware that he cannot influence her any more.

She tells them the truth.

How fascinated these two men of God are to hear of her deflowering, their eyes feverish as they push and push her for more detail. They lap up her every word as she describes how Tassi put his knee between her thighs to stop her closing them; how he put his hand over her mouth; how much it hurt; how she tried to scratch his face and pull his hair; how he undid his laces and thrust his penis towards her; how she grasped the thing so tightly that her nails cut into its flesh, drawing blood; how she flung her penknife at him and drew more blood. So much blood, everywhere, hers and his, but more hers.

They are drooling like hounds over a carcass by the time she's finished.

That event, which happened a year ago now, is sealed in a caul. She feels nothing in its recounting, as if it happened to someone else or was an invention, a subject concocted in her imagination to render in paint.

The only time the caul's membrane is breached, for the briefest of instants, is when she sees a look on the face of a young scribe who's come to record her words. He glances from his papers towards her with greyish limpet eyes, his mouth set in horror. For the first time she sees herself reflected in someone else, and it rattles her.

The two judges prod, as if she is the one on trial. Had she acted carnally with others, they ask, seeming disappointed that she hasn't further lurid details for them. They wonder why she gave herself to Tassi again after the event – occasionally they use the term 'violation', once or twice 'despoilment', often 'deflowering'. Not once do they refer to it as 'rape'. Rape is *her* description. That was what it was. Words can be as misleading as Tassi's painted artifices.

'He promised to marry me.' Her voice is devoid of emotion.

'The midwives will have to make an examination.' It is the nondescript one who says this. 'They will send us their report.'

They need no further explanation. The three of them creep out in silence, the limpet-eyed clerk giving her a forlorn backward look before the door is closed.

Her father sidles round, seeing if he can squeeze anything from her. 'What did you tell them?'

'The truth. What else would I tell them?'

'You know, all this would go away if only you would accept Tassi's hand.'

'I'd rather die,' she replies blankly. 'It would all go away if *you* dropped the charges.'

He looks at her in shock, as if she has suggested he drink hemlock.

'I've accepted an offer from Porzia to go and stay with them.'

Orazio looks forlorn. He pleads with her to remain, telling her, as bait, he intends to have her *Judith* returned. He has said it before, and she knows he hasn't the power to achieve this. Quorli's widow apparently has a docket to prove that the painting came into her husband's possession legally. 'I will have Tassi charged with its theft.'

'Do as you please.' She has accepted the loss of her painting, as she has accepted the trial – stoically.

When she is packing her belongings to go to the Stiatessis', the midwives arrive, a pair of stone-faced harridans. They prod their cold, hard fingers into her – a grim further molestation. Her body no longer belongs to her. She is a doll, a puppet, the Epiphany witch, La Befana, the stuff of children's dreams and nightmares.

She imagines the two judges slavering over the midwives' report that deems her officially no longer 'intact'. The term puts an image in her mind's eye of her body fragmenting, parts falling from her, until she is indistinguishable from the ancient, limbless stone goddesses of Rome.

35. At What Price

March creeps into April and then May. The city is once more filled with light and birdsong. Its vibrant colours, a thousand vegetable greens, are set against the edifices of golden travertine that rise up into the startling blue of the Roman sky. But everything, to Artemisia's eye, is muted.

She has waited and waited for the legal process to crawl forward. It is months now that poor Zita has languished at the Tor di Nona. They intend to hold her until everyone has been questioned, or so Giovanni believes. He and Porzia were the last to testify in support of Orazio's claim. She will not call it *their* claim, as her father does.

Had it not been for the Stiatessis these last months, she might well have flung herself into the Tiber. They have given her refuge and she sleeps in a pretty room at the top of their house, with a view into the gardens of the Santo Spirito Hospital, where she watches the nuns flit through the cloisters like doves.

Artemisia rarely leaves this sanctuary. On the occasions she does venture out, to buy groceries or go to mass, she has to steel herself for the pointed fingers and blunt stares, ignoring the lewd jibes and cruel comments that spill from twisted mouths.

Piero's friendship keeps her going. He sends her pigments from Florence in return for small works of art. Unable to tackle any more profound topic, she has been painting the Stiatessis' pets: a little black dog with raisin eyes, called Lola, who has taken to sleeping on her bed; a hound that uncannily resembles Giovanni with its whiskers and long nose; and a hoopoe that languishes alone in the garden aviary, making its strange insistent call, *ooop, ooop, ooop*. Despite its apricot plumage and pert crest, the hoopoe makes her sad. He lost his mate a while ago, Porzia had told her, and has been calling for her ever since.

For what seems an age the judges have been hearing Tassi's witnesses. A trickle of information reaches the Stiatessi house daily. Artemisia is learning of how, evidently, she has slept with half the young men in Rome: Geronimo Modenese; the wretched Nicolò Bendino; that hideous Francesco something or other, whom Father used as a model for a devil in the back of a painting once, years ago. She has had them all, and more. She has shared a bed with men she has never heard of. She has committed despicably filthy acts and whored herself about since before she could count to ten. Nicolò Bendino, she learns, delivered letters from her to her multitudes of lovers, letters written by her – a miracle, since she can neither read nor write.

Tassi's hatred of her burns in every rumour.

She might have been married to him by now and avoided all this. She would rather be decomposing in her grave. She knew in the moment she rejected him the price of that union was too high, even if it meant the return of her stolen *Judith*.

She would laugh in the face of all the stories she hears about herself if she didn't know what they mean: she will soon be forced to prove the truth of her own testimony.

She can hear them discussing it downstairs, the Stiatessis and Orazio, whom she refuses to see.

'We must make her change her mind.' Her father's voice runs high with upset – or is it guilt? she wonders. 'They will torture her, break her fingers. She may never paint again.'

She cannot paint anyway. Her drive is depleted, any emotion at all impossible to summon. She has lost the raw passion that spurred her to create her best work. Her ambition to see her paintings on the walls of the great palazzi seems merely the idealized dream of a distant youth.

'Don't say such a thing.' Artemisia can hear, even from upstairs, that Porzia's voice is wet with tears. She is a woman given to emotion – she wept when her grandchild developed his first tooth and then again when he took his first steps and even when the cat had another litter of kittens. Her surfeit of sentiment baffles Artemisia in her numb state.

'Don't lose heart, Orazio. We have right on our side. We can win this. Your honour will be restored, I'm sure of it.' Giovanni is ever the optimist.

At what price? Artemisia is tempted to shout down the stairwell.

The front door slams and she watches her father's hunched shape from the window skulking back to the grim apartment. He turns, seeming to feel her eyes on him, and she slides into the shadows out of view.

She waits for it all to be over.

When she is alone in the house someone comes to the door, a gentle knock. She hesitates, standing still as stone in the hall. The knock comes again and again. Something catches her eye. It is Zita, looking right at her, framed in the window – or a version of Zita, if she had become a wraith.

Artemisia flings open the door. Zita is scrawny and pallid, her pillows of snowy flesh deflated. She can't look Artemisia in the eye as she hands over a package. 'Porzia's cushion and blanket. I washed them.'

'When were you released?'

'It's been a while now.'

The knowledge hits Artemisia that, if Zita has been released, all the testimonies must have been heard. Dread hooks in her belly. The trial must be imminent.

'Did they hurt you?'

She shakes her head, saying, 'Let's not ever speak of it.'

'Will you come in?' Artemisia stands aside but Zita doesn't move.

'I haven't time.' She glances over her shoulder to where a cart is waiting half visible behind the wall. 'My husband.'

'He came back!'

'Yes.'

'You must be glad to be reunited.' They speak as if they hardly know each other.

Zita smiles, nodding, a hand running over her belly. 'Missed my monthlies.' The old spark gleams in her eye. 'Always been so regular.' She flicks her eyes heavenwards. 'I am surely forgiven.'

'Oh, Zita!' Artemisia knows that above all Zita yearned for more children. 'I am glad for you.' How simple to be you, she is thinking, finding joy in the ordinary path of life. But she knows that this is not entirely the case – Zita has her own demons.

'I must go.' She hesitates, as if she wants to say something more, but makes just a small unintelligible sound, half sigh, half cough, before turning and walking down the steps.

Artemisia wonders what she chose not to say. She feels sorry for Zita's ordeal but not sorry enough to try to rekindle their friendship. It had been a lopsided amity: they had nothing in common except the trouble that her father and Tassi visited on them.

She remembers Zita talking of the things her husband said to her: *You're both the prettiest and the stupidest little thing I have ever met*, curious as to how she can love him so much.

But what does Artemisia know about love?

36. The Ring

Artemisia is given a day's warning. *Signorina Artemisia Gentileschi, daughter of Signor Orazio Gentileschi, painter of Rome, is hereby notified to appear before the Illustrious and Excellent Lord Geronimo Felice, deputy, the Illustrious and Excellent Lord Francesco Bulgarello substitute deputy, and the Magnificent and Excellent Lord Porzio Camerario, substitute judge at the court of His Supreme Holiness, on the fourteenth day of May in the year of Our Lord sixteen-twelve on the hour of terce, at the Tor di Nona . . .*

The anticipation is torment. Her mind churns with the torture she will inevitably undergo, an internal knot drawing tighter with the sluggish passing of each hour. It is impossible to comprehend what the pain will be like. Pain, she is learning, is an abstract concept, only understandable in the moment of experience. They say that nature makes mothers forget the pain of childbirth, or they would never want a second child – they would all take the veil and the nunneries would be filled to the gunwales.

If she allows her thoughts to run unchecked, the grim anticipation makes her bowels loosen and her throat constrict, her breath shortening until she feels faint. She thinks of the Virgin Martyrs facing torture – far worse agony than she faces – with placid equanimity: Saint Lucy, her eyes little pools of jelly cupped in her palm; Saint Catherine on the breaking wheel, smiling; Saint Agatha, her severed breasts on a plate.

Saint Agatha puts her in mind of that pilfered cake and Zita's light fingers that, in a roundabout way, allowed events to unfold as they did. But to think of it so is to blame poor Zita and absolve Orazio. She will not absolve her father – ever.

She lies awake all night, grateful for the comforting presence of the little black dog, Lola, who tucks her warm, woolly body into the crook of her arm. Her fear expands in the dark. She counts time by the two-hourly bells, and watches as the day seeps through the cracks in the shutters. The sounds of morning begin: a single set of footsteps descending the stairs; the back door opening as the big dog is let out into the yard. The hoopoe is making its plangent call. Lola pricks her ears and jumps down to scratch at the door. Artemisia drags herself up to let her out, returning to bed.

Then comes more footfall on the stairs and the giggles of the children, the Stiatessis' eldest grandson and her own little brother Marco, who, like her, refuses to go home. The voices of the family breakfast thread their way up to her and with them the smell of warm bread, causing her stomach to grind, but even that will not tempt her downstairs.

As the prime bells sound, Porzia creeps in with a soft greeting, opening the shutters a little to allow a dim, filtered light into the room. She sits on the side of the bed and strokes a gentle hand over Artemisia's forehead, as if she is an invalid.

'I've been thinking.' Her voice is little more than a whisper. 'Didn't Tassi give you some kind of ring when he promised to wed you?'

Artemisia remembers now, the ugly too-big ring, a man's ring, with the initials AT engraved on a flat piece of jade. She had tried to sell it, along with the earrings he'd sent her from Florence, but the jeweller wouldn't take it, said it wasn't of any value, though he offered a fair sum for the earrings.

'Do you have it?' Porzia is asking.

'I don't know. Why?'

'It would add weight to your testimony – given he has denied the betrothal.'

'He's denied everything, hasn't he? Denied ever having come near me at all.'

She pulls herself out of the bed and across the room, rummaging in her chest, glad of the distraction. 'Will you come with me?'

'Of course. I wouldn't dream of leaving you.' She hesitates a moment, looking down and away. 'Your father will be present. You do know that, don't you?'

'I've been trying to put it from my mind.'

'The separation is a source of suffering for him.' Porzia means well in her frequent attempts to reunite father and daughter.

'Please don't. He suffers because he can no longer count on me to finish off his paintings.' The force of her own scorn surprises her. Misfortune has worked away at her, making her hard and abrasive as pumice.

'I understand.' Porzia makes a soothing sound, a kind of hum, and Artemisia waits for her to say something about how she will think differently when she has children of her own. But she doesn't.

What she says is: 'I think your father has had difficulty

coming to terms with the fact that you are the better painter.'

Porzia takes her in her arms, where she, at last, having let no one near for months, allows herself to be held. 'I know. I know. I know,' murmurs Porzia, though she couldn't possibly know, but Artemisia is soothed, nonetheless. 'All you need do is tell the truth.'

'Yes.'

She breaks out of the embrace, continuing to search the chest, her fingers finding the ring at the bottom. She holds it up so Porzia can see. 'He gave you *that*.' Her disdain is apparent. 'And your father saw it?' She takes the ring, scrutinizing it, seeing the initials, with a snort of indignation.

'Father was the one who brought it to me.'

'Any woman could have told him that the man wasn't serious, offering you an ugly thing like this. It's not even gold. But never mind – the judge will be convinced. And the etched letters – well, Tassi won't be able to deny that, unless he says you stole it. But who would steal a thing as worthless as this? It would be more at home through a hog's snout.'

Artemisia finds herself laughing. 'I can't wear it. It's much too big – I suppose I could hang it from my chain.'

'No, you must wear it on your hand, because when –' She stops herself abruptly. 'Then they will all be sure to see it.'

'You *can* say it.' Artemisia meets her gaze. 'When they knot the Sybille round my fingers. We both know that is what they'll do. There's little point in pretending otherwise.'

'Oh, sweetheart, God has made you stronger than most. I thank Him for that. You never know, Tassi might

322

change his testimony and it' – she still won't say the word, *torture* – 'might not be done.'

Artemisia wishes she had even a fraction of Porzia's hopefulness. 'There's this too.' She hands over her embroidery bag.

Porzia looks puzzled for a moment but, on finding the handkerchief inside, the bloodstains now brown as rust, and seeing Tassi's stitched initials there, a shadow falls over her. 'Your blood?'

Artemisia nods.

'You poor, poor girl.' The sight of it seems to render the assault more real for Porzia, who looks distressed and tries to pull Artemisia into another embrace. But Artemisia feels brittle. She can't stomach pity, never could. 'We'd better keep it in case. To add weight to your account.'

Porzia stuffs it out of sight, briskly changing the subject. 'Now, what will you wear?' She sorts through Artemisia's few clothes, drawing out a plain dark wool dress. 'This?' She holds the garment up to the window, seeing a spot of dirt, rubbing the fabric together vigorously to remove it.

Artemisia doesn't care what she wears, is glad not to have to decide about anything. As if she is a child, she lets Porzia dress her in whatever she deems suitable, lifting her arms so she can be laced tightly in. Though she is still thin with worry the flesh of her breasts spills over the starched edging of the bodice.

'That won't do,' says Porzia, searching through a pile of linens, producing a partlet to cover every inch of Artemisia's skin. 'That's better.' She then clips a small crucifix around her neck and scrapes back her hair, pulling it tightly into two plaits, which she pins in a roll at the nape of her neck. A cap is found to cover her head and an iron to press her skirts, which have sat crumpled in the bottom of her chest for weeks.

'You couldn't look more demure if you were a nun. Have you any other shoes?' Porzia looks at the two pairs, indoor and outdoor, that Artemisia owns. Both are covered with paint. 'Never mind, I'm sure I have some that will fit you.'

She leaves the room, returning with a pair of grosgrain slippers. They are a little tight, but Porzia seems so happy with them that Artemisia doesn't complain.

When Porzia stands back, saying, 'You'll do perfectly,' Artemisia fends off a new surge of apprehension, knowing that they are about to leave for the Tor di Nona.

Artemisia wonders what Porzia is doing when she tears a little piece of paper from the corner of the summons letter and dampens it in the washbasin. 'Give me your hand.' She slips the ugly ring onto Artemisia's finger and wedges the roll of wet paper inside the band to hold it in place. 'There. That will do.'

A residue of paint still clings to her cuticles. The fear returns to her, sudden and overwhelming. 'I don't know how I could face this without you.'

'I only wish it could have been avoided. If you'd come to live with us when your mother died,' Porzia looks wistful, 'things might have turned out differently.'

'I would probably have resisted.' Artemisia summons up a smile. 'You know how headstrong I was, even then. I wanted to paint. I would have been a terrible handful.'

Porzia returns her smile. 'Perhaps you would.'

Without a word, the two women go downstairs and out

into the waiting carriage. Though it is only a short walk to the Tor di Nona, Giovanni had insisted that Artemisia be shielded from the crowds. He presses a pastry into her hands. It is dusted with a coating of fine sugar. The smell alone sets her mouth watering. It is delicious, sweet and buttery, and feels like the last thing she will ever eat.

Giovanni is right: there is a throng at the gates waiting for a glimpse of the infamous Artemisia Gentileschi. They hear a frenzied drone of shouting, angry mouths spewing hate, as the carriage passes into the yard. Artemisia leans her temple on the window, watching the condensation of her breath making patterns on the glass.

Orazio is waiting as they dismount.

Artemisia won't meet his eye.

Her heart begins to beat fast and heavy. The grosgrain slippers are already rubbing.

Porzia brushes a few flecks of powdered sugar from her dress and they enter the building.

37. The Sybille

Artemisia is led to stand before Tassi. The irony strikes her, right between the eyes, that it seems – the two of them standing face to face, with the judge looking over – like a marriage scene.

He has doused himself in that horribly familiar scent. She doesn't allow it to take her back to that day. He may smell the same but he looks unfamiliar, has cropped his hair and shaved off his beard, exposing his hollow cheeks. The razor has left an angry-looking cut on his chin. Only the snake eyes are unchanged. They try to grab her. She avoids them.

She can feel the burn of her father's gaze on her back and stands straight, square-shouldered. He'd tried to pull her aside at the bottom of the staircase but she was thankful for a guard's summons, so she didn't have to listen to his lecture.

All she heard of what he said was the word 'meek'. He'd like nothing more than for her to have the air of a sacrificial lamb. But if she gives in to even a splinter of weakness, she may fall apart altogether.

She breathes slowly and steadily, forcing her thrumming heart into line as the day's proceedings start with the oaths and formalities.

Tassi is asked if he has anything to add to his previous deposition.

Apparently he has already undergone several days of questioning. She keeps her eye line beyond his shoulder, towards a stained-glass window. Colours spill from it, so rich and beautiful they could tease tears from a stone.

His response is firm and measured. 'I do not have anything to add or subtract.'

Now she looks at him, firmly, grimly.

'Signor Tassi, would you finally cease with your obstinacy' – the judge's tone is edged with exasperation, which Artemisia hopes is a good sign – 'and tell the court the truth about whether you violated Signorina Artemisia Gentileschi, who stands before you, about which you have been questioned many times.'

Tassi, in the face of Artemisia's unwavering stare, seems unable to maintain his poise. 'I . . . I . . .' He takes a long inhalation. His skin is slick with sweat.

'Speak louder,' says the judge.

His head is nodding slightly, his mouth moving, as if trying to form his confession. His gaze vacillates over Artemisia like a dying candle. Is it too early for her to smell triumph? The entire room holds its breath, waiting for him finally to admit his crime. She had expected more resistance – they all had.

'I . . .' He draws himself up, as if tugged by a puppeteer. 'No, signore, I have spoken the truth and I am telling you that not only have I not violated the said Signorina Artemisia' – he is not looking at her now but directly at the judge – 'but I have never had sexual relations with her.'

There is an audible gasp from the assembled company.

His lie is a trick as convincingly rendered as one of his

perspective drawings. She understands how they are done, with lines and lies and the pretence of light.

She swallows.

Dread begins to well in her.

She knows what this means.

'You maintain that you contradict the lady's testimony?'

'She can say it to my face that I have had relations with her – deflowered her' – he makes a small huff of sardonic laughter – 'and I will still say to her that she lies.'

The judge turns to Artemisia. 'Do you stand by the testimony you gave? Will you confirm it as the truth before the witnesses here present?'

Artemisia clears her throat. She feels herself waver. 'Yes, signore, what I said in my testimony before your lordship about the person, Signor Agostino Tassi, here present, is the truth.' She summons all her reserves of stoicism. She will *not* be meek.

Her voice is clear and strong and absent of all emotion, her posture holding firm, as she begins to relate, as asked by the judge, the circumstances of her defilement . . . 'He was a friend of my father . . . used to frequent our house . . . I trusted him. It couldn't have been further from my mind that he would violate me . . .' She tells of the first perspective lesson. The company listens on in rapt silence. 'And on the second occasion –' Her voice cracks slightly, her mind swilling with those images of him, snarling, the memories suffocating her.

She seeks solace in the colours of the glass window.

Clearing her throat, she begins again. 'And on the second occasion he came to teach me, he came upstairs, uninvited, to my rooms. I did not realize his intention until he grabbed me violently and threw me to the bed . . . I struggled.' She waits a moment, and feels the entire room wait with her. 'It was rape.' The word rings around the space like a curse uttered in church.

She continues with the details, telling also of the marriage proposal, finding strength in the fact that, whatever happens, it will be better than being wed to him.

Tassi interjects, attempting to cast doubt but is silenced, emphatically. When she has finished, a notary reads her previous testimony in its entirety. So they must all hear again of her ordeal.

She doesn't listen.

Now Tassi is called on to respond. His demeanour is shot through with scorn. 'It is not true that I have raped her or that I have had relations with her . . .' And he begins to list all the men who are supposed to have been with Orazio Gentileschi's daughter. On and on he goes. 'Everything she has said is untrue.'

She points towards the Bible, on which she had sworn earlier, and looks with a challenge at Tassi. 'I say it is the truth, and if it were not the truth, I would not have said it.'

Tassi casts his look briefly to his knitted fingers.

Artemisia can see, from the side of her eye, one of the prison guards preparing the Sybille. She tastes bile in her throat. It takes every shred of her strength to contain her outward poise.

'Are you prepared to stand by what you have said under torture?' The judge says it to her in a casual manner, as if asking someone whether they prefer red or white wine.

'Yes, signore. I am ready to confirm my testimony in

whatever way is necessary.' She makes a backward glance, instantly wishing she hadn't.

Porzia holds a handkerchief over her mouth and Giovanni is clasping her hand, his face the picture of horror. Her father is glistening with sweat, like a guilty man. Artemisia feels the blood drain from her face and suddenly feels fragile as glass. 'Even under torture.' Her voice is barely audible.

The judge is now saying his piece and calling the guard over with his instrument. Artemisia lifts her hands up, absolutely still, as if in prayer, holding an image of those placid Virgin Martyrs in her mind.

The guard proceeds to wind the knotted cords about her fingers crushing them together. It is uncomfortable but bearable.

She tells herself to breathe.

The judge drones on, admonishing her to beware of unjustly accusing the man before her.

'I have told the truth.' Her voice sounds steadier than she feels.

The guard adjusting the cords looks briefly towards the judge who nods, commanding him to proceed.

He tugs on the running string.

A searing twinge shoots up her arms, into her shoulders, down her spine.

A cry catches in her throat.

Time seems to suspend itself.

The strings tighten.

A new spasm erupts, intensifying.

She might vomit.

She hears a click like the snap of a wishbone, almost fainting with the new convulsion it brings.

She drifts on agonizing waves, floating away up into the vast space of the roof where the pain cannot reach. She floats there with the painted angels, vaguely aware of the judge asking if she wants to change her testimony.

Another sharp snap brings her back.

'I stand by every word.'

Blood is flowing. Her blood.

The cords bite further into her flesh.

She tries to drift away again, beyond the pain but she is stuck with the thought of her fingers broken and useless – all her abundance of talent without the means to express itself.

Her hands shake uncontrollably.

The Sybille creaks, a notch tighter.

She holds her breath.

A notch tighter.

Crack, crack, crack.

Blood is trailing down her wrists, into her sleeves.

A notch more.

A splat of red lands on Tassi's face. He wipes it into a crimson smear.

She thrusts her shattered hands towards him, surprised she can speak but they are her words. It is her voice. 'This is the ring you gave me when you promised to marry me. See your initials there?' The engraved letters are clogged with blood.

Tassi accuses her of lying.

The judge asks her to confirm once more her spoken testimony.

'It is true, it is true, it is true!'

The force of her own cry shocks her, exploding from

the deep well of rage she has suppressed for months, a sleeping monster awoken. Why are they not binding Tassi's fingers? Why are they not testing *his* version of events?

The injustice serves to fuel her rage further.

Tassi can't look at her, doesn't dare. 'It is not true. You are lying through your teeth.' Derision drips from him but he is fighting to maintain his composure as he registers the increasing incredulity on the faces of the judges. He makes an attempt to add something but is silenced by the upraised hand of the interrogator.

Artemisia, on the contrary, looks him right in the eye, where she can see a tiny woman reflected back. It is her. 'I've told the truth.' She will not break and set him free with his lies.

She staggers slightly and a guard has to hold her upright. She can feel the air in the room shift. The gathered company are horrified to see her suffering so.

The judges peer at the initials on the ring – the worthless piece of brass – now engraved in blood.

Blood drips down into the white cuffs of her shift, transporting her back to that day, her blood then, and the painted blood, rolling in runnels along the creases of the bed linen, Holofernes' blood. In places it is raspberry bright, running to black in the shadows. She closes her eyes, taking a deep inhalation, and an image emerges from the darkness, generated by the sheer brute force of her hate.

It is a new *Judith*, almost identical yet crucially different, better, more bloody, more violent, the women crueller. Fuelled by the volleys of pain rattling through her fingers, down her wrists, to her elbows, the image clarifies. This

Judith looks at her victim with a terrifying expression of detached brutality.

This Judith inhabits her.

She knows now, with absolute certainty, that she will render this image in paint even if she has to hold the brush between her toes, between her teeth, even if she has to spit the paint onto the canvas. This new Judith will come into being.

She can feel it quickening in her belly – her masterpiece.

She barely notices the judge command the Sybille be removed.

She becomes aware of the effect on the assembled company, of the sight of a young woman, hands still set in prayer, blood drooling to the floor from broken fingers. They will be thinking of the suffering of the saints.

She registers the sympathy of the officials – every one of them, even the scribe.

She is guided to a chair where someone, a physician she supposes, brings a bandage to wrap her shattered hands, wiping them first very gently with a cool, damp cloth.

Her fingers are hideous, like the talons of some terrible bird, a vulture, or a harpy, swollen and blue beneath the blood, several at strange angles. The physician wraps them carefully, tightly, each to a splint, more pain exploding through her each time he does so.

While her hands are tended, Tassi mounts a passionate defence, trying to prolong the proceedings. 'Don't let her go.' He thinks he can change their minds. 'I want to ask her some questions. It is my right.'

Stained with desperation, he passes a notebook to the

interrogating judge, who peruses it before discussing briefly in whispers with his colleague.

Now the physician has set her bones, the pain settles into a deep throb.

Her imagination is aflame as her new painting continues to take shape, vivid as reality in her mind's eye. She sees each small detail, as if through an eyeglass. Judith has her knee on the bed to gain force behind the blade she wields. It is heavy and razor sharp. It slices an artery emitting a spray of blood that spots her breast and the golden damask of her dress. Her brow is screwed in determination. She can see the whites of his eyes.

'Very well,' the judge says to Tassi eventually, having scanned the notebook.

Artemisia is politely, apologetically, requested to remain. She asks for a drink and a boy holds out a cup, realizing with a mortified blush that she can't take it.

'Put it to my lips,' she tells him and the whole room is horrified once more as she is obliged to sip like a baby.

The judge asks her if she is ready. She nods and he begins to read out Tassi's questions. Each one is ever more outlandish, about the men she is supposed to have been intimate with, about the violation itself, about the colour of her blood, whom she did and didn't tell of what happened – on and on.

She answers each question clearly, truthfully.

Tassi hasn't even the courage to look at her and his petulance escalates with each response. He will not accept he has lost.

The officials become increasingly impatient, rushing the final few queries. Their minds were made up half an hour ago, everyone assembled knows as much, and Tassi's further questions have served only to crystallize their decision.

The judge returns the notebook to Tassi and enters into a swift discussion with his peers.

He stands to announce the sentence.

Someone at the back of the room shouts, 'Lock him up.'

The judge asks for silence before his pronouncement. 'Signor Agostino Tassi, I hereby command that you be taken from this place to the Corte Savella —'

Tassi's composure disintegrates. He stands, striding to the bench, waving his fist: 'This is wrong. You're wrong.' Two guards manhandle him roughly back into his seat. The judge looks right through him, continuing: '— and there you will be imprisoned for two years . . .'

Artemisia stops listening. Two years or two hundred years, it makes no difference to her. Her honour is restored. She is beyond caring. Her entire mind is taken up with her new *Judith*.

Finally, she is allowed to leave. Porzia comes to help her, a protective arm offered. She kicks off the uncomfortable slippers to descend the wide stone steps. She cannot remember mounting those same steps that morning, though she must have.

The courtyard is bright, everything bathed in a resplendent golden light, paving stones warm under her bare feet, birdsong serenading them as they approach the waiting carriage. Just as she is about to climb inside, she hears a sound, a cough, behind her.

Turning, she finds herself face to face with her father.

He beams, brimming with triumphant pride, and opens his arms to embrace her. 'You were extraordinary.'

'You make it sound like a performance.' She shows him her bandaged hands. 'You got what you wanted.' He can't look at them.

As she enters the carriage, she is filled with an over-whelming sense of liberation and a surge of strength. She has been tested and survived. Her future unscrolls before her – she can see it now.

It only dawns on her in this moment that she is truly free, that she is mistress of her own fate.

38. Invidia

Rome, nine months later . . .

Rome wears its winter coat. The cool light has stripped away its gilding to flat grey, matching the sky. A bitter January breeze blows up off the Tiber, running in eddies through the narrow streets, agitating last night's discarded litter. A cascade of sound rattles across the city, marking the morning – time here is carved up relentlessly by the chime of bells.

Orazio trudges across the bridge, his face hidden in the hood of a dark wool cloak. Once over the river he moves in a south-easterly direction, through the Campo di Fiore. Shutters and doors begin to creak open and the early hawkers call out as they trudge into the day with their barrows. The canvas corners of the market stalls whip up, snapping in the wind, like ships' sails, and a winch squeals, as it hauls a vast slab of marble up onto the portico of a new building. New and half-built structures, armoured in scaffolding, seem to have sprung up everywhere suddenly, changing the city beyond recognition.

He skirts the Palatine Hill, where soaring ruins and broken pilasters fight hopelessly against nature and time, continuing past the vast drum of the Colosseum. Echoes of the ancient city, crumbling – the ghost of a painting beneath a painting.

Once he would have noticed every detail: the quality of the light and the way it glimmers on the wet banks of the low river, the particular colour of the water, not the exquisite blue-green of a summer midday but a sludgy umber. He would have registered the crow-like shadows cast by a pair of priests bustling along, cassocks flapping, and the bright clump of berries peeping over the wall of a garden, the exact magenta of a cardinal's Advent robes.

But he sees none of this, is too entangled in the misery of his thoughts, his mind stabbed through with regret. He wonders if he can still call himself a painter when he hasn't held a brush for months and his reservoir of inspiration has run completely dry.

The building he seeks is unremarkable, a dull square of old red brick, its door pockmarked by time. The latch scrapes, hinges complaining as it swings shut behind him and he is enveloped in the quiet. He won't be recognized here.

Inside it is colder than out and he wraps his cloak tightly about his body. The air is thick with incense and his boots clack against the rough flagstones, drawing unwanted attention from a pair of women. They take a brief look at the stranger before returning to their prayers. Inferior frescos line the walls, depicting familiar scenes: an *Annunciation* and an *Assumption*, both Virgins pink-cheeked and ill-proportioned, sit either side of a chipped and peeling *Baptism of Jesus*.

The confessional is an unembellished wooden box with a threadbare velvet curtain half obscuring its interior. It is vacant and no one appears to be waiting, so Orazio enters and draws the curtain. Almost immediately the confessor comes, settling in with a rustle of fabric beyond the wooden grille.

The priest clears his throat to indicate his readiness.

Orazio makes the sign of the cross, but it is a few more moments before he is able to speak. 'I have committed the sin of envy, Father.'

'Envy,' repeats the confessor back to him. He sounds surprised, as if he has been expecting something much worse. 'It is human to succumb, as long as you repent from the heart.'

'But this is no ordinary envy . . .' Orazio finds, now he has begun, that the words come untrammelled. 'I am an artist, not a young man, and as such have become quite used to understanding that some of my profession have greater gifts than mine. But it was when I recognized an ability in one close to me, a pupil . . . an ability so far beyond my reach, that I tumbled into the ugliest of resentments.

'I would watch that brush scratch out a few lines, adding a little of this colour, a little of that, until life took shape, until figures occupied the surfaces of those canvases with blood coursing through their veins. They were beings who lived, who suffered, who loved, who sinned, whose skin gave under touch, and bruised, and itched, who were warm, who existed, as do you and I, Father . . . as do you and I.' Orazio's hands are wringing. 'And the beauty, such soaring loveliness could only have been a gift from Our Lord.

'I should have been pleased, for this painter was my own offspring, whom I myself had taught to paint. But all I could see in it was God's derision, my own deficiencies

339

exposed in the cruellest of ways, such divine mockery to give these extraordinary gifts to my daughter – a woman.'

The icy air is seeping through Orazio's winter cloak and his hands are numb with cold. He hugs himself, rubbing his arms to generate a little warmth, and wonders if the priest on the other side of the grille has a charcoal burner under his feet.

'You *have* sinned, my child. If you repent you will be absolved.'

'But I haven't told you everything yet, Father.' His breath makes a pale cloud.

He spits out his sins, on and on. 'And then, in the aftermath, my daughter began to paint the most brutally violent of scenes, a grisly festival of gore: Judith slaying Holofernes.'

'A biblical scene.'

'That painting – that piece of shameful sacrilege – I recognized, even in its unfinished state, as a work finer, more alive, more replete with truth, than anything I could ever have produced. I hated her, Father. I hated my own daughter for her brilliance.'

'What's done is done, my child. All you can do now is repent. And you are here. That is the first step to redemption. Our Lord is a forgiving master.'

Orazio has to inhale sharply to prevent himself from succumbing to sobs. 'She has a new life . . . as a painter. She has commissions.' He is boiling inside once more, his envy refusing to be quelled. 'Commissions that should be *mine*. All this achieved because of *me*. *I* taught her to paint, raised her as a painter.'

'You cannot change Our Lord's will. If He makes it so, then so it will be.'

A long pause ensues. Orazio feels shame enveloping him, like a shroud.

'You should give thanks to Him for bestowing on your daughter such a gift.'

Terror seizes him. 'Am I going to Hell?'

'If you do penance for the sins you have confessed, you will find He is a merciful master. But first you must truly accept His will.'

The priest lists his penance. It seems so little: a few incantations to absolve him when the burden of his sins feels so vast.

As he stands to leave, his body painful and stiff as it unfolds, the priest says, 'One more thing, before you go.'

'Yes, Father?' He stoops down to the screen, seeing through it, a single black bead eye catching the light.

'You might consider also asking *her* forgiveness.'

Orazio is confused a moment, thinking he is referring to the Holy Virgin, until realization alights. 'My daughter?'

'I am not versed in the ways of the world, but I do know the power of forgiveness.'

The bells have started to ring, and the priest douses his candle. The smell of the burned wick emanates through the grille. Mass has begun by the time he quietly slips out into the day.

He hears a whistling, as if someone is trying to attract his attention. When he looks around, the place is empty.

It sounds once more.

Twit, twit, jug, jug.

Birdsong.

He searches for the singer, eyes rummaging through the leafless trees. The clouds are as dense as gruel, the frigid air making a mist of his exhalation.

It is much too early in the year for a nightingale. But that is the song, no mistake.

39. Her Angel

Florence, three months later . . .

Piero hovers, vast wings reaching out behind him, a breeze riffling through his snowy plumage as he sways gently, suspended in air. A fly dithers. He swipes it away with an arm.

'Keep still,' Artemisia says. 'I won't be long, now.'

Her husband is hanging from a rope attached to a joist. She studies the way the early morning pours over his goose-feather wings in blushing folds and catches in the pale drapery of his tunic. Dabbing the tip of her brush into carmine, she mixes it into a smear of lead-white and touches the colour onto her canvas, standing back to appraise it. The light is different in Florence, warmer, where it reflects off the red earth. She mixes in a touch more of the red, layering the colours in fine strokes to create the feathered effect.

Her angel is taking shape, while the Virgin crouched beneath him remains a vague bluish blur. She has yet to find a model to sit for her and can't help but think of Zita. Those days in the via della Croce, Zita's girls and their constant racket, her brothers and little Luca, all of them creeping round Orazio for fear of his temper, seem distant. Once the court case was won, all those who had jeered at her, or spat at her, or refused to serve her in the market behaved as if none of it had ever happened. Within a month she was married and gone.

She doesn't miss much of her old life, only her brothers, but Giulio will be arriving in Florence soon to take up a position as her studio assistant. Marco is still happily installed with the Stiatessis. Francesco went to Naples several months ago to work with a painter there, leaving Father to 'stew in his own juice'. That was how he put it in his letter. The letter Artemisia was able to read, thanks to Piero's patient tuition.

Her life has changed beyond recognition, and she too. It is almost impossible to remember the girl she'd been two years ago.

'Shouldn't we go? We don't want to keep them waiting.' The rope creaks, Piero swaying back and forth, as he adjusts the harness. 'This is digging in.'

Artemisia is deep in contemplation, stippling colour onto the canvas, breathing life into her angel.

'Artemisia!' He has caught her attention. 'Get me down from here.'

She stretches out her hands, joints clicking as they unknot. The pain is fading and the scars are turning silver. One finger will always be deformed, curling in towards her palm like a talon, a constant reminder of her fury, source of her inspiration.

She unties the pulley rope, lowering Piero slowly to the floor and tossing him a robe. He comes to stand beside her.

'This is good, Arti. Are you happy with it?'

'Almost.'

They have fallen into an easy rhythm together. No one questions the legitimacy of their marriage. Piero says one day she might even come round to the idea of mother-hood. He thinks they would make good parents. Artemisia cannot imagine that day, not yet, while her new life is still unfolding. She had never thought beyond her desire to paint and now she is earning her living as an artist. That dream is achieved.

'There's the cart,' he says. They can hear wheels rumbling outside and a horse's whickering, the jangle of a bridle.

'You take the other end.' Piero has hold of the carefully wrapped canvas by the door. She helps him with it. It is not heavy, only large.

Excitement opens inside her, like a spring leaf unfurling.

She will never lose the thrill of being paid for her work. If her *Judith* pleases the grand duke's overseer, then the grand duke himself, the payment will transform their lives completely. Their rent will be paid for an entire year and there will be enough to give Giulio a stipend. She is looking forward to being able to buy better materials, even, perhaps, a little lapis, which trades for more than gold these days.

She takes in the scenery as they trundle down the steep slope towards the river. This city, her new home, with its russet roofs and ochre render, the pale shape of its cathedral nestled at its heart, has beguiled her. There is an intimacy to Florence that is lacking in the grand splendour of Rome. Florence's secrets must be discovered. It is a place where you can turn a corner and find a masterpiece, loitering there unannounced. Here she has encountered two hundred years' worth of beauty, works of art she could only have tried to imagine before.

The Palazzo Pitti stands on its own, away from the jumble of streets, an enormous edifice of rose-gold stone. A thousand arched windows watch as they approach, raised brows suggesting they don't belong in a place like this.

The cart pulls up at a side entrance where the trades-men make their deliveries.

'Not here.' A provisioning clerk gestures at them to turn around. A twist in her gut tells her he is going to send them packing and they will discover that the whole thing has been a mistake. 'You need to go round the other side, through the arch.' He points vaguely towards where the high wall disappears around a corner.

'Carlo always used to sneak me in through the kitchens,' says Piero.

They enter through the archway, as instructed, to be confronted by the main entrance gilded in sunshine, a great studded oak door, strapped with iron braces, liveried guards on either side. 'This can't be right.' She had expected some kind of workshop or studio.

Piero shrugs. 'It's where the clerk told us to come.'

They are waved through into a splendid marble hall with an endless, chessboard floor. 'I'm not sure about this.' Piero and she look at each other. She is resisting the urge to turn tail when a slender young man in black satin and velvet steps towards them.

Removing his cap, he bows. She wants to laugh, tell him he has mistaken her for someone else. 'Signora Gentileschi?'

'Yes.' She has a moment of euphoria to hear him use her maiden name, her painter's name.

With another deferential bow, he says, 'It is a privilege to make your acquaintance.'

She must be in a dream, this silk-clad man paying hom-age to her. It is all she can do to contain herself and introduce Piero. 'And this is my husband, Signor Stiatessi.'

'This way, if you please.' More servants magically appear

to carry the painting. And they set off over the chessboard, smoothed by generations of Medici feet, and into a long corridor.

She would like to stop to look at the pictures along the walls but the young man is moving at quite a pace. Another corridor, a flight of stairs, along a galleried landing, and they arrive at an interior pair of doors that is swung open by two sentries.

They step into a vast chamber, more works of art on its walls calling for her attention, as they hurry across the space, and through another pair of doors, and yet another, traversing increasingly small rooms. She wonders how she would ever find her way out alone, imagining she would need to leave a trail of thread, like Theseus, and is glad of Piero's hand holding hers.

Eventually they arrive in a modest chamber where a man and a woman are standing with their backs turned, looking out of a window. The woman's dress is embroidered with gold and the man's jacket is of dense crimson velvet. The pair turn in unison. The woman is tall and smiling with a fine-boned face. The man is taller with a thick beard and curious hooded eyes.

They seem to be waiting for something.

The slender young man whispers, 'It is customary to curtsey before the grand duke.'

She manages a muffled apology, dipping down, thinking they have been brought to the wrong place.

'Never mind that,' says the woman. 'My son and I have been looking forward to this, haven't we?' The grand duke is nodding.

Artemisia realizes now that this is Carlo's mother. Had

she looked properly she would have seen how greatly she resembles him. 'We were expecting to see your overseer, my lord.' She hopes she has used the correct address, suddenly doubting herself.

'I instructed Signor Riggoberti to bring you directly to me.' The grand duke is pointing to the slender young man, and she has made yet another misapprehension – *he* is the overseer. 'I was keen to see this one for myself.' His eyes are twinkling.

Artemisia can feel the tick of her own pulse in her temple.

Her *Judith* is being placed, with great care, onto a waiting easel beside the window. The sackcloth wrapping is stripped away. It falls to the floor. Artemisia feels faint. She doesn't look at the painting, but watches the expression on the grand duke's face, on his mother's, as they both flinch.

Dismay gouges out her heart.

Her confidence drains in an instant. They should never have come. Who did she think she was, believing her work would stand up in this place?

'I don't know what to say,' utters the grand duke.

His mother makes a small sound, a kind of 'oh'. Shock is splayed over her face. 'This is . . .'

Artemisia has a falling sensation, a great plunge into nothingness.

'This is all your own hand?' he asks. She is surprised no mention is made of her sex.

'It is, my lord, all mine.' She can't look him in the eye, keeps her gaze down on the beautiful tiled floor, waiting to be dismissed, to be told to take her aberration out of their marvellous palace, imagining Piero and she, lost for eternity, wandering through the endless marble chambers and corridors of the Palazzo Pitti, seeking an exit.

Piero places a hand on her back, an invisible support.

The silence is dense, the only sound their breath.

Mother and son begin to speak heatedly to each other. It takes a few moments for Artemisia to understand that they are in dispute about where to hang her painting.

'It pleases you?' she says.

'Pleases?' The grand duke is looking at her strangely. 'It speaks the truth. The truth pleases me.'

Her heart dilates.

'Carlo was right about you.' The duchess holds out her hands to take Artemisia's, inspecting them. She is horribly conscious of her deformity, wishing she had worn gloves, but the other woman lightly strokes her talon of a finger. 'I heard about what happened. I'm so terribly sorry.' She looks directly at Artemisia for a long moment, her expression full of upset. 'But you have risen above it.'

They fall to silence once more.

They are gazing in wonderment at her *Judith* and Artemisia is soaring up, up, aware of the strength of the wingbeat at her back, carrying her inexorably towards her future.

Author's Note

Disobedient is a work of fiction. However, the major events of Artemisia Gentileschi's life that I describe are based in fact. Gentileschi was raped by her painting teacher, coerced into accepting his hand in marriage, only to discover he already had a wife. She was then forced to prove the truth of her testimony under torture.

Despite this, and perhaps even because of it, Artemisia Gentileschi went on to find great success as a painter. She was the first woman to be admitted to the prestigious Accademia d'Arte in Florence. Her career took her all over Italy and also to England, to paint commissions for Charles I and his queen, Henrietta Maria.

Soon after the trial she married Pierantonio Stiatessi, about whom very little is known. Gentileschi's authentic voice can be found in her letters, a number of which still exist; several are between her and her lover, Francesco Maria Marenghi, who was also in friendly correspondence with her husband. This led to my distinct characterization of Piero. The letters offer an intimate insight into her ambitious nature and her libertine lifestyle. The court transcripts of the Tassi trial also provide a full account of the terrible ordeal that is recounted in my novel and her testimony, another place to find her own words. The greatest insight into Artemisia Gentileschi, and in my mind the truest echo of her voice, though, lies in her work and the subjects she chose to paint – an often bloody litany of female heroes.

For all her great success, Artemisia fell into obscurity. This was partly because her style of painting went out of fashion but also because of a general disregard of female painters. In 1876 the records of Tassi's trial emerged, causing some interest in her over the decades that followed. But it wasn't until the late twentieth century that her work was properly considered as having a place in the canon, with her becoming something of a feminist symbol for the world of renaissance art.

I stumbled upon Artemisia Gentileschi some years ago when, as is often the case, researching something else. It was her *Judith Slaying Holofernes* that grabbed my attention with a force I was unable to resist. I wish I could say I had first discovered the work in its full, vivid glory on the walls of the Uffizi but that would not be true – it was a fuzzy reproduction in a book. But even this inferior facsimile took my breath away with its unremitting violence, its composition drawing the eye to a catherine-wheel of blood spattering the foreground, runnels of it coursing over the bedclothes, smearing into the white linen, the terrible howl on the victim's mouth.

It made the other Judiths I had encountered: Cranach's placid, bovine young woman, Botticelli's coy sylph and even Caravaggio's eroticized girl, also depicted in the act of beheading, seem strangely detached and feeble, hardly capable of killing a mosquito. Not so Gentileschi's two matrons, muscular and efficient, fearless, flushed with effort as they overcome the supine man, one holding him down while the other hacks off his head. There is no turning away from the brutal and messy business of murder.

As my interests lie in women who have found forms of

expression through adversity, a subject I have returned to constantly in my fiction, my curiosity about the artist was sparked. Female painters were a rarity at the time, and all avoided controversy in depicting subjects such as this – all except Artemisia Gentileschi. This masterpiece was created when she was only seventeen. And when I learned it was also aged seventeen that she underwent the terrible ordeal of her rape and torture, I came to a visceral understanding of the genesis of the work.

Feminist art historians often seek to resist the idea of Gentileschi's art as merely a response to the events of her life. They want her work to stand up and be counted on its own and not as something shaped by the actions of men, which it does. However, to encounter that unflinching, blood-drenched painting and to deny that it is an expression of the artist's personal rage is to deny its intrinsic power. In my mind this work is an act of revenge, through which she articulates not only her fury but that of all women subjected to violence at the hands of men. It is a ferocious howl that echoes down the centuries.

The creation of this work forms the trajectory of my novel. I depict the progress of my protagonist from a fearful Susanna under threat from two lecherous men, to a courageous blade-wielding Judith. It is as if the two paintings – the *Susanna* and the *Judith* – bookend Gentileschi's early life.

But my view is biased. Her story resonated with me because I too experienced rape at a similar age. I was sixteen when I was attacked by six men who left me for dead. The police doubted my account too. Chiming as it did with mine, for years I wanted, but found myself unable, to tell

Gentileschi's story. As writers we are told to write what we know but this was a topic too close, too terrifying, too cloaked in shame, for me to consider living with it for the endless months it takes to research and write a novel.

It wasn't until some time later, when I watched Christine Blasey Ford testify before the US Senate Judiciary Committee, that the idea arose once more. Blasey Ford was similarly subjected to disbelief and humiliation when she described her sexual assault as a teenager. And even though many did come to believe her testimony, the man in question would go on to be elected to the Supreme Court. I watched, as gripped and appalled as I had been on first encountering Gentileschi's masterpiece, feeling the force of forty years of my own unexpressed rage welling up. All around me women were beginning to hold their abusers to account. I realized I had been silenced by misplaced shame for too long. However hard it would be to confront my own demons, I felt compelled to tell the story of Artemisia Gentileschi's defiance and her refusal to accept victimhood.

So *Disobedient* came into being.

Elizabeth Fremantle 2022

Acknowledgements

I am ever grateful to my editor, Jillian Taylor, whose commitment, patience and insights I value enormously. No one knows better than she how to tease my disjointed ideas into something resembling a novel. I am indebted, as well, to the team at Michael Joseph and Penguin: Press, Marketing, Sales, Rights, Art. Without their unerring work behind the scenes there would be no book. Many thanks to Hazel Orme for her tactful and astute copy-editing, as well as Beatrix McIntyre and team with their scrupulous eye for detail and Holly Ovendon for her inspired design.

Heartfelt thanks go, too, to my agent Alice Lutyens and the team at Curtis Brown. I am also greatly appreciative of Dane Millard and our long conversations over lockdown walks that helped me develop my ideas, Stephanie Glencross whose sensitive advice is always welcome and Simona Style, with her invaluable knowledge of all things Italian.

I must also mention my little dog Lola, whose quiet presence beneath my desk was a constant reassurance and who died during the writing of this novel.

He just wanted a decent book to read ...

Not too much to ask, is it? It was in 1935 when Allen Lane, Managing Director of Bodley Head Publishers, stood on a platform at Exeter railway station looking for something good to read on his journey back to London. His choice was limited to popular magazines and poor-quality paperbacks – the same choice faced every day by the vast majority of readers, few of whom could afford hardbacks. Lane's disappointment and subsequent anger at the range of books generally available led him to found a company – and change the world.

'We believed in the existence in this country of a vast reading public for intelligent books at a low price, and staked everything on it'
Sir Allen Lane, 1902–1970, founder of Penguin Books

The quality paperback had arrived – and not just in bookshops. Lane was adamant that his Penguins should appear in chain stores and tobacconists, and should cost no more than a packet of cigarettes.

Reading habits (and cigarette prices) have changed since 1935, but Penguin still believes in publishing the best books for everybody to enjoy. We still believe that good design costs no more than bad design, and we still believe that quality books published passionately and responsibly make the world a better place.

So wherever you see the little bird – whether it's on a piece of prize-winning literary fiction or a celebrity autobiography, political tour de force or historical masterpiece, a serial-killer thriller, reference book, world classic or a piece of pure escapism – you can bet that it represents the very best that the genre has to offer.

Whatever you like to read – trust Penguin.